HIGH TIDE
in
CHERRY GROVE

HIGH TIDE

in

CHERRY GROVE

HAROLD BROWN

High Tide In Cherry Grove

United States Library of Congress
Certificate of Registration Number: TXu-2-255-399

ISBN: 979-8-9853898-0-7
Printed in the United States of America

For Sharon Lee O'Connor Murphy

My Ms. Calabash

1.

PROLOGUE

Lyles Morrison was born and raised in Charlotte, North Carolina. He graduated from Mecklenburg County's Biddleville High in 1966 near the top of his class. Most schools there were still segregated. His was an all-black one where he had excelled in both track and basketball.

Between the years 1964 and 1973, under the Selective Service and Training Act, the U.S. drafted over two million young men into the military. Three out of every five conscripted were from the lower end of the working class. Many were still teenagers. Lyles was drafted a few months before his nineteenth birthday. By the end of 1967, he had served five months in Vietnam. Then in combat, Lyles received a bullet wound to the right shoulder. At the rank of Private 2nd Class, he was awarded a purple heart and discharged from the military shortly after being returned home.

Lyles Morrison learned a lot from his experiences in Vietnam. His most helpful was maintaining a sense of sanity with the benefits of marijuana. And, like most vets coming home from that war, he continued to smoke it regularly once back in North Carolina.

In March 1968, along with his girlfriend Tammy, Lyles purchased for $400 one pound of Mexican "weed" from a street dealer. It was a poor quality compared to what he had enjoyed in Nam but still enough to last him throughout the rest of the year. Driving home, he was stopped by a city police officer for exceeding the speed limit. An illegal search and seizure took place. The young veteran was charged for "possession with intent to distribute a controlled substance" and "contributing to the delinquency of a minor." Tammy was three months shy of eighteen.

It was not until the late 1960s, that brought with it widespread use of marijuana by the white upper and middle class, did the public develop more lenient attitudes towards its use. Unfortunately for Lyles Morrison and literally thousands more like him, the U.S. Congress was slow to respond. Up until its passage of the Controlled Substance Act in 1970, marijuana was included right along with other stimulants and depressants as a "Schedule One" controlled substance. As such, it fell under the provisions of the Boggs Act of 1951 which set mandatory sentences for drug convictions. No matter how trivial the offense, courts and judges were prohibited from suspending a sentence or paroling a convicted defendant. For Lyles Morrison's first offense, the mandated penalty was a fine in conjunction with serving not less than two or more than five years in prison. He was a wounded veteran recently back from a brainless war. Justice was definitely blind in his case!

The Control Substance Act became effective May1, 1971. Potential penalties remained, but it repealed mandatory statues and differentiated marijuana from addictive narcotics like heroin and cocaine. With no minimum sentence imposed on judges or prosecutors, law enforcement agencies were provided with a powerful tool against the importation and distribution of drugs. "Plea Bargaining." And, with the creation of the DEA January 1, 1973, interdictions along with incarcerations increased over the next decade. Understandably, as demand rose and prices increased, so did the amount of drugs produced and smuggled into the United States. Opportunities to make fortunes were there for those willing to take risks. There was no shortage of that category.

Following the careers of these individuals is intriguing. It's the primary purpose of this text because entrepreneurs in the trade were persons of mixed races who first challenged the dangers mostly because of personal circumstances. Few of them actually set out to be labeled criminals. Rather they pursued the reward of wealth with a sense of adventure. The exploits of some ended well. Others were not so fortunate. For them, punishment for offences committed sometimes depended on which side was injured.

A matter of convenience plus competition led to the formation of alliances by foreign bodies producing the drugs. In Colombia and Mexico primarily. Like corporations or businesses, once these entities were formed, management was driven by achieving growth and greater returns. With success came notoriety. But without the consideration of dissolution, their eventual demise was inevitable.

The role of principals within these organizations as a part of this story is unavoidable. But their histories in drugs have been well recorded, so the focus of this writing is to introduce other lessor known characters. Normal men and women with different but ordinary backgrounds who entered the trade seeking to better themselves. And like the marijuana and cocaine they smuggled, their ventures are intoxicating.

2.

LEANN AND JESSIE

Lamar Talbert was a hefty 6'2 marine veteran who had lost a large part of his right foot to an improvised landmine in Vietnam. Although honorably discharged by the Navy in1968 along with a purple heart and a bronze star with the "Combat V," the injury had left him pretty much unemployable, particularly at the time as a handicapped black man in Columbia, South Carolina. When he left the corps, he had a wife named Mary who he had met while on leave after training at Parris Island, and Jessie, a six-year-old son from their honeymoon.

The disabled veterans' pay was pathetically inadequate, even with Mary's occasional assistance as someone's house cleaner. For nearly eight years after he left the service, Lamar struggled to support the family with on and off jobs. Finally, in 1976, after going without work for four months, Lamar began to supplement his government check by selling drugs in his neighborhood. He worked from a street corner across from a vacant lot used for his stash. Walking with an impairment from the lot to buyers waiting in their cars at his corner soon earned him the nickname, "Stumble."

The Talbert's family quality of life improved dramatically over the next two years. They transitioned from near poverty to upper middle class. The timing could not have been better. Jessie was fast growing into a physically fit young man well liked in his high school. He made good grades and played junior varsity football as an aggressive lineman. The boy loved and respected Lamar for his sacrifices as a marine and often spoke of becoming one.

In the mostly segregated black communities of Columbia during the seventies, the sale of "hard drugs" such as heroin and cocaine were controlled by the Higgins brothers. Both were known to the locals only by their nicknames. The oldest and worst of the two was "Higgs." His younger brother by two years was named for his attire. "Topcoat." The men purposely advertised themselves as South Carolina inner city drug bosses. They survived as such by an earned and well-known reputation. Employed thugs for dirty work. If one of their street dealers cheated, a severe beating or much worse was certain. Police never charged either of the Higgins brothers with the occasional brutal methods they used for the management of their dealers. Nor their hired henchmen. Rumors were that Higgs and Topcoat had City Hall's paid for protection, so long as they confined their sale of drugs to the blacks.

Stumble was one of the Higgins brothers' least successful dealers when it came to his supplier's returns. His acquired success and affluence among the neighbors were brought to the attention of Topcoat by a jealous friend and supposed confidant. Stumble was apparently shorting payments to the Higgins by secretly passing crack *double ups*. Topcoat advised his brother of Stumble's offence. In the world of selling your boss's drugs in a designated territory, the sin was nothing less than stealing from family. Any show of tolerance by the Higgins and the habit might spread. An example had to be made.

Stumble was working his street on a frosty December morning. Two *morons* were lined up for buys. The second car waited it's turn and then pulled up to the curb. It was an older model, four door sedan with dirty windows. Stumble knew the car as one belonging to a nearly burned-out addict named Horton. He always brought heroin. But, as the driver's window lowered, he saw Higgs at the wheel with a 12-gauge Bushmaster already raised. Higgs shot once directly into Stumble's chest. The kill was over with that one shot. An example was still needed. Higgs opened the door, exited, pumped another round into the chamber, and then literally blew Stumble's face away. Higgs calmly stepped back in the car, closed the door, raised the window, and drove off slowly. It was not the first time he had committed murder, but years later, taking Stumble's life would make for his own.

At the time of his death, everyone in the neighborhood knew who had killed Stumble, but not a soul whispered even a suspicion. Justifiably so! Consequences were well known. The murder warranted a short paragraph on page two of *The State* newspaper and not even a mention of Lamar's military service or medals. A brief investigation by the cops had written it off as the robbery of a street dealer gone bad. Moved to cold case files in less than a month.

Lamar's son, Jessie, was devastated by the loss of his father. An initial grief quickly turned to wanting revenge. Jessie was a smart tenth grader, and the manner of Stumble's death left little doubt in his mind who was responsible.

Mary feared for her son's safety. If the Higgins thought for a minute Jessie was a threat, his death would be next. For that reason, Mary moved them shortly following the funeral from Columbia to her mother's home in Darlington, South Carolina. Her mother had relocated there years earlier and loved the community amenities that came with a small town.

Darlington was about 70 miles from Colombia and far enough so that Jessie, starting in a different school, might make new friends there to help him get over the loss of his dad. Even with the relocation, early on Jessie continued to lament and resent his dad's murder. Took months but the pain of his loss eventually passed. Memories remained. When football started that fall, Jessie carried his aggression to Darlington's opponents. He was his coaches' favorite lineman. The team ended the season with 9 wins and 1 loss.

Mary's best friend in Columbia was Leann Fox. They were high school classmates in Columbia, and Leann was Jessie's godmother. A circumstance that eventually had a long history of consequences.

When Mary's husband was killed, Leann was first to arrive at the home, and she stayed there with Mary and Jessie two days after the funeral. Five days and nights. Leann offered to stay longer but Mary, with thankful hugs, insisted she was okay there with just Jessie. Even after the move to Darlington, the friendship remained strong between the two girls. Leann visited regularly. Jessie called her Aunt Leann.

Leann was an occasional user of cocaine. Occasionally at parties with friends, she would do a short line. Because of her close friendship with Mary, Stumble would often supply her with small baggies. After he was killed, Leann was unable to provide occasional freebies to her friends. Loss some consequently. She and Mary became even closer. As well, with no children of her own, she loved her godson.

The move to Darlington had been a blessing. Not long after they had relocated, Mary succeeded in finding employment with the Darlington County recreation department. Unfortunately, she lost her mother to pancreatic cancer the year following their move. With her mother's passing, Mary devoted herself to work and to Jessie. She watched him grow with pride.

Two years passed. Jessie was a senior and had played his second and last season for the Darlington Blue Devils. He was a well above average student liked by everyone, and because Jessie somehow managed different girlfriends, envied by a few. He had grown to six feet tall, and his mom would remind him he took after his dad in both size and personality. He was devoted to her. Always respectful and liked being the man of the house, especially when strong muscles were required. His future looked good. Recruiters for the University of South Carolina were definitely interested in offering him a scholarship.

Mary's position with the county required inspection visits to school playgrounds and city parks. She liked the job, especially the occasions when responsibilities required her to leave the office. Tragic outcome! Mary was returning in the evening on state highway151 from a visit to a county planned facility in the nearby town of Hartsville. Driving west, the sun was setting directly in the roadway. At an estimated 50mph, she rear-ended a stalled logging truck. Skid marks were measured at only18 feet. Mary was pronounced dead at the site of the accident.

For Jessie, the loss of his mother was catastrophic. Devastated this time was an understatement. Leann arrived the morning after the accident. Hard to tell which of the two were the most distraught.

In Darlington, Mary had regularly attended The First Baptist Church. Her service there was packed with sadness and tears. Jessie contributed more than his share. Leann's new boyfriend, Trevor, came. She was visually upset, unstable, and stayed supported physically and emotionally by him almost the entire time.

Jessie had expected Leann to stay like she had done when his father died. Instead, with a reddened face from crying, she left her car for him, gave a long hug, and returned to Columbia with Trevor. Too damn much for an eighteen-year-old to take. Losing his dad, his mom, and now maybe Aunt Leann as well to some total stranger. All those he cared about most. For the second time in his life, grief turned to anger.

Mary's Baptist preacher was last to leave Jessie at the boy's home late that evening. For a sleep aid some nights, Mary had kept a pint bottle of "Old Stage" bourbon in the cupboard. Once left alone, Jessie finished half of it mulling what to do next.

With all the memories of his mom everywhere in the house, the whiskey didn't seem to help. He decided to leave and took Leann's car along with the rest of the bottle. Hours later that night, he was stopped by a county deputy sheriff for speeding. Jessie was clocked at 105 mph on highway 151 less than a mile from where his mother was killed. He was obviously drunk.

Jessie spent the rest of the night and the following morning in a county holding facility. Word of his arrest quickly spread. His high school counselor, who also doubled as an assistant football coach, tried to have Jessie released into his custody. Apologetically, the sheriff refused. Jessie was eighteen. An adult in South Carolina. A hearing before a magistrate was already scheduled where bail for his release would be set.

Jessie's school counselor placed his second call in a week to Leann Fox in Columbia. She was listed on Mary's records as the person to contact in emergencies. He explained Jessie's current circumstances including the part about a 3 p.m. hearing before a magistrate. It was nearly noon. Short notice, but Leann replied she would be there in two hours.

In the past six months, Leann's situation had changed. She had met Trevor and quickly fallen in love with him. She thought he was magnificent. Sent from heaven. A few dates and they were intimate. It didn't seem to matter to him that she was nearly ten years older. Plus, she very much enjoyed being with a younger man that was great in bed.

The last week of November, Leann moved in with Trevor. They had been living together for six weeks. Spent their first Christmas as a couple in his nice waterfront home on Lake Murray. Upscale neighborhood. But it was his property, his house, and their relationship was fairly new. Still, she had to ask a huge favor. Coming home from Mary's funeral, she prayed he would understand a request. Allow Jessie to move in with them. Her godchild had no place else to go.

Trevor's first response was to ask if Jessie's stay would be permanent. With Leann's assurance that the boy would be off to college by fall, he consented to the move.

Leann gave him a big hug and whispered a much more grateful response would come that night. She was very appreciative of Trevor's compassion. A new home would be just what Jessie needed after the tragedy of first losing his father and now his mother.

What followed the next morning was totally coincidental. Trevor's private phone rang at 10 a.m. Leann overheard his part of a brief and cheerful conversation with someone named Juanita. Afterwards, Trevor explained the call involved a business opportunity in Florida that would require his stay in the state for a considerable period of time. Possibly a month or more and leaving in just two days. Leann was saddened with the news, but under the circumstances, her suggestion that Jessie move to Columbia was perfect timing. Even advantageous, Trevor assured her.

The lake property included a large house along with three acres of surrounding grounds. Everything required upkeep. For that, Jessie's presence could prove useful since Trevor's extended absence was probable. One more important consideration. It was something he had only a short time ago told Leann. Until just last Easter, Trevor had been a major part of the marijuana trade in South Carolina. No longer and even then, nothing to do with cocaine or heroin. But as a local drug dealer in the past, he left out the part that he knew who had killed Jessie's father.

The phoned message from the school counselor advising Leann of Jessie's arrest came a little over an hour after Trevor had consented to the Miami, Florida trip. Even with a tight schedule ahead, Trevor drove Leann to Darlington. And, before leaving Lake Murray, he phoned his lawyer in Columbia to ask for legal assistance on Jessie's behalf. Must have worked too. There was no appearance before a magistrate. On arrival and before 3pm at the county detention center, he and Leann were allowed to bring Jessie back to his mom's home. Since he was departing for Florida in less than two days, Trevor didn't stay long. He apologized to Jessie for leaving and spent several minutes giving Leann hugs and kisses goodbye.

Later that night during dinner, Jessie thanked his aunt for busting him out of jail. He wanted to know what strings she must have pulled. The sheriff had walked up to his holding cell and said, "You're free to go, Son. The charges have been dropped."

Leann smiled with a knowing look. "Don't thank me, Jessie. It was Trevor. He made one call for you before we left Columbia. Apparently, he has important friends!" She knew better than to tell Jessie that she had only recently learned how Trevor had achieved his remarkable success.

The following day Leann, a state welfare officer, the coach, and the preacher from Mary's church met with Jessie at what had been his mother's and grandmother's home. Since he was no longer a minor, they explained that the state could not interfere with a move to Columbia. If he wished to, Jessie could live with his godmother, Leann Fox. There, he would have to start with a new school, finish his senior year, and hopefully stay out of trouble.

Leaving all the friends he had made in Darlington weighed on Jessie's decision. He had a choice. Stay or leave. The assurances from his aunt Leann that he would love his new home helped him to make up his mind. Leann was thrilled when he agreed to move.

After the others left, Leann and Jessie spent the rest of the day packing for him. They boxed everything else of importance for storage. What remained would make for a large garage sale over the next couple of days. In late evening, Leann made a compassionate attempt to help remove some of her godson's emotional distress. For dinner, she cooked a pair of thick rib eye steaks with baked potatoes and salad as sides. Jessie had barely eaten since his mom's death. He finished his steak and half of hers. That night, before going to his room, he turned toward her and softly said, "Thank you, Aunt Leann. I love you!" She cried!

3.

TREVOR

Trevor Lamont Dunbar was raised by a single mom. His dad was a "drunk." She had to divorce the bum when Trevor was barely four. Afterward, they lived with his grandparents in a two-bedroom, one bath home on the outskirts of Blaney, South Carolina. He could not remember ever seeing his father again. Blaney was a very rural community about 15 miles from downtown Columbia. His mom found local work as a housekeeper. In 1964, she was employed as a maintenance night worker in a recently opened Elgin watch factory. The little town of Blaney changed its name to Elgin.

The Vietnam War ended just under four years after Trevor graduated from Lugoff-Elgin High. He finished his senior year as a very strong, 6'1" lineman on the football team. Consequently, he was tough, healthy, black, and more than eligible for military service, but his lottery number saved him from the draft. Instead, Trevor went on to attend a local technical-vocational school in Columbia. His grandparents had bought him an old ford pickup for his graduation gift, so he was able to commute from home. At school, he was training to be an auto mechanic. He also worked part time at a Texaco station in Elgin, but still he struggled for money. Nearly always broke!

With so many Nam Vets leaving the military because of the war and jobs being scarce, the government had introduced a lucrative support program to help veterans earn a higher education while they transitioned back into civilian life. There were lots of them at the technical school. Nearly all smoke marijuana, a habit most brought back from Vietnam. By the midterm of Trevor's first year, probably three quarters of the students were recreational users. As well, some of the vets were snorting a relatively new drug to Trevor. Coke!

Trevor saw an opportunity to earn some extra cash. During his senior year at Lugoff-Elgin High, a classmate buddy of his was buying as much as a pound of weed at a time and breaking it down into *nickel bags*. He was making a killing before he was caught. The cops tried to turn him on his source. He refused to give up whoever it was. In court, he was represented by a good lawyer. That, his parent's pleas, and because he was a month shy of eighteen and still in high school, helped a local judge to give him only a year's probation with a $1,000 fine. No jail time but he was expelled from school. His name was Link, a nickname for Lincoln. Last name was Rollins.

4.

LINK

Lincoln Rollins had a troubled history as a teenager. He was raised as an only child in Lugoff. His dad worked for DuPont and his mom worked part time day care. The family had a nice little ranch style home off highway 34 just outside of town. His parents were very tolerant minded "born again Christians." From the time he was two, they spoiled him which might explain his teen history. Trouble followed him. When he was thirteen, he and two others were caught shooting out streetlights with BB air rifles. When he was fourteen, he was arrested by a county sheriff's officer along with another kid for lighting cherry bombs in mailboxes. Arrested again a year later for shoplifting. He failed the tenth grade. He was kicked off the varsity football team for fighting. Even so, his parents bought him a used Mustang for his 17th birthday. Three weeks later he was ticketed for speeding and cited for driving with an open beer can. Just a month after that, he totaled the Mustang in a ditch. Caught selling drugs in his junior year of high school at Lugoff-Elgin did not surprise anyone but his parents. They shelled out a healthy chunk of change for his lawyer. Afterwards, Link moved in with his Uncle Tracy in Columbia.

Hope was that the move might help Link to straighten up. His family prayed he had finally "learned his lesson." At least he was working and not selling drugs. Unfortunately, his uncle was a night watchman at the Columbia Mall. Except for weekends, Link had nights to himself.

A year and a half had passed since Link was expelled. Trevor found him circling around in a nice Chevrolet Impala at the Sunset End in Lugoff, a local hangout with curb service and outdoor parking that was mostly patronized after dark by teenagers.

Parking in the far back was for *making out*. No matter that everyone was too young to buy alcohol. There were plenty of backdoor bootleggers. Trevor asked Link to join him in his truck to talk some business.

"Can do, Trevor." Walking over, Link chuckled while pointing to Trevor's hat. "Hey, man, I'm a Falcons fan too! Have to get me one of those."

In 1972 the Atlanta Falcons had ended their seventh NFL season 7&7. The team had failed to improve on previous seasons since the franchise was formed. Consequently, Trevor replied with a tone of frustration. "It's getting old pulling for a bunch of losers. Been doing that since the seventh grade. If they don't at least make the playoffs next year, I'll give you this damn hat."

"They'll get better. Just you wait and see. Look at me and my ride, for instance. After all the crap that I went through, I'm living proof anyone can make a comeback."

Trevor nodded an acknowledgment but with a curious expression. Thought to himself, maybe Link's back in business.

Once they were in the truck, Link listened to what Trevor described as a chance to make some real money if he could just lay his hands on some weed. Trevor was convincing. Link liked what he heard. He had known Trevor since elementary school. They were good friends then and through most of high school until he was kicked out. Link could trust him. Consequently, he told Trevor something only one other person knew. "Trevor, I'm still working, but I'm not a street pusher anymore."

Trevor's look showed he had no idea what type of work Link was talking about. Link laughed and with a tone of bemusement said, "Man, I'm running weed now."

Trevor hesitated and then replied with a wide smile of doubt. "No way. You're shitting me?"

Trevor had heard rumors of guys who would travel to Miami, Florida and return with as much as 20 lbs. or more of marijuana. Link went on to explain he had become just such a runner by becoming a partner with someone really smart. "I got lucky as hell, Trevor."

Link told how he was made to get a job after moving to his uncle's place in Columbia. Work was part of his probation. "Spent eleven damn months pumping gas and washing cars, Trevor. You know what that's like. Sucks! Took it longer than I should have before I decided to start dealing again. Had to come off probation first. But this time, none of that nickel bag stuff. I wanted to make some real money."

Trevor interrupted. "So, what did you do? How in the hell do you go from dealing to a runner?"

"I told you I got lucky. Visited with my old source for help. Let him know I wanted to move some volume like him. Maybe it was a show of appreciation for keeping quiet when the cops tried to turn me on him. I think he figured he owed me for that. Said he could possibly help me out if the person supplying him was agreeable. Said I'd have to wait a week or more for a phone call. If the call came, it would be to set up a meet."

"Link, this is fantastic. No way you would be here telling me all this unless you were contacted. What happened?"

"I was told the call would be from someone named Thomas. Nickname, TB. Supposed to be from Florida. My uncle Tracy works a night shift, so I made sure this guy was only to phone after 11 p.m. on weekdays. Trevor, I stayed up late by that phone for almost a week."

"But he did call, didn't he? You two must have hooked up."

"Called six days later around midnight. I grabbed the damn phone on the first ring. He wanted to meet the next morning at the new McDonald's on Hardin. I had to tell him I had no wheels. Total silence! I thought he had hung up. Then he says, 'Okay, I'll pick you up in front of your uncle's house. Nine o'clock sharp. Be there!' The man knew where I lived, Trevor. And who I was living with."

"Damn! Somehow he must have checked you out."

"You think? That and a lot more. Really smart white dude. He knew my whole story. Even my probation officers' name. We spent an hour at McDonald's. I answered a lot of questions. Looked me straight in the eyes for answers. Next, we went someplace else that I can't tell you about. Already told you more than I should have."

"You can count on me. None of this is going out of my truck. I know how to keep quiet."

"You sure better, Trevor. This is some serious shit we're talking about."

"Not to worry, Link."

"Okay, here's how it went down. Because I already had a record and was just coming off probation, he convinced me how stupid I would have to be to deal on the streets. Too many people you connect with. Way too much risk. Sooner or later, I'd be caught again. And I'd probably go down hard a second time around. So, he was not remotely interested in me as a local dealer. He wanted somebody for something else. Help."

"Beginning to make sense now. He was running the stuff, wasn't he?"

"The man's ass was worn plum out. Been running for years. Said he needed some R&R. Business was just too good! Also, I could take some of the risk off his back."

"And you're a runner now?"

"Yeah. And that's the way it happened. There is a lot to learn before you go off on trips. He is an incredible teacher. One more thing I'll tell you. Don't you ever repeat this. His name is not Thomas, and he's not from Florida. Only the guys he supplies think otherwise. He's local."

"No shit?"

"No shit. Let's you and I for now just call him my boss. I call him that most of the time anyway. And now that he has me working for him, I think he's looking to expand a little."

Link continued to explain. His boss sold some to inner city street dealers, but the majority went to the colleges. At schools like Benedict, Allen, USC, and even Clemson, he supplied campus dealers. Then, Link, without revealing the details of how, described an even better part! His boss had arranged a way of doing business where he remained practically anonymous. "Helped me do the same, Trevor." Explained they both carried fake identification cards. "Dealing high quality weed too.

So good that a pound goes for $400. Even more at upstate Clemson. Broken down into one ounce bags, sells for twice that on campus. More than two times the price of the Mexican crap."

Still staring at Link with a look of admiration, Trevor said, "Hell, if I can get 10 lbs., that means it'll sell for nearly $8,000 at my school."

To that, Link replied with a smirk, "I don't drive all the damn way to Florida for a measly 10 lbs. And remember what I told you. Dealing the small bags is risky. Get a grip and try this on for size. Boss is paying me $1,000 per trip plus expenses. Just for making the runs. I have keys to two cars. They're just alike. Both have a secret storage compartment and come with the job. All I do is drive to Miami for an overnight stay at a motel. Nice prepaid pet friendly place. Usually before six or seven that evening, someone with keys to the car I drove down takes it. He leaves an identical car fully loaded for me. Next morning, I drive home a thousand damn bucks richer. Slick as hell and with hardly any risk. Just drive and switch cars. Boss handles sales and everything else."

"That's one hell of a lot of money, Link. I had no idea it was that much. And for doing practically nothing too. Come on, man. I want in on some of this action!"

"Not up to me. Stay cool and we'll see. And just so you know, here's where I'm coming from. I'm planning to learn a lot. Someday I'm going to be supplying my own dealers like my boss does and making a lot more. Your idea about the tech school just might be a start."

Trevor's imagination ran wild. There were lots of technical schools across all of South Carolina. Also, with all the vets scattered in, they had a potential for access that he knew Link and his partner had not considered. Link said as much, and he planned to talk with his boss about it.

Trevor and Link were both excited now. A damn lot of money could be made if they could pull this off. They walked over to Link's car to share a half pint of bourbon. A toast of sorts. Link had taken the first swig from the bottle and was passing it to Trevor when their car lighted up from behind. Trevor thought cops for sure. Link looked in the rear view and then lowered his head sideways towards Trevor. "Not the cops, Trevor. It's a white ford pickup. Got to be Sonny. He's trouble, so take this and watch my back." Link handed Trevor a roll of quarters bound with electrical tape. Trevor nodded his understanding. Next, Link folded his right fist with another bound role under his left shoulder, leaned back and looked to his rear-view mirror.

The doors on either side of the truck opened. Sonny stepped out from the driver's side and his friend, KJ, from the other. Both walked up to Link's half opened window. Sonny leaned close and smiled. "Hey, Link! What's happening?"

"Not much, Sonny. Me and Trevor here just talking some. How come you light me up like that and block us in?"

"Here's the 'why,' Link. Me and KJ need to score some weed! How about you help us out with a dime or two. 'Old time's sake,' if you know what I mean?"

"Can't do that, Sonny. I've been clean ever since I was caught. You know? Probation and all the crap that goes with it. I'm not looking to do any time over some smoke. Maybe you need to try someplace else?".

"That so, you say! And I was thinking you were my friend. What about these nice wheels you sitting here in? Must wash a whole lot of cars for a ride like this. And I heard you quit that job. So, you can see why I have my doubts, and if you are my friend, then you won't mind stepping out and letting me and KJ check a little for ourselves?"

Link lied, "The car belongs to my old man. And so, yes, I do mind"

Sonny smiled again and then, with his right hand, waved his truck keys in Link's face. "Your old man's car? Interesting. Not a scratch on it yet. And I do mean yet! You get my meaning?"

Trevor leaned forward in his seat and decided it was time to add a little to the conversation, "Sonny Boy!" Then paused. "Listen some, Sonny Boy! First you light us up and now you're talking some shit. Sounds to me like you and KJ looking for trouble, not weed? If that's what you want, asshole, Link and I can help you out right here, right now.".

Sonny's smile disappeared. "Well, if it ain't Trevor butting in? This here was supposed to be between me and Link. And maybe I might let you call me 'asshole.' But you call me 'Sonny Boy,' and I'll be coming round there and hurting you some kina bad!"

Trevor whispered to Link, "Watch KJ for me," opened his door, stepped out, and looked over the Chevy's hood at Sonny. "Sounds like lots talk to me, Sonny Boy"!

Sonny was maybe an inch shorter than Trevor, but with some gut, a broad body, muscular arms and chest, he outweighed him by thirty pounds at least. And, when it came to fighting, he had a real dirty reputation. So, with fist closed, he began to slowly walk with obvious confidence to the front of Link's car. Trevor did the same but as they both rounded fenders and were a little less than six feet apart, he moved slightly forward, casually lifted the Falcons hat with his left hand and tossed it over to Sonny's shoulder. "Catch Sonny!" Sonny glanced at the distraction for a split second. He never knew it was a mistake. Trevor, with his right fist of rolled quarters, swung a full round uppercut to Sonny's chin. He knew immediately it was a home run and then some! Made a surprising loud crack-like sound followed by Sonny falling backwards to the ground with a hard thud.

KJ started to come around but stopped cold when Link jumped out behind him. Thinking about it, KJ held both hands up and open while backing towards Sonny's truck. "I don't want none of this, Link!"

Link pointed to Sonny on the ground. "KJ, you need to make better friends. March your ass over here and get Sonny's keys. Move that damn truck! Then come back and get this moaning piece of shit out of our sight." KJ shook his head obediently.

Link followed KJ around and waited for him to take the keys. He looked down at Sonny. The poor bastard was up on one elbow but still moaning. Blood coughed from his open mouth. Link grinned at Trevor. "Christ, Trevor! He's still half out and maybe missing some teeth."

Trevor returned the grin. "You think?" Grinned again. "Maybe we better leave before some cops show up."

Link gave a thumb's up. "You got that right. Let's get a move on!"

A new relationship had started that night between two old friends. A much stronger relationship! Almost brothers! Neither knew where it would take them. Like many at times, both of these young men simply dreamed of making a lot of money. No harm in that when supplying something that millions of people enjoyed?

Later that evening, Link assured Trevor he would talk to his boss about the tech. schools. "You have to be patient, Trevor. No way he will do anything without checking it out for himself first. And it makes no difference that you and I are old friends. You can bet he's going to check you out too! So, it will take a little time."

"I'm good with that. Just like you were though, I'll be staying close to my phone every night until I hear back from you."

Something Trevor did not tell Link was that he had probably figured out who he had partnered with. Elgin was a small town. Less than 500 residents. Trevor had grown up there. He knew practically everyone. A year or more in the past, one person in particular who he did not know aroused his curiosity. There was this white guy maybe in his mid-thirties. He drove a nice 1969 Chevy Impala 4 Door. Always carried his dog with him. Very friendly Irish Setter! He would gas up at the Texaco station and then would wait while having his car washed. He sported a year-round dark tan. Trevor recalled at least twice when the guy came for gas and service only to return a few days later with an empty tank and a dirty car. Okay, who the hell was he? The station owner called him Ken. Thought he was a farmer. Maybe that explained the tan. Trevor worked full time at the station during the summer. Once, on a Tuesday morning, Ken came in for service. Trevor washed his car and made a note of the odometer. It read 78,347 miles. That following Saturday, he pulled in for service again. Shortly after, Trevor checked the odometer. It read 79,834 miles. Trevor thought, that explains the tan and so many miles on a car only three years old. The distance to Miami and back was about 1,300 miles. Only now, after Link had shared his new profession, did Trevor make the connection between the two of them.

A week after he and Link met at the Sunset, Trevor was introduced to Kenneth Bayne. Alias, TB. It seemed everyone had a nickname. His was Kenny, but he preferred Kenneth. Link had already shared everything with him. Kenneth had seemed hesitant at first. He did not particularly appreciate Link blowing half his cover before coming to him. Told Link as much with some stern warnings and that he would have to think on it before meeting his friend. In truth, he had been considering expanding distribution to some of the predominantly girls' colleges, possibly because there might be some side benefits. Instead, moving into the technical schools with all the vets there was a much better idea business wise. Kenneth had six years of military service with two tours in Nam. You could work with vets, especially as middlemen.

Expanding business to the tech schools would require more transport from Florida and that meant some help. He remembered Trevor from the Texaco station. Link swore by him. He agreed to a meeting at his farm. Link knew why. Kenneth had left the army with a final rank of Sergeant First Class. He could read you like a book. Trained well, he wanted to make sure Trevor knew who ran things, controlled the money, could follow orders, would never question his authority or decisions, and most of all, keep his mouth shut.

The meeting went well. They were seated across from one another. Trevor was coming from nowhere, broke, and agreeable to whatever Kenneth discussed with him. On advice from Link, he had dressed neatly. Even though Trevor was unable to hide his excitement, he still managed to stay restrained and attentive. He took every question seriously. He tried to answer each with precision and honesty. Kenneth sensed the qualities he needed to see. Trevor would have made a pretty good soldier. A half hour had passed. Link was there but had remained quiet. Finally, Kenneth opened a drawer in a side table and pulled out a perfectly rolled joint. Handing it over to Trevor with his left hand and flicking a light from his Zippo with his right, he smiled and said, "Welcome to the team."

Link smiled too and said, "Damn, Trevor! You scored a touchdown." Kenneth laughed. Later they were all stoned. Everyone was laughing. It was, in fact, the start of a strong and incredibly profitable comradeship. Unfortunately, like so many others in this line of work, it was short lived!

5.

KENNETH

Kenneth had signed up with the army right out of high school in 1961. He trained at Fort Jackson. He liked serving in the military and re-upped in 1964. He began his first tour in Nam as an excited optimist ready to kick some ass. He left the army in 1967 thoroughly discouraged and morally changed. He had seen a lot of action his second tour. He was tough as hell but going through just that in Nam had damaged him. From that day forward, he wanted to always strive for a better life. Put himself first for a change instead of some senseless war.

Returning home late November 1967, he discovered that his mom and dad had sold most of the farm where he was raised. They had been too embarrassed to tell him how badly they needed the money. His dad's health from smoking two packs of Camels a day had advanced into late-stage emphysema. He probably had less than a year to live. Making matters worse, his mom was an overweight diabetic. Together, with the money from the sale of the land and their small savings, they had moved into a retirement home in Camden. It was about 20 miles from the farm.

Out of 156 acres, only 26 remained around the old, one-story home. It was badly in need of fresh paint. Still, leading to the house, there was a drive lined with pecan trees. Further back, there was a wooden barn with a rusted tin roof, and around the barn about 15 acres of fenced land, once cleared but now covered with high weeds. Also, there was a half full irrigation pond in the very back. There was cleaning up and repair work needed everywhere. No matter! Kenneth looked out over the property from a screen porch on the side of the house and thought to himself. Beats Nam on a scale of 1 to 10 by ten.

Over a period of six years, Kenneth had saved a little more than $9,000. He had planned to use the savings to invest in some kind of business for himself. One thing he knew for sure. He did not want to work for anyone. Months passed. Nothing cropped up, so he spent most of the time working hard on the property. He painted the house and barn both outside and inside. He repaired the pump to the water well feeding the irrigation pond. He managed to get the tractor parked in the barn back into good running condition. He plowed under the field of weeds. Every day he worked on something. Kenneth had spent a little less than $2,500, but now everything about the place was shaped up and invitingly nice to see. It was its old self and more. Then, on May 27, 1968, his dad passed away.

A funeral for his dad was held on a Thursday morning at the Wateree Baptist Church in Camden, SC. Along with about 30 people from the church and retirement home, none of whom Kenneth knew or could remember knowing, a first cousin from his mom's side came. After a graveside service, the ladies of the church served lunch. Classic! Fried chicken, coleslaw, macaroni and cheese, sweet potatoes, and rolls. Ruth, his mom, was surrounded with friends at her table, so Kenneth set apart with his cousin Jake. Both had served in Nam and the conversation quickly turned to their experiences there. They had a lot in common. Later, as the crowd began to leave, Kenneth's mom walked over to explain she was returning to the retirement home with some of the other residents. She was fine but a little tired and needed some rest. She hugged Jake for coming such a long way for his uncle's funeral. She asked about his mother, Sarah, who was ill and could not be there. She almost insisted he follow Kenneth to the farm so at least to see the old place once more. He might even stay there for the night before returning to Miami. "For one thing, it's too long a trip to begin now," she argued. Jake had planned on just driving back as far as Gainesville and finishing the trip to Miami the next day. When he glanced over at Kenneth, he saw an approving invite followed with a comment.

"Sure, Jake. Come on! I've got a fridge full of beer." As it turned out, the two war vets had a lot more to talk about.

Kenneth showed Jake around the outside grounds and then the house.

He was proud of his work pointing out in detail some of the repairs he had made. Jake was familiar with almost everything from visits back when they were both kids. Casually mentioned that he had a little four-acre farmhouse of his own near Gainesville. Then he asked if you could still catch catfish in the irrigation pond.

"Sure can," Kenneth replied. "Want to try your luck? There are some big ones in there."

Jake declined. "No thanks. Rather just sit out on the porch and have a beer."

After the two of them had been on the porch for nearly two hours sharing stories and now enjoying their fourth beer, Jake leaned over and inquired, "Kenneth, no offence but can I ask you something personal?"

The beers were working on Kenneth. "Yeah. What the hell? Fire away!"

"Did you smoke much dope in Nam?"

Kenneth's grin gave him away so much that an answer was not really needed. Still, he joked. "Only three or four hundred joints my first tour but at least a thousand my second time around."

They both laughed. Jake pulled an opened pack of Lucky Strikes from his shirt pocket. Taking one out, he offered it to Kenneth with his left hand accompanied with a light from his Zippo in his right. It was a perfectly rolled joint, not a cigarette. Later they were stoned. They devoured the leftovers his mom had insisted they take home from the church dinner. The fried chicken was incredible!

The following morning was a cool day for May. Spring like. Kenneth and Jake decided to have their coffee on the front porch. Kenneth, for the second time, thanked Jake for sharing such great weed the evening before. It had been a while since he had enjoyed himself so much.

Jake shrugged. "Glad you liked it. I'll leave a bag with you. I've got lots more back home. You can't beat the Jamaican I'm getting. And I deal a little."

"Making any money?" Kenneth asked.

"Just started the middle of last year a few months after my discharge. Could be making more but I'm playing really safe. Sales took off right away. Hope you understand. I'd rather not tell you exactly how much I'm clearing. Let's just say it's up in the five-figure range. Thinking about expanding my business too."

"You've got to be kidding me, Jake. If you're making that much a year, why in hell are you driving a six-year-old Chevy pickup?"

"You noticed that. Good! Part of playing safe is looking average. But Kenneth, not a year. Five figures a month!" Jake saw Kenneth's look of curiosity explode. He paused for a few seconds. Guarded as always with the business he was in. Instinctive too, from Nam! But this was family all the way back to when they were kids. Safe enough! Then he asked, "Why come you so interested, Kenneth?"

Kenneth explained how he had saved some $9,000 in hopes of going into business for himself. Months had passed. He had found nothing, and nearly a third of his savings was gone. The farm was nice, but with only 26 acres, it was hard to justify the expense. He needed an income. Regardless of the risk, clearing $10,000 a month or more sounded way too tempting. A fortune in fact. More in one month than he had saved in six years. What's more, there had to be a local market around Columbia for that Jamaican. Damn, it was good!

Jake understood Kenneth's situation. It was similar to his own experience after being discharged. Once again, he reminded himself, this was family. Jake told Kenneth maybe they could work something out. Maybe! No promises at this point. The details to be discussed would require him to stay another day or possibly two. There was a lot to explain; especially how you go about finding a safe way of exchanging your marijuana for cash. You wanted to avoid being involved with hard core crooks. College kids were best if you could remain anonymous. They were easily turned if caught. Jake wanted to look around. Check out some of the campuses.

Finally, if all seemed okay, Kenneth would have to come to Miami for a week or so. He needed some training!

Late that afternoon, Jake drove into Columbia with Kenneth. They visited the grounds of three schools located right in the center of Columbia. They were within a mile radius of one another. Allen University and Benedict College were small with what appeared to be all black students. The University of South Carolina was huge by comparison with an enrollment of nearly 12,000. The surrounding community was old with mostly two story, wood framed houses. At least half had several cars parked front and back. College student rentals. After two hours, they had seen only one campus cop, and they had driven past a parked city police car. As night fell, a place called Five Points seemed to be the center of everything. Lots of bars, food, dancing, and if you could smell, marijuana. They went into what appeared to be the most crowded place in Five Points. After a beer, Jake wanted some time to mingle alone with the crowd. He suggested Kenneth do the same and meet back at the truck in about an hour. Without questioning why, Kenneth agreed. For him, an uneventful two more beers passed the hour. Jake was already sitting in the truck when he got there. "What now?" Kenneth a s k e d.

Jake started the truck and said, "Home cousin, home." Twenty-five minutes later they were driving down the farm's driveway. Sitting with two more beers at the kitchen table, Jake pulled out an ounce bag of weed from each of his pants pockets. In less than an hour and shy forty bucks, he had scored twice. He emptied both bags into separate bowls. Studying each, he smiled. One was supposed to be Colombian. The other one's nationality was unknown but supposed to be "really good weed, man." Both were Mexican. Even a fairly poor grade of Mexican. Probably dried, pressed, and smuggled as bricks. Stems, leaves, and seeds with the buds passed through a blender. The leafy parts crumbled when slightly squeezed. This stuff was old too. He looked over at Kenneth while, oddly enough, shaking his head in approval of the purchase. "Kenneth, this place has the potential of a dealers paradise. Money to be made here. In Miami, we flush better shit than this down the john." And a few seconds later, "Kenneth, pack up! You've got to go back with me."

6.

JACOBS MORGAN (JAKE)

Jake had left the army for good after serving one tour in Nam. It was December 1966. He was able to make it home for Christmas with his mom. Moved back into his old room. His dad had owned a profitable plumbing company in Miami but died from cancer when Jake was just 16. Sarah, his mom, sold the business for a good bit of money, paid off the mortgage on their house, and placed what was left into a retirement fund.

Jake graduated from Miami Edison High in 1960. Right away and possibly because his dad had served in the military, Jake joined the army. He was discharged from active duty in 1964. A year later, as the war in Vietnam required, inactive ready reservists were first to be called up. Jake was no exception. His tour in Nam lasted 13 months.

His mom was proud of his service and hoped he might have stayed with the military. Make a career of it. So, Jake told her about some of his combat experiences ending with how damn lucky he was to have made it out in one piece. Like so many others back home in the early years of the Vietnam War, Jake's mother had no idea how bad it had been for the boys over there.

A few months passed after coming home. Jake had been unable to find work that would have paid much more than minimum wage.

He toyed with the idea of college. His high school grades were pretty good, and he had made an above average SAT score before joining the army.

He reacquainted with a couple of old high school friends. Both were now in their senior year at Miami Dade. Jake was invited to one of their fraternity parties. Later that night, his friends had to pull him off one of their frat brothers he was beating the shit out of in a hallway. After finding out Jake had served in Nam, the guy had asked him how it felt to be a murdering SOB. Pulling Jake off probably saved him from killing the idiot. Making matters worse, some of those at the party had agreed with the stupid asshole. Ignorant bastards! Several, including his two friends, were high on weed. The fight, if you could call it that because the jerk never knew what hit him, ended Jake's thoughts of college. But the party had given him an idea.

It was easy to score marijuana in Miami. Jake had even been given a couple of bags of great Jamaican from a friend he knew well. His nickname was Little Mac. His dad, Mack, had worked for Jake's father in the plumbing business. Now, Little Mac supplied street dealers. Visiting him the next day at his home, Jake inquired about the wholesale price of 10, maybe 20 lbs.

"For that much and cheap, you got to deal with my guy. Name's DB. Young black dude like me. Works for a supplier that came out of the military. Supposedly brings his stuff in through Melbourne. Other than that, neither of us know squat about him. Before you do this, Jake, you better think hard about it. DB says the people the weed comes from are real bad asses. Who knows? Mexicans maybe. Says if you mess with them, might get hurt really bad." He looked back at Jake for a reply.

"Don't worry, I'll do right by them, but if I need to, I can take care of myself." Jake had gone through months of combat in Nam. He knew what being scared felt like and this sure as hell wasn't it. Not even close!

Little Mac shook his head. "Alright then, he contacts me every other Saturday. That's day after tomorrow. You know I'll stand up for you cause we go back some. I have to tell him where you live, give him your phone number, and some of our history. Say you're just out of the army too.

If everything looks good, he'll call you. Might as well know now, you'll have to pay upfront. He'll tell you where to make your pick-up."

Jake agreed and thanked him with a handshake. "I owe you one, Little Mac. Won't forget this!"

Three days later, Jake got a call with instructions. Strange though. Not from DB. The caller spoke with a northern accent, and he wasn't in Miami.

To make the buy, Jake had to travel to a marina in Key Largo. It was a three-acre lot encircled by a six-foot-high chain length fence. Passed inside through a double wide gate. Sign at the top read, " Sunset Marine and Storage. Open 5 AM. Close 10 PM." Sign at the bottom read, "Beware of Dog After Hours." Front two acres were for covered boat storage. Long sheds almost full. The acre behind was for parking. The marina backed on water with double wide ramps, two boardwalks and about 30 slips. There was a house trailer along the water at the far end of the property and a small, two-story bait and tackle shop positioned between the docks. Captain's Watch on top. Charter service signs were posted at the front of each walk and on the shop. Grounds were neat. Kept well. All in all, the place was first class.

Turns out, the dealer wasn't scary at all. Just a very tall, heavy-set man, unshaven, maybe about 220lbs. Hoarse voice. Both arms were tattooed, and he was baked almost brown from too much sun. Muscular as hell too. Obviously fit and probably a weightlifter. Ex-navy CPO in his early forties working out of the marina's bait and tackle shop. Sign above the shop's door read "Manager." His name was Peter Ingram. Introduced himself as Pete. Retired from the navy after twenty. Served his last deployment to Nam on the destroyer USS *Higbee*. Saw a little action.

Jake showed his military ID. Pete already knew he was just out of the army but having a service record in Nam made a hell of a difference. Established a quick trust. Both were vets. Asked Jake if he liked to fish? The answer was affirmative, so Pete had to show off his 24-foot Grady-White charter fishing boat tied in a nearby slip. Name on the stern side read, *Drifter*. Chesapeake model cabin cruiser powered by two 125HP Mercury outboards. The boat and both engines looked new.

Nice little express cabin up front with a marine toilet and V bunks. Clean as a whistle. Rigged with two stern rod holders and a rear facing harness seat. Jake suspected he used the boat for something besides just charter fishing.

Afterwards, Jake made his first bulk purchase. Two thousand in fifties for 16 lbs. of Jamaican. That was a wholesale purchase price according to Pete. Street value was about four times that. He had Jake make the payment up front and then leave to wait at a certain phone booth for instructions. "Just a precaution," Pete explained. "Never keep the stuff here."

Jake drove about two miles to a corner phone booth by an ESSO gas station. He sat there for ten minutes before the phone rang. Following what he was told to do, Jake picked up his 16lbs of marijuana from the unlocked trunk of an old Plymouth in the same marina's parking lot he had left before. It was separated and loosely placed into four paper bags. Fresh! Mostly buds with a few narrow leaves. Looked good.

There was a young black man at the door of the tackle shop watching. Jake had not seen him earlier. Pete was sitting in the seat at the back of his Grady White. He stood and gave a slow salute. Jake returned the salute with a nod of thanks. The two of them had connected! Jake unknowingly had met his first real friend since Nam. What he did not know at the time was that a purchase of this size would have been made out of Miami. An exchange of money for a drop by DB. Nothing more!

The meeting with Pete was arranged for a reason. Jake had been introduced to someone who was much more than just a bait and tackle shop manager with a side business. Pete was running a major marijuana operation, and he was shopping for help.

Jake didn't waste time with Miami Dade. His ex-navy source, Pete, had advised him there was too much competition in Miami. With emphasis, he included himself in that category. "We work with lots of guys like your friend, Little Mac. Hope you understand!" Pete suggested that the University of Florida was a different story. "Weed is an in-thing with the college kids and not nearly as much law to worry about there. If anyone you sell to should ask, tell them your Jamaican comes out of Melbourne. Lie a little!"

The following morning, Jake took about an ounce worth from one of the bags. He made a dozen perfect joints using the same manual roller he had used in Nam. Next, he placed them in the back of an empty lucky strike pack, filled in the remaining space with real lucky strike cigarettes, then put the pack in his shirt pocket. Same way he and others had carried weed in Nam. After hiding the bags of marijuana in a garage overhead storage trunk, he borrowed his mom's car and made the trip to Gainesville. The drive took six hours.

Jake spent the next three evenings at some of the local bars near the university. He introduced himself to most of those he met as Richard Boyce from Melbourne, Florida. His friends called him Dick. Not one person he met ever asked for identification. Mostly just young, naive college kids. Incredibly trusting. Mixed in with the crowds were quite a few guys sporting long hair. Among those, beards, headbands, and necklaces were popular. Jake humored himself thinking. Good thing for the beards because otherwise, you might mistake one of those dudes for a gal. Jake bought more than a few rounds of beer. Hinted around that he had some great weed. Twice he accepted invites back to a couple of rental houses to share some of his "smoke". Out of caution, he stayed away from dorms.

By the end of the third night of drinking beer, passing joints and getting stoned, Jake had found and gained the confidence of two students, one full time and one part time, wanting to deal some of that damn good marijuana he had shared with them. Neither knew the other. They lived off campus. Separately, Jake had offered to front both with four lbs. Each had jumped at the chance to deal a little and make some money. He took their phone numbers and driver's license info explaining he would contact them with where, when, and how to make pickups and payments. After each payment, another drop would be made. All they really knew about him was his name and where he was from. Richard Boyce from Melbourne. Each would have to return $1,000 to him after their sales were completed. $250 per lb. Broken down, they could make more than twice what they had to pay him.

Finally, before leaving, Jake explained he was just a runner working for some bad ass people back in Melbourne, and they should take working with him very seriously. He made sure both understood the consequences if his suppliers were ever ripped off. He laced that message with hard core profanity to make it crystal clear! Very convincing lies.

On a softer note, if all went well, this was just the beginning. They stood to make a hell-of-a-lot of easy money. Jake would arrange for his payments from them by first phoning and then sending "his man" to pick up the money. Whatever amounts of marijuana they needed next would be included by a note with payment for the earlier delivery. Afterwards, and another phone call, additional deliveries would be made by the same man. Jake would make contact for the first drop within the week.

Leaving Gainesville for Miami, Jake was feeling confident of his three new employees. He had kept his third a secret from the other two. A pizza delivery boy struggling to work his way through his first year at the university. Made a perfect cover for pickups and deliveries. Jake had noticed him bringing pizzas into one of the bars. Later, Jake ordered a pizza and then recruited him for the job. Over just one beer and a shared joint, he easily convinced the young freshman to work as a courier because a single collection and drop paid $150. That, Jake argued, was more than he made in a week trafficking pizza. The guy also liked the idea of some free grass.

Three days later, he was back in Gainesville phoning his dealers for their first shipment via a pizza delivery. Returning again in only two weeks, Jake was surprised to hear one had sold out by the third day and the other within the first week. To keep up with demand, their notes ask for either larger supplies or more drops. They were both excited and happy little campers to hear from "Richard". Leaving another 4 lbs. with each of them by way of his pizza boy, Jake phoned with assurances that the next drop was coming soon, and it would be much larger. Jake realized then that he was on the brink of making some real money. He reminded himself to be careful. Keep the horse in front of the buggy, Jake. This isn't a game!

After returning to Miami, Jake called Pete. He anxiously asked if he could make another purchase of as much as 80 lbs. There was no response. Jake took the silence wrong and backed off some. "Pete, if you're uncomfortable with that much, how about 50 lbs.?"

Another few seconds passed before Pete replied with an answer. "Jake, you said you like to fish. If you can take a little time for R&R, how about coming down to Key Largo for a few days? Stay in my house trailer at the marina if you like. Fish a little. Maybe mix some pleasure with business. Depending on the weather, we could even try for swordfish."

Again, Jake was taken off guard. Without thinking, "Sounds great to me, Pete. When?"

"The rest of this week is supposed to be nice weather. Can you make it tomorrow?"

"I'll be there around noon. And thanks for the invite. Hope we can catch some. My mom loves fish."

What Pete had in mind had very little to do with fishing. His setup was ideal. His offshore connection provided what was an unlimited supply of incredibly good marijuana. In just a year and a half, operations had grown significantly in the areas around Miami and Key West. Now they wanted him to expand further north. Pete was pretty sure he had come across the right person to start the move. He had checked Jake out thoroughly by way of a Miami law firm. Now he would check out his sea legs too. Go after swordfish and maybe something more!

7.

THE KEYS, JUNE 1, 1968

The trip to Miami took Jake and Kenneth two days. They had driven as far as Gainesville and stopped there overnight. Jake explained he had some business that required his attention. Had to make some calls. Leaving Kenneth at the motel, he was gone for an hour. When he returned, Kenneth didn't ask any questions.

Arriving in Miami at Jake's home the following afternoon, Kenneth's aunt Sarah was surprised and thrilled he had returned with Jake. She apologized for not being at his father's funeral. "The trip would have been too hard for me, Kenneth. So sorry I could not be there for you and your mother, but I can barely see anymore. How is Ruth holding up?"

Kenneth assured her his mom seemed to be doing remarkably well, especially so with the support of her friends from the retirement home and her church. Otherwise, he would not have left.

"Aunt Sarah, Dad suffered towards the end, so his passing was almost a blessing. Also, because of her diabetes, Mom was having a difficult time caring for him. As for me, I just needed to get away with his loss coming so soon after Vietnam. Hope you can put up with the two of us for a while?"

Sarah Morgan smiled. "Boy, you stay as long as you want. Just make yourself at home. We have a guess room. Jake can use some company.

Pay no attention to our dog. She's a beautiful golden retriever. Jake's dog, Annie. Friendly to everyone."

The next morning, after Aunt Sarah's pancakes and sausage breakfast, Jake took Kenneth out to the garage. It was large enough for two cars and set back separately from the house. Jake asked, "How do you like it?"

Looking around and then referring to a clean 4 door Chevrolet sedan taking up half the garage space, Kenneth replied, "Nice big garage. Is that your mom's car?"

"It was Mom's, but her poor eyesight keeps her from driving. She gets around the house well enough. Still a great cook too! She's having a fried chicken dinner for us tonight. Come over here and I'll show you something." Jake opened the car's back door, lifted the floorboard carpet a little, then turned a small spring latch fastened at the base of the rear seat. Leaning across and pulling the carpet again, he turned a second latch to the seat on the opposite end. With a hefty pull up and what sounded like a pop, the seat lifted completely out. Kenneth leaned inside to see. Jake had rebuilt the bottom of the seat and the area underneath so that it extended a foot into the trunk. It was a good size compartment lined with half inch-thick fiberglass as was the base of the seat.

Jake tapped Kenneth on the shoulder and waved at his work. "See how I molded the seat's fiberglass bottom to fit in real snug? Airtight when I hook it down! Plus, I clean up with alcohol and then soapy water after every run. When I started out, I bought my first marijuana by the pound. Now my haul arrives here in 10 kilo bales sealed in plastic bags with tape. I wrapped them again with heavy foil. Humidity control and no oxidation are the essentials. I can carry twelve bales in the car. That's two hundred fifty pounds a run."

Kenneth was impressed with the car's storage compartment. But he was even more impressed with the amount Jake mentioned. "Cousin, you'll have to show me how to make one of these."

"Will do, but this little trick is one of the easy things I want to teach you. Come on. Let's go for a ride." They spent several hours driving around Miami. Cruised through Miami Dade University three times. They stopped and visited two different bars where students hang out.

Jake talked constantly about which ones to watch and what to look for. More than once, he said, "You have to be careful, Kenneth." Returning home, Jake pulled up to but not inside the garage. "Got another little something to show you." Kenneth followed him into the garage. Jake closed the door and flipped a light switch. "Come over here, look around, then tell me what you see."

Kenneth walked over and did as Jake instructed. "Search me, cousin. I don't see anything but a work bench over there, lawn mower, that toolbox, water hose on the wall along with all that gardening crap, and a storage trunk up on the rafters. Am I missing something?"

Jake grinned. "You're standing on it. Remember I told you my marijuana arrives in ten kilo bales. Move over some." Jake took out a crowbar from the toolbox and slipped the curved end under a small piece of rebar barely exposed in the concrete floor. Pulling up, he slid off a two-foot square slab of reinforced concrete. Cut to fit the space just three inches below the slab, Jake had installed a hinged, plywood trap door. Reaching for a handle on the door to open it, Jake said, "listen." Then a pop just like the car seat had made when opened. The base of the door was lined with fiberglass. Beneath was a hollowed-out space about five feet square and six feet deep, also lined with fiberglass. "It's airtight, Kenneth. Look at what you were standing on and did not smell a thing. Each of those weigh 10 kilos." Looking inside, Kenneth saw it was about half full of bales of marijuana wrapped in foil. "I can store 50 of those when it's full," Jake bragged.

"That's a humidifier gauge attached to the base of the door, and the open jug hooked at the top of the wall holds a gallon of glycol. My Jamaican keeps best at 70% humidity. With the car or my truck all locked up and parked right on top, you would never know this place was here. Pretty safe, Kenneth. I keep quite a bit of cash down there too."

"Damn ingenious. No garage, but I have a barn with a tractor inside."

Jake thumbed up his approval. "Should work and your farm is a hell of a lot more rural than suburban Miami."

They spent the next day repeating what they had done the day before. Kenneth proved to be a fast learner. His military training kicked in.

He paid attention to every detail his instructor offered. That evening in a bar, Kenneth pointed out some kids sitting at a table. "They're all stoned, Jake. Careless too. Maybe even walking around with a joint or two. And the guy way back in the corner is watching all four of them. Cop, you think?" Jake nodded an affirmative smile.

On the third day, Jake woke Kenneth early. "Rise and shine. We're taking a trip."

Still in his shorts, Kenneth looked puzzled. "Where?"

"Kenneth, you're going to like the next couple of days a lot more than trolling Miami. Pack up. You'll need a swimming suit too. Or maybe not? We're heading south to Key West. Jam packed with peace loving kids. Mingle some and learn a lot while having fun. I'll tell Mom we're out for some R&R. Take my truck."

Key West was indeed a lesson of the times. Music about love and peace was everywhere. Joan Baez, Simon & Garfunkel, Peter Paul and Mary, Bob Dylan, and of course, The Beatles. War was bad! Getting stoned, solving the world's problems, watching the sun set, and having sex, were favorite pass times. A few stupid kids dropped "acid." You could spot them in a crowd. It was easy to join in with groups. If you disliked the president and hated the Vietnam War, nobody was a stranger. Kenneth and Jake were careful not to mention they were vets. Half the kids were back-packers and campers. Jake had the foresight from previous visits to reserved two motel rooms. The accommodations proved to be an advantage. Both met a likable girl and spent great evenings with them. So much so that Kenneth persuaded Jake to spend one extra day. Jake already knew why. Before leaving, Kenneth and his new friend, Patricia Chauvin, exchanged numbers, addresses, kisses, and a promise to see one another again. She had just finished her freshman year at LSU. Damn good looking. Free spirit. Half Cajun. A great accent when she talked.

Spending a few early summer days and nights in Key West was a crash course education in college campus life for Kenneth. He thanked Jake for the lessons.

Jake joked, "Key West is one hell of a classroom. Seems to me you enjoyed your homework too."

Kenneth with a big smile replied, "Oh man, I sure did. I really liked her." And then after a pause, the smile faded. "My only regret was I couldn't tell the truth about my military service."

"Yeah. Not coming out with whole truths comes with the territory of what you're getting into. You have to be able to handle that part."

"Jake, I handled two tours in Nam. This will be a walk in the park. I would just like to see her some more. You know what I mean?"

"Sure, but it's time for you to meet someone not nearly as pretty. We'll be making a stop on our way home. I have rooms for us at a Holiday Inn. Let's just say the next few days will be your final lessons before you return to Columbia."

Kenneth offered another one of his puzzled faces but said nothing. Whatever Jake had in mind he had been planning all along.

It was almost noon when they stopped at a Holiday Inn just off US 1 in Key Largo. Jake checked them both at the desk. Asked for two upstairs units next to one another. "Once you get settled, come on over and I'll explain this stop."

Kenneth gave a weak salute. "Just be a little while. I'd like to call Mom. Check up on her and let her know we're having a nice time. She would be thrilled if I were to say, I met a nice girl."

Jake took a few minutes in the bathroom to freshen up. Kenneth knocked and entered just as he picked up his phone.

"Calling Aunt Sarah?"

Jake shook his head. "No. I need to, but this is business." Kenneth overheard one side of a short conversation, part of which was explaining why they were a day late and ending with, "Great! That works for us. We're both recovering from some late nights in Key West, so a few hours of sleep sounds just right. Be there at seven this evening. Weather's looking good I hope?" Hanging up, he asked, "Is your mom okay?"

"Doing well. I was right too. She wants to know when the wedding will be. Hey, what's going down at seven?"

"Going fishing. Have you ever caught a Swordfish? Not this trip but maybe another time, we'll go after Marlin or Tarpon."

"No. None of those. Just catfish. Are we going out tonight?"

"Best part. Fits in with our trade. Remember I said we would be meeting someone? Final lessons? That was my partner on the phone. He's looking forward to meeting you. We will be up most of the night, so get some sleep. I'll wake you at six. It's warm but wear jeans, a long shirt, and the jacket I told you to bring. It can get chilly out there. Oh, almost forgot. Pack up too. We're leaving the motel."

Kenneth walked to the door. Turning his head half around, he chuckled and said, "Well, I hope we catch some fish. Hell, you never said you had a partner."

They pulled into the marina at seven sharp. Parked in the back. Jake waved to a large rough looking man standing 5 yards out on a boardwalk. Before they could walk over, he was untying dock cleats to a sleek looking boat in the first slip. Name on the bow read, *Drifter*.

Jake shook his hand and motioned to Kenneth. "Pete, meet my cousin, Kenneth Bayne."

Extending a right hand with a hard grip, "Good to meet you. Names Pete Ingram. Come on you two. Let's get going. Thirty miles to the shelf and it's best if we're there before night."

It was a calm evening with a slight overcast of high clouds. Pulling out of the marina, Kenneth spotted several other fast boats ahead. Before throttling up, Pete pointed to them. "Season got started a little over a month ago. Guys trying to make a little money with this good weather. Lots of charter craft taking visitors fishing. Light SE wind. Doesn't get any better than this. We're about an hour out, so enjoy the ride."

Jake offered Kenneth a bottle of Dramamine. "Need any of these?" Kenneth declined. The two 125HP Mercury outboards tilted the bow upward as Pete increased the speed. Along with the two motors, most of the weight was in the stern. Even so, Pete planned out at a little less than 15 knots. He increased the speed to thirty. Sea was calm with low gentle swells that the boat seemed to cut through to the next with a smooth forward lift.

Kenneth smiled toward Jake and Pete. The speed and the wind in his face was exciting. "Damn, I like this!" They all laugh.

Jake opened a Coleman cooler to his left side and took out three Buds. "These make the trip even better and a lot shorter." The beer tasted too good. Went down fast. Of course, it was a three-beer ride to the shelf.

An hour out to sea, Pete slowed to almost an idle speed. As night fell, Kenneth was surprised how dark everything became. Cloud cover. No stars or even a moon if it was out? All you could see out there were the running lights of maybe a dozen other boats off to their right. He wondered how far away they were.

Pete rigged two rods with what looked like 10-inch slabs of meat. Kenneth asked, "What kind of bait is that?"

"Bonita," Pete replied. "We'll troll with it at about 7 knots for an hour or two. Heading's northeast. Going after swordfish. Just wait until you hook into one of those babies." He cast out maybe 20 yards and then free spooled line out another 60 with the speed of the boat. "Swordfish run much shallower at night. We're fishing around 80 feet deep. I like night trolling more than bottom fishing during the day. Right now, we're over about 1,600 feet of water."

Jake cast his rod to the other side. Both were placed in the rod holders at the rear. "Relax a little," Jake said. "You'll know if something hits. Takes a lot of luck to hook a swordfish."

Beginner's luck? Twenty minutes passed. Jake's rod tipped 45 degrees over. Line sang off the reel. "Fish on!" Pete yelled. He slowed the boat to idle speed.

Jake motioned Kenneth to the harness seat, strapped him in, and with some effort, placed the base of the rod in his harness. "Okay now, hold the reel in your right hand and keep your left hand on the rod a foot higher. Let him run some. Strong fish. Takes time to wear them down. Then you will have to pull up and reel down. He's not going to swim to us. You have to bring him in. Got it?"

Kenneth's expression was less than reassuring. The rod was still doubled over and the fish seemed to be going straight down. "Christ, Jake, how big is this damn thing?"

Pete yelled. "100 lbs., maybe more! Hell, you outweigh that fish. This is the easy part."

Kenneth began to pull and reel. Ten minutes later, he looked back at Pete. "I think this damn fish is winning. Easy part, my ass"! Pete and Jake were both enjoying a beer. And grinning!

A half hour later and at 9:30 that night, Kenneth caught his first swordfish. He had finally managed to bring it to surface and then along the left side of the boat. He was dripping in sweat, but in truth, that was the easy part. Rather what seemed to be the least dangerous part. Pete jerked a long gaff into the side of its head and then had to hold on for a minute or two until he managed to bring it up and parallel with the bill. Jake rolled out a mat across the stern's floor and then handed Pete a fish bat. Struggling to hold on to the gaff with just his left hand, Pete swung the bat hard against the back of the swordfish's head. It rolled slightly over and remained still. Making sure, he hit it again. Jake handed him a short gaff that Pete hooked in the fishes' mouth. Next Jake, after a couple of slippery misses, managed to get a rope around the tail. Together, with Pete holding on to both the short gaff and the bill; Jake with the rope and tail; they lifted it in the boat and onto the mat.

Pete reckoned it weighed 180lbs. "Swordfish steaks from the grill tomorrow night fellows. We're running a bit late, so better get to it."

Jake retrieved gloves, a meat hook, knives, and a hacksaw from a tool-box. While Pete finned, Jake sawed off the broadbill and tail. Working together, it only took minutes.

Pete stood, gloves off, wiped his hands on a towel and looked at his watch. "Jake, you two stow it away. I'm going to rev her up and get under way."

Jake opened a long cooler that stretched across the back of the stern and removed two large bags of ice. Still sweating, Kenneth helped Jake place the fish in the cooler and ice it down. " Pretty early, isn't it? Why leave with just one fish?"

Jake pointed at the bow. "Not leaving, cousin. Going! Final exams, remember? You're riding with your instructors. Pay attention."

Kenneth looked towards the bow. They were running at 30 knots again. Looking back, he could only see the faint lights from one other boat. The rest were gone. They were still heading northeast. Far away to the left, you could make out a glow of light on the horizon. Miami.

Pete kept an eye on the compass. He maintained his heading and speed for another 30 minutes and then slowed to an idle.

Kenneth glanced at the compass. The horizon lights from Miami were due west. Nothing else was out there. "How far out are we?"

"Thirty-five miles," Pete replied with confidence.

Pointing to some faint lights on the horizon to the east, Kenneth asked, "Is that the Bahamas?"

"Bimini Islands," Pete replied while stepping inside the cabin and taking the mike attached to a short-range VHF radio. Powered on, it was already set to channel 16. Pete adjusted the wattage to one. "*Lucky Too, Lucky Too, Drifter*. Over." Seconds passed.

"*Drifter, Lucky Too*, here. Channel 71. Over." Pete changed to channel 71. "Have you in sight, *Drifter*. We're a mile to your starboard. Over."

Running lights appeared out of nowhere on their starboard side. "Roger that, *Lucky Too*. Thanks. Nice night? Over."

"Nice night, *Drifter*. Out." Code words for all clear.

Pete tum to starboard and throttled up to 15 knots. Minutes later, they slowed and sided up to a beautiful boat that looked twice their size. Pete throttled back into neutral.

Jake pointed. "It's a 41-foot Hatteras. Twin cabins. Out of Bimini. Captain has a place in Port Royale. Names Hank. Has two crewmen with him. Both Jamaicans."

A black guy standing on the bow of Lucky II cast a line to Jake. Another standing in its stern cast one to Kenneth. Following Jake's lead up front, Kenneth looped his line to a cleat at *Drifter's* stern. Seconds later, they were tied up to the Hatteras. A neatly dressed man wearing a captain's hat backed away from *Lucky Too's* helm, climbed down to the deck and strolled over towards them. "Evening, Pete. The usual?"

Shaking hands, "Sounds right, Hank. How's Martha and the kids?"

Hank motioned to his crew. "Jerome, you and Casey better get to it." Both men disappeared into the Hatteras cabin. "Doing just fine, Pete. Come visit. Can't be all work and no play."

Pete smiled and then stepped back and partially pulled part of the swordfish out of the stern's storage cooler.

"Damn!" Hank complained. "We haven't even had a shark hit."

Pete was enjoying himself. "It's not far from here. Cruise over to Key Largo sometime and I'll give you and Jerome some lessons."

Both were laughing as the two Jamaicans began carrying 10 kilo bales up from the Hatteras cabin and handing across to Jake. They were off loading them two at a time. Pete stepped into *Drifter's* cabin and started storing the bales as Jake passed them inside. Kenneth wanted to help. Jake handed him a pair of binoculars. "This will only take a few minutes. Keep a watch for any running lights. Same as Hank's doing."

Pete came out of the cabin ten minutes later. Now he was the sweaty one. "We're loaded. Let's go! Thanks, Hank. Give my best to the family. I'll call in a couple of weeks. Same time."

With those go orders, Jake and Kenneth began releasing lines to the cleats. Pete handed Hank a heavy duffle bag. Jake winked at Kenneth and whispered, "That's three hundred and fifty grand bound for our bank in the Bahamas. Most of the proceeds from our last trip. We just loaded another 700 kilos!"

Kenneth stared inside the cabin. Smiled back at Jake. "Have to ask, do the two of you go fishing like this often?"

Jake nodded an affirmative, then reached for beers from the cooler. Handed one each to Pete and Kenneth. "Sorry, but I'll have to explain later. Hard to talk much over the engine noise."

Untied, Pete pulled away from the Hatteras. They all waved goodbye. Hank saluted them! Pete turned southeast and throttled up. The Grady-White planned quickly with 1500 lbs. up front. Ignoring the extra weight, Pete increased their speed to 25 knots. The two Mercury outboards seemed louder this time. He looked over at Kenneth. "At ease, Soldier. We've got two hours of this. We're 65 miles from base."

Hour and fifteen minutes later the running lights of several other boats began to appear. Kenneth figured they were the same ones they had left behind. They ran at 25knots for another thirty minutes. Pete slowed to idle speed and picked up the binoculars.

44

"We're about 7 to 8 miles out," Jake volunteered. "Watch the horizon."

Kenneth obliged. Thought he could see the flicker of a light. Green. Pete offered the binoculars. With the glasses the light was crystal clear. Pete increased their speed back to 25 knots.

Leaning close to Kenneth and speaking loudly, Jake tried to explain over the noise. "The light is from the marina captain's watch. Green means the coast is clear. Pete's guy is there. Probably been watching us coming for five minutes. Standing in the watch, he's 35 feet above sea level. On a clear night like this, he can see everything on the water 12 miles or more out. We're good to go, cousin."

A few hundred yards from the marina, Pete once more slowed to idle speed. Motored in with no wake to the slip nearest the bait shop. His spotter was waiting there with two metal platform trucks ready to load and haul. A big German shepherd sat by his side. Tail was wagging. A 20-foot cargo truck with its rear doors open was parked next to the bait shop. The truck was white with large painted signs on each side that read "Homestead Plumbing" Phone number underneath.

With all four of them working, they unloaded the *Drifter's* 700 kilos into the very back of the truck's cargo area. Took under 10 minutes. When they had completed the transfer, Jake slid a metal door down from the inside roof of the truck completely concealing the haul. Kenneth latched the door down to the floor of the truck's bed. He was sweating again. They all were. But they weren't quite finished. Pete's helper motored around a forklift with a flatbed full of plumbing equipment, including sinks and commodes, and lifted it into the rear of the truck. Pete and Jake shoved it to the back. Another two flatbeds were loaded, and the storage area seemed nearly full. Barely any room to move around. You would never suspect there were 700 kilos of Jamaican marijuana completely hidden away inside.

Jake introduced Kenneth to Pete's friend, Bucky Givens. He was Kenneth's height, 5'11", black, and looked to be not more than 25. "Call me Buck." Shook hands with Kenneth and then looked at Pete. "Did you catch anything?"

Pete was already on the bow of the Grady-White washing it down with a water hose. Yelled over. "Show him!" Together, Jake and Kenneth retrieved the swordfish and carried it to the dock's cleaning station.

Pete bragged, "Is that fish enough for you, Buck? Fresh steaks tomorrow night. You're coming, so ask Ned to close for you. Let's get going, you bums. Cleaning up here doesn't take long. Jake, you and Kenneth go on ahead to my house and get showered. Buck, park the truck in the shed, lock it up, and then get to work on that swordfish. I'll help as soon as I'm through here and then join up with you two in Homestead. Be there in an hour or so. On the way, stop at Tony's Pizza in Florida City.

They stay open till two. I'll call in an order for us."

Jake motioned Kenneth to come. He had to unlock the gate at the marina's entrance. Once outside, he locked it again, hopped back in their truck and headed north. Explained that they were going to Homestead where Pete had a really nice place.

Kenneth had to ask, "Jake, do we leave that cargo truck full of marijuana just sitting in the marina?"

"Think about it. Several things to consider. It's out of sight and locked in a shed. Buck stays at the marina in the apartment above the bait shop. Let's the dog out when he sleeps. Check your watch. Hardly any traffic traveling across old Dixie Highway right now. Homestead is 25 miles. Look a little silly for a plumber to be on this road after one in the morning. We'll make the run sometime tomorrow afternoon when *US* 1 is busy as hell."

Kenneth sat silent, and as Jake suggested, thought for a moment. Of course, he was right. Stupid question. Hell, these guys knew their business. Team players watching each other's back. Professionals too. All night, neither Pete nor Jake showed any sign of being nervous. Casual as if taking a walk in the park. In just over six hours, they had traveled what was practically a round trip to Bimini, caught a 200 lb swordfish, and smuggled 700 kilos of quality Jamaican marijuana ashore. I owe them for even considering letting me join up.

8.

PETE

Peter Ingram was born May 15, 1927, in Norfolk, Virginia where his dad was stationed and serving his fourth year of active duty in the Navy. He was deployed three months prior to Pete's birth. Like so many Navy wives, Pete's mom already had her hands full with a three-year-old son. During those times, an enlisted serviceman's family had its share of disadvantages.

Nevertheless, Pete's dad made a career out of the navy. After serving 20 years, he was rated a Senior Chief Petty Officer. Typical of navy life, Pete was raised in Norfolk, Virginia; San Diego, California; Pensacola, Florida; and Jacksonville, Florida. The family moved often, so Pete never had a chance to make any lasting friends. His dad, however, devoted most of his off-duty shore time to the kids. He was an avid saltwater fisherman, a capable sailor, and a great instructor. By the time they were in their mid-teens, both of his boys were nearly his equal as seamen and in size. Pete was stout, tough, strong as hell, and grew to a little over 6'3".

Just days after Pearl Harbor, Pete's brother joined the marines. He was 18 years old. He died in combat sometime in the month of January 1943 during the Battle of Guadalcanal. Six months later, Pete's dad was killed on the USS *Helena*, a light cruiser torpedoed in the Battle of Kula Gulf.

Pete turned eighteen two weeks before finishing high school. Ignoring his mother's wishes, he enlisted in the Navy the day before graduation. Three months later, the world war was over. He regretted missing the opportunity to somehow avenge his brother and dad.

Young, right out of high school, and with the war over, Pete initially rated a ship's serviceman. Thanks to his dad's seamanship training, he eventually qualified for Quartermaster and ended his navy career as a Chief Petty Officer Operations Specialist. He served aboard two cruisers, one amphibious assault ship, and six destroyers. He saw action on the USS *Kidd* during the Korean Conflict and on the USS *Higbee* during the Vietnam War.

Except for once in Japan, he was stationed in the U.S. for all his shore duties. Naval Station Mayport in Jacksonville, Florida was his favorite until by chance, he was reassigned for a short time to NAS Key West during the Cuban Missile Crisis. The navy had set up a temporary shore command to assist in ship navigation for the blockade around Cuba, and Pete was considered one of their very best Operations Specialists.

The dispute with Russia lasted only two weeks, but while waiting for new orders, Pete got to remain in Key West for another month. He loved it. With little or no base work to do, Pete fished, worked out, and visited bars at night trolling for the opposite sex. In the process, he made his life's best friend.

One evening in early November 1962, Pete was enjoying his second beer at a downtown Key West bar. Place was crowded. A couple of guys, one white and one black, walked inside. No one was sitting at the two barstools next to Pete. The guy in front asked, "Those seats taken?"

"No. They're all yours. Rest your chops," Pete politely replied.

Sitting down next to Pete, the white guy waved to the bartender. "Sir! Two buds when you can."

His friend had taken the other seat. Guy beside him to his right rotated around, looked for a moment and said, "Boy! Is your ass lost or something?" He was wearing a Georgia Bulldog hat. Without waiting for an answer, Bulldog stood while lifting his drink off the bar. "Get your black ass away from me before I make you eat this damn beer bottle!"

The guy sitting next to Pete looked over and leaned forward. "Hey, man. He's with me. We just want a beer. No trouble."

Bulldog stepped across and closer. Two of his friends left their seats and joined behind him. Both were also wearing Georgia hats. You could tell. They had all been having a few drinks too many. "Well, that's just too bad, 'nigger lover.' You brought trouble in with you! And now, I'm going to stick my beer bottle up both your sorry asses. In here or outside, fart face? Your choice."

Pete rose slowly. Barefoot, he was 6'3", but he was wearing navy issued boots. Towering figure of a man in a navy T-shirt filled to capacity and then some. Walked over, smiled, and gently laid his right hand on bulldog's shoulder next to his neck. Speaking softly while his grip tightened, "Guess you don't hear so good, do you? They said they were with me."

Bulldog opened his mouth trying to speak, but Pete's thumb looked as though it was already well back into his throat. He sank to his knees in pain. A little blood dripped out the side of his lips. Face turned a deep red.

Pete stared at the other two. "You should take your friend out of here. I think he needs a doctor." They were wide eyed with hesitation. "If we ever see any of you Georgia puppies around here again, a doctor won't be able to help." He loosened his grip. Bulldog sank the rest of the way to the floor. His friends lifted him by both arms. Bulldog's feet were dragging as they carried him out.

Pete's barstool neighbor extended his hand to Pete. "Sir, thank you! Thank you so much! I thought they were going to beat the hell out of us."

Pete returned the handshake. "Name's Pete. Glad to assist. He deserved what he got, but I should leave. Maybe disappear for the evening. Lots of people saw what went down. The cops here don't appreciate any kind of altercations."

"Okay. But we still owe you big time. My name's Hank Bayman. My cohort here is Jerome. We have a car on the comer lot. Come with us. I've got a place where we'll all be safe. Least I can do there is offer you a drink. Or, if you like, we can drop you at your base?"

Pete looked at his watch. Crap! Night was early. He had hopes of finding some feminine entertainment. These two didn't fit with his plans but running into the police were a poor alternative. Instead, a couple of drinks sounded good. "Alright, let's get out of here."

Hank left a C-note on the bar. Bartender nodded his head with approval and placed a finger to his lips. As far as he was concerned, nothing had happened. Pete saluted a thank you.

The car was a solid white 1961 Cadillac convertible with red leather interior. Top was down. Jerome took the wheel. Hank sat shotgun. Pete jumped in the back seat and stretched out. Jokingly told Hank he would keep his head low until the coast was clear. Damn nice ride but it only lasted 5 minutes. The safe house was parked in the Marina. A 66-foot Chris-Craft Constellation. Hank waved at it as they climbed aboard. "Dad's boat." Pete managed to keep his cool. Damn nice yacht. Name on the side was, *Lucky*. There were two crewmen. One asked if they would like refreshments. Pete noticed an accent. "Sure would," Hank said. "What's your pleasure, Pete?"

"Jack on the rocks if you have it." Finally, Pete's curiosity got the best of him. "Hank, I apologize for asking, but what does your dad do for a living?"

"We're farmers. Jamaican farmers. We're all from Jamaica."

Pete was returned to base at 3am the next morning. Jerome drove him. It was a memorable evening. The drinks were one thing, but Hanks' crew served food for hours. The two of them got along as if they had known each other for years. Inevitably, as often happens on a boat, their conversation got around to fishing. Hank already had a charter scheduled for the following night and asked Pete to join him. "Going after swordfish, Pete. If you've never caught one, you're in for a treat. Just be at the marina before six this evening."

Pete arrived by taxi late in the afternoon. He was an hour early. A little before midnight he landed his first swordfish. Weighed 135lbs. Actually, the swordfish hooked him. From that night on, they were his favorite sport. They arrived back at the marina just before daylight. On the way in, Hank had convinced him to have dinner with them. "Grilled Swordfish steaks, Pete. This time don't take a taxi. I'll have Jerome pick you up at the base. I'm sorry we have to sail home tomorrow."

Their third evening together went as well as the first two. Simply said, they enjoyed each other's company. On top of that, Pete polished off two thick cuts of grilled Swordfish. Finally, at the end of another late night, Hank encouraged Pete to visit Jamaica during one of his navy shore leaves. He had called his father and told him about the bar incident. Of course, his dad wanted to meet the man who had saved his son's life. Hank was straight up about it. Wanted to get to know him better. The invitation was an open one. Pete promised he would take him up on it. In any event, they both decided to stay in touch. Neither thought that three years would pass before the promised visit was kept.

Pete completed 19 years of service in June 1964. At the time, protest against U.S. involvement in Vietnam had spread across college campuses nationwide. Most of the servicemen in the military were pissed at the lack of respect they received for their sacrifices. Pete was particularly offended because of the loss of his brother and dad in the service. He had finished what was supposed to be his final deployment before returning February 1964 to San Diego for shore duty. With the action heating up in Vietnam and maybe to spite the protesters, he volunteered for an extended tour of duty.

The destroyer USS *Higbee* had been readied for action earlier that year. He was an experienced operations specialist and was deployed on her June 30, 1964. He spent most of the remainder of his service in the South China Sea. Pete received his discharge from the navy October 1965, when the *Higbee* saw short duty as Station Ship Hong Kong.

Mostly because of his navy career, Pete was single and unattached. His memories of good times in Florida and especially Key West were not forgotten. He liked to envision himself becoming another Earnest Hemmingway; except for the part where he ended it all by suicide. Only fishing and the ladies because he was no writer.

Within a month after his discharge, he had temporarily moved into a small upstairs apartment in Key West. Toward the end of his third week there he managed to get into a fight with a couple of long-haired peace lovers. They lost, but the place was crawling with them, so Pete was thinking of moving on. First though, he wanted to see if he might reconnect with Hank. Mostly on Hank's part, they had corresponded some over the past three years. Pete sent a few postcards and Hank, in turn, wrote letters back. Once he had included pictures of himself and his two sons holding a string of yellow tails. Comment on the back read "eat your heart out." He always ended with his telephone number and asking Pete when he was getting out of the navy.

Pete called long distance to Jamaica. A woman answered. A thought flashed through his mind that it might be a wrong number but what the hell. "Yes Ma'am. This is Peter Ingram. Could I speak with Hank?"

"You most certainly may, Pete. I've heard all about you. Read your cards too. You have to come visit us. Just a minute, I'll get him." Pete overheard her a few seconds later in the background, "Sweetie, you're not going to believe this. It's Pete."

The conversation with Hank lasted a quarter hour. There was way too much to catch up on over the phone. Even so, Hank was trying. He knew Pete had spent eighteen months out of the last three years aboard ship, and that he had been stationed out of San Diego. Pete explained how he was recently discharged and that at the present, he was fooling around in Key West. Asked if Hank and his crew might be coming there any time soon?

"No, Pete, but since you're free, why don't you come to Jamaica? Love to have you as a guest. You'll get to meet the family, we can catch up, fish a lot, just gel out and relax. What say you? You've got to do this. Remember your promise."

Pete politely lied. "Hank, thanks so much for the invitation. Mighty gracious of you but I can't take advantage of your hospitality like that."

"Come off it, Pete. That's bullshit! And I told you my dad wants to meet the man who saved my life."

He was right. It was bull. He was dying to visit. Hell, I'm going to Jamaica! "Okay, Hank, what's convenient for you?"

"Tomorrow, Pete. Pack for a couple of weeks. There's a flight out of Key West International in the morning. Pan Am to Miami and then to Jamaica. Departs at 9am I think but call and make sure. A ticket will be waiting for you at check in. You'll need your passport. We'll pick you up on arrival."

Pete thought, unbelievable! Talk about a nice thing for Hank to do. Sitting here for weeks being crapped on by a thousand war haters, and a guy all the way from Jamaica offers a friendly hand. He had spent over twenty years in the navy and could not remember having something like this to look forward to.

The Pan Am flight departed for Miami at 8:55 that morning. Pete was booked first class. Changed planes in Miami and arrived at Sangster International early that afternoon. It was not until looking at his ticket before boarding that he knew exactly where he was going. Montego Bay! Sounded good to him. He had sailed all over the Caribbean in a destroyer but had never made a port stop in one of the islands. He breezed through customs. Hank was waiting with a handshake. Another Cadillac convertible too. This one was baby blue. "My wife's car," Hank explained.

"We live near Negril, Pete. Small city only about 30 miles to the southwest of Montego Bay, but the drive takes an hour. Enjoy the scenery. There's a cooler with cold beer in the back. Help yourself."

Pete did both. The route was a curvy coastal road all the way. Perfect weather for December. Top was down on the car. "Never going to beat this, Hank. Thanks for having me."

In fact, the ride and the scenery were just the beginning. Hank's place was a plantation house overlooking the coast. Private driveway through an ornamental iron gate. As they drove in, there were white wooden fences closing off large grass fields on each side. Horses were mulling around the one on his left. The home was an incredibly beautiful two story with a plush garden and a fountain in front. The driveway circled around to steps where Hank stopped.

"Pete, come in first and greet the family. They're all anxious to welcome you. Leave your luggage in the car. I'll drive you over to the guest house after they finish with you. That's it just over to your right. Give you a chance to freshen up before dinner. Walk back over about seven. Dress casual. This is Jamaica. Hope you don't mind but we're putting on a welcoming spread for you. Dad will join us. He loves great food, and he also wants to finally meet you."

Pete was introduced to Hank's wife, Martha, and their two teenage boys. She politely extended her hand and welcomed him to their home. "Pete, I'll show you around this evening. Go on and rest a bit for now. We just want you to relax and enjoy." She was an attractive and gracious hostess to say the least.

The guest house was as nice as any place Pete had ever stayed. Railed patio in back overlooking the Caribbean. After washing up and changing, Pete took a beer from the fridge, walked out back, and for a while just relaxed. Nice view. He thought, how lucky can you get?

Dinner that evening was splendid. The main course was a combination of spiny lobster and crab cakes. Hank's dad had arrived just before the table was served. From his appearance, Pete's first impression of him was Earnest Hemingway in the flesh. Back from the dead maybe! Tanned, full bodied man, maybe 65 or 70, with a head of gray hair and a short gray-white beard. Casually dressed wearing loose trousers and a colorful short sleeve shirt on the outside. Without hesitating, introduced himself. "Pete, Carl Bayman. Welcome to Jamaica. You and I have lots to talk about. Hank may not have told you, but I'm a navy vet too. We'll get to that and more later. Better eat first, or Martha may get annoyed with us"

Dinner ended with a slice of key lime pie for dessert. The boys had homework, so Hank helped Martha clear away the dishes. Carl invited Pete to the den. "Hank, join us when Martha is through with you in the kitchen. Come on, Pete. Let those 'girls' do their job."

The den was finished in stained hardwood. There were filled bookshelves on either side of the door. Both the left and right walls were hung with framed ancient maps of the Caribbean. Four leather cushion seats and a center table were arranged toward a curtain covering the back. Carl drew the curtain opening floor to ceiling windows with a clear view of the sea. "Nice night. I never get tired of looking at that wonderful sea. Would you like a cigar, Pete? They're real good Cubans. There's brandy here if you prefer."

"I could enjoy a good smoke, but only if you're having one."

Carl opened a teakwood box on the table. Took out three and a cigar cutter. Trimmed the end of one and offered it to Pete with his left hand

and a light from his zippo with his right. Pete accepted, then drew and puffed until it was well lit. "Thanks, Carl. Really tops off Martha's great dinner."

They settled back in the leather chairs. Without asking again, Carl poured two glasses of brandy. "Pete, let me tell you a little about myself before Hank comes. My son has heard it all anyway."

"Not much to say about my early years. Born and raised in New Haven. I remember those winters being very cold. Made me love Jamaica even more. I told you I was a navy vet. Hard to believe now but I signed on in 1916. Three months in, I started submarine training. First served on the USS *KS* as a seaman. After the U.S. entered the war, we were assigned convoy escorts around the Azores. Never saw much in the way of action, Pete, but I can tell you it was miserable duty. Rough seas, cramped wet quarters, crap for food, and a tiny head for the seamen that smelled to high heaven. A lot more I could say of those times, but altogether, it was worse than you can imagine. Memories of it still wake me some nights."

Pete interrupted. "Carl, why the hell did you choose submarines? In those days it was dangerous just to be on one, and a hell-of-a-lot more in combat!"

"Pete, I was only 19. What the hell did a 19-year-old know back then? We were all a little crazy I guess, especially those poor souls that served on the ground. But it worked out well for me in the long run. Shortly before the war ended, I was made third class Petty Officer. Reassigned to the USS *K7* stationed at Key West Naval Base. Served my last year and a half out of that base. Early on, a few ASW patrols but after the war, training duties only. Lots of shore time with leaves too."

"Those days in Key West changed my whole life, Pete. I wouldn't be sitting here with you and family today if not for the time I served there. Fell in love with the Caribbean. Never wanted to leave it and never did. Raised a son and daughter here in Jamaica. Now I have six grandchildren too."

"Except for the kids, your story sounds a lot like what happened to me. It was the Cuban missile thing three years ago that got me assigned to NAS Key West. Great duty place and met Hank there. Damn Caribbean is catching. Like I said, no kids yet that I know of, but I'm still young."

There was a single knock on the door and Hank walked in. "Uh-oh! Is Dad telling you war stories?"

Carl answered the question. "Not so much war stories, Son. Just a little of this old man's interesting history. Sit with us and have a cigar."

Carl offered his son a cigar. "That's enough about me for now, Pete. I could carry on all night, but I'd rather learn about you. Anyway, we've got the rest of the week ahead of us before leaving. Tell me about yourself. I already know you can handle a bar fight."

Pete spent the next half hour talking about himself beginning with how he had joined up after the loss of his dad and brother. Went on for a while about the action he had seen on the USS *Kidd* and the USS *Higbee*; then some of his favorite station times; finally for Carl's benefit, told a few humorous stories of bar fights. The night drew on and ended with Hank asking his dad to go fishing with them in the morning.

Carl declined but invited them both to the farm the day after. "What do you think, Son? Should we give Pete a tour and teach him a little about Jamaican agriculture?"

"Absolutely, Dad! I'll fish him in while we're on the boat tomorrow. Be a good catch too! Pete, rise and shine by six in the morning. We'll have breakfast at the marina. Suppose to be nice weather but bring a jacket in case. Maybe fresh tuna for dinner tomorrow night."

Pete thanked Martha for serving such a fine meal, said his goodnight to everyone, then made the short walk back to the guest house. It wasn't quite ten, so he poured a whiskey from the bar and sat out on the patio. Clear night lit with a million stars. Curious though. Hank had said pack for two weeks. Something must have come up because Carl mentioned they were leaving before the end of a week. Just hoped the timing of his stay had not turned into an inconvenience for them. He would have to volunteer an early departure while fishing tomorrow. Whatever the case, catching some tuna sounded good.

Pete woke at five and was waiting outside for Hank before six. They made a fifteen-minute drive from the house before pulling into a marina. It was located on the Negril River just north of the city. A sign at the entrance read "Bayman's Marine and Storage." Hank waved toward the sign. "Not mine. Belongs to Dad"

Jerome was waiting for them with a 25-foot Cris-Craft Cavalier tied to the dock. A counter in the cabin was set with sausage-egg biscuits, coffee, and cinnamon rolls. Just the right servings for an early morning outing on the water. They enjoyed a few minutes eating before Hank took the helm and started the inboard engine. They passed under a bridge and met some rough water around the inlet jetties. Once they cleared, Hank increased speed and motored out and parallel to the coast for nearly half an hour, then slowed to about three knots while Jerome let out two rods rigged with feathered jigs.

Pete was not new to tuna fishing. Off and on he helped Jerome with the chumming. By midday, they had landed four yellowfin tunas in the thirty plus pound range. Lost two yellowfins at the boat and a big blue-fin. As they reeled in their rods to return home, Pete looked off to the horizon. "Hank, I'm having the best time I can ever remember. What a day. Thanks for having me. I won't forget this! And about packing for two weeks. Your dad mentioned you guys had to leave in a few days. Just let me know when it's time to go. I'm good with whatever is convenient."

"I have a little explaining to do, Pete. Truth is, I have a lot to explain! For reasons you'll come to understand, I haven't been completely up front with everything. Last night, after you left, Dad and I talked. Let's just say he was impressed. You more than lived up to his expectations."

"I liked him too. Interesting guy you have for a father."

"Thanks. Here's what we talked about. We want to make you a busi-ness proposal. If interested, your packing for two weeks or more will become crystal clear. It's not something to discuss over engine noise, so for now, let's go back in. Once we get home and clean up a bit, I'll join you at the guest house. Okay?"

"Hot Damn, Hank! Of course, it's okay with me. Let's get moving."

Pete's curiosity was killing him. Whatever was going on, it had to be good. Beer in his hand; wind in his face; thinking all the way to the marina he could never afford a nice boat like this on a navy pension. Maybe if he could earn some extra cash working with Hank and Carl, it might be possible?

9.

CARL

Hank showed up at the guest house a little after four. He brought along of those Cuban cigars. Pete poured two bourbons, and they walked out onto the patio. Nice breeze and still a couple of hours until sunset. Both men stood for a moment looking out over the Caribbean.

"Pete, everything I'm about to say to you is confidential. You'll understand why soon enough. I'm sure by now you've figured that the family is well off. I can tell you it's all thanks to Dad. You'll visit the big farm tomorrow. Covers nearly 1,200 acres. I also own a somewhat remote and much smaller farm. It connects to the back side of his. Combined, we have about eight hundred acres of cultivated croplands. Dad has a home in Negril. In Montego Bay, he owns Bayman's Financial Service. It's a small but successful brokerage firm with a select clientele. He also owns some recreational and commercial properties in the Bahamas. Here in town, he owns the bank, a restaurant, two bars, and half of a sizable resort. Also, the marina you saw."

Pete interrupted. "Interesting and more, Hank! He's a regular nice guy. Not an ounce of pretense in him. You're one lucky son."

"I agree. I have a lucky sister too. Janice. She has four kids. She's raising them in Coral Gables. Her husband is an attorney and has his own law firm in Miami. He's well connected with both local and state officials. All of our stateside legal matters are handled by him or one of his associates "

"Carl mentioned he had six grandchildren. Quite a family!"

"I think so too. One reason I mentioned Janice has to do with Dad. He's leaving this Friday. Flying to Miami to close on a property in Key Largo. Plans to combine business with pleasure and spend time with Janice and the grandkids."

"I see. It's just Carl that's leaving?"

"Not exactly, Pete, and I'll come to that. Last night, Dad pretty much talked about himself up until he left the Navy. He was discharged in June 1920. He had made up his mind to stay in Key West. After more than a year, the warm blue waters were in his blood. With his savings and some borrowed money, he started a charter fishing business. That didn't turn out so well. By early that next year he was broke, and the bank was about to repossess his boat."

That's one tough story, especially after all the crap he went through serving the country in those stinky submarines. Lousy payback, Hank. And still, he built all this in Jamaica somehow from scratch?"

"Well, to some extent, but in a way, he owes it all to the good old U.S. government."

"You're kidding me?"

"Pete, he was smart, a good seaman, and it was the beginning of pro-hibition. Cheap Rum could be had from boats anchored just beyond the three-mile limit. Dad started taking chances at night smuggling it to shore. With his experience at sea, he was damn good at it. Claims he sometimes made three runs a night and occasionally did that in the fog."

"Must have been risky as hell. What about the Coast Guard? Shore patrols?"

"Way Dad tells it, they were pathetically understaffed and cruised around in slow boats lit up like a Christmas tree. Says he often ran without any lights, especially if he spotted one."

"Hank, it still took some balls. Did it alone, man against the sea kind of thing. Have to be brave as hell. And he's your dad. Proud of him, aren't you?"

"I respect my father more than anything. I could go on all evening about him. Instead, let me try to sum it up for you. I'm going someplace with this, and it involves you."

"Keep talking. I'm all ears."

"Well, it wasn't long before Dad bought a much bigger boat and began working out of the Bahamas. Bimini Islands to be accurate. Barely sixty miles from Miami. By the end of 1923 he was supplying smaller boats along a good part of the Florida coast. He was making quite a bit of money, Pete, and just when you would think it couldn't get any better, the U.S. government helped him again."

"Payback and then some. How, Hank?"

"Early in 1924 they extended territorial waters to twelve miles. Tough on small boats coming that far out for cheap rum. Cost a few lives the way Dad tells it. Even so, there were still plenty of guys who would take the chance, especially if they were bringing in good whiskey and gin. Sold for a lot more and made it worth the risk. Dad was early to recognize the market had changed. He transitioned to English Gin, Canadian Whiskey and Vodka. Good quality stuff too."

"That's true to this day. I like Jack Daniels, and I don't care if it costs more even on my budget."

"Story gets better, Pete, and that's where Jamaica came into play. Most of his supplies came through Jamaica, and its north coast offered a direct route into the Gulf of Mexico. In mid-1925, he expanded his operations and opened a second front into the states. Montego Bay, Jamaica to Plaquemines Parish, Louisiana. Thirteen hundred miles give or take. Dad had to purchase a much larger boat. With it and by the end of the year, he was smuggling contraband worth a fortune and clearing as much as three hundred thousand dollars each run."

"Hell, Hank. Per trip! That was an unimaginable amount of money in those days. But Prohibition ended. What happened then?"

"Ended in 1933, but Dad saw it coming with the start of the Great Depression. Sold everything to do with the business in 1929. Bought the farm and took up residence right here in Negril. After nine years of smuggling, he was very rich. But there's something else you should know about him and it's pretty impressive."

"I'm already impressed, Hank, but go on."

"Dad's got a great big heart. When he started operating out of Jamaica and making all that money, there was a huge disparity here between the wealthy and the general population. Too much for him to ignore. No way he could just sit and do nothing. The infrastructure for the poor was pathetic. No shortage of places or people in need of a good Samaritan. With all that cash coming in, Dad became that and more."

"So, he decided to return some of his good fortune?"

"Shortly after beginning his operations in Louisiana, he started taking half of the proceeds from each run and spending it on some needed projects, He concentrated the money in the two parishes around Negril. Westmoreland and Hanover. Pete, he's a local hero. Put up the funds for the elementary school and the high school; the hospital; a park and recreational facility; and several housing projects. He's mostly responsible for a first-class fire department in Negril, and as well, the police facilities. All that and more."

"Not what you would call keeping a low-profile, Hank. On top of everything else, he's a philanthropist."

"You could say that. It was about the same time that he met my mother. She loved and worshiped him for all his good deeds. Beautiful lady and he was devoted to her. Sadly though, I never really knew her. She died in 1938 giving birth to Janice. Dad never remarried."

"I can understand. When you love someone, you never completely recover from their loss. I still think about how the war took my father and brother. I wonder if that's why I've never married."

"Ready for the good part of all this, Pete?"

"If there's more? Carry on, but what you've already explained will be hard to beat."

"You're wrong. Try this on for size. The family tradition of helping the locals continues today, and I'm going to follow in Dad's footsteps."

"Not possible, is it? Not in these times?"

"Pete, tomorrow we'll visit the farms and I'll show you some of what Dad referred to as innovative Jamaican agriculture. Are you familiar with ganja?"

"No?"

"Hindi for marijuana. We grow marijuana. A lot of it!"

Pete was quiet. At first maybe, a loss for words. Just a puzzled look at Hank before he spoke. "I remember when we first met in Key West, you said you were farmers. Arriving here I thought you and your dad must have been successful at it. 'Innovative Jamaican Agriculture!' Explains a lot. I'm not only appreciative, Hank, I'm enjoying every detail of all this."

Hank smiled and gave Pete a minute to recover by pouring both another bourbon. The conversation on the patio lasted until an hour after the sun set. Hank had continued with the rather incredible history of Carl Bayman.

Carl had attempted to make a go at farming when he first started in the early thirties. He raised and harvested sugarcane, bananas, and cacao beans. Mostly bananas. Harvesting them was hard, labor-intensive work. It took a little over a year for each tree to mature and bear fruit. Making matters worse, sugarcane and especially bananas were the principal crops on many of the Caribbean Islands and some of the Central American countries. Results were a huge over supply of both. Even on sizable farms like his, breakeven was the norm. But it was Jamaica and Carl recognized a more profitable market to be explored.

Most Jamaicans were very poor by American standards. As such, they often found relief in one or two local commodities. Cheap rum and cheap ganja. The latter was even part of a religious movement. Simply put, ganja was illegal but completely tolerated. As a compliment, Jamaica offered an ideal climate for growing cannabis. The season was long enough that plants could be allowed to grow to a full floral stage. The benefits for the farmers were quality and quantity.

Carl's farm had over three hundred acres of pure stand banana groves. The trees were perennial. With tilling, they allowed for mixed cultivation. In 1935, Carl tried it. He blended two fifty-acre groves on the very most back side of the farm with marijuana plants. Eight months later, the farm was profitable. Over the course of another five years, he experimented with different strains, fertilizer, spacing, and rotations. He also introduced mixed cultivation with the cacao trees. By the time the U.S. entered WWII, he was a top producer of quality Jamaican marijuana.

Carl only sold in bulk within the country. His operations were virtually risk free. Almost all of what he produced was consumed in Jamaica. Content with not being greedy, he never personally exported. Part of the reason for keeping a lower profile was that he was raising two kids.

Carl invested a portion of the profits but continued to contribute more than half to parish projects and local charities. Meet him on the street and you would never know it, but within the two parishes around Negril, he was practically revered.

Hank and Pete had just finished enjoying their third Jack Daniels when Martha rang a dinner bell on her porch. "Time flies, Pete! Let's continue all of this in the den after dinner. Dad will be joining us again tonight. There's more to explain, especially the part of me following in his footsteps and where we hope you will fit in."

"I'm starving. Let's go! After all this, I'm looking forward to spending another evening with your father."

Martha served baked tuna with side dishes. Delicious! The boys politely alternated asking Pete questions about the Vietnam War. Good table manners kept Pete from telling the kids like it really was.

Once more in the den, Carl wasted no time asking Hank to update him with regards to Pete.

"We went over most of your background in Key West and the startup here in Jamaica. Left plenty to talk over with you tonight. No details yet on where we're going with this."

"Good. I'll fill in some blanks for you, Pete. Bear with me if I double up on something my son has already told you."

"Carl, I know enough about you already to make me respect whatever you have to say."

"I'll get to it then! The Great Depression hit here in Jamaica harder than the states. For reasons of my profession up until that time, I had avoided banks. Thank God for that too. Truth is, I was loaded with cash. Stashed it under the mattress sort of speak. I bought a lot of my properties here and in the Bahamas for pennies on the dollar, and there was plenty left over."

"Dad, I went over some of your deeds with the Jamaicans starting in the mid-twenties."

"Thanks. Sharing my good fortune paid off though. Things got so bad that in 1934 there were riots. Damn rebellion started right next door in Westmoreland parish and then spread some. Farm labor went on strike.

Everywhere except me, Pete. Locals remembered all my help, so I was spared. Even protected!"

"World War One in submarines, rum running out of Key West, and then kept from harm's way during a rebellion. You've got a guardian angel looking after you, Carl."

"Maybe so. Hope she stays with us with what we're about to do. Consider this. On my farm and Hank's, we raise around thirty-five tons of ganja a year. Good at cultivation and processing too! Best on the whole damn Island, I think. Partly for family reasons, I've stayed out of the export business for the past thirty years. That, some connections, and because lots of the farmers in Jamaica grow the stuff, keeps the authorities away."

"Thirty-five tons, Carl. Hell! That's a lot of marijuana."

"Yeah, and mixed in with the other crops, profitable even in Jamaica. Sells really cheap here, Pete. Locally, we only gross about twenty-five dollars a pound. I keep about half the net for the family and give the rest away. May sound generous to you but ten times that and much more is needed here. Just look around. These people are poor!"

Carl paused for a few seconds as though reflecting on what he had just said. Hank politely continued for him. "Two things happened to make Dad and I think seriously about exporting part of our ganja. First, since Jamaican independence in 1962, the Jamaican Labor Party has held the majority in parliament. They're market friendly and Dad is a major supporter with high up connections. Second, starting about the same time as independence, a good portion of what we produced on our farms began to be purchased and smuggled into the states. We sell in bulk, Pete. A kilo goes for about fifty U.S. dollars. Street dealers in the states make ten times that. Can you see where we're going with this?"

"Like you said. Follow in your dad's footsteps. Consider it a compliment for saying this. You're just a chip off the old-block."

Carl laughed. "He may like to think so but I'm smarter. Been planning a change for a couple of years. My idea. Let Hank in on it this past summer. And now, Pete, we want you to become a part of the team!"

Second time that day Pete was lost for what to say. There was a moment of silence. Carl and Hank were both watching for his reaction. Leaning forward and slowly shaking his head in approval. "I'm in! Whatever it is you want me to do? I'm in."

Carl offered a handshake. "Just the response we were hoping for, Pete. Tomorrow, we'll give you a tour of the farm. Never hurts to know both ends of an operation like the one we're proposing. Unfortunately, I have to fly off to Miami the day after. I'll leave it to Hank to explain your part in this business."

"After Dad leaves, there will be plenty of time to go over some details. Weather is still looking good, so hopefully we can do that during another fishing trip. And then, if the weather still allows, we'll be taking the Constellation on a voyage to the Bahamas. How does that sound?"

"Like a dream come true, Hank. Why me of all people?"

"Don't sell yourself short. Dad was first to bring it to my attention. You're a seaman. A damn good one. Your skills are exactly what the job requires."

Carl nodded. "You remind me of myself, Pete. Hey fellows, can we call it a night? Get an early start in the morning. Hank, best you don't spend too much more of the evening with the two of us instead of Martha. She can be understanding to a point! See you both at the farm after sunup."

The farm was gated. Red clay roads harden with crushed limestone that wound over gently rolling hills groomed with what appeared to be the stumps of banana trees on one side and stands of cacao trees on the other. They passed by a dozen or so small row houses. Hank pointed to them. "That's quarters for our hands that stay here year-round, Pete. During harvest, we have to bus in more workers."

Carl was waiting on the porch of the main farmhouse as they drove up. He hopped in the back seat. "Good morning, boys. Drive on, Hank. This little visit will take about an hour. Afterwards, we can go into town for breakfast."

Hank drove another two hundred yards beyond the house and through a patch of thick woods. He stopped and unlocked a second gate. The road opened out and through more banana groves and cacao trees. Both were well tilled. "We're on my property now, Pete."

"Sorry to ask but where's all the marijuana?" Then, pointing before Hank could reply. "And what kind of trees are these?"

"Cacao trees to answer your second question. Beans from its fruit are roasted to make cocoa and chocolate. As for the marijuana, it's out of season. Three months ago, it was growing right here beneath the canopies of the banana and cacao trees. It's called 'mixed cultivation.' We plant the seedlings in March and harvest in early October. Afterwards, we harvest the bananas and cacao beans and till the land. The stalk of the banana tree is cut each year. They're perennials. It's December now, Pete. Come back next September and you'll see everything lush and ripe."

From the back seat, Carl tapped Pete's shoulder. "Don't worry. In those two big barns by the sheds over there, you're about to see a whole lot of marijuana."

"The sheds are for drying," Hank added. "The barns are for curing first and then packaging. Thirty-five tons takes up some room when it's handled and stored properly. Processing takes us a little more than two months."

The first barn was filled with fifteen hundred bales, each neatly wrapped with orange plastic. They were stacked four high and eight deep on reinforced shelving that lined the barn's walls.

"Each bale weighs ten kilos, Pete. Any more than four high will damage cured marijuana. We have to be careful packaging too. Dad's been at this for years. The growth time under tree canopies and the way we process takes longer than most, but our quality is hard to beat."

Carl boasted. "Best on the whole damn island. What say we take a look at the other barn, Son? Then drive him through the fields. I'm ready for some breakfast."

HIGH TIDE IN CHERRY GROVE

The tour of the second barn and the rest of the farm took another thirty minutes. Afterwards, they drove to Negril. Over breakfast in a private room at Carl's restaurant, Hank continued to explain their operation. Pete asked lots of questions. He was an anxious learner. It showed!

They dropped Carl off at the bank. "Enjoyed the morning, Pete. My house is a short walk from here. Sorry to have to cut out so soon but I've got business to take care of before I leave tomorrow." Carl reached out to shake hands goodbye while smiling; "Welcome aboard, Pete. See you in the Keys next week."

As Hank drove away, he looked over at Pete. "I already know what you're going to ask. The answer is we will be meeting up with Dad later part of next week in the keys. Key Largo. But let me ask you something?"

"As usual, I'm a good listener, Hank. Let's hear it. Before I forget though, thanks for the morning's tour and breakfast too."

"Hell, I enjoyed showing you around. Did you happen to notice that about a quarter of the shelves in our second barn were empty?"

"I noticed but were they supposed to be full?"

"Two hundred bales worth. Two thousand kilos. They're already loaded on the Constellation."

"And we're sailing her to the Bahamas, right?"

"Bimini to be exact. Dad has a nice house in Port Royal."

"Hank, that's a lot of marijuana."

"Yep! But it's well under *Lucky's* load capacity. Room for more but I like a safe ride. Even so, I'm glad to have someone with your experience as crew. Jerome, Casey, and Ray, our galley steward, will be coming along with us. How does our little sea cruise sound so far?"

"Stability on the seas along with a good crew is the only way to sail. What's the weather forecast like?"

"Real good. Light wind out of the southeast. Say, is it okay with to drop you off at the guest house for the rest of the day? I'll have dinner sent over for you this evening. We'll be sailing Saturday, and I want to spend some quality time with Martha and the kids before we leave."

"Sure enough, Hank. I've got lots to think about. Suppose we don't go fishing tomorrow? That can give you more time with them."

"No. We'll still rise early and fish in the morning. Mix business with some fun. The trip will give us a chance to discuss how you will be fitting into operations with Dad and I."

Early the next day, they enjoyed another fishing trip together. Towards the end of the morning, discussions turned to business. Hank had estimated it would take the Constellation a little less than four days to reach Bimini. After docking at Carl's house in Port Royal, he explained how they would go about transferring their cargo from Lucky. "Big house on a cut canal, Pete. Private too. Dad owns vacant lots on both sides and there's a two-car garage in back that we've modified for safe storage. On top of that, we recently bought a 41-foot Hatteras. Great for offshore fishing and perfect for running loads offshore at night."

"Sounds all good, Hank, but where will we be running to?"

"Okay. Here we go. This is where you come into the game. We'll be running fifteen miles out from Bimini and meeting with you, Pete. Transfers will be in good weather at night under the cover of charter fishing. The business side of Dad making a trip to Miami is to close on the purchase of a marina in Key Largo. Also, a nice home in Homestead. You'll be in total charge of both and operating out of the marina"

"Hank. I can do this. Makes my day! It may take a little while to set up. No problem though. Just like Carl back during Prohibition. Only now it will be me, and I'll be smuggling marijuana instead of rum."

"Pretty close to the way we figured you in. It will take some time to work out the details on your part. First, buy yourself a boat for charter fishing. We'll supply the cash. Consider it a sign on bonus."

"Oh, hell yes! I know exactly what I need. A good size Grady-White with strong outboards. Fast and dependable with a two hundred mile plus range."

"Sounds about right. Figure in the size with running as much as two thousand pounds. And, if Dad or I come to visit, we can try to catch swordfish with you."

"Remember I told Carl he must have a guardian angel watching over him? Well, right now I think that same angel is hanging around me."

"That may be, Pete, but you'll need some help besides her. The mechanics of the operation stateside will be to get things started strictly as a bulk supplier. Stay in the background. Put space between yourself and the street dealers. Remain anonymous as possible. Any ideas?"

"By chance, to get things cranking, I may know just the person to bring onboard. Best of all, he's from Miami. Name's Bucky Givens. Goes by Buck. He served as a ship's serviceman on the USS *Higbee* during my last tour. Before we were deployed, the two of us were occasional drinking buddies in San Diego. Smoked a little grass together too."

"And he's not in the service anymore?"

"No. He worked in the ship's galley. A cocky first lieutenant caught him baking cookies spiked with Mexican hash. Pissed half the crew off when he brought Buck up on charges. He received an 'other than honorable discharge,' Hank, but he was a good hand and we got along well together. I stood up for him at the hearing. It didn't help much, but he thanked me before leaving. I can look him up."

"Your call, Pete. Hey, we're almost back to shore and I promised Martha another evening together before leaving. Anyway, we'll have lots of time on the Constellation."

"Okay with me. Family always comes first."

Back at the house before noon, Hank loaned Pete his car and suggested he spend the rest of the day learning his way around Negril. "Maybe visit a bar or two after dark. Plenty of action around if you're inclined to get lucky. Just be in good shape and ready to leave midday tomorrow."

Pete dutifully obeyed both of Hank's instructions that evening. The next morning, he was happily refreshed for the trip. They set out for the Bahamas early afternoon, December third. They reached Bimini on Pearl Harbor Day. Pete had spent much of his life on the sea but never in the comfort of cruising for days on a yacht. Even with their cargo, there was plenty of space and little real work. Nothing like his time on destroyers. He enjoyed every minute of it. And Ray was a good cook!

They arrived dockside at Carl's home in Port Royal just before sunset. Around midnight, the five of them offloaded four tons of marijuana to pallets. Eight pallets each with fifty bales and weighing a half a ton were carried by forklift into an oversized, three-car detached garage set towards the back of the house. The rear wall of the garage was equipped with heavy steel shelving allowing the pallets to be placed four across and two high. Once all were in place, five feet across the back side of the garage was taken up. Even so, it was only half full with room above for eight more stacked pallets. Hank and Jerome next concealed it with four separate sections of well fitted, floor to ceiling, wood shelves. Working together, Casey and Ray filled the shelf space with assorted tools, garden equipment, tackle boxes, and a dozen or more rods and reels for offshore fishing. When they had finished, Jerome drove inside a Ford pickup followed by Hank in a Mustang convertible. While sliding the garage doors down he couldn't resist asking Pete what he thought of it all?

"You wouldn't know it was anything but a plain old big garage, Hank. Nice piece of work!"

"Sorry to disappoint you but I had nothing to do with any of this. All Dad's doings nearly a year ago. Remember he told you he started planning the operation long before I knew anything about it."

"Never ceases to surprise you, does he? Carl's really smart."

"You're right as hell about that. Come on. Let's get some rest."

"Sounds good, Hank. I'm tired. It's past two, so maybe I'll sleep in."

Pete woke at ten in the morning to the smell of bacon cooking. He found Hank already at the kitchen table waiting on Ray to serve. "Good morning. Sorry if I'm late. Slept hard and sound all night. Felt good!"

"No problem, Pete. Your timing couldn't be better. Jerome and Casey left for the Port Royal marina with the Constellation an hour ago. After securing it, they'll be coming back with the Hatteras. Dad called and would like for us to meet him in Key Largo before five. We'll leave after breakfast. Just you, I, and Jerome. Seas are slightly choppy ahead of a front coming tomorrow afternoon. That was when we had planned to go. Not a problem now with the Hatteras. Four hours max. If we wait, the weather could set us back days, and I promised Martha I'd be home within two weeks of our leaving Jamaica. Christmas time, you know?"

"Like I've said before, best to always first consider the weather and family. Looking forward to the Hatteras too. Not to mention meeting up with Carl again after seeing this handy work and learning how I fit into his plans."

They made it to Key Largo before five. Pete took the helm all the way and loved it. The seas were not even white capping. Breeze out of the east and cool. For the last quarter mile, they motored at idle speed. Lots of other boats around. Carl and an older black guy named Ned were waiting for them at the marina in front of a two-story bait and tackle shop. Pete, Hank and Jerome waved. Carl grinned and saluted.

Weather was coming, so Jerome and Ned stayed with the Hatteras to secure it while Carl showed Pete around his newly acquired marina. Hank had seen it all before the purchase but strolled along as company. Pretty common set up with covered storage sheds for boats, a double wide concrete ramp into the water, and two boardwalks with adjoining slips. Above the tackle shop there was a small apartment with a combined kitchen-living area, bathroom, and a circular stairway to a captain's watch on the roof. The whole place seemed to be in top notch shape. Even so, Carl had prepared a list of improvements for Pete. The list included adding a double-wide house trailer off to the backside of the property and enclosing the whole place with chain-link fencing and a gate.

"As for the trailer, Pete, I've already picked one out to be delivered in a few days. We'll need the extra space when we make a fishing visit, and you'll want some full time help around here besides Ned. Oh, in case I forgot to mention, Ned comes with marina. We go back a long way and I guarantee he's a good man you can trust. We'll be leaving you behind to get acquainted with the place. Call yourself a manager if you like."

"Dad, it's after sunset, so for now let's take off for Homestead. We've had a long day and I'm hungry. Great restaurant in the town for dinner tonight, Pete, and we'll show you the house. Plenty of room for us there in what will be your permanent quarters. You'll like it."

They dined in one of Homestead's downtown restaurants. In season for Florida and the place was nearly full. They drove to the house after eight. Pete liked it before they unlocked the door. Nice and located on the outskirts of town. First class ranch style with four bedrooms and three baths. It was set at the back of a large, wooded lot. Hank pointed out a two-car attached garage. "Guess what our plans are for the garage?"

"Not hard to guess. Storage I bet?"

Carl replied for his son. "Yes, but not like in Port Royal. I've drawn up the plans for you. Concealed underground cellar with climate control. Cars parked on top. Space beneath large enough for five hundred bales"

"Carl. The Hatteras, my boat, a marina, and this house. You're spending a hell-of-a-lot of money!"

"Might seem so, Pete, but consider this. Within two years or less, we plan to be moving more than half what we grow in Jamaica through the Key Largo marina to Homestead. Bulk sales of twenty tons! Gross proceeds should come to around twelve million. That could double if prices go up, and I'm pretty sure they will because marijuana is increasingly popular in the states. Also, we're working on strains that will make major improvements to our quality."

"Carl, that's moving a lot of marijuana and all that cash too. Thanks for your confidence but this is more than just a little new to me."

"Well, as for the money, don't worry. Sale proceeds will be transferred offshore through the Bahamas to my bank in Jamaica. The harder part of your end will be setting up distribution here in Florida. You'll need help and my advice on that is to take your time. Do you play poker?"

"Sure. During deployments quite a bit and pretty good too."

"Sounds corny but maybe think of it this way. You're working as a house dealer. You hold all the cards and all the chips. Those you'll be bringing into this game are just players coming to the table. Strangers at first, so never show your hole cards until you're sure of who you've been dealing to. Bottom line, keep some distance. Try to put layers of anonymity between yourself and the streets."

"Dad, I've pretty much already told him not to hurry and some tricks on being careful. He has an ex-navy friend in Miami to begin with. Like you and Ned, they go back some. Pete plans to search his buddy out for starters and go from there."

"I like the sound of it, especially working with former service members. With the right choices, it's like keeping everything in the family. And Pete, there's another thing I need to let you know when it comes to family. Put you a little at ease with this. One of the best law firms in Florida is available should you need it. Connected all the way up. My brother-in-law knows your name, and you'll have his phone number. Hope you never have to use it."

"I'm not sure I should be feeling this way, Carl. Hell, I'm excited. Not worried in the least. I'll be careful, but I'm busting a gut to get started."

"Me too. Long time ago but I still have memories of my days running rum here in the Keys. Looking back now, best damn adventures ever. Kept the adrenalin flowing. Maybe I'm trying to relive some of it before I'm too old."

Hank chimed in with a laugh. "Cut it out guys! Next thing you know you two old farts will be hugging. Let's have a bourbon and relax. A toast is in order."

Standing on the opposite side of a bar in the living area, Carl poured three glasses of Jack Daniel's whiskey and passed two over. "I have to compliment you, Pete. Not once have you asked, but you must want to know?"

"Not sure I follow you."

"Aren't you curious what share you will get from this?"

Pete shrugged his shoulders and smiled back in reply.

"We'll make sure your cut of the profits covers lots more than just expenses. Something along the lines of a seventy-thirty split after my cost. Enough for you to share with anyone who works for you. It's important to keep everyone in the operations happy"

"I'm enjoying myself so much that I'd almost do my part for nothing, Carl. You should know! Compared to being stuck on a cramped floating target in the middle of the ocean, this is like a dream come true."

"Funny, I thought you might have felt that way the first time we met in Hank's home. Even so, there is something about my seventy percent that I want you to understand. It's important to me. I'm not doing this for myself. I'm too old for that, and I've got more money than years ahead of me. From my take after expenses, Hank and his family will get a portion. All that's left goes to the people in Jamaica, Pete. Every penny!" Carl raised his glass. "To a successful venture and those who it will help most!"

10.

BUCK, JUNE 12, 1968

As he drove to Homestead to join Jake and Kenneth, Pete's mind drifted back to his startup. Two and a half years had passed. It seemed more like yesterday. His best move was finding Buck. With no money, black, and impaired by a navy OTH discharge, Buck had been left with little choice but to survive as a street dealer. Risky business pushing Mexican weed by the bag, but he was smart and knew his way around. Navy training helped. Disciplined, tough, and a little scary when he wanted to be. He had been at it for eight months when one evening a pickup stopped in front of his rundown apartment. Big white dude inside the truck with sunglasses on and wearing a cap. Not good he thought at first. Under-cover narcotics cop maybe but then, low and behold, out stepped Chief Petty Officer Pete Ingram. They hugged at his door.

A rewarding friendship had been renewed at that moment. With Pete as the guide, they spent the next two days together. The surprise, especially coming from someone as straight as Pete, was the business proposal. Exactly the stroke of luck Buck needed to crawl out of his hole. Pete, of all people, wanted to become a big-time dealer in the marijua-na trade about which he knew practically nothing. But somehow, he had made the right connections along with the backing it took to start a major operation.

The marina and the Homestead house were perfect. A well thought out setup for safely smuggling in and then temporarily storing large amounts of marijuana. Beat the hell out of local competition. Most smugglers working the coast would meet up with a cargo ship beyond the twelve-mile limit and then make a high-speed run for shore. You had to risk the weather, coastal patrols, and once you made land, local law enforcement.

From the house in Homestead, all that was needed was the experience and know-how for downstream distribution. Buck could provide that in spades! Like the back of his hand, he knew how street dealing worked. And topping the cake with icing was the best damn marijuana he had ever tried. High quality Jamaican. Much better than the Mexican crap going around.

January 1966 was the beginning of what was to become one of the more successful marijuana trades in Florida. Pete was a fast learner and quickly came to realize that the business of "dealing," like most other businesses, could be divided into three parts: production, transportation, and distribution. The last of these was the riskiest in terms of getting caught. Hank and Carl handled the production. No problems upstream. Transporting all of it required some travel on open seas, but with dependable crews and capable crafts running almost always in international waters, pretty damn safe. End line distribution, however, ultimately required hands on meetings with perhaps hundreds of buyers while moving as little as an ounce at a time. Street dealing! Individuals working from a corner or an alley, a car, and even an apartment. Profitable, but risky over time and a path Buck knew they had to avoid.

Only through bulk sales of marijuana, in the range of twenty to forty pounds and sometimes more, were the chances of exposure greatly reduced. Setting that up was not a lot different from the way's prohibition worked when smugglers supplied the speakeasy. The illicit liquor store or nightclub, by the bottle or the glass, sold to the public. Buck pretty much followed the same methods. First, he assumed a new name. Called himself DB. Short for Donald Bates. If asked, he partnered with a single outfit run out of Melbourne. Talked about them as if they were Mexicans. Came on with a "screw with us and you'll get hurt!"

During the first few months, Buck carefully chose a few locals with some experience in the marijuana trade to supply as middlemen. Ten to twenty kilos each of excellent Jamaican. They, in turn, sold smaller amounts in quantities of a few pounds or more to the street dealers. From there it was broken down into bags and even joints. Little Mac was his first such middleman. Took him off the streets. Buck never disclosed his true identity to him or any of the others he recruited, even when he had to help with an initial setup. Afterwards, he arranged receipts and drops by phone. Outside of that, Buck remained pretty much of a mystery person to all of them. Purely business relations. With middlemen as go-betweens, end of the line street dealers barely even knew he existed.

Pete supplied the cash, kept the books, and generally supervised the business, especially the offshore part of the operation. Timing could not have been better. Marijuana's popularity was amazing, especially with the younger generation. Cultures had changed overnight. One year into dealing, they had distributions in Fort Lauderdale, Miami, and Key West. Pete was making two monthly offshore meetings with Hank and the *Lucky Two*. He was bringing in eight hundred kilos a trip.

Making Jake a part of the team expanded their business north to Gainesville. Initially, Buck was his instructor showing him how to first find and then set up middlemen all the while remaining pretty much anonymous. They needed a nearby base to work from, so with Pete's okay, they bought a small farmhouse near a crossroad town called Archer. Purchase was deeded to Richard Boyce, a Melbourne, Florida resident. The property included four acres of land and was located about ten miles southwest of Gainesville. Just the two of them constructed a temporary storage site there. Perfect because the house was set back in a field a hundred yards off the highway and the place was enclosed with a barbed wire fence and a gate. Neat and pleasant to look at if you were passing by. Just another little rural house in the country.

Not by coincidence, Jake's first middleman was his former pizza delivery boy. A week later, he and Buck added a freshman dropout from the university and a long-haired hippie type named Archie. They had to assist all three with getting started. Within another six months, Jake finished adding operations to Tallahassee. By the end of the first year, The University Florida and Florida State were practically gold mines. Jake was running four hundred kilos a month to Gainesville and supplying a total of nine middlemen there and in Tallahassee.

Pete arrived at the Homestead house a little after two in the morning. He carried in a cooler full of fresh swordfish steaks. Found Jake in the kitchen making a bowl of toss salad. Two large pizzas were already on the table. Smelled good! Kenneth was in the living area enjoying a drink at the bar. He offered to pour Pete one. "Thanks, but I'm going to clean up first. Smell a little too much like swordfish. You two go ahead and eat but save me some of that pizza."

An hour later they were all together in the sunroom. Pete finished off the last slice of pizza and then turned toward Kenneth. "I guess you know your cousin, Jake, thinks pretty highly of you. Your time and experience in Nam speaks for itself where I'm concerned. We plan to make you part of our team. Still a lot more for us to talk about but it's after three. Let's turn in. I'm beat! Start fresh in the morning."

Kenneth slept like a rock and didn't wake until past ten in the morning. Pete and Jake spent the rest of that day at the house with him explaining how and why their methods required dealing strictly in substantial quantities. Buck arrived in the Homestead Plumbing van at five in the evening. While helping to unload to storage the eighty bales, Kenneth got his first look at what they called the "cellar." A larger space than the one in Jake's garage but identical in the way it was sealed and disguised. At dinner that evening they all welcomed Kenneth with a toast. Fresh grilled swordfish was incredible.

Buck drove Kenneth in and around Miami the following day. Pointed out some of the areas his men supplied. What to look for, and as well, what to watch out for. Teacher and student time together. Jake stayed with his mom at their home. Took the time with her by explaining he had to spend the following two weeks in army reserve training. Buck dropped Kenneth there late in the afternoon. Received a big hug from Aunt Sarah and was rewarded for his return with a second fried chicken dinner that night.

Later, after his mom went to bed, Jake went over the itinerary for the next couple of weeks. "Kenneth, tomorrow you and I will be making a run to Gainesville. Carrying a full load and Buck will follow us with another. I doubled down supplies to my dealers before leaving for your dad's funeral, but with all that we've been doing, they are probably running low now. I hate playing catch up."

"Going to my farmhouse. You'll like the place. Smaller but it's similar to your home in Elgin. Buck's helping me out with some late deliveries. We'll be busy taking care of business. Good opportunity for you to see how to deal with middlemen both in Gainesville and Tallahassee. They think they know me, Kenneth. They don't really. Not even my real name. I work with them the same as Buck does with his dealers here in Miami. Collections, drops, and orders are all arranged by phone. Always play it safe. Your opportunity to watch and learn from the pros.

"Who do you say is calling when you phone?"

"Made up a name. Richard Boyce from Melbourne. I'm supposed to be working for some bad ass Mexicans. Thanks to some connections Hank's dad has in Miami, I even have a driver's license and army I.D. to complete my cover. Suggest you come up with a name for yourself. We'll get you some identification cards to boot."

"How does Thomas Boyce sound? Make like we're brothers. Maybe I'll call myself TB. You can be RB."

Jake with a smirk. "Whatever! Breakfast with Mom in the morning before we leave. Making collections and deliveries out of Gainesville takes about three days. After that, we'll leave for your place. It'll take you a month or more setting up. I can spend a week with you before I have to come back. First thing we'll do is get you a car for transporting. Maybe get started on your barn too."

"How about finding some help to deal the stuff Jake?"

"That too if time allows. I'm taking two bales with us just in case we get lucky, and a good candidate pops up. Best not to hurry, Kenneth.

Doing it right takes some time but believe me it's worth it. Are you curious about that yet?"

"Well, you know I can't help but wonder, but I figured it was impolite to ask. Hell, I'm just thankful you guys are bringing me onboard."

"Sounds familiar. I was the same way. Just so you know, the rest of our team appreciated that about you, and it did not go unnoticed. Let me lay it out for you but keep your shorts on. Don't piss in your pants."

"Try not to!" Kenneth laughed. "Carry on, cousin!"

"Okay, but this will take some explaining. Pay attention!"

"Yes Sir!"

"Shortly after he retired from the navy, Pete started working with Hank and family. That was a little over two and a half years ago. Hank's dad, his connections, and his money, was then and still is the key to our entire operation. Someday you'll meet him. Name's Carl. He lives in Jamaica. Interesting guy with lots of history."

"Like the godfather?"

"No. More like a patron. A real good person, Kenneth. Better man than me by far. I'll come to that but try not to interrupt or I'll never get to the best part."

"Right away, Pete made Buck his first partner. They served in the navy together. Good friends and a stroke of luck. Buck came off the streets of Miami and knew how to deal marijuana there. Taught Pete a lot and it was Buck who almost single handedly started up sales and distribution in Miami. Thanks to Hank's dad, they had the best damn marijuana around. By the time they brought me in, they were working from Fort Lauderdale to Key West and supplying seven hundred kilos a month to a dozen middlemen."

"I saw what that much marijuana looked like on Pete's Grady White. Hell of a lot but you guys were moving it smooth as silk."

"Thanks, but consider this next because it may help you to know what to expect on your end. I joined the team a little over a year ago. It was in April and just six months after I was discharged. Kenneth, we're currently selling almost fifteen hundred kilos a month. My part of that out of Gainesville is around four hundred. Business is good and getting better too. Hopefully, you'll do as well in Columbia within a year. Like I told you at your farm, the crap they're smoking in your kicking grounds doesn't come close to what we offer."

"I won't let you down, Jake. Trust me, I'll be careful, but this is a dream come true compared to Nam."

"You've got that right, but remember we get jail time instead of medals for what we're doing. So now you're ready for the payoff?"

"Locked and loaded."

"Alright, gross sales are coming to plus or minus seven hundred, fifty grand a month. Out of that, Carl's and Hank's cost of production and transportation runs a hundred grand a month. Just so you know, almost a third of that expense is for protection both in Jamaica and the Bahamas. Includes some local law and a few politicians where needed. Between the family and Pete's end, we split what's left seventy-thirty. Do the math! Thirty percent comes to almost two hundred grand a month. Our team is making over two million a year and growing!"

Kenneth just stared at Jake with his mouth half open.

Jake went on. "Pete's take is forty five percent. Sounds like a pretty big portion, but out of that, he takes care of major expenses. Covers Ned, the marina, the boat, housing, the cars, and a lot of inevitable incidentals. Another five percent we set aside as savings in case of an emergency. Leaves Buck and I twenty five percent each."

"Wait a minute, Jake. Make sure I'm following you. Do you mean twenty five percent of two million?"

"Pissed in your pants yet?"

"Hell yes!"

"I told you it was five figures per month back at your farm. Started out making much less before becoming a full partner. This year, I'll clear a cool half million. So will Buck. Pete makes a little more than we do."

"Christ sakes, Jake! What do you need me for? You're rich!"

"The family, Kenneth. We have to grow to meet their expectations. Carl's expectations to be specific. On his end, he gives Hank, Martha, and grandkids fifteen percent. Truth is he doesn't keep a cent of what's left. Gives it all away to Jamaicans. Community infrastructure projects and an endless number of individuals. Kenneth, he's a philanthropist. A damn hero. Wants to do more too. Lots more! That's why we want you to join up. Expand us to the Carolinas."

"Does Carl know you guys are letting me in?"

"You bet he does! Pete keeps the family informed of every move. Apparently, military experience counts a lot with Carl. He manages the cash too. You saw the transfer from the *Drifter* to Hank's *Lucky Too*. Moves on through a bank in the Bahamas to Carl's bank in Jamaica clean as hell. Carl and Pete keep records of our share. Invested for us. Not just sitting around gathering dust. I've already got a stock portfolio making even more."

"Unbelievable, Jake. And you stumbled into all this by sheer luck!"

"We all did. That's why the boats on the families' side are named *Lucky*. Here's how your end of the money works. Damn fair too! You'll start out on the team the same as I started. Rookie in training at first. Pay grade is a thousand a week plus expenses. Afterwards, when you're moving quantities, you become a junior partner. Pay grade increases in proportion to your percentage of what I and Buck sell. From what I saw in Columbia, you might make a full partner with the two of us in a year. Once you do, it's a simple three-way split."

"So, I need to build up my part to four or five hundred kilos a month. To do that, I'll need to make a trip every week."

"Not at first, but if you want an equal share in a year or so, you will have to put some miles in. Seven hundred each way. Never said this was easy. Damn profitable though."

"I'll need a good car."

"We'll just make sure it's a sedan that we can modify. One other thing. You'll have to get yourself a nice dog."

"I like dogs, but what the hell do I want with one?"

"You'll see the answer to that and more tomorrow. It's after midnight. Time to turn in. Mom will fix an early breakfast for us. We load and take off after that."

The next morning Jake came to breakfast in his army khaki uniform with the rank of Staff Sergeant on the sleeve. Aunt Sarah looked at him with obvious pride. Half an hour later, Buck arrived wearing navy blues and a utility jumper with three stripes. Seaman's rank. The German shepherd was in the back seat of his car. Thanking Jake's mom with cheek kisses, they all said goodbye. Outside, with the garage door closed, they packed twelve bales into the rear compartment of Jake's car and latched the seat down. Placed a half-folded blanket on top and let Annie, the golden retriever, hop inside.

Damn this is brilliant, Jake. You're both on the road in military fatigues. Nice disguise!"

"Thought you might like it. Pete's idea. And remember, we have a military I.D. as well. If for any reason we're ever stopped, perfect excuse to be on the highways going or coming. Those big, tail wagging dogs compliment the back seat. Not likely to ever be searched. Ready to roll?"

"Hell yeah, but wish I had brought one of my old uniforms."

"You'll have plenty of opportunities to do that later. You should wait until we get you some new identification cards. Thomas Boyce, wasn't it?"

They drove to Gainesville with the windows half down. Beautiful day and mild for Florida in June. Kenneth's mind played with him. A thousand a week for joining up to start with. Not bad, not bad! Going through all that shit in Nam for a measly nine thousand in savings. If he worked his butt off with these guys, he could make fifty times that in a year. Sure, there was the risk of being caught. In Nam, there was a much higher risk of getting yourself killed. Scared as hell there most of the time. Instead, this deal was exciting. Damn if he wasn't enjoying himself. Thinking about it some more, he was having fun!

11.

OPERATIONS, FEBRUARY 14, 1972

It was almost dark by the time Kenneth and Link finished storing twenty-four bales of marijuana in the barn's cellar. It was modeled after Pete's garage cellar in Homestead except for a tractor instead of a car parked on top. He and Link had both completed separate runs to Miami and returned home by late afternoon the second day. Ten kilos per bale. Over five hundred pounds. Kenneth was stocking up ahead of some needed R&R. Jamaica! Link had a date and reminded his boss it was Valentine Day. Kenneth gave him a calendar day and time for his next run and waved goodbye to him as he left. Link's black lab had its head half out the back window. The lab and Kenneth's setter practically loved each other. The setter chased their car to the end of the driveway.

Kenneth walked back to his house ready for a Jack Daniel's after the long trip. Returned minutes later to a porch table and chair. Time to relax with a drink and plan tomorrow's distribution route. Generally took a while since he tried to avoid using the same place too often for collections and drops. Separate locations for each because collections preceded a second phone call providing the dealers where to find the drop. It was always TB calling. Worth the extra safety precautions and it was hardly a crime to find a sack of money lying in the trunk of a car that wasn't yours. At least that's the way a good lawyer would argue it in court. Kenneth avoided the malls. Instead, he preferred the parking lots of grocery chain stores like Food Lion, A&P, and Piggly Wiggly. Often shopped for a few things while waiting.

Kenneth's dealers like working with him. The quality of his marijuana was unbeatable, and his price left them with plenty of room for profits. Going on four years now and only one of his middlemen had run afoul of the law. Apparently, that was the result of him cheating on his girlfriend. Her stupid way of getting even. Street dealers were not as fortunate. Half dozen or so arrested but none with more than a bag or two in procession. A middleman rule they were required to follow.

The family was pleased with how things had progressed. Combined he, Jake, and Buck were moving seventeen hundred kilos a month. That kept Pete busy as hell making regular offshore runs to meet with the Hatteras. But even with busy schedules, there was time for fishing trips out of Key Largo plus one week stays in Jamaica every year at Carl's resort. Always the penthouse! That was the R&R Kenneth was looking forward.

Three days later, Kenneth had completed distributions and collections. On the morning of the fourth day, he drove to Charlotte and caught an Eastern Airline flight to Miami. Pete, Jake, and Buck met him in the terminal. They all boarded a Pan Am flight to Montego Bay. Flew first class. Smooth, enjoyable trip together and they arrived before five.

Hank was waiting for them at customs with firm handshakes and hugs. Hour later they checked in at the resort. "Have a drink and rest a bit. Jerome will pick you guys up in front around eight. Having dinner with Dad at his home tonight. He's busy as hell but still looking forward to your visit. Has some news to share with you. Just like the past couple of times, consider tonight's dinner as a partners meeting. The rest of your stay will be all about resting up and enjoying yourself. It's peak fishing season!"

Dinner that night started with drinks, more handshakes, stories, and lots of laughs. Carl's home was an elegant Victorian style two story. After hosting a steak dinner, he asked for a few moments' attention. "Okay, gentlemen, we're all friends here at this table, so I'll make this little speech short, sweet and to the point. As far as I'm concerned, there has never been a business relationship better than the one we share. And it pleases me to sum up for you a successful year." As you know, our wholesale price is way up. Thanks to your hard work and the quality of our product, we averaged three hundred dollars a pound. In round figures, gross sales came to over seventeen million dollars. We deducted from that sum two and a half million for the cost of production, transportation, and what I always refer to as legal expenses. After those cost adjustments, Pete, your team's share was four million, three hundred and fifty thousand."

Carl stood and raised his glass. They all followed his lead. "Congratulations, gentlemen. Well-deserved and all Jamaica thanks you." Carl emptied his glass and turned to Hank. "Explain why Son. Update everyone on what we've achieved on this end. Also, acquaint them with our sinsemilla experiments."

"Pretty hard to top seventeen million but here goes. And I hope you fellows will be as proud as we are with what I'm about to share with you. This year, we doled out eight million dollars to people and projects in Jamaica. Over half of that amount was for the completion of two brand-new children's orphanages in Kingston. I know none of you have kids, at least you don't think so. Now you're all the patrons of four hundred boys and girls in Kingston. Congratulations again, Dads!"

Another toast followed. Then Hank handed Pete a photo album of the kids. Carl looked on and sat quietly beaming with pride. Jake, Kenneth, and Buck gathered around Pete as he flipped the pictures and commented. "Wow, they're beautiful. Healthy looking and all smiling too."

Carl couldn't help but reply. "Pete, the three of you are making a lot of money. So is Hank. But just look at those kids. They're happy! The family's doing a good thing here. Took two years from start to finish but the facilities and dormitories are first class. Someday we'll visit them, and you'll see for yourself. And remember that guardian angel you thought was watching out for me? Well, she's smiling on all of us now. Those kids too."

Hank added, "Dad's right about that, and I can promise you we are unique to this business. There's plenty of competition out there but not even one doing what we do with the money."

"Speaking of our competitors, Son, might be a good time let them in on our cultivation plans for next year."

"Coming to it next. As you all know, in terms of quality, we've always tried to stay a little ahead of the rest of the players in the game. With this year's October harvest, we may turn out to be two, three, maybe four years ahead. Buck, you speak some Spanish, don't you?"

"Some. Helps in our marketplace."

"Ever heard of sinsemilla?"

"Yeah. Marijuana without seeds. Thought that was a myth. Have to have seeds to grow marijuana."

"You do, Buck, but both male and female plants are grown from those seeds. The male plants fertilize the female plants. After that is when the female plant buds make the seeds. Nature at work if you know what I mean. Jerome heard about a couple of locals growing just the female plants in their backyard garden. He and Dad visited one and were impressed with what they found. The technique supposedly came from India."

"Don't drag this out, Hank. Get to the good part. They're hanging on every word."

"Keep your britches on, Dad. I'm enjoying every minute too."

"Last year, we isolated one small field and experimented with pulling out all of the male plants. Labor intensive at first but wow, did it pay off. Instead of setting seeds in the flowers, the female plants continued to mature, flower, and produce floral bracts covered with resin. Guys, the quality of that ganja doubled. And come this October, we'll deliver to you out of Bimini marijuana ten times better than anyone else sells."

Carl had to smile. "Hank may be exaggerating just a little, but here's the bottom line. Nobody will even come close to competing with our marijuana. Get set for your wholesale prices to climb. Volume right along with it!"

Pete leaned back in his chair. Took a deep breath. "Carl, Hank, you two are incredible. Business is already good, but demand on the streets and quality go together like bees and honey. Even if we charge more, sales will increase a lot from where we are now. To make that happen, the boys here will need some help. Pretty much working their butts off already."

"True enough," Carl agreed. "It's the reason I approved of Kenneth adding two runners to ease his load. Seven hundred and fifty miles each way will wear on you. But neither of his new guys had any military. I consented only with the condition of keeping the family and the rest of you secret. How are they coming along, Kenneth?"

"To early to say about Trevor. We just got his identification cards. His first trip was with me. Dropped him at a motel in Miami before going on to Homestead. I will say this about him. He follows orders, no questions asked. He recently made another trip with Link. The only connection in Miami that both of them will ever have is which motel they stay at for switching cars. With the way Buck has arranged to park a car in the lot with a full load and letting them exchange their car for it, they stay completely in the dark as to how the rest of our operation works."

"Link has on occasions asked questions. I've cautioned him not to be even remotely curious unless he doesn't like making thirty or forty grand a year. But the truth is, Carl, bringing Link on has made my part much easier. Everything considered, I'd say it's working out well. Once Trevor starts making trips on his own, I'll be able to concentrate three quarters of my time on distribution. With the extra time, I can handle more."

Carl looked around the table. "How about you, Jake? Need some help too?"

"Possibly. I'm looking in Gainesville for the right person to assist with runs. Even after I find someone, I'll keep this end of our operations a total mystery. Like Kenneth's recruits, pickups here in Miami made at a motel with a car switch and then delivered to Richard Boyce's farmhouse in Archer. I'll take the shipments from there and continue to supply the dealers same as always."

"Sounds good," Carl replied. "You okay with these changes, Pete?"

"Technically, I guess. Not much choice if we're going to increase sales. Let me add something for thought. It's only as safe as those you employ to make these runs, so contingencies need to be made in case something goes wrong. On your end, Kenneth, I would suggest you make plans to abandon ship if either Link or Trevor get in trouble. And it's best to be ready to lawyer them up if that happens. The drug detectives have recently become pretty good at offering deals to get to higher ups."

Kenneth smiled at Carl with a confident nod before answering. "I'm ahead of you on both points, Pete. That's probably why Carl is grinning. At his suggestion and a referral by his son-in-law, I put a South Carolina attorney with connections and experience in these matters on retainer. A damn healthy retainer too! Also, I purchased a neat little fishing cabin on a nearby freshwater lake to serve as a safe house if needed. Bought it in Thomas Boyce's name as a precaution. Added a storage compartment beneath the place's pump house. It's less thirty miles away from my farm, so I can empty my barn's cellar and move   everything to the cabin in a couple of hours if I have to."

Jake interrupted. "Damn smart move, Kenneth. Here in Florida, we already have legal help if needed, but I really like your idea of a remote safe house nearby in case of an emergency. I'll do the same thing somewhere close to my farm. Small expense and worth every penny."

"Dad, sure is a comfort to be working with such careful friends."

Carl nodded and said, "Yes, indeed it is. We chose our partners well. And, Jake, there is a final bit of news I'll pass on to you and Kenneth. Buck and Pete are already onboard with this. Ned has been my loyal friend for almost fifty years. He had two grandsons. Both served in Vietnam. I've known those kids since they were toddlers. Thank you all for attending the funeral of the youngest when he was killed last year. Very sad occasion under the circumstances because their father, Ned's only son, lost his life during World War II. Afterwards, Ned helped to raise both boys. Losing the youngest of the two was incredibly hard on him."

Pete, Buck, Jake, and Kenneth slightly bowed heads. "I didn't know any of this," Kenneth said. "Damn, wish I had."

"Thanks, but here is why I'm telling all of you now. Ned needs a favor. I was honored with his request. His oldest grandson is being discharged in March. Name's Danny. Ned would like for us to employ him when he gets out. Damn good man! Totally trustworthy and a perfect fit with the extra work Pete and Buck have going."

88

"Looks like our company's staff is growing, Dad. Do you have any more changes to bring up?"

"One more thing, Son." Carl passed out a bound folder to everyone at the table. "Your individual portfolios prepared by my brokerage firm. I would ask that you review your report later tonight at your leisure. For now, I promise you will be happy with your investments. If you have any questions, save them for the fishing trip tomorrow. I'm coming along."

The waters off the western end of Jamaica were a sports fisherman's paradise. As the sun was rising the next day, they arrived at Carl's marina and boarded a 38-foot Hatteras with Jerome at the helm. Weather was perfect. Fishing was great! Another four days of pure enjoyment followed. Mornings were spent fishing and required midday naps after returning. Afternoons were passed at the resort's pool. Restaurants with great food and drinks completed the evenings. Carl covered everything including ladies for the afternoon's poolside and evening's entertainment.

Reluctantly, they were scheduled to fly back to Miami on the sixth day of their vacation. Carl asked Pete to spend an hour with him at his home before leaving. Hank was already there when he arrived. Over coffee, "Pete, have you looked over the investments?"

"All first-class blue chips from what I can tell, Carl. I can name some of the best with good returns like Amoco and Mobil Oil, Chase Bank, Consolidated Edison, and Duke Power. Everything's okay, I hope?"

"Rest easy. Those big corporations are doing well. Except for the little downturn two years ago, the markets have been moderately fruitful for over ten years. But I learned back in the thirties good times don't last forever. Out of caution, I plan to move your team out of most stocks later this year. Changing over to interest bearing certificates of deposits. Maybe gold too because it's easy to store and there's no way it can go down in price. Just guessing, Pete, but if I'm right, we'll be liquid and in a perfect position to take advantage of cheap real estate if a recession or worse occurs. Except for buying gold, same thing I did during the Great Depression. Paid off big time for me. And, even if I'm wrong, we'll still be making a decent return from the interest."

"Carl, I feel like our money is in good hands. With your bank transfers and investments, clean as hell too! Whatever you decide, we're good with."

"Thanks for your confidence. Once you're back in the states, update the rest of the guys. Still, there is one last thing I want to make sure you're aware of before leaving. This part especially worries me considering my daughter and her family in Coral Gables."

"Whatever, Carl. You know I've always said families come first. Tell me because if something bothers you, I'm concerned too."

"Back in the early twenties when I started running liquor shipments, the enterprise was pretty much a gentleman's game of chance. Kept the adrenaline flowing too. The romance of the business changed in the mid to late twenties. Gangsters started taking over the business. Having a load hijacked at sea became a real threat. There were some lives lost. Making matters worse, the coast guard added speed boats and World War 1 naval ships to the fight. Those difficulties combined to cause a few of my competitors to be either caught or robbed. In 1927 ships with illegal liquor started being seized 34 miles from shore. My operation in the Gulf of Mexico had more than one close call. Not wanting to push my luck, I sold out in 1929 and took up permanent residence here in Jamaica."

"That was almost the same story Hank told me six years ago, Carl. He didn't mention the gangster part, but I've heard some stories."

"Do you remember I once asked you if you played poker?"

"Yeah, I remember. Still do when time allows, and I can get out to Vegas for some fun."

"Well then, if you're good at the game, you know when it's time to take your winnings and leave the table."

"Most of the time. Not always. Where are you going with this?"

"Just paying attention to changes that affect our business. Pretty much like I did back in the twenties. Year before last, Nixon signed legislation they called the 'Controlled Substance Act.' Along with that, congress has added some racketeering statutes to seize property. Another one called the 'Kingpin Statute' targets suppliers. My son-in-law tells me legal challenges are getting serious."

"Is it time to abandon ship?"

"No. For sure, not yet! I'm just giving you a heads up. Hank and I are totally safe here in Jamaica. Pretty much the same in the Bahamas.

That protection cost but it's well worth it. As an added precaution, I've set up an intermediary legal contact between my daughter's husband and you. Keeps him out of the picture much like your middlemen do for you in the trade.

"Smart move for the family, Carl. I'm good with this little procedural alteration. Anything else?"

"Maybe. With our offshore safeguards and how we operate, its you guys taking all the risk. Safe for now I think, but if circumstances change like they did in the twenties, be prepared to cash in and quit playing."

"Absolutely! Mind if I discuss this with the team?"

"Counting on it. Get going or you'll miss your flight."

Handshakes passed around. Pete thanked Carl for a great vacation and especially the evening treats to which Hank gave a wide grin. Followed up with mentioning he was already looking forward to next year. Jerome drove Pete back to the resort to pick up the others. When they arrived back in Miami, Pete pulled his team aside and went over every detail of his morning's meeting with Carl. They all listened carefully while nodding heads in agreement. After handshakes, everyone departed for home, rested, and ready to deal some of this new seedless marijuana.

A month back in Elgin, Kenneth invited Link and Trevor for an afternoon cookout at the farm. The dinner was just an excuse. Most of the evening would be spent going over the procedures they were to follow in the event of an arrest. Kenneth had carefully thought out every detail of legality when busted with a car full of marijuana. For each of them he had typed a brief copy of rules not to be broken, steps to take if involved with law enforcement personnel, and a cover story to minimize their offence if caught with a shipment.

"Link, Trevor, before our dinner, we're going to go over these instructions I'm giving to you. I want them memorized and then burned. If something unfortunate happens to either of you on the road, these simple things can save your butts."

Link asked, "Boss, we're being careful. Are you worried about us?"

"Part of my job is to worry! Let's go over this." He handed a single page to each of them. At the top of the page in caps was an attorney's name and phone number. Charles Whitfield. Attorney at Law.

"The first rule I insist you follow is to never carry a firearm on you or in your car. Never! Complicates everything and gives law enforcement a big leg up if caught with one. Don't screw up on this."

"The second paragraph is a copy of your Miranda Rights. Learn them by heart. They're your best friend. You can thank the U.S. Congress and the Supreme Court for this six years ago. Basically, it lets you keep your mouth shut. If you are ever questioned by police, the third sentence of those rights is always, and without exception, your only reply. Ask for your lawyer. Nothing else! No matter what they say to you, ask for legal representation. Over and over again, if necessary."

"The last part of the page is the story to tell your attorney. Stick with it. A believable tale designed to reduce you to a small naive player in the drug trade. If not in the eyes of the police, then perhaps in the minds of a jury. You're just a driver being paid well for trips to Melbourne. Arriving there, you spend a couple of hours at a theater. While enjoying a movie, someone takes the car and returns it. You drive back to Columbia and go to another movie. Same thing happens and your payment for the trip is left in the trunk. You suspect something crooked but why ask? Like biting the hand that feeds you. The money for the trips is just too good. Any questions so far?"

"How do we say our instructions come to us?" Link asked.

"By phone. Caller's last name is Barker. Memorize the name but only if Whitfield wants to know."

"And the car. Where did it come from?"

"Melbourne, Florida. Given to you by the same guy that calls. And, I'll remind you again, answer these questions only if asked by your attorney, not the cops."

Trevor with a puzzled look. "What about the hidden compartment beneath the back seat filled with marijuana?"

"Sealed inside tight as a drum. How could you have known? Back when you worked at the Texaco station, you washed my car dozens of times without finding a hint of a secret compartment. If not for Link and I showing it to you, would you have ever guessed it was there"?

"I reckon not. Thinking about this, except for Melbourne instead of Miami and a theater instead of a motel, damn near what we do. Why Melbourne though?"

"The people I buy from tell me some big-time smugglers operate the coastal shores there. The Barker brothers. Better for the cops to make that connection and they'll believe your story even more."

Link looked at Kenneth. "The way I see this playing out is Trevor and I have no idea what's in our car, what happens to whatever it is, who takes it, and no way of connecting you to any of this, Boss."

"Smart way of summing it up, Link. But it's for your protection as well. Commit your attorney's phone number to memory. Charles Whitfield is on a retainer to Thomas and Richard Boyce. Someday that may even become your names, and you'll have identification cards to prove it. Law enforcement doesn't care about small-time street dealers or unsuspecting runners. They want whoever supplies you. No guarantees but with a good lawyer like Whitfield by your side, your worst case may mean serving a little jail time. Then probably probation. Remember your sentence a couple of years ago, Link. Not much more than a slap on the hand."

"So, we spin this story to the lawyer. He takes it from there, and that's all we know?"

"Correct! He's another reason for making Melbourne the false hub of operations. His retainer comes by check from Seacoast Bank. They're headquartered in Melbourne. The name on the account is Thomas Boyce."

"Amazing. This sounds bulletproof. Hope we never have to use it."

"Me too, Link. Taking precautions though is a safe way to go."

Kenneth added an incentive. "One more thing you'll appreciate."

"What else, Boss?"

"If either of you are ever caught and you follow these rules, your paychecks don't stop. You'll be on a pension plan. Weekly deposits of half what you make now and the other half when released. If you spend any kind of real time in the pen, at least you'll have plenty of money when you get out."

Trevor extended his hand to Kenneth. "Thanks. Takes the pressure off by giving me something to hold on to if I'm locked up."

Kenneth shook both Trevor's and Link's hand. "Glad you two like the plan but there's a catch. Money stops if I'm caught!"

"Little like your insurance policy, Boss?"

"Right again, Link. Nothing wrong with looking after myself. Enough of this. Let's have a drink and put some steaks on the grill. I'm hungry!"

12.

EXIT, MARCH 12, 1977

Kenneth tossed a leather suitcase into the back seat of his new ford crew cab. The annual holiday in Jamaica was the reason for packing. Because of business delays, he was leaving two days late. Everyone else had gone ahead, so after arriving in Charlotte, he flew alone to Montego Bay. The three-hour flight offered time to reflect on his future. Something he seemed to be often doing these past couple of years. It was time to leave the business. Some lessons in life were piling on.

Kenneth's mom had passed away. Congestive heart failure complicated by diabetes. Ned had died in 1974. Heart attack as well. His loss was hard on Carl. Ned's grandson, Danny, quickly filled the void at the marina. And, with the end of the war in Nam, there were plenty of vets looking for opportunities to make a new start. Coming from that hell hole, marijuana was no stranger to them. Buck had recruited two for help on his end and Jake had recently added his second to assist with not only runs but distribution as well. All were carefully screened. Nevertheless, the increase in numbers brought a greater chance of exposure. Always a concern of Pete's. Kenneth worried too, so planned to discuss it with the rest of the team.

There were other considerations. Maybe the most important one was Patricia Chauvin. Over eight years had passed since they first met in

Key West. After graduating from LSU in 1972, Patricia entered graduate school at UVA. Majored in geology. During that period, her studies, distance, and Kenneth's work prevented them from maintaining anything more than a causal relationship with benefits. Mostly kept in touch by phone.

After receiving her master's degree in geology, Patricia was employed by Shell Oil in New Orleans. During the following two years, visits by Kenneth became more frequent and the relationship grew serious. Then this past Christmas, she asked him to spend the holidays with her in Lafayette and finally meet the parents. He accepted the invitation. Glad he did because they apparently liked him. A lot according to Patricia. An engagement was inevitable, but there was a problem. Maybe a major one. She had no idea how he had really achieved his success. Only that he was engaged in real estate and the stock market.

As usual, Hank was waiting at customs.

Shaking hands, "Sorry I'm late arriving, Hank. Business delays."

"No apologies necessary. Do wish you could have come earlier. The annual meeting was at Dad's home last night. I'll have to bring you up to date while we drive to Negril."

"Did I miss much?"

"I'm afraid so. Whole lot. The family is selling the farm and getting out, Kenneth. Would you believe a church called the Ethiopian Zion Coptic is buying it?" They're closing the purchase in November.

Kenneth tried to hide the rush of a pleasant surprise. His answer to the complications between business and Patricia might be in the works. Instead, he pretended a worried look. "Have to say, Hank! I didn't see this coming. Is it some kind of trouble on our side of the operations?"

"We think so. More than just one reason though. In fact, several things. I'll explain but not here. Come on, let's go!"

The drive from Montego Bay to Negril would take an hour. Once in the car, Hank handed Kenneth the customary bound folder containing his year end portfolio summary. "Brought this along for you. At least we can start your trip out with some good news before I get to the bad. Check it out later though. For the ride, I'll try to fill you in on the latest."

"I'm listening."

"Okay, you saw how Ned's death affected Dad last year. Took it hard. They were the same age, Kenneth. Dad's seventy-nine and still sharp as a tack, but even before losing Ned, he had been going downhill physically. Hasn't been to sea in two years. Now he's moving about slowly and not getting out of the house much. Thing is he knows this better than any of us."

"Crap! I love that man. Anything I can do to help? Anything!"

"No, Dad's had a good life. He's just pissed at being old. Last spring, during my sister's visit, we gathered at his house for a discussion of the family's future. Right up front tells us he only has a few years left at best. Goes over the fact that the safety of our farming and transport business coexist with his political and legal connections. He's sure the latter parts can't be passed on. Without him, the families at risk here in Jamaica, the Bahamas, and maybe Florida too."

"I can understand that. Carl has spent half his life building business relations. We're all vulnerable unless he's with us."

"There's more!"

"What else?"

"You may already know this because it's something Dad mentioned at last year's meeting. The drug smuggling business is changing. And now it's changing much faster than we thought it would a year ago, and not for the better either."

"Is it cocaine? That shit is becoming pretty popular lately."

"You guessed it! Did you know that coke in a pure form has been around in the states for more than a century? Abused too! Would you believe some say a long time ago, they put it in Coca-Cola?"

"No kidding?'

"Not kidding a bit. Bad stuff all the way back then too. We're good people, Kenneth. Like you, I take a cut, but the family is mostly in this business for helping Jamaicans. Especially kids. The orphanage for example. Plus, as you know, Dad gives all his share away. Let me put it this way. We've never considered that smoking marijuana was dangerous. People can use it for recreational fun, and it's safer than alcohol."

"I'm onboard with that because I drink a little. I'm still young and most times, I like five o'clock bourbons along with a good joint."

"Well coke can make the equivalent of a twenty-year alcoholic out of someone really quick. Worse than heroin in terms of addiction. Works on your brain. Makes you feel smart and full of energy. Kenneth, they don't just smoke the stuff. Inhale it straight up, ingest it, and even inject it into veins. After a little bit of time, the craving for another high becomes fierce, so you can understand why it's spreading like a plague."

"I've already seen a little of what coke can do back home. One way users shoot the crap is called 'crack.' Melt the stuff so they can inject it with a needle. An intense and faster high but apparently even more addictive that way." Kenneth thought he best not tell Hank how he had become familiar with the drug. Link was into cocaine through his nose. Something he refers to as 'doing-a-line.' Trevor, on the other hand, stayed clean of it."

"Okay, so you know a little about it, and like I said, everything may be changing. Our marijuana sells on the streets by the ounce. Damn cocaine sells by the gram. Big time money maker for the bad guys. Colombians are bringing the coca paste across their border from Bolivia and Peru. Buying it real cheap in those countries. It's processed into cocaine powder and flown to Panama. From there, it's somehow transported into the states. A lousy kilo can go for over fifty grand. Several times that when cut and sold on the streets by the gram."

"Maybe I'm wrong, but I've heard the Colombians are much worse than just bad. Some of the stories make them out to be ruthless killers."

"Not just made-up tales, Kenneth. Territorial idiots. Kill one another and anyone else they think threatens their business. That last part is one of the reasons why Dad decided it was time to get out."

"But we don't compete with them."

"Not directly. But the Bahamas might be a problem. You know Dad has connections there. They're well compensated for their assistance?"

"Sure. Part of the business to keep us safe."

"Well, the short hop from Bimini to Florida has been one of the keys to our success. Now Dad's friends on the island tell him the Colombians may be looking for an easier cocaine route to the states. And apparently, they don't care what it cost."

"I hope you don't mean Bimini!"

"Can't be sure. Doesn't matter. If they start using the Bahamas, you can bet it will make our operations there much more dangerous. On top of that, law enforcement will have to start concentrating right in our backyard. Also, there's this new branch of Feds working in government called the 'DEA.'

DEA. Short for Drug Enforcement Administration. They just got started a few years ago, but now they're becoming fairly effective."

"Not good, Hank. Nixon's so-called 'Controlled Substance Act' keeps potential penalties for marijuana right up there with the bad stuff. And I've read that the federal judges are sentencing offenders to longer prison terms unless they cooperate with the authorities. If that's the case, our legal guys may not be able to help much."

"Almost like Dad laid it out to all of us last night. And he brought up the fact that two of his grandkids are already in college and the rest are close behind. As he put it, time to stand down for their benefit as well as our own."

"I couldn't agree more under the circumstances. Made a bundle of money too. But just how and when do we go about shutting down?"

"We're almost to the resort, Kenneth. I'll let Pete and Jake explain how they plan to do that. One last thing you should know though. It's March. We didn't plant a new crop. Fields are bare except for the banana and cacao trees. By September the barns will empty too. Shortly after that, our Bimini house will run out of marijuana."

"That puts a time frame on it for me. Maybe this December, we should all plan to reunite here in Jamaica. Celebration party!

"Good way to end it. I'll run the idea by Dad.

The resort was nearly full of the usual tourists. Kenneth had arrived an hour before sunset, skipped checking in at the desk, and took the elevator to the top floor penthouse. Pete and Jake were waiting for him. Pete waved a half salute. "Good to see you made it, sergeant. We're having a bourbon. Want one?"

"Sure do. Where's Buck?"

Jake laughed. "Remember that good-looking dish he grew so fond of last year."

"Hard not to remember her. Too well-off up front to forget."

"They took off for the beach this morning. Before leaving, Buck packed a few things. Said he may not see us for a couple of days. Hell, I think the kid is in love."

"That can happen to any of us. Hope it works out for him."

"How about that drink, Pete? I need one. On the way here, Hank went over some of what went on at the meeting with Carl last night. Sorry to talk business right after walking in, but I'm anxious to hear how you two plan to close our company down."

"No problem, but first look over your investment's report while you have a bourbon. I think this year's returns will surprise you. It may also help to understand how Jake and I plan to move on. Having dinner at Carl's restaurant at eight, so we have two hours before leaving. Take your time and enjoy."

Hank had already said that the portfolio was good news. Now Pete hinted the same, so instead of taking his time, Kenneth thumbed straight to the summary. Column one showed last year's positions and the value of each of those investments as of December 31, 1975. The column to the right side did the same for the year ending 1976. The two rows filled nearly all the page with listings of assets in real estate investment trusts, stocks carried over from the previous year, cash converted during the year to newly acquired stocks, interests held in various Florida coastal properties, bank accounts, and ended with gold purchases measured in kilograms. Balances were underlined at the base of each column. Just over six million dollars in 1975 had grown to seven and a half million during 1976. Kenneth looked towards Pete and whistled out loud. Both Pete and Jake returned thumbs up.

"Now we can discuss shutting down, Kenneth, unless you want to stare at your money some more."

Taking a large sip of his bourbon and then laughing, "Pete, I'll save that for bedtime tonight. Pretty much like a dream anyway."

"Well, if you're ready, here is how we plan to move on. Business as usual for the next six months. No need, as we see it, to share any of our intentions with the help before then. Doing so might just stir up problems and complicate a quick and clean break."

"I think so too. Saying nothing is probably the best policy. What then?"

Jake replied to the question. "More or less we'll just be honest with everyone, but let's keep it strictly to those on a need-to-know basis. The short explanation will be we lost our supplier, so we're quitting. Getting out and going straight. The truth if you think about it."

"Sounds good to me, Jake, but this might fly like a lead balloon with Link and Trevor. They're enjoying the good life too much to just walk away. Not just runners anymore as you know. Together they've built up a small clientele of their own. Trevor is the brains behind the two."

"That may or may not be a problem," Pete said. "Jake and Buck seem to think some of their guys could behave the same way. Buck plans to work on a solution of sorts just in case. He'll have six months to work it out. If successful, he can share it with you and Jake."

"Good, but can I ask how's he going to pull this off?"

"Simple really, Kenneth. Over the years Buck has come to know a couple of our competitors working the Florida coast. Made a friend of one after the guy and his crew had a close call with a coastal patrol and had to dump a load at sea. With Carl's approval beforehand, loaned him two hundred kilos so he could get back on his feet."

"That's impressive! Never hurts to make friends, especially if they owe you one."

"Way Buck and Carl saw it too. As a precaution, they know practically nothing about us and only know Buck by his street name. DB. Short for Donald Bates if you recall? The leader of the group is named Russell. He and his partners move a fraction of what we do, but they're young and want to grow. Apparently got their start a few years after the so called 'Steinhatchee Seven' were busted in seventy-three. West coast of Florida operation you may have read about?"

"Yeah, hard to forget. Made headlines, Pete. They were careless, and I'm beginning to see where you're going with this. Offering our guys an alternative source if they want to keep dealing. Am I right?"

"Buck thought of the idea right after the meeting last night. He says these kids are bringing in 'Colombian Gold' from meeting with fishing trawlers way the hell offshore. Not as good as our Jamaican sinsemilla and risky on their part, but they have an endless supply. A good size trawler can carry seventy tons or more and can hang fifty miles out."

Pete continued. "Hank believes this crew has to be brave or stupid to run that far out to meet a cargo ship and then come back in with nothing more than the cover of night. Except for that, Buck was impressed with the onshore part of their operation. Good cover. Said it was similar to our marina but with a big warehouse for boat storage and repairs."

Jake rolled his eyes. "I'm not sure but add this thought to their operations! For 'Colombian Gold' in large amounts, they have to be dealing directly with the Colombians for their supply! Both stupid, brave, and maybe careless too if they are? But since we're getting out, how they obtain their goods is not our problem. And think about what we have, and they don't. Over the years we've built one hell of a distribution system. They have nothing even close to it, so Buck is convinced this crew will jump at the chance to work with our people."

"Is Carl okay with this idea?"

"Hank discussed it with him this morning. Carl's onboard so long as we keep some distance from them and keep our identities safe. Let Buck handle everything!"

Kenneth looked at his friends. "And we're all agreeing to closing out by the end of the year?"

Pete and Jake nodded a yes.

"And to Buck turning our distribution operations over to these new guys?" Pete and Jake nodded again with a smile.

"Okay! I guess that's it. Something else to think about though. On the way here, I suggested to Hank we have a big Jamaican reunion come December. It's been one hell-of-a-run, so a major celebration party is in order."

"I'll raise a glass to that now and a lot more come December," Pete answered. After the toast, he added. "Maybe you'll want to freshen up Kenneth. We'll be leaving for dinner in an hour."

"Yeah, but I think I'll take a bath rather than a shower so I can take my investment report with me. Great reading material and best to look it over sober. After all that we've decided on here, I plan to enjoy dinner tonight along with several more drinks. Hard to believe I'm so rich!"

Dinner at the restaurant that evening was more than the usual special occasion. Almost as though the closing of their business was a pressure relief. A clean escape was in the works and sounded good! Carl was in best of spirits. Still, you couldn't help but notice his physical appearance. The years had caught up with him.

The party lasted three hours. Everyone had enjoyed one too many drinks, stories, and laughs. Jerome drove them back to the hotel. He had to help Kenneth to the elevator. Pete did the same for Jake.

It was early afternoon the following day before they recovered. Hank arrived with news that a storm system was expected to move in over the weekend. Fishing trips were out. Instead, he had a request from Carl. A favor! All of them were to join his dad and board a chartered flight that evening from Montego Bay to Kingston. Spend two days there. Carl wanted them to see firsthand what they had accomplished. The orphanages! First day, visit the one for boys. Second day, the one for girls. Of course, they complied. Anything for Carl, especially if he was up for the trip. It turned out to be one of the most self-rewarding and memorable occasions of their times in Jamaica.

13.

BREAKING UP, NOVEMBER 17, 1977

Kenneth watched as three dump trucks entered his farm's driveway and then went to the front entrance of his barn to empty their loads in piles. Supposedly this was soil for the raised foundation of a new barn once the old one was demolished. The structure was coming down, but the fill was for the drug cellar beneath and then some. Basically, a cover up. Appropriate description in this case Kenneth thought, but just one of the steps he had taken recently to "cover his tracks".

As planned, Kenneth and the rest of the original team had shut down. The excuse, told to anyone who needed to know, was they had lost their supplier. Without that connection, they had decided it was time to go straight. Getting out of the business themselves but turning the entire distribution system they had built over to their worthy and loyal employees.

On Kenneth's end, the worthy and loyal employees were Trevor and Link. A month earlier, he had explained the situation to both. The smuggling operations from Jamaica were over. Even so, a new source was available if the two of them wanted to carry on. Good stuff too! "Colombian Gold." Not for him though. He was quitting the business. Thinking about getting married and maybe even raising a family. In truth, he was already engaged to Patricia.

Kenneth had contracted for the barn's demolition a week before December. However, the drug cellar still held around three hundred kilos of Jamaican sinsemilla. One hundred and twenty thousand dollars of value to Kenneth and worth over twice as much on the streets. As a parting favor and to keep the transition smooth, Kenneth offered it all to Trevor and Link. They gladly accepted his generosity. Damn nice bonus!

A year earlier, Trevor had used some of his earnings to buy himself a home on Lake Murray. He loved the place. It was located about twenty miles west of Columbia and included a three-acre wooded lot. While there were other lakeside homes nearby, the size of his property made for considerable privacy.

Using their transport cars with hidden compartments, it took just two trips for him and Link to move the three hundred kilos of marijuana to Trevor's lake house. Initially stored it in the home's basement.

Trevor already had a boathouse and dock under construction. He copied Kenneth. Within a month of its completion, a drug cellar was added underneath. In place of a tractor, Trevor parked a boat on its trailer inside. The concealment was even better than Kenneth's.

Sadly enough, the "end-of-game" reunion never took place. A month before the planned date their patron, Carl, took a turn for the worse. He was hospitalized in Montego Bay for three weeks and passed away two weeks before Thanksgiving Day. According to his wishes, he was cremated. The family erected life-sized bronze statues of him at the entrances to each of the orphanages in Kingston. Without ceremony, his ashes were interred beside those of his wife at a family gravesite in Negril.

A few weeks later, on December 6, Hank and family held a memorial honoring Carl's life. Pete and the rest of the team attended. A sad occasion but several hundred Jamaicans came to pay their respect to the man that had devoted much of himself to helping them. Lots of tears were shed. Pete spoke a few words of praise and ended with, "I'm proud to have known this man. I'm a better person for it."

After the service ended, Kenneth invited Hank, Pete, Jake, and Buck to join him for drinks and dinner that evening. Had some news he wanted to share.

Without a thought of waiting, Jake guessed out loud right away. "You and Patricia tying the knot?"

"Got to! She just found out she's pregnant," Kenneth replied with a guilty look.

Buck chimed in with a smile, "I can relate to that. Wanda's in the same shape but a couple of months ahead. Time for me to man up as well."

Pete slapped both men on their backs. "Congratulations, old boys. Damn good reasons to celebrate. How about six at Carl's restaurant. I already know Buck's little honey, and I want to hear more about this girl of yours, Kenneth. Have to meet her."

"You will and soon too," Kenneth started to explain.

Jake interrupted, "She's a winner, Pete. Louisiana Cajun bloodline. Way too good a match for the likes of Kenneth."

Except for Carl's absence, dinner that night was almost the closing celebration they had hoped for. Hank and Jerome joined them for most of the evening. Kenneth announced the wedding date he and Patricia had agreed on. "It's set for early January. You're all invited. Sorry for the short notice, fellows, but it's at the family's church in Lafayette with lots of her relatives attending. She doesn't want to be showing."

"Of course not!" Pete said. "Oh! Sorry if you took that wrong. I was referring to the date. No matter about the timing now that we are all kind of retired. And the sooner the better because I'm looking forward to a good time. Hank, if you like, you and I can stay over a few days and do a little duck hunting. Supposed to be great in Louisiana."

"I'm game for that," Hank replied. "Martha will be there too, Kenneth. She loves weddings. First though, I have to ask. How much does your fiancé know about all of us?"

"I came clean with her this past spring. Explained we were reluctantly closing shop on what had been a very profitable business involved in smuggling marijuana out of Jamaica. Could not believe her reaction."

"And it was?" Hank asked.

"Hilarious and excited! Said here she was thinking she was marrying someone in a boring financial business. Successful, but boring! Then, while enjoying what would be our last cigarette because a baby was on the way, she insisted on hearing all about our history. Laughed a lot and loved every minute of it! Especially the part about your dad's devotion to helping the Jamaicans. She expressed her admiration of him right off."

"As we all have," Pete said.

"I'll say one more thing about her. Patricia already knows Jake, but now she can't wait to meet the rest of you. Hank, like Jake told you, she's a winner just like your Martha, so we can count on her support and confidentiality."

Hank shook his head with approval. "Sorry to leave early fellows but I promise Martha I wouldn't stay late. Enjoy your evening and I'll meet up with you tomorrow for Pete's little surprise."

Jake and Kenneth looked at one another and then to Pete. Both asked together, "What surprise?"

"Not a big deal. Sort of an announcement of my own."

Kenneth laughed. "Don't tell me you're getting married too?"

"Not hardly. Hell, I turned fifty last May. Too damn old to settle down now. I'll just stick with playing the field and watching tamed kids like you envy me with my girlfriends."

"Okay, what's the surprise?"

"My new house. You'll see it tomorrow. I bought a place in Montego Bay. Nice dock out back with deep water access. I'm moving from Florida. Making Jamaica my new home. Buck also plans to do the same and settle down right here in Negril. Raise kids. Like he just admitted, his intended already has a head start on that part."

Buck smiled and said, "Wanda and I picked out a lot on the river. Almost directly across from Bayman's marina. We're going to build a house with lots of room. She wants a big family."

Pete ended that memorable evening with a toast. "To Carl! A better man than any of us and a man we shall never forget."

The next morning Jerome drove them all to Montego Bay. Kenneth and Jake had flights booked from there the following day, so Pete convinced them to stay their last night with him at his new home. He was proud with every right to be. The place was incredibly nice. Kenneth felt a tinge of envy. He was going to miss Jamaica and the times he had shared with his friends there. Couldn't be helped. Patricia had other plans for the two of them.

January 7, 1978, Kenneth and Patricia married in the First Baptist Church of Lafayette. Not a small wedding. Large crowd of family and friends. Pete, Buck, Hank, Patricia's two brothers and one of her cousins served as ushers. Jake was Kenneth's best man.

A reception followed. Later, while Patricia was changing for their departure, Kenneth spoke privately with Jake. "Just want to let you know, Patricia and I will be making our first home here in Lafayette. Starting up a small oil and gas exploration company."

"Don't say?" But what the hell do you know about that kind of business?" Jake inquired.

"Not a thing but the family does. That's how they convinced me to give it a try. Patricia's brother already has an office here and works as something they call a 'landman.' Her dad's a petroleum engineer with thirty years of field experience, and Patricia has three years with Shell as an exploration geologist. All of that time working the onshore portions of the Louisiana-Texas gulf coast."

"Okay, but how do you fit in?"

"On the investment side mostly. I plan to bring a good chunk of start-up money to the table, and except for what I've told Patricia, her dad and brother think of me as skilled in financial matters. Some truth to that because I learned a lot from Carl along those lines. We all did."

"Another adventure, Kenneth. First a soldier, then a marijuana smuggler, and perhaps maybe you'll be an oil tycoon! You'll have to write a book someday."

"I'm telling you all of this for a reason, Jake. I owe you way back for bringing me onboard with your group. So now, if you want to join up with us, I can make that happen."

"Thanks, but I'll have to pass. I still have Mom to look after, and Florida is where she wants to stay. I have caregivers with her 24/7. Besides, I'm close to the Keys. They're like my home now. I'll probably buy myself a recreational place in Key Largo or one of the islands nearby. That said, if you and your new business partners will allow me to invest, I could offer some start-up cash too. No strings attached either, come boom-or-bust."

"I don't have to ask them. I'm the financial genius, and we're looking for investors."

"So how much do you plan to pony up, Kenneth?"

"One cool million. As you know, I can afford it."

"Well then, put me down for about half that amount. Blind trust. No questions asked, no matter how it turns out. You can send me the paperwork once everybody's interest is settled. Just refer to me as a silent partner. Make me an oil tycoon too! Another John Rockefeller."

Kenneth's eyes rolled a little. "That's stretching your expectations a bit I think?" Shaking hands on the deal, they both laughed.

14.

THE TAKE OVER, 1978

Link and Trevor never thought to question Kenneth's explanation for quitting the business. Besides, the story went over especially well with Trevor. The opportunity to take over everything came as a pleasant surprise. He loved it. For one reason, Link was so far out in left field on cocaine, he pretty much did whatever Trevor instructed. With Kenneth gone, instead of being mostly just a runner, Trevor would become the new boss of the whole damn business. Lots more than just a major image change! He knew a huge amount of additional money came with the title.

"Hugh," in Trevor's mind, was making maybe five or six thousand a week split two ways. Instead, by August, Trevor and Link were running four hundred kilos a month from Florida to South Carolina. They were clearing almost twenty grand a week!

Except for a minor adjustment or two and some added street pushers, methods were pretty much the same as when Kenneth ran operations. Sellers for the colleges, universities, and tech schools were still their best customers. Even better, they remained practically anonymous and known only by their adopted names. During trips, and as well with distribution at home, Trevor had assumed Kenneth's alias, Thomas Boyce. Link was Richard Boyce. Brothers supposedly. Each carried a Fort Jackson military ID, a Florida driver's license, car registrations, and proof of insurance. Both of Kenneth's transport cars came with the false documents. Whenever driving them, they were Florida residents with Melbourne addresses. All the faked papers and identifications were supplied with Kenneth's help. It was part of taking over his operations with the idea being, as he explained, the people they supplied would have no way of knowing there had been a change in management. Still the same mysterious TB from Florida and the same lawyer on a retainer. Actually, transferring the names was another part of Kenneth's "clean-getaway".

Another plus for Trevor was no more dealing with unknown smugglers. For years, Kenneth had kept him and Link in the dark when it came to who, how, and where their marijuana arrived in Florida. Now they had been personally introduced to the outfit to be used as a new supplier. On his and Link's side, their aliases were used. They were from Melbourne, but ran marijuana to a connection in Columbia, South Carolina. A friend of Kenneth's named Donald Bates made the introductions. All together, they met in Florida with four young white dudes: Russell, Eddie, Ronnie, and Steve. The obvious head of their operation was the guy named Russell. Second in command was Ronnie. Both seem anxious to meet the two of them and to do business. The meeting took place at Russell's home late in the afternoon. A nice waterfront house in a place called Port Salerno.

Trevor quickly came to understand that Russell was an accomplished seaman. Had to be! They were meeting with a ship well out in the Gulf Stream. Sometimes, they even traveled at night more than fifty miles offshore. Bringing in bales of marijuana with each trip. Very much needed to expand their distributions. They were well equipped with high powered speed boats, a cabin cruiser, and a private docking station onshore with an inconspicuous, enclosed facility for warehousing and transfers. Altogether, a well-planned and safe smuggling operation to work with according to this guy, Donald.

Everything went so well that Trevor suspected Donald must have played an important role in Kenneth's operations. He decided not to ask.

As time would tell, it was the first meeting with these new marijuana smugglers that turned out to be a game changer for Trevor. They had agreed on a price, the way they would connect, make exchanges, and generally just work together. Partly as a boast but also as a show of competence, Trevor offered Russell a courtesy of sorts with a polite question. Went something like this, "Russell, would you like to see a bit of the way we transport back to the Carolinas? You'll be impressed."

"You bet I would. Thanks! Ronnie, take Richard out to the dock and show him around the boat. Cruise around some if he would like."

Trevor's 1975 Ford Granada was parked in the front of Russell's driveway. Light green four door sedan with a dark green vinyl top. Fort Jackson sticker on the back bumper. Left comer of the rear windshield had a U.S. Army sticker beside an American Flag. The windows were down with Kenneth's Irish setter sitting in the back seat.

"Does the dog bite?" Russell asked.

"No, but he may lick you to death."

With that reassurance, Russell opened the driver side door and slid inside. "Nice car, Thomas." Looking back, he noticed a hanger with a military dress uniform across the right rear window. "You guys army or something?"

"You might think so. I'll explain but first step out and take a look in the trunk."

Trevor opened the trunk with his car key. Neatly placed inside over the spare tire well were a partially open green duffel bag filled with military attire, a Fort Jackson tote, two pair of army boots with nice spit shines, a large bag of Purina Dog Chow along with a dozen or so cans of Friskies, and a case of Pabst Blue Ribbon beer. Russell gave a questioning look. "Sorry, but I must be missing something."

Trevor smiled. "Exactly, Russell! You're supposed to miss something. Including the dog, it's all part of a travel disguise. Richard and I both carry army identification cards to go with this stuff. When making runs to Columbia with a full load, everything you see is made up to look like we're just coming back from spending a 'leave' in our hometown of Melbourne. Now, I'll show you the best part."

Trevor opened the driver side back door. The Irish setter, tail wagging, hopped out and sat to the side without even a command. Leaning inside,

Trevor lifted the floor carpet just enough to expose two spring latches along the base of the rear seat. He flipped the latches. Turning toward Russell with a grin, he pulled the seat up. There was the usual pop of the sealed compartment beneath being opened.

Russell stared inside. "Damn Trevor. Outstanding! No way anyone would look for this."

"Holds a little over 200 pounds. Lined with fiberglass and airtight. I'm showing you all of this so you know you're not working with a couple of amateurs. Our methods are safe as hell. Been hauling on 1-95 for years. Both Richard and I have encountered traffic jams at times due to road work or wrecks. He's never been stopped by the law. I have though and it was my first just last year in Georgia. No reason for the pull-over except that I was black and driving this nice car. Happens to us!"

"Yeah," Russell acknowledged. "I know how it is down here."

"It was actually a sheriff's deputy. Checked everything. License, title, registration, insurance. Pissed me off but played it cool even when asked to open the trunk. Paid off too. Before waving me on, he petted the dog, thanked me for my service, and apologized for the inconvenience. Said they were trying to interrupt drugs coming from Florida. I almost laughed. He was inches away from 220 pounds of marijuana and never knew it."

"I like that story, Thomas. Got to get me a car set up like this, especially now that we plan to move more products. Hope you don't mind me asking but there's a leather case in the bottom of that storage compartment. What's it for?"

Trevor reached for the case, moved to the car hood and opened it. Russell whistled out loud. "About forty thousand in C-notes. Donald told us what your price would be even if we haggled a bit. Drove all this way to meet-up and introduce ourselves. Since things went well, Richard and I would like to carry some desert back to South Carolina. A hundred kilos would do if you can spare it?"

"We can, and for starters, I'll price it at a discount. Got to wait though. We have a boat and motor repair shop along with a marine storage business in a big warehouse. Fenced all around and shuts at eight. Private property, completely quiet, and no traffic a couple of hours after closing. Very safe! Hope the delay isn't an inconvenience?"

"No problem. How about you choose the place and I'll treat all of you for dinner? Celebrate making new friends. Get to know each other better. Take the Granada if it's okay to leave my dog here. Drives like a dream."

"Sounds perfect! Just Ronnie and I though. Steve and Eddie have some work tonight. We'll meet back up with them at the warehouse. Let's get a move on and see if Richard has enjoyed his boat ride?"

While having dinner at a seafood restaurant that evening, Russell explained to Trevor and Link a little about his team and their setup. Link had done a "line" earlier and was pretty much spaced out, so the conversation was mostly between Trevor and Russell.

"Ronnie remodels and repairs boats, Trevor." Ronnie tried to say something, but he had a mouth full of fried shrimp, so Russell kept talking. "And by the way, he can work with fiber glass if you get my meaning. Eddie and Steve are inboard-outboard engine mechanics. Good ones too!"

"How did you guys meet up?"

"The four of us graduated from the same high school in 1971. Hung out together as friends. We still are."

"Sounds like all of you go back a long way. Brothers in a way like me and Richard." Trevor was being careful not to use his or Link's real names. He hoped Link's coke habit didn't cause him to forget.

"Sort of, I guess. After high school, I went off to the University of Florida. Finished there with a BA in business two years ago. Managed to graduate while smoking a lot of grass my junior and senior year. Some great marijuana was going around campus. Jamaican, I think."

"I take it you weren't drafted?"

"No. I'm 4F. Bad heel spurs but no complaints. They probably kept me alive. Ronnie lucked out with his lottery number. Steve and Eddie weren't so fortunate. Both were drafted. Somehow, Steve managed to serve stateside for two years. Then he got the hell out. Eddie went to Vietnam but came back four months later. Took a bad round in the knee. Now he's our disabled vet."

"I noticed his limp at your house."

"Yeah, but considering that hell hole, it was one of those million-dollar wounds. What about you two?"

"Neither of us. Richard had a little criminal history. Juvenile stuff but his records were made available to the local board. As for me, I won the lottery just like Ronnie."

Trevor was more interested in his new suppliers than talking about himself, so he purposely moved the conversation back to about them. "After you finished college, all of you must have joined back up somehow?"

"Not right away. When Eddie was discharged, he got himself a real estate license. Tried selling houses for a living. Meantime, Ronnie, and Steve opened an engine repair shop here in Port Salerno. They were working out of a rented garage. Bottom line! None of them were really making it."

"Sounds like my story. Grew up poor as hell. I never knew my dad. Washed cars and pumped gas for peanuts until I was almost twenty."

"Sorry about that. I had it much better. Parents were divorced but my dad worked for Florida Power and Light nearly twenty-five years. He did okay, I guess. Totally paid for my education, so I never worked when I was at the university. Growing up, we fished offshore a lot. Way the hell out too. He taught me everything I know about the sea."

"You must have done something right since then. That home of yours on the water is pretty nice."

"Thomas, it was my dad's 'pride and joy.' He died working a power outage a few years ago. Miss him a lot. Left me everything in his will. Except for the house, it wouldn't have been much, but it was a work-related accidental death and FP&L paid off big time. That's how all this got started."

"You mean the money?"

"Yeah, for the most part. Eddie, being in real estate, found out about a property on the St. Lucie River that had been in foreclosure for almost a year. Scheduled for an auction on the courthouse steps. He went to Ronnie and Steve with a business proposition. Idea was the three of them would go in together and borrow enough to bid on it. If they won, plan was to turn the place into a marina."

"Must have worked, Russell. Sounds to me like that became the storage business we're going to visit tonight?"

"It is but the banks laughed at them. Think about it. They wanted to get an upfront loan to bid on a foreclosure and afterwards put the place up as collateral. System just doesn't work that way."

"Something tells me they came to you?"

"Yeah, but only after the banks said no. When I came home from school, Ronnie and I started hanging out together. He approached me because of my inheritance. Once I had a chance to look at the property, I agreed that if I could buy it at auction cheap, it was too good of an opportunity to pass up. Hell, there was this great big warehouse included and the location was only a couple miles from the inlet. Figured that if things didn't go well down the road with the three of them, I could sell out and still get most of my money back."

"So, you own a marina?"

"Totally at first! All with my money too, so I only agreed to the deal if I became the manager. Boss really."

"You already know my next question. How do you go from running a legitimate business to running marijuana?"

"Luck! Starting out we worked our butts off to get things going. Cleaned everything up! Renovated the warehouse to include some office space and added more than twenty boat slips along with a larger dock. Advertised our new business too. Damn near put all my inheritance into the place. Did everything right. First class! Even so, nine months later we weren't even breaking even. Steve and Eddie stayed a little busy repairing motors, but Ronnie and I didn't have much to do. Sat around a lot. Truth is, I was already thinking of selling out. About then, opportunity knocked."

"Along came somebody I bet."

"Two guys early one morning. Motored up to our dock in a 34-foot Bayliner. Right off, tied up and came inside. Impressed with their boat, Ronnie and I both stepped out of the office to greet them. Smaller ones' name was Luis. He introduced the other guy as Juan. Much bigger unshaven dude about our age."

"Mexicans?"

"We thought so. Luis said they were looking around for a boat slip. Also wanted to check out our maintenance shop, so we gave them a tour. Steve and Eddie were both there working on some outboards, so we introduced them too. Long story short, Thomas. They weren't Mexicans and they weren't really interested in a boat slip."

"They were looking you over?"

"I told you we advertised. That's where they were coming from. Read our ad in the newspaper. After a ten-minute tour, Luis asked how our business was doing. He already knew the answer because the slips were nearly empty and there were only twenty or so boats in storage. Pretty obvious things were slow. I said not very good, but we're pretty new here."

"I can almost guess what happened next, Russell. They were in the marijuana business and looking for runners like us?"

"Not exactly. Wanted to talk in private, so the four of us went to my office. Luis did all the talking. Real damn polite too. Found out Juan didn't speak English too well. Mostly just Spanish."

"Then, they were Mexicans?"

"Think for a moment, Thomas. Tomorrow, you and Richard will be driving back to Carolina with a load of answers to that question."

"You have to be kidding me! Colombia?"

"Yeah, and not the one in South Carolina where you haul to. Anyway, this is how our meeting in the office went. Luis was straight up about it. Said they were looking for a Marina set up like ours. Already knew what I paid for the property at auction. He offered to buy me out on the spot for twice as much. Cash too!"

"Awful tempting but you must have turned them down."

"Hell no, I didn't turn them down. No way! Remember, I said at first, I owned it. Not anymore. Have to be nuts to walk away from a chance to almost double my inheritance in less than a year. Plus, making the deal even better, they wanted to know if we would stay on and run the place for them."

Trevor interrupted. "This gets better by the minute! Don't stop. Got to hear how it ends. I'm ordering another round. Ronnie, ready for a draft?"

"Sure," Ronnie replied and glanced at Link. "Get on with it, Russell. One more beer and it'll be time for us to go to work. Getting late and Richard is looking a little tired."

"No, not tired," Link replied. "Between the two of us brothers, I'm more than just the younger one. The silent partner too. Don't let that fool you though. Listening to every word. Go on with your story, Russell."

"I sold the whole place to them. Lock, stock, and barrel. But before agreeing to sell, and right there in the office meeting, I did something I'll never regret. Said to Luis, I want to take you up on your offer, but that's way more than the place is worth. Truth is, most of the time like today, just sitting around. We're losing our tails. Nearly broke and when the fishing season ends next month, things will probably get worse."

Ronnie couldn't help himself. He was leaning off the edge of his chair. "Hey, here comes the good part. Let me tell the rest!"

Russell nodded. "Glad to. You're on!"

"Okay. Picture this, you two. This man, Luis stands up, leans over, and puts one arm each around Russell and me. Says, amigos, you're wrong. This place is a gold mine. If you'll come to work with my people, all of you will become very rich."

Russell smiled and added. "That's pretty much how it all started. Within a few weeks, they had us running our first ship to shore load of Colombian Gold. After that, we began working on distribution. Sales increased slowly at first but now with you and some others, we're growing like hell!"

Trever lied a bit. "Sounds a lot like what happened to the two of us. Just got lucky. Met someone who put us to work. Now he's retired and we run things from Florida to his dealer in the Carolinas. Travel there about once a week to connect, stay overnight and then come home to Melbourne."

"Looks like we're going to be doing a lot of business together, Thomas. Something you need to know though. Before I could meet with you and Richard, I had to run it by Luis. He's pretty much boss of everything from the offshore to here, but there's a higher up he answers to in Colombia. It's a well-run, big-time organization, and they're careful about who they work with.

"Well, my brother and I must fit in. We're here and about to drive off carrying more than two hundred pounds of paid for marijuana."

Russell shook his head with a smile. "Yeah, 'fitting in' is one way to look at it. Ronnie and I first considered ourselves as joining up. Not anymore. Hell's bells, Thomas, fact is we were recruited."

"What's your point, Russell?"

"Point being, sometime soon, you will have to meet Luis. Juan too! Luis likes to get to know the people he works with. Best way to do that is to ride out with us. Are you up for a little sea cruise?"

Trevor didn't hesitate. "Hell, yeah. Say when!"

"Good. I'll give you a heads-up, maybe even the next time you come down for a load. Arrive a couple of days early and I'll make a seaman out of you. Earn your 'sea legs'. It'll give me a way to say thanks for showing how you transport back to the Carolinas. Take a few hours for an offshore trip with us and you'll get.to see how we operate. Make a new friend out of Luis too. He's the person you want watching your back."

"How so?" Trevor asked

"Let's save an answer to that next time you come down. Drink up. It's time for us to go to work, and you two still have a long day on the road tomorrow. Stay at my house tonight. There's plenty of room. You and Richard can leave after breakfast tomorrow."

"Thanks for your offer. Beats the hell out of a motel because we never hit the road at night. Much safer to blend in with all of the traffic during the day."

Trevor's and Link's trip back home with a supply of Colombian marijuana was nothing more than routine. The ride from the restaurant to the marina in Trevor's Granada had taken less than ten minutes. Eddie was waiting at the gate to let them in. Once inside the warehouse, they were given a brief tour of the facilities. Afterwards, Russell asked Trevor if he could show his guys the car's storage compartment. All of them were impressed, especially after Trevor retold the story about his stop by a sheriff's deputy looking for drug smugglers. Loading up the marijuana and latching the seat down was followed by a round of handshakes and back pats. New friends and partners. One hell-of-a-successful day, Trevor thought.

He and Link had a good night's rest at Russell's home and left at nine the next morning. During the ride, Trevor discussed the probability of taking an offshore boat trip with Russell.

Link didn't think much of the idea. "Trevor, you go ahead if you want to, but I'll pass on this one. Everything just seems to be moving too fast now. We've got a great thing going, and I don't see the advantage of adding risk to the game"

"Maybe, but apparently it's part of the deal. Way Russell put it, this Luis fellow from Colombia has to know who buys his goods. Also said he was someone you wanted watching your back."

"I doubt he's another Kenneth," Link replied.

"We'll see. No sense in both of us doing it anyway. We never take trips together like this one. Next time I make a run, it'll just be me, Russell, and the fish. Probably be fun."

Link laughed. "You think? We'll don't get yourself caught. Might end up on the wrong end of the line bro. Bait! You and I are damn good at what we do on our own turf, but we've got zero experience with the ocean, much less some foreigners."

"You know me. I'll be careful. Leave it at that." Truth was, Trevor figured knowing the people you were in business with worked both ways. Maybe even more if they were from another country. How would he know? Raised in Elgin, South Carolina, so knowing anything about the rest of the world never was in his cards.

Link made the next trip to Port Salerno a week later. Returned with a full load. While storing it at the home on Lake Murray with Trevor, he told him about a chance meeting at the warehouse with the man they called Juan.

"Trevor, this Juan is built like a tackle for the Falcons. Arms bigger than my legs. He's about our age. We shook hands but he never cracked a smile. Talked some too but I couldn't make sense of what he was saying. More Spanish mixed in than English. Kind of the scary type even when he says nothing."

What Link had described gave Trevor an idea. In high school, two semesters of a foreign language were required to finish with an academic degree. During his junior year, he had taken Spanish. Liked it and made good grades both semesters. Teacher praised him all the time. Her name was Cindy Sullivan. Damn good looking and well-built for a white woman. She had encouraged him to take an advanced course during his senior year, but he chose football instead. Since then, Trevor had forgotten a lot, but now he wondered if speaking some Spanish when meeting with these Colombians might prove impressive?

Cindy Sullivan's name was listed in his phone book. Seven years had passed, and he doubted she would remember him, but he called her anyway. "Cindy, this is a voice from the past. Been a long time and"

Cindy interrupted. "Trevor Dunbar. Can't believe it. Been years. Como estas?"

"Muy Bien. Gracias! But please, Ms. Sullivan, those years have cost me my Spanish."

"Not so, Trevor. Maybe some missing verbs, nouns, and adjectives but most of it is still somewhere in the archives of your mine. Especially you! My best student ever as I recall. What can I do for you?"

"Depends! How busy are you, Ms. Sullivan.?"

"I still teach full time at Lugoff-Elgin. Why are you asking?"

"I need a refresher course in a bad way. Actually a 'crash course'. I'm in the real estate business with a very special client looking to buy coastal properties in Florida. This guy is an incredibly wealthy Mexican. Problem is, he only speaks Spanish. You see where I'm coming from?"

"Yes, and please, Trevor, call me Cindy for heaven sakes. I'd love to help you. I'm free after five most weekdays and my weekends are open. What did you have in mind?"

"Some of both if you're willing to spend a couple of months bringing me up to speed. I can double your normal hourly charge for the inconvenience."

"It's true then. I heard you were doing so well that you bought a place on Lake Murray. Congratulations, Trevor. This couldn't come at a better time for me. South Carolina teachers barely make enough to get by, and my old clunker of a car needs to be replaced. But the high school is a public facility for students. We'll have to work out of my apartment."

"Great Cindy. I have your address from the phone book, but I've got to work this weekend. Can we start next Monday?"

"Okay, then. And Trevor, if you're serious about working two months at this plus doing some homework on the side, you'll be more than just back to speed. I guarantee you'll be as fluent as me."

15.

LUIS AND JUAN

Trevor was taking his turn at making a trip to Port Salerno. He had arranged one extra day in his travel plans to arrive early for a scheduled offshore run with Russell. Left on a Thursday. Halfway to Florida, it started to rain. Big storm moved in over the weekend. Came home that next day with a full load, but the weather had canceled his chance for a sea trial and to meet Luis and his big companion, Juan.

Coming back to Columbia, Trevor thought perhaps missing the meeting worked out for the best. Two weeks before another trip would give him more time with Cindy. He liked Spanish. She promised to make him fluent too.

Two months passed. During that time, Trevor had made four runs and Link five. Still no meeting with the two Colombians. Russell had explained in an apologetic way that they were busy as hell in the Bahamas. Something to do with setting up business there. Fine with Trevor. He and Link were making a killing. After expenses, twenty-five thousand a week. Their only problem was hiding all the money!

Trevor and Russell were becoming good friends. Still, he kept his and Link's real identity secret. Twice he had joined in for offshore runs. Smooth operation. Using the Bayliner manned by Russell and Eddie, they met and tied up to a "mother ship" fifty miles out to sea. Its hands loaded them with eighty bales in less than ten minutes and they were off. Coming in, Ronnie and Steve ran point guard in a fast boat staying three to four miles ahead and ready to make radio contact if there were any signs of trouble. Once, Russell said coastal patrols were checking everyone coming to shore, and they had to dump a load overboard.

Trevor purposely began staying an extra day or two in Port Salerno. Russell was keeping his promise when it came to making him a seaman. The two offshore smuggling runs were an important part of Trevor's training and staying with Russell at his waterfront home was even more helpful. There was a Santa Cruz 28 Express Cruiser moored at his dock. Except for bad weather days, they used it and the Bayliner to take tourists out on guided tours. Trevor went along as part of the crew and received mariner instructions from Russell on each occasion. Excellent learning experience. Early on, Trevor was at the helm of the Express Cruiser confidently enjoying himself.

The trips with visitors aboard took time, and there was little money to show for the work. Worth the inconvenience because it was a deliberate way of regularly having the boat with its crew seen in the bay and offshore area. Worked as a well-designed disguise whenever they were coming in with a cargo of marijuana. Appeared to be just another workday for the marina guys. Proof of that came during drinks and a joint one night at Russell's home. He shared a story with Trevor about an encounter with the coast guard.

"Thomas, remember when we first met, you told me about being stopped in Georgia by a deputy sheriff."

"Yeah, I do. Hard to forget that little scare."

"Well, I've got one better. About a year ago, Eddie and I were coming in with a full load. Engine cut out on us three miles from the inlet. Later found out it was a bad ignition switch. Anyway, Eddie was in the back trying to find the problem when off our port side the coast guard pulled up. Recognized us right off and asked if we needed any help. Played it cool as a cucumber. Said, 'sure could use a tow to the marina.' They tossed me a bowline to tie off and towed our Bayliner all the way to our dock. I untied and yelled a loud 'thanks, fellows.' They waved back and left. Ironic as hell. Your Georgia lawman was inches away from two hundred pounds and never knew. Our coast guard helped us smuggle in eight hundred kilos and never knew."

Earning his seamanship abilities with Russell's help was a major accomplishment for Trevor. At the time he had no way of knowing that achieving fluency in Spanish during the same period was much more to his advantage. Spending two hours with Cindy on weekdays and twice that on weekends paid off in more ways than expected. His Spanish returned quickly, and a month into studies, the sessions with her turned sexual. When he wasn't traveling to Florida, the Saturday and Sunday lessons were at his lake home. Great learning Spanish in bed with an excellent teacher in both categories.

Mid-April, Trevor was making his fifth trip to Florida. Seven hours driving there were spent listening to tapes supplied by Cindy. Homework she insisted on if he missed regular instructions because of traveling. Now, true to her assurances, his Spanish was practically flawless. Perfect timing too. This trip down, Russell was confident there would be a meeting with Luis. Because of that and his acquired friendship with Russell, Trevor had decided it was time to reveal his true identity. Trevor Dunbar, not Thomas Boyce. In a way, he was looking forward to everyone's surprise with his confession.

Trevor arrived in Port Salerno at three in the afternoon. Drove straight to Russell's home and parked out front as usual. He was expected, but still as a courtesy, he rang the doorbell. Two men answered. From the sheer size of the younger one in back, Trevor surmised he had to be Juan.

Without hesitating, the one in front reached to shake hands and introduced himself. "Thomas, my name is Luis. My compadre here is Juan. We finally get to meet, and please accept our apology for the delay. Welcome and come in."

Trevor accepted with a nod and stepped inside to shake hands with Juan as well. It gave him the few seconds needed to recover his thoughts from the unexpected introductions before saying, "Thank you! Real pleasure to meet you both because Russell has said so many good things about you two. I take it he's not at home?"

"No. He and his crew are at the marina making some preparations for tomorrow. They'll join us later. You've had a long trip. Take a load off and relax, Thomas. Let's sit at the bar and get acquainted. We're already having a drink. Would you care for one?"

"Yes, thank you. In fact, I was already looking forward to a 'jack-on-the-rocks' when I arrived." Joining them at the bar, Trevor thought to himself that Russell's description of the two was right on. Juan was the quiet, serious one. Luis, on the other hand, wasn't a loss for words and had a polite personality.

Juan, in the role of bartender, handed Trevor his drink. Luis raised his glass as a toast to the occasion. "Tell me about yourself, Thomas. I like to know the people we work with."

Luis's comment instantly caused a memory to return to Trevor. Like the first time he met Kenneth, this meeting might be more of an interrogation than a "get acquainted." Best take extra care to play it straight and be completely honest with them. With that as his guidance, Trevor recalled for Luis his childhood days being raised by a single mom, never knew his father, always poor from pumping gas and washing cars for a few bucks; and growing up as a black in a small country town.

Luis interrupted just once saying to Juan, "Compadre, ustedes dos tienen mucho en común creo. Los tiempos dificiles hacen de ti un hombre."

Juan replied with a simple nod in agreement, and Luis offered an apology to Trevor for his reversion to Spanish.

Trevor had understood every word and considered the comparison of Juan's hard times a compliment. His glass was empty now, so Juan poured another for him.

Taking a sip, Trevor continued his story with how he came into the marijuana business, first as a runner and then a dealer. Luis was particularly interested in his ways of disguise during transporting and his methods of anonymity when dealing. Trevor had to elaborate on both of those in detail for him.

Trevor had talked for the better part of an hour. Luis finished the last of his second drink with a swallow and turned to Juan. "Que piensas, compadre?"

Juan slightly cocked his head to his shoulder and looked directly at Trevor while answering the question. "Es joven pero inteligente. Siendo honesto con nosotros también. Tipo de persona en la que podemos confiar. Me gusta el!"

"Juan liked your history, Thomas. So did I."

From Juan's comments. Trevor knew he had made a good impression on both men. Never would be a better time than now to let them in on some secrets. "Luis, there's a couple of things about me you and Juan have to know. My name is not Thomas. It's Trevor. Trevor Dunbar, and I'm not from Melbourne. My home is in the Carolinas."

Luis responded, "Well, that's news. What about your brother, Richard?"

"His name is Link Rollins, and he's not my brother. Best friends. Link and I go all the way back to grade school."

"Did Russell know who you really were?"

"No, but I can tell him when he gets home."

"Maybe not, Trevor. Leave that to me. I'll decide when it's time for that. Tell me though, why you kept this from all of them in the first place?"

"Maintaining a false identity has been our way of dealing in marijuana since we started. Always works to our advantage, especially on the streets. When we first met Russell and the others, they were strangers and we saw no reason to change."

"Luis again consulted Juan. "Estás bien con este?"

"Si, te dije que era inteligente."

"Good, then. Anything else, Trevor?"

Relishing the moment, Trevor figured it was perfect timing but apologized anyway saying, "Si, y espero que me perdones por no haberte dicho antes. Hablo y entiendo perfectamente el español."

Luis leaned back on his barstool with an obvious look of astonishment. Then he leaned forward laughing, extended a handshake to Trevor and said, "Damn if you aren't full of surprises for a country boy!"

Juan reached across the bar with his right hand and gripped Trevor's shoulder. It was the first time Trevor had seen him smile. With his left hand, Juan raised his glass and said, "Bien hecho mi, amigo. Bien Hecho!"

Homerun way over the fence, Trevor thought. They passed another ten minutes of conversation in Spanish ending with the noise from a car pulling into the driveway. Had to be Russell. Luis asked if his friends knew he spoke Spanish. When Trevor replied "no," he requested they keep it between the three of them just like his and Link's true identity. Trevor wondered why but nodded an agreement.

Russell, Eddie, Ronnie, and Steve all came in. After greeting everyone and making themselves a drink from the bar, Russell suggested they go over tomorrow's offshore run before going to a restaurant for dinner. Trevor learned that Luis and Juan would be accompanying them on the trip out but not returning. Planning the trip offshore was more a matter of synchronization than anything else. Took less time than it did to finish their beverages.

They cruise the Bayliner through the Saint Lucie Inlet at 8am the next morning. Starting at the marina, Russell placed Trevor at the helm, then stayed beside him during the two-hour trip explaining safety procedures and rules of navigation. The lessons weren't necessary. From lots of previous excursions, Trevor was already a competent seaman.

Fifty-five miles offshore, they tied up to a fishing trawler with the name *Paso Seguro* painted along its bow. It was Trevor's third visit to the ship, but he had not been invited aboard until now. Luis suggested a quick tour while the crew loaded the Bayliner. Trevor accepted the invite and took notice of two things in particular while on the trawler. Coming onto the bridge, he was introduced to a Captain Rene who had immediately saluted Luis. Interesting because the pecking order was obvious. More impressive was the trawler's hole filled with crates and pallets instead of fish. A huge amount of marijuana which made it clear that Russell's involvement in this operation played only a small part.

As Trevor was about to climb back aboard the Bayliner, Luis asked if he had ever visited the Bahamas?

"No, Luis. Miami, Florida is as far south as I've ever been. Truth is, except for Vietnam, most of the kids I finished high school with have never even been out of South Carolina."

Luis replied, "In time then, I'd like for you to join me there for some fun and relaxation. Maybe meet some of my friends?"

"Seria honrado, Luis."

"Take my business card. Call if you need to get in touch."

"Thanks." Trevor placed it in his wallet without looking. "Let me return your courtesy." Trevor took a short pencil from his pocket and removed a personal card from the wallet. It read, Thomas Boyce with a Melbourne address and a Florida phone number. He wrote another number on the back of the card while explaining, "This card is just more of my fake disguise, Luis, but the number I've written on the back is unlisted and connects to my home in South Carolina. Please call me anytime you wish."

"I'll see that my office secretary has this. Have a safe drive home."

Untied and with Trevor again at the helm, the Bayliner set course for Port Salerno. Luis and Juan saw them off. While the two of them were still waving from the deck of the trawler, Juan joked. "Pretty obvious you like him. First time ever you've invited any of them on our trawler."

"I may have plans for him someday, Juan. He works in the Carolinas. Those states are a weak link in our distribution chain. I'll speak to David about him."

Juan Valencia never questioned his jefe. Besides he liked Trevor too, and as Luis had pointed out, they shared some things in common. Trevor never knew his dad. Juan was an illegitimate Afro-Colombian kept by his mother and given her last name at birth. He and Trevor grew up poor and both still managed to finish high school, but the similarities between them ended there. The quality of life for the lowermost class in the United States would have been considered not just sufficient but comfortable in Colombia.

Juan's childhood of stark poverty was in a third world country. Unimaginable contrast to Trevor's hardships. Instead, his earliest memories were of a tiny makeshift shanty in San Javier; a mountainous, densely populated area on the western edge of Medellin. Locals called it "Comuna 13." It was basically a squatter's settlement in place of anything resembling adequate housing. Large parts were slums. "Barrio bajo" in Spanish. Home for him was a fourteen by eight-foot shelter built from scraps of tin and plywood with corrugated plastic for a roof. The tiny space had to accommodate Juan, an older brother by seven years, and his mum. Add that to what were generally messy conditions without clean water or decent sanitation for a complete picture of Juan's circumstances during his early years as a child.

Colombia's caste system placed the family into the lowest social status levels. In Comuna 13, they were isolated at the outer rims of the hillsides, and even there, limited by invisible gang borders. Juan grew up in an environment of drugs, guns, extortion, prostitution, and murder.

Salvation for Juan was school and his brother, Jose. A basic educa-tion, even in San Javier, was available and free. Juan was a high school graduate or "bachiller" meaning he completed his elementary, secondary, and upper secondary education. As well, he nearly finished a freshman year in the Medellin extension of the National University of Colombia. Without his brother, none of this would have happened.

Like Juan grew up to be, his brother, Jose, was tall, black, muscular, and very strong by his mid-teens. Attributes inherent to their mum as well. It was those obvious physical qualities that prevented him from completing high school. He was prime gang material and "force-re-cruited" shortly after his sixteenth birthday. Probably because of his impoverished history, gang life was a good fit. Six years later and only twenty-three years old, his membership had grown to one of five in command of nearly two hundred. They controlled a fifth of San Javier. By Jose's orders his brother, Juan, was untouchable, and the shanty was replaced with the first and second story of an apartment house.

Juan was eighteen when he graduated. Class of 1972. By then, the family was benefiting substantially from Jose's participation in gang criminal activities. Juan envied his brother's income and local status. Juan was a big man and physically fit from running up the steep stair-ways in the hillsides of Comuna 13. As well, Jose had trained him in the use of firearms. Primarily for all those reasons, he wanted to join. His mum wouldn't allow it nor would Jose, the family jefe. In those days, territorial gun battles at night between drug-running gangs fighting for street control were commonplace in Comuna 13. You stayed in after dark. Sometimes in the mornings, there would be a dead body or two lying in one of the steep stairways or a narrow alley. José knew the dangers too well and literally commanded Juan not to become a part of it. Instead, since money was not an obstacle and could be used as a means of influence for entry into Colombia's higher education system, Juan was enrolled in the Medellin campus extension of the Universidad Nacional de Colombia, January 1973.

Luis Rojas Alfonso Castillo was born in Medellin August 12, 1941. He was Mariana and Sebastian Castillo's seventh and last child. Luis's father was an attorney having received his Bachelor and Master of Law degrees from the prestigious Universidad de los Andes, Bogota. His age at the time of Luis's birth was forty-six. Mariana was eleven years younger.

Sebastian Castillo began his law practice in Medellin when the city's population was less than 150,000. By the time Luis was entered into pre-school, his dad's firm had established itself as one of the most successful in the province. Colombia's caste system played an important part in that achievement. The family's ancestry was one of well-educated, white, Catholics. Along with race and religion, classes of social status were linked to education, wealth, occupation, and power.

These were the family circumstances Luis was raised in. His was a sheltered life from childhood through adolescence even though those years were one of the most violent periods in Colombia's history. Recorded there as *La Violencia* and fought mainly in the countryside, it was a time of brutal civil war brought about by political feuding between Colombia's liberal and conservative parties. Aware but fortunate to avoid it all, Luis spent grades one through twelve at Saint Ignatius Loyola College located in the La Plazuela area of Medellin. The school's location in the upscale center of the city helped it to serve as a well-protected refuge for the highest classes of conservative Catholics. At the age of eighteen, Luis enrolled in his father's alma mater in Bogota where he completed his Master of Law LLC in 1965. His dad's health was failing. Consequently, Luis returned to Medellin and joined as a partner in the law firm.

Sebastian Castillo's clients consisted of politicians, businessmen, and substantial land barons. Of these, one of the most respected and profitable was the family of Fabio Ochoa Restrepo; a businessman and cattle rancher but best known for breeding Paso Fino walking horses. Fabio Ochoa's two marriages produced a dozen children. Unfortunately, Sebastian's law practice inherited three of them along with the family patriarch, who together in the mid-seventies, opted for a path in drug smuggling. They were Jorge Luis, Juan David, and Fabio Jr., co-founders of the Medellin Cartel.

Luis Castillo's dad passed away in 1967. He was only seventy-two but lived his life as a heavy smoker and died from lung cancer. Luis replaced his father, but over the next four years, the firm lost most of its political and business clientele. Sisters and brothers blamed Luis for their decline in prosperity. They all sold their inherited share of the business to Luis for "pennies on the dollar." In reality the loss of clients was a result of governing by the National Front. The four-year periods when liberal presidents were serving culminated in a socialistic agenda for land reform. It also led to high unemployment and inflation. These conditions brought about even more complications for Columbia such as the formation of paramilitary groups, crime syndicates, and rural guerrillas. All considered, not exactly a healthy climate for economic success in Medellin, Colombia. Instead, crime prospered and Luis, by necessity, followed the money.

By 1972 Luis's credentials as a criminal defense attorney were recognized as exceptional. On more than one occasion, he was invited as a guest speaker at the National University of Columbia. To accommodate student attendance, lectures were conducted during evening hours in the Humanities and Economics departmental facilities. In Spanish, the official title for the building was Facultad de Ciencias Humanas y Economicás.

The university was located just two miles east of San Javier and bordered on its west side by the heavily forested Parque Natural Cerro El Volador. As a safety precaution, students and faculty were advised to only move around in groups after nightfall.

April 27, 1973, Luis began what was to be three classes of instructions on the application of Colombia's legal system to juveniles ages sixteen and under. It was both a sensitive and controversial subject for all Colombians but especially for a young audience composed of more liberal leaning students. The auditorium held two hundred and was nearly packed. The two-hour lecture ended at 10 p.m.

Three students remained behind to personally introduce themselves. Two wanted to challenge and argue the police policy of incarcerating minors for just about any felony. Luis politely assured them the criminal codes and judicial procedures that applied to those circumstances would be addressed in the next lecture.

Having waited for his turn to speak, the third student softly introduced himself. "Professor Castillo, my name is Juan Valencia. I'm just a freshman at the university, but I came tonight because of your subject matter. I grew up in one of the roughest areas of Comuna 13."

Luis was immediately impressed. Coming from that environment into the university was practically impossible. Rare at best, especially for an Afro-Colombian, and this quiet, well-mannered young man was huge. Six foot three or four and built like a gorilla. "Congratulations for your university enrollment, Juan. I'm familiar with the conditions in San Javier because I've had the opportunity to represent a few clients from there. Your being here tonight as a student is a pleasant surprise. You escaped?"

"Thank you, Professor. It's still my home though. I live there with my mum and brother, Jose. He's the one responsible for my being here."

"How did he manage that if I may ask? And please, call me Luis. Just a guest speaker here and certainly not on the faculty."

"Okay, Luis, but the explanation must remain between you and I."

"Trust me, I'm an attorney."

"Well, then. 'Money' is your answer. Simple, Luis! Make a donation to the university or even the right people and welcome to January's registration."

"I have to admit I'm aware of the university's financial needs. Sometimes exceptions for the right and wrong reasons are made. Should give your brother credit in any case. Successful businessman, I take it?"

"Depends on how you measure success. He's a gang leader in Comuna 13."

"I see! Explains the confidentiality request too." Luis raised his index finger in an instructive manner. "Try to stay out of trouble, young man. Keep clean and don't follow in his footsteps."

Juan nodded an agreement and left. Watching him leave, Luis thought to himself what a remarkable student to have met. Honest and straightforward to a fault. He gathered up his notes and papers and arranged them in the proper order before placing everything in his briefcase. Glanced at his watch. Running later than he wanted to.

Luis left the building by the rear entrance. Light rain was falling. Faculty parking lot was 150 yards further back and you had to follow a paved path through a tropical garden-like area to get there. Halfway, he saw it was a mistake.

It was late at night, raining, and the walkway was deserted. Suddenly, he heard fast footsteps from behind. Turned his head to look and saw two men coming towards him. Both were holding sticks. No, more likely clubs. Thinking fast, he immediately decided to stay on the path and run. Couldn't. Another man had moved out of the brush in front. Damn gang members for sure, so he reached for the wallet in his back pants pocket and prepared to give it to them.

In the next moment, time just seemed to have stopped. Not a second passed between a staggering blow from behind to his right shoulder, the sound of its bone cracking, and finding himself in the path on both knees.

In real pain now and with something like a glassy gazed, Luis saw all three of the men were standing over him. One commanded the other two. "Los dos lo terminan! Prisa!" Obediently, both raised their clubs. Luis instinctively tried to lift his right arm and fend off blows. Never happened. Teeth, hair, and blood from the nearest assailant literally splattered everywhere. Startled and hesitating, the other one with a club turned too late in defense. There was a repeat of blood and teeth again, and even more than the first. Their commander backed some, then ran like hell leaving his companions. One was conscious but withering on the path. The other wasn't moving at all.

Luis saw a giant of a man standing over them. He also held a club. His was dripping blood. In that instance, Luis recognized it was Juan Valencia. Juan tossed his club off into the brush and knelt beside Luis asking, "You okay sir? Stay still. Help will come."

A minute passed before two policia came hurrying along. They had seen someone running from the area. More campus security arrived shortly afterwards. Ambulances were called for Luis and the two attackers. While waiting, they questioned both him and Juan. Luis was loaded into an ambulance and taken to the hospital. He did not have a chance to thank Juan.

Luis suffered a severe clavicle fracture. He spent three nights in a hospital room on painkillers with a badly bruised and swollen shoulder. The doctors had to wait until the swelling went down before, on the third day, they fitted him with a figure-eight splint to immobilize his right side for the next four to six weeks.

Early the first morning of his hospital stay, a Major Castro with the Colombia National Police came for a statement. After recounting the assault for the officer, Luis asked about Juan.

"Mr. Castillo, he told us what happened. I'm pretty sure that student saved your life. Before the club attack, you were preparing to hand them your wallet. Said so in your statement. Sorry to say if you had, it would have made no difference. We already have a confession from one of the men. The other is in a coma. They were not there to steal anything. It was part of a gang initiation."

"Mierda," Luis replied. "It never occurred to me. I'm familiar with some of those gang's 'rites of passage.' Have to commit a crime to join."

"Think about what you heard, Mr. Castillo. One instructed the others to finish you off. And like I said, we have a confession. They were going to club you to death! We have all three in custody facing attempted murder charges."

Major Castro left. Luis reflected on the events. Here he was a criminal defense lawyer and some of the very types of people he had defended tried to kill him. And Juan, an Afro-Colombian from Comuna 13 stepped in at his own risk to save him. Have to look this Juan Valencia up at the university when I'm better. He's earned more than just a grateful thanks. Hell! The man saved my life.

Two months later, Juan was leaving a 10 a.m. biology class when he found Luis waiting for him in the hallway. Luis extended his right hand and a broad smile. "Good morning, Juan."

Juan returned the smile and a soft handshake. "Well blow me down, Mr. Castillo. Good to see you. Looking well, but how's your shoulder?"

"All healed, thanks to you! Sorry I haven't gotten around for a visit before now. This thing laid me up for a while. I had to take it slow and easy."

"I understand, Mr. Castillo. They came down pretty hard on you."

"Yes, and according to a police detective, it could have been much worse if you hadn't stopped them. It's the reason I'm here. Offer you my sincerest thanks. I believe you saved my life."

Juan shook his head negatively saying, "No need for all that, Mr. Castillo. I'm glad I was there to help. Truth is, I kind-of enjoyed busting those bastards. Wish I could have gotten all three though."

Now Luis was nodding his approval. "One talked. Police arrested the third one in San Javier. A gang leader too! They're locked up now and facing a two to five prison sentence. Means we can forget them, Juan, but I'll always remember what you did. Here, take my card and 'for Christ sake,' call me Luis."

Juan took the card. In bold letters it read simply: "LUIS CASTILLO, EL ABOGADO." In smaller print at the left bottom corner, there was a phone number and address.

Luis pointed to it and said, "I'm at your service if you ever have need of me, Juan Valencia."

"Thank you, Luis."

"I have to go now, but there is one more thing I'm curious about. The night I was attacked, you left the building five minutes before me. Hell-of a coincidence you happened to come along when you did?"

"It was raining, dark, and late. Not a good night to be out! Times like that are the reason I kept half a baseball bat in my backpack. To be honest, I hung around to watch you leave. Stayed low and followed about forty yards behind. Saw what was coming too. Just wish I had been a little closer. Maybe I could have stopped that first hit."

With his mouth open in amazement, Luis stared at Juan for a moment. Looking back as he turned to leave and said, "I'm indebted to you. Memorize that phone number. In your case, I'm available 24 hours a day."

It was late October that same year when Juan's life took a painful turn. It was the end of his second semester at the university. He had studied the night before for a final exam in his economics course. Hated it but made good grades anyway. Finished the test that morning and was jogging home. It was a three-mile run, and he paced himself to make it in under thirty minutes.

As he came close to San Javier, police cars and ambulances raced by. Not an unusual scene unfortunately. Then, as he rounded the corner to the street near his home, everything was blocked off. Looking ahead he first was alarmed, but that quickly became panic. Police were moving in and out of his home. Several were standing outside questioning neighbors. Juan instinctively ran towards the house, first dragging one and then two policemen with him. Half-a-dozen more police, some with guns drawn, were about to confront him when a neighbor yelled. "Ese es su hijo! Ese es su hijo!"

Juan was finally stopped and held feet from the front door. It was wide open, and he could see inside. One of the policemen holding him said, "Don't go in, Boy. Stay back! Nothing you can do! Don't go inside."

Those cautions weren't much help. Juan's brother was lying face up and stone cold at the foot of the staircase covered in blood. Jose was obviously dead. Struggling but still being held back, Juan pleaded, "Where's my, mum. Is she okay?"

The same officer lowered his head but with eyes held up towards Juan. "She's gone too, Son. Both are gone."

Juan moaned a long "no, please no," and slumped to the front steps.

Hours passed before the bodies were removed. Later Juan learned Jose was shot seventeen times. Not just a gang killing but a gang message. His mother was found upstairs beneath her bed. She had apparently tried to hide. The person that killed her had to kneel on the floor to point the gun. From that position and probably only a foot way, he shot a defenseless woman twice in the head.

From that day on, Juan's character changed. He almost never smiled again. He wanted revenge. One of Jose's friends told him who carried out the assassinations. Members of "Los Alcazares Soldados," a local gang that controlled several of the San Javier districts besides the one they were named for. And they were well known for brutality. Territorial disputes between Juan's brother, Jose and their leader had sometimes occurred. His name was Gusta Lopez Garcia. Word in Comuna 13 was that Gusta ordered all of the Valencia family to be killed. Two weeks later, Juan's absence from home that morning proved to be a deserving end to Gusta Lopez's life.

16.

CAREER PATHS, NOVEMBER 2, 1973

For Juan, his brother's death was a game changer. During most of Juan's life, their relationship had protected him from the adversities of growing up in Comuna 13. It was much worse now. For certain he was still on "Los Alcázares Soldado" hit list. His chances of survival in his old neighborhood were not good. Added onto that, the family's money train came to an abrupt halt when Jose was killed. Juan, big and tough as he was, had never worked for a living.

Juan endured a period of mourning at his home with little sleep, all the while with the appearance of a paramilitary fighter. Thanks to Jose, there were several weapons hidden in the house. Juan kept two handguns on his person. One in a shoulder holster and another at his hip. As well, there were three short barrel pump shotguns with extended magazines close at hand. Prepared himself for a gunfight.

And so, for a day or two, Juan was hoping Jose's assassins would try something. Dreamed of killing them all but they had time on their side. The gang's smart move would be to stand down at least a month before taking him out at an opportune time. The realization was slow coming, but eventually Juan knew he had to leave San Javier. Question was where to go and with what? Answer to the last part was to sell the home for half its worth in cash and get the hell out as fast as possible. Take Jose's car. He wondered if Luis Castillo might help him with the other.

Eight days after his family was killed, Juan was packed and ready to leave for a rented apartment on the eastern side of Medellin. Before going, he made a phone call. Luis Castillo's secretary answered.

"Bufete de abogados, Castillo. Juanita hablando." Juan gave his name and asked if he might speak with Luis.

"Ciertamente, señor Valencia. Un momento por favor."

Moments later, Luis responded. "Juan, it's a nice surprise to hear from you. Doing well, I hope? Is there something I can help you with? Anything at all?"

"Perhaps, if you have time this afternoon, I'd like to stop by your office. Just talk with you if it's convenient? I have your address."

Luis's experience as a criminal defense attorney immediately kicked in. Juan was not requesting a social visit. "Juan, I'm always available for you. Anytime this afternoon is fine."

Luis's office was one of several on the eighth and top floor of a downtown professional building. Juan arrived there at 1pm and took the elevator up. He found Luis's name and occupation on a door at the end of the hallway. Inside, there was an impressive receiving room with seating for guests. At the front desk, he introduced himself to a handsome lady who turned out to be Juanita. She apparently served as a secretary and receptionist. Over an intercom, she said, "Sr. Castillo, Juan Valencia para verte." He replied, "I'll be there in a moment."

Juan took the time to admire the facilities. To the left, there was a glass enclosed conference room furnished with a long mahogany table surrounded by eight high-back leather chairs. On the right side, there was a small but unoccupied office with a desk, chair, and credenza.

Luis stepped out through a pair of double doors with a smile and his right hand extended. "Juan, great to see you! Please come in."

With that greeting and the handshake, Juan complied. Inside at one end, Luis's had a large desk with seating for two in front. There was shelving behind the desk with rows of thick books. On the opposite side of the office, four chairs were placed around a small marble coffee table. In a corner, there was a fully stocked bar. The walls held numerous framed photos and diplomas. His office was designed to give an impression of competence and success. The scene accomplished that easily.

Luis offered Juan a chair and then sat behind his desk. He knew Juan must be there for a reason but decided to put him at ease and begin with some pleasant conversation "Tell me how you've been. I know the second semester just ended at the university. I'm anxious to hear how you did in your first year."

Before answering, Juan removed a small, unsealed envelope from his shirt pocket and handed it across the desk. Apparently, Luis was not aware of Jose's and his mum's death. Juan understood. Not surprising for the times in Colombia. Practically the murder capital of the world. In any case he waited for Luis to read the contents of the envelope. It was a 3x6 inch article from the largest newspaper in Colombia, *El Tiempo*. Juan had cut it out from page four in section two. In just two short paragraphs taken from a police report, it described the brutal murder of Jose Valencia and his mother, Gabriella Ana Valencia.

Luis read the clipping. Still holding it, he placed both hands on his brow. He looked directly at Juan while slowly moving his head back and forth in a negative manner. "I'm so very sorry, Juan. I've been away and I did not know. Is there anything, anything at all I can do to help?"

"Probably not, Luis. I wanted to tell you I've dropped out of the university because of this. They were killed just as exams started. I took an 'incomplete' in everything but economics."

"I can fix that for you."

"Thank you, but no. Even if I wanted to, I can't go back. I was proud to be in the university for the family. No point in it now."

"I see but maybe with time to heal, you might change your mind."

"Perhaps, if it were that simple. For one thing, I don't have much money. Remember my brother paid the bills. More importantly though, I know the gang that murdered them. For some reason they wanted to kill us all. Not just Jose. I'm still on the list. I left Comuna 13 this morning. This afternoon, I'm moving into an apartment on the east side. Otherwise, you would soon be reading about me in the obituaries."

"I've got high up connections with the police. Let me see if they can help. What gang was it?"

"They're an especially bad bunch. Ruthless sometimes and everybody in San Javier knows it. Call themselves 'Los Alcázares Soldados.' Leader's name is Gusta Lopez."

Luis hesitated. Lean back as if in shock before saying with a grimacing facial expression, "Oh my god, Juan! I'm so sorry! Please, I'm so sorry! Oh my god!"

His reaction caught Juan off guard. "What's wrong, Luis? Are you okay?"

"No! I'm not okay. Gusta Lopez is in Bellavista prison. He was the one on the path that got away. The police arrested him a day later and charged him with attempted murder. I was called to testify in court, but a detective Castro said he made a plea deal before the trial. He's serving eighteen months for attempted manslaughter."

Juan's mind exploded with the realization that it was his intervention in the attack on Luis that led to his family's death. Now the son-of-a-bitch that had them killed was serving a lousy eighteen months. He knew gang members wore prison time like a badge of honor. Practically revered for enduring the hardship. Once Gusta Lopez was released, he could move back into his leadership role.

Juan took a moment to control his anger. After a deep breath and then releasing his fist from a tight grip on his chair's armrest, he said, "Don't apologize, Luis, especially for what these bastards did. This Lopez is still calling some shots from his cell. That has to be the way it came down on Jose and mum. He won't quit until I'm killed. That's the way it works in Comuna 13."

Luis was still putting the pieces together. He couldn't help but admire how Juan was able to keep his cool. Two things were bothering him. Still holding the newspaper clipping, he looked to check the date of the murders. They were killed on the day after Gusta Lopez was transferred from a city holding facility to Bellavista. Too damn much of a coincidence, so he told Juan what he was thinking.

"Makes sense, Luis. The timing is obvious. It lets everyone know the assassinations were in retaliation for his conviction. Also, my stopping

those three at the university that night was an embarrassment for Alcazares Soldado. Remember their chickenshit leader ran leaving two
behind. To save face, I'm surprised they didn't try to get you as well"

"Exactly? It's the other thing that troubles me. One confessed but
I was prepared to testify in court against all three. Probably the reason
for a plea deal. Something tells me I was on the hit list that day."

"No way! If you had been, we wouldn't be talking now."

"I may be alive because I wasn't here. I've been in Miami, Florida for
the past two months on business. Came back two days ago. That's why
I had not heard about all this. Wait one second. We'll see." Luis pressed
the intercom button. "Juanita, you said Miguel Ruis called about a week
ago wanting to speak with me?"

"Yes sir. I told him you were out of the country but would touch base
soon after you returned."

"Get Miguel on the phone for me, Juanita. If he's busy, say it's important I speak to him right away."

"Who's Miguel?" Juan asked.

"Gusta's lawyer. Court appointed. He brokered the plea deal."

Intercom buzzed. "I've got Miguel on the phone for you"

"Put him through, Juanita." Phone rang. Luis pressed the speaker
button and answered. "Good afternoon, Miguel. You called last week,
but I was away. Not important, I hope?"

"Possibly not. A courtesy matter really. You recall I had to represent
the men that attacked you?"

"Yes."

"Well one of them was a badass apple. That's putting it politely. When
I bargained the plea deal with him, he kept bringing up your name.
Wasn't asking about your health either, if you know I mean. Very disturbed man, this Gusta Lopez. Anyway, probably nothing but maybe
you should watch your back for a while."

"Will do, Miguel. And thanks for the warning. I'll be careful."

"Luis, do you carry a weapon?" Juan promptly asked.

"No. Never even fired a gun. Wouldn't know which end to point.
Maybe I should follow Miguel's advice if you think I'm in trouble?"

"An Alcazares Soldado gang leader like Gusta doesn't make idle threats. No doubt about it. He plans to have you killed. Damn right you're in trouble. Question is how to stop him. It's a hell hole, but he's safely tucked away in Bellavista. No way to get him there, otherwise I'd personally kill the son-of-a-bitch."

Luis sat back in his chair. It was a habit when he was concentrating before speaking. "Not necessarily, Juan. In the criminal law business, you work with people on both sides of the legal system. I have two things in mind. Do you know how to use a firearm?"

"I was raised by a gang leader in Comuna 13. He taught me from the time I was ten. I'm well trained with guns, but I've never had reason to use one until now. Why do you ask?"

"I'm sure you don't have a permit?"

"Not hardly, but I've been carrying my 9mm everywhere since Jose was killed."

"Everywhere! Mind if I see it?"

"Sure." Juan reached behind his back with his right hand and brought out a gun. He checked the safety, removed the eight-round magazine, ejected a round from the chamber, and handed it to Luis while explaining, "This is a semi-automatic 9mm Smith & Wesson Model 39-2. Damn good weapon!"

"It's light! Looks heavy but feels light, Luis said. Pointed it at the wall and sighted down the barrel. "Juan, could you teach me how to use this thing?"

"It weighs less than two pounds without a magazine full of cartridges. And yes, I can teach you."

"Thanks, I may have a proposition to offer you. Let me make a call first. It will take a few minutes. The bars open. Fix yourself a drink if you like."

"I will. Can I get one for you?"

"Yes, I need one after all this. Straight scotch-on-the-rocks for me. Luis buzzed Janita on the intercom. "Juanita, get me Hernando Cubides on the phone. As always, say it's important."

While pouring drinks at the bar, Juan asked, "Another lawyer?"

"Yes and no. Hernando and my father were close friends. An attorney but doesn't practice. Works out of Bogota. He's the Minister of National Defense."

Luis stood and walked over to the bar. Sipped his scotch before saying. "Juan, we've got a little time, so listen up. I'm calling Hernando for the both of us. Gun permits in Colombia are restrictive and take time. Exceptions are made for special circumstances such as personal protection and private security personnel. If you're not going back to school, would you consider coming to work for me?"

Luis held his hand up to stop Juan from replying. "Wait for some details before you answer! After I speak with Hernando, we'll have temporary weapons permits faxed to us. He's the only person that can waive rules and fees. When you leave this office, that 9mm will be legal to carry. Juanita and I will be leaving with you. I want you for my bodyguard. Permanent position! In addition, your assistance will be required in certain cases that I have to deal with in Colombia. The United States as well. I've recently become involved in some work there. We'll discuss that later."

Bodyguard, Juan thought. He liked the sound of it. "It would be my honor to protect you, Luis. Hell, yes and thank you. I'll take the job." With his left hand, Juan raised his glass as a toast to his new "jefe" and extended his right hand to seal the agreement.

Luis did the same and said, "Done deal." Juanita buzzed the intercom. "I've got Hernando for you."

"Relax, Juan. This will take a moment. Step out in the lobby if you would and give Juanita your identification cards. I'll explain why after I take this call. As Juan left, Luis picked up his phone without using the speaker. A habit of keeping the conversation private when speaking with someone in politics. Twenty minutes passed before he came out and apologized for taking so long. Luis turned to Juanita and introduced Juan as their new employee.

She stood and shook his hand with a grip like a man but addressed Luis. "May I ask what's going on, Mr. Castillo?"

"Hernando's secretary is holding for you, Juanita. She requires personal information for the three of us. We're all being issued temporary weapons permits by fax. I'll explain after you finish with her. Juan, do you have any spare firearms?"

"Yes sir. Right outside. My brother's car. I have an arsenal in the trunk. Plenty of ammunition too!"

"Good. You said you were moving into an apartment later today. You work for me now, so I'm asking you to reconsider. My father passed away a few years ago. He owned a 2,000-acre hacienda about thirty kilometers south of Medellin. Dad often commuted to the office from there. It's a half hour drive all the way on route 25. After his death, the family forced the sale of the property and divided the money. I managed to keep the ranch house on a 70-acre plot. That's where we're going. Okay?"

"Seriously, Luis? A ranch-house? I grew up in a shanty half the size of your office, so it's more than okay with me. Do I follow you there?"

"No. Not if there is room for me in your car. I'd feel safer being with you. Leave my BMW in its parking space. What are you driving?"

"A 71 Buick hardtop. Plenty of space."

"My plan is to close the office for a week. We can stay at the ranch. Should be safe there and you can teach me how to use that 9mm."

"Juanita, if you're through with Hernando's secretary, I'll explain what's happened."

"Please, Mr. Castillo. I'm worried!"

"It seems one of the gangs in San Javier may be planning to use us for target practice. We'll all be alright, but we need to take precautions for the time being. It's one of the reasons to close up here for a while."

Luis took another five minutes to explain to Juanita the events that lead to the danger they might be facing. Without interrupting, she listened carefully. When Luis finished, he instructed her to gather up whatever she needed from the office and prepare to join them the next day at the ranch for an extended stay. They would be conducting business there.

"Thanks, Mr. Castillo for making sure I'm safe as well. Knowing all of this now, I need to tell you about something that happened a week ago. Didn't think much of it then but it could be related. Closed the office at five. As I left the building for my car, there was a black sedan parked in one of our reserved parking spaces. Four unsavory looking young men were just sitting there inside. I decided to tell the driver the spaces were reserved, and they would have to move. When I did, he replied they were waiting for someone. I asked who? He pointed to our reserve sign with your name and said, 'This lawyer man.' I told him he would have to make an appointment. Then I told him to move, or I was going to call security."

"They left?" Luis asked.

"Yes, and cursed me as they drove away. Driver gave me the 'finger' too! You know me. I flipped the old 'bird' right back at him."

Luis looked at Juan. He was shaking his head acknowledging the obvious. "Perfect timing, Luis. They were there for you."

Juanita saw how both men reacted to her story and anxiously said, "I can be ready to leave when the fax comes. Anything else?"

"Yes. See if you can reach Pedro on the phone. Tell him to expect us at the gate around ten. That will allow for Juan and I to have dinner and time afterwards to meet with someone at the restaurant. Juanita, pack whatever you need to bring for yourself from your apartment. Be at the ranch around eight tomorrow if you can. Plan for at least a week."

"Who's Pedro?" Juan asked.

"The ranch caretaker," Take a seat, or better still, help Juanita if she needs any assistance. I have a few things to pack. Juanita don't forget your Rolodex. We may have to make lots of calls."

The faxes arrived just after 3pm. Juanita faxed back an acknowledgment and a thank you from Luis. As they were preparing to lock up and leave, Juan asked for a paper bag. Juanita handed him one from her desk drawer and watched as he concealed his 9mm inside. "Is that necessary?" She asked.

Juan smiled before saying, "Probably not but if there is a black sedan waiting for us, I prefer to have 'hands on' and ready if needed."

They left the office without an incident. Luis had requested an armed security guard to be present in the parking lot. Juanita drove away first. Thankfully, everything seemed normal as he and Luis left in the Buick. Luis looked at his watch. "We're making an early departure. I asked that guard to be on the lookout for a black sedan. If one comes around, he's to take down the license and call the police."

"Smart, Luis. If he spots them, we'll know if our playing it safe paid off. Half an hour drive to your ranch? I may need to stop and gas up. Okay?"

"Sure. First though, we're eating at a great Medellin restaurant. Five minutes from here on Callie 10 east. Family owned. Belongs to a client of mind. I made several calls before leaving the office. We have reservations!"

"Dinner reservations? You do remember there is a whole damn gang out looking for us, and we're stopping for dinner?"

"Would not have normally. We're meeting someone there. I told you in my law business, I sometimes represent clients who can help on either side of the legal fence. Have you ever heard of Julio Fabio Ochoa Restrepo?"

"Yes, of course. Everybody knows who he is. Big time Colombian rancher with several haciendas. Cattle breeder but practically famous for the horses he raises."

"That's right, but Don Fabio Restrepo is also a prosperous business-man and respected for his integrity in all of Colombia. He inherited some of the wealth from his father, but his prosperity has since grown many times that. The restaurant we're dining at is one of several he has in Colombia. The Don is regarded as an outstanding citizen and stays well connected with the right people in government. My father was good friends with him and his wife Margot. Dad served the Don as the family's lawyer for more than twenty years."

"You're still connected with them, I assume?"

"More than just connected. Without their continued support after my father died, my financial means would have been severely limited. Even more so today. I would not have my office, or my ranch were it not for their assistance."

"I'm not sure I understand why? Like your father, you're a successful lawyer. Still young too."

"The short answer is siblings. I have six. Not one of them has ever worked a day. They're all older than me, and my mother raised them as spoiled rich kids. After Dad passed away, they fought over every penny in the estate. My father had named my oldest brother as executor. By the time everything was settled, most of Dad's money had disappeared.

I use my share of what was left from the inheritance and some borrowed cash to keep the ranch and a few acres. I've had little or no contact with them since."

"I just want to be certain, Luis. Who exactly will we be meeting at the restaurant?"

"Julio Restrepo and his son, David. We'll have to wait a bit. They can be there by seven. David is the Don's oldest boy. In his mid-twenties. He and I returned from Miami together three days ago."

"I'd like to go there with you someday. Anywhere in fact. You mentioned the United States of America. I've never even been to Bogota, much less out of the country."

"There is a lot I have to tell you. If things work out with the Restrepo family, you'll be traveling quite a lot. The next few years may be the chance-of-a-lifetime for both of us. I haven't forgotten you saved my life. Sorry you paid such an awful price for that."

"Thanks, I'm better now. Meeting with you today has helped. No way I'll sleep tonight. Been depressed ever since Jose and Mum were killed. Now, I'm excited as hell! If I ask too many questions, just tell me and I'll shut up."

"We're near the restaurant, Juan. It's a few blocks further on the right. We'll have some privacy there for a couple of hours before our friends arrive. Once we're settled in with a drink, I'll explain most of what you need to know."

The restaurant was upscale and already busy. Luis gave his name at the door. They were escorted to a small but private dining room. After drinks were served, Luis requested the waiter give them some time before ordering.

Luis waited a moment for privacy before saying, "Juan, I spent the last two months in Florida at the request of Julio Restrepo. He wanted legal representation there that he could trust with very delicate matters and had asked me to open a law office in Miami. Thanks to an idea you gave me at the university, I succeeded in doing just that."

"Mighty kind of you to say, but there's no way I could have helped? Just a first-year college freshman."

"But you did! To practice law in Florida, you must pass the bar exam. I'm accredited from one of the most prestigious universities in South America. For admission to the exam in Florida, my credentials don't amount to a row of beans. You have to be a three-year graduate of a law school accredited by the American Bar Association. International degrees don't count. However, there was an alternative method, and that's where you helped. If you've been awarded a Doctor of Jurisprudence degree from a law school recognized by the ABA, you're eligible."

"Awarded. You mean like a gift?"

"Pretty much. I provided my educational qualifications to a Florida law school along with substantial donations to the right people. A month later, I framed a degree from the school on my office wall. Kind of similar, if you remember telling me how you gained admission to the National University of Colombia."

"Not surprising. Money talks in the states as well as Colombia. So, that was all it took to open an office in Miami?"

"Not quite. I still had to study like hell and pass the examinations for admission. Finished those just last week. There's more. Before taking the oath, you must provide evidence of good moral character. That was easy for me with my connections here. Now, I'm licensed to practice in Florida. Already have an office set up in Miami."

"Miami, Florida. All I know about it is the pictures I've seen on TV. Girls in bikinis. Does that have something to do with the 'delicate matters' Julio requires there? Has David gotten some honey in trouble?"

"Nothing as simple as that. A year ago, Don Restrepo sent his son to the states in search of thoroughbred horses for his ranch. He also plans to open a restaurant in Miami similar to one in Bogota. Respectable undertakings for the family, but while in Florida, David became involved in something besides horses. Smuggling! At first it was whisky but it's something much more lucrative now. The potential income was enough to interest his younger brother Jorge and gain the much-needed support of Julio."

"Luis, you're not talking about smuggling marijuana, are you?"

"Yes."

"Wow! The respectable Restrepo family is getting into the marijuana business. I love this. How do you fit in?"

"I'll explain but be careful when you implicate the entire family. Without question, Don Fabio Restrepo is the patriarch. Even so, he was reluctant to be involved when considering his wife Margot and the other children. In Florida, I'm working strictly with David as his business attorney in America. But my specialty is criminal defense. It's not exactly a legitimate enterprise they're contemplating, so quite a bit of legal counseling can be helpful. With my advice, Julio is trying to avoid direct ties to the operation. Hopefully, my appearance with any of them in a U.S. courtroom will never happen."

"I hate to change the subject, but what has all this got to do with a gang from Comuna 13 out to kill us?"

"I'm coming to that, but let's slow down and order dinner. There will be time for another drink before we're served. Colombian steaks are the house specialty."

Juan could not remember ever having a better steak dinner. Topping it off, Luis had ordered a bottle of wine. While enjoying that, the conversation turned to sports. Both men were naturally fans of the Colombia national football team. The Central American and Caribbean Games were still two years away and were being played in Santo Domingo. Made little difference to Colombians. Their team hadn't won the Gold Medalist since 1946, and the anticipation of winning again only intensified every four years. Luis suggested they attend the games in Santo Domingo.

Juan raised his glass for the second time that day. "Watching from the stands instead of a TV would be an experience to remember, Luis. I'd really like to go with you someday!"

Luis responded with his glass and a handshake. Laughed and said, "Consider it done, if we're still alive!" He paused after his weak attempt at humor. "Maybe we better get back to business. You wanted to know what my association with Julio Restrepo has to do with our current problem. I'm sure you've never been to Bellavista prison. I have on occasions had to go there representing someone on appeal. It's a very nasty and dangerous place. In the case of us versus Gusta Lopez, I think he is exactly where we want him. I intend to ask a favor of the Don. Wish I didn't have to because favors must always be returned. The situation we're in leaves no choice that I can see."

Their waiter approached the table. Luis stood thinking maybe their host had arrived. Instead, it was a phone call from Juanita.

"She wouldn't call unless it was important. I'll be back in a moment. Enjoy your wine."

Juan followed instructions. Sipped wine and reflected on the day's events.

There was still the danger from the Alcázares gang, but his fortunes had taken a turn for the better. He was employed as a bodyguard by someone he admired. In that capacity, he would soon be staying on a ranch well removed from Medellin. The possibility of traveling outside of Colombia in the near future was hard to imagine. Something else. Luis had included him when he mentioned the future being a "chance-of-a-lifetime." A little later in the conversation, transporting Colombian marijuana into Florida was mentioned. Now, and here at this restaurant, they were to meet with the very people planning to be involved in that venture. Plus, at the request of Julio Restrepo, Luis had just opened an office in Miami. In his mind, Juan connected all the dots. He was not sure of his part in the operation, but somehow, he was going to be included in the business of smuggling marijuana. A chance to make lots of money. Maybe a ranch of his own someday? Hell no! A hacienda!

Ten minutes passed before Luis returned. His earlier smile had been replaced with a serious facial expression. "Bad news?" Juan asked.

"Yes, I'm afraid so. There is a brokerage firm at the other end of the hall from my office. A good friend of Juanita's works there as a secretary. She called Juanita at home to ask if she had heard what happened? Our security guard is dead."

"The one that was looking out for us when we left?"

Luis nodded with an affirmative. "Maybe it was my fault. I asked him to watch for a suspicious black sedan in the parking lot. He was supposed to take the license and call the police."

"I remember you telling me that. What went wrong?"

"Apparently, he did as I suggested and called the police. It was five o'clock though. Workers were starting to leave the building for their cars. According to Juanita's friend, witnesses said he walked to the driver side of the sedan, looked in, turned back, and tried to walk away. For no apparent reason, two men got out with pistols and shot him in the back several times."

"What about the police?

"They arrived a minute too late. For now, that's all Juanita knows. I asked her to try and contact Major Castro. Once she does that, we'll receive a status report tomorrow morning."

"If we had not left the office early, it would have been you and I lying dead in the parking lot. I'm your bodyguard, Luis, but four against one is poor odds when our lives are at stake. It's not over either. These killers are just following orders. What do you think we should do?"

"It's nearly seven. We'll wait as planned for Julio and David."

Julio Restrepo arrived promptly at seven. His sons, David Ochoa and Jorge Ochoa were with him. Julio greeted Luis with a handshake. Next, Luis introduced Juan. "Julio, this is the young man that saved my life at the university. Now, for certain, he has done it again. That's why I ask to meet you here."

Julio made an up and down observation of Juan and grinned. "I can sure see how. Damn Juan, you're huge! In terrific shape too. Luis told me you busted two heads with a bat that night. Thanks for that. One look at you and I'm surprised either of them survived. But Luis, what's so important now? This big fellow saved you again, you said?"

Before Luis could answer, the waiter knocked and came in. "Compliments of the house gentlemen." He placed a tray set with a small ice bucket, glasses, a bottle of scotch and a bottle of bourbon on the table. "Will there be anything else, Mr. Restrepo?"

"No thank you," Julio replied. "That should do. Everyone, help yourself." Each man politely took turns pouring themselves a drink. Julio apologized for the interruption. "Okay, Luis, what's the problem?"

From his shirt pocket, Luis removed the newspaper clipping Juan had given him. He handed it to Julio and waited without saying anything.

Julio read the clipping and passed it over to his sons. Then he leaned forward towards Juan. Son, someone killed your mother and your brother?"

"Yes sir."

Luis knew an explanation was needed and thought he was better suited for that than Juan. For the next ten minutes, he recounted for Julio and his sons the motives and circumstances that lead to the murder of Juan's family. He named Gusta Lopez Garcia as the leader of the Los Alcázares Soldados gang in Comuna 13, and as the same man convicted of trying to kill him at the university. Luis went on to describe in detail Juanita's account of four men waiting for him in his reserved parking the day Gusta was transferred to Bellavista prison. Made a sign of the cross and thanked god for being away in Florida with David. Finally, Luis credited Juan for coming to his office today with that newspaper clipping and the story of his loss; else he would not have put all the pieces together and taken the precaution of leaving early. Instead of him, he told how the security guard was killed at five this evening by four men in a black sedan. Luis ended with, "Mr. Restrepo, this Gusta Lopez won't give up until he has his revenge. Is there any way you can help?"

"Of course, I can help, Luis, and thank you for giving me the opportunity. I'll have some friends look into this for us. When you called this afternoon, your plan was to leave Medellin for the ranch. Tell Pedro to expect two men in my employ to arrive there by ten this evening. He's to accommodate them. Also, it'll be best if you mention they will be armed. This article says your brother was shot seventeen times, Juan. Would you allow me to keep it?"

"Yes Sir. I'm honored you asked for it."

"The honor is mine to meet the man that saved the life of my friend and attorney. Luis tells me you're working with him now. From your looks, I'd say you and Jorge are nearly the same age. We have a couple of hours. If you like, you might take some time to get acquainted with my sons. Share some stories of growing up in Comuna 13 with them. In Medellin, I'm sure they've enjoyed a more privileged life than you."

"I have some operational changes to discuss with you, Luis. We'll need to make some phone calls too. Let's go upstairs to my office."

Luis and Juan left the restaurant two hours later. Luis drove because of the number of drinks Juan had consumed while sharing his history with Jorge and David Ochoa. Apparently, the three of them got along famously for almost two hours. It was obvious they were somewhat inebriated. Luis and Julio were amused by their condition.

At a little past ten they turn off route 25 into a driveway. Pedro was waiting for them. Luis waved to him as he unlocked and swung the gate open. Just inside on the right there was a bunkhouse with a porch across the front. Two men were watching from the porch. Both were standing and armed with assault rifles. "Julio's men," Luis pointed out. "We're safe now, for sure."

Two hundred yards further, they pulled into a two-car garage con-nected to the ranch house. They entered the home from a side door inside the garage. Luis gave Juan a quick tour before excusing himself for the night. The place was spacious with a large center living area connected to a den, dining room, and big kitchen. There were four bedrooms, two each at either end of the house off hallways. The décor was western. Juan had never imagined staying in something so nice. Woke the next morning lying on a bed in a guest room. Looked at his watch. It was nearly 8am. He was still dressed. Thought to himself, maybe I had a little too much to drink. Some bodyguard he was. Hell, Luis had to drive.

Juan saw that someone had retrieved his luggage from the car and left it in the hallway. Good thing too because he needed to freshen up. Afterwards, he found Pedro preparing breakfast in the kitchen. Luis was having coffee on an outside patio and waved for him to join.

Luis smiled and jokingly said, "Good morning, Juan. Feeling worse for last night's party?"

"My apologies, Luis. I think maybe following Mr. Restrepo's instruc-tions to get acquainted with David and Jorge went too well. Between the three of us, we polished off most of the bourbon and half the scotch. Have to say, I like those two."

"Nothing to be sorry about. Have some coffee with me. Last night at the restaurant may have solved our gang problems. Also, Julio has accepted you as part of our business plans. Said as much in his office.

Today, I'll speak to Hernandez again. A defense minister can expedite just about anything government wise. You're going to need a passport."

"For real?"

"Yes, for real. Over the next few months, Julio and Jorge will be very busy setting up the business here in Colombia. The goal is to be operational in one year. After last night's meeting at the restaurant, my own involvement in all of this is becoming something more than just legal counseling. David and I will be working together in Florida establishing a distribution network. You're coming with us!"

"As your bodyguard?"

"Here in Colombia, yes. Not so much in Florida. You'll have to give Julio credit for including you there. For one thing, he figures since you were raised in Comuna 13, the drug capital of Colombia, your knowledge of dealing in marijuana is more advanced than ours. David and I are novices. One of your contributions will be offering advice."

"You mean like a consultant?"

"Yeah, but don't get too big headed over that part. There's more. Julio took one look at you and decided if we needed one, the fit was perfect. Our 'enforcer.' Give yourself credit. David and I couldn't scare a fly, but you can. Proved yourself with a baseball bat that night at the university."

"I can handle that with ease. Shouldn't say this again, but I sort of enjoy busting heads. By the end of a week staying here with you on the ranch, you'll know there is something else I'm really trained for, thanks to my brother. Weapons! Pistols, shotguns, or rifles. You name one and I can use it."

"Good to know, but hopefully necessary only as a last resort. By that I mean self-preservation when threatened by someone like Gusta Lopez or betrayed by an associate. Carefully consider the last part. The one thing that Julio Restrepo demands is loyalty. I expect the same from those working with us. Are we clear on that?"

"Absolutely! Whatever is called for and only at your command. You're my jefe!"

"Okay, that's settled. Juanita will be coming soon. She can bring us up to date on the office shooting. Afterwards, she and I have some office work. Need to make some calls. While we're busy, I've got something in mind for you. Can you ride, Juan?"

"Ride what?"

Luis made his customary gesture by leaning back in his chair and smiling. "On a horse. This is a ranch, remember?"

"I'm not sure. Never have been on a horse but I'd like to try. Can't be very hard, can it?"

"Let's have some breakfast and visit with Juanita. Afterwards, I'll have Pedro saddle up a couple from the stable and bring them up front. Spend the morning riding with him and you'll be a real cowboy."

Now Juan laughed. "Maybe I'll buy a hat and boots to match? Even better, a holster for a single action 44. Look like your real bodyguard then."

Juanita arrived shortly after breakfast. There was a small efficiency apartment above the garage that had once served as a maid's quarters. Pedro took Juanita's luggage there as usual. She had worked with Luis at the ranch on several occasions. With a notepad and pen in hand, she joined Luis and Juan on the patio.

"Coffee, Juanita?" Luis knew without asking and was already pouring her a cup.

"Yes please. I do have some news about the guard's murder." Juanita began reading from her notes. "Major Castro's call came at 7am this morning. After a car chase yesterday that ended in San Javier, they captured one of the men. The driver of the black sedan. Three others got away, but he assured me not to worry. Apparently, after questioning as Major Castro put it, this driver gave the rest of them up. Arrest warrants have already been issued. All of them were members of Los Alcázares Soldados."

"That's good news!" Luis responded. "Juan, do you think this changes our situation?"

"It's hard to say. This police detective may be confident of catching them, but I guarantee you, if they're still alive, they left Medellin last night. Best thing they can do is leave Colombia or join one of the guerrilla movements. They screwed up big time. Even their own gang members would not let their mistake go unpunished. I'm just not sure how this foul up will affect Gusta Lopez."

"Remember Julio is having someone look into that for us. Until we hear from him, we're safe on the ranch. Just in case, and later this afternoon, I'd like to start my training on how to use a firearm. After your riding lessons, set something up with Pedro for me. He'll understand it has to be as far as possible from the stables."

"Anything else to report, Juanita?"

"I'm afraid so. The guard left behind a wife and three kids."

Luis lowered his head. "Damn shame. I feel somewhat responsible. Do this Juanita! Keep my name out of it but make sure all the funeral expenses are taken care of. Then quietly find out what his family's circumstances are. Insurance and whatever else I need to know? We'll go from there with any help that's required."

Juan had listened carefully to Luis's response. This man never ceased to impress him. He offered friendship and loyalty where none was required. Smart and humble in an admirable way. Now he had shown a charitable side. With just one small act for Luis at the university, Juan's whole life had changed. A passport along with travel to the states seemed certain. Once there, the opportunities for success would be an adventure enjoyed. From that day on, Luis deserved and would have his allegiance.

17.

THE START OF A CARTEL

The morning of November 2, 1973, Juan rode his first horse. Pedro had saddled a seven-year-old stallion named Glory for him and a mare named Mia for himself. Pedro was a good riding instructor. An hour into lessons and Juan was galloping all over the fields obviously enjoying every minute. He fell in love with horseback riding from that day on. Dreamed maybe someday?

Another five days followed with more riding for Juan and weapons training for Luis. With the help of one young stable's boy, Pedro was both grounds and housekeeper. Juanita pitched in as the cook. Also, she and Luis spent each morning working in his den which served as their temporary office. As instructed, Juanita had brought along a polaroid camera and used it to take Juan's photograph for his passport. The photo and application were carried by courier to the defense minister's secretary in Bogota. On the afternoon of the fifth day, the same courier returned with Juan's passport. An amazing feat considering Colombia's bureaucracy.

Each day an issue of *El Tiempo* was left at the front gate. While they were having breakfast the morning before Juan's passport was delivered, Luis received a call suggesting he read a relevant story on page two of the newspaper. He did so and a minute later nodded his approval while handing the paper to Juan.

In the left corner at the bottom of the page, an article described the death of a reputed gang leader named Gusta Lopez. He was found in his cell at Bellavista prison with seventeen bullet wounds. The report went on to suggest that evidence taken from the mouth of the victim indicated his brutal demise was the result of a feud between two Comuna 13 gangs. The proof was stuffed down Gusta Lopez's throat and included the coincidental times he was shot. It was a two-week old *El Tiempo* newspaper piece about the murder of another gang leader shot seventeen times at his San Javier home. His name was Jose Valencia. The murder of Jose's mother was not mentioned. Police were questioning inmates and investigating leads.

Luis had waited for Juan to finish reading before volunteering an answer to an anticipated question. "The call just now came from an associate of Julio Restrepo. A week ago, I mentioned to you that our problem was right where we wanted him. Bellavista prison. The guards on the walls are armed but those inside do not carry weapons. On the other hand, some inmates serving long sentences have firearms. Very common dilemma at Bellavista!"

"I have my revenge, Luis. Indebted to you for that."

"Not so much me. Remember, self-preservation! No doubt, we're both beholden to Julio for this. Someday one or both of us may be asked to repay the favor."

"I'll do so gladly. In fact, I'll look forward to that opportunity. Thanks to Don Julio Restrepo, I have justice now! Repaying him would be welcomed."

Juanita left the ranch for El Dorado International Airport in Bogota on the third of December. Her destination was Miami, Florida. It was her second visit to the city. She had spent most of the previous October working in the downtown area to establish an office for Luis's legal practice. This trip, her immediate responsibilities were to make sure the office was fully operational in time for Luis's arrival a week later. As well, she was to finalize the purchase of a large residential home in Coral Gables. Very expensive too! The house was located in Gable Estates with a dock in back that provided deep-water access. It had six bedrooms, five baths, separate maid's quarters, and was spacious enough to accommodate her, Luis, Juan, David, and guests. Supplied with almost unlimited funds by Julio Restrepo, Juanita proved to be amazingly capable of her task. Everything was ready with one day to spare.

Luis, David, and Juan arrived at Miami International December 12, 1973. Juanita was waiting for them at customs. Ostensibly, David was there on his father's behalf to manage the final construction phase of a family restaurant to be followed by its opening. In the same manner, Luis was tasked with exploring other business opportunities in south Florida. In truth, for both Luis and David, this was to be the beginning of a company explicitly designed to bring Colombian marijuana into the United States. At home, Julio Restrepo and his son, Jorge Ochoa, were directly involved with setting up the enterprise. Years later, and even though he was the family patriarch, Don Julio Fabio Restrepo's personal association through family with what was to become a famous drug cartel was doubted and considered no more than a personal embarrassment for a respected citizen of Colombia.

By inquiries, Julio Restrepo familiarized himself with marijuana smuggling operations working the coastal waters of Florida. Someone was involved with transporting large amounts of Colombia's highest quality cannabis, *Santa Marta Gold*. It was grown in northern Colombia's Sierra Nevada region of Santa Marta. Its proximity to the coast added a convenience for exportation by sea and included easy cooperation from local authorities when properly compensated.

Julio thought it best to learn from a successful rival. He used his influence to identify who in Santa Marta made the purchases and paid officials for protection. Most commonly associated with the large acquisitions was an American known as "Captain Ray." He could be contacted through his Miami attorney, Bernie Claxton. By way of a third party, Julio arranged a meeting for Luis with the lawyer after the Christmas holidays. For reasons Mr. Claxton did not explain, the meeting had to be reset for mid-February.

Juan spent the rest of December in Miami taking English classes scheduled by Luis. In a short period of time, he was able to understand someone talking in the language but could only manage to speak it with a mix of Spanish. With that ability, Luis asked that he acquaint himself with some of the city's black population involved in marijuana. He reasoned that learning procedures followed by the local trade would be a smart approach to begin the process of setting up their own business.

Juan quickly became amazed with the popularity of the drug among a diversity of Americans. Most blacks just liked the high from smoking it. As well, it was prevalent on college and university campuses, almost universal among veterans returning from the Vietnam War, and enjoyed as a recreational compliment to alcohol by many of the general adult population. Demand was so strong that price didn't matter. His report to Luis was simple. Invest two thousand pesos in Colombia and it would earn two hundred U.S. dollars in Florida. Whatever your cost back home, multiply the return by twenty. This place was a smuggler's paradise.

Luis came to the same conclusion but from a survey of coastal circumstances. His arrived with reminders from David who too often said, "I told you so." During January, while Juanita kept an office presence, the two of them together explored the east coast of Florida while enjoying more than a dozen day and evening charter cruises. They made a simple observation. From Key West to Jacksonville, there were thousands of boats constantly moving in and out of inlets, coves, canals, lagoons, and along the inland waterway. Because of all the traffic, an understaffed coast guard was severely handicapped. It was practically impossible to tell if any one craft out of such a huge crowd might be hauling contraband. Nearshore conditions were perfect if a method of delivery into that environment were properly concealed. Instinctively, as a lawyer, Luis knew exactly what was required. Experienced seamen with both a right and a reason to travel Florida's offshore coastal waters beyond the U.S. territorial limits. Professional fishermen!

Something else Luis observed. The Vietnam War had changed the United States. Many of the young soldiers returning home to Florida were disillusioned with the norms of the society in general. Some, having endured the savagery of that conflict, wanted more than just a pat-on-the-back for a job well done accompanied by an honorable discharge. Mixed in with the vets were a flood of unthankful kids in their late teens and early twenties bent on escaping the old parental guidance for a more enlightened life. Drugs! The soldiers had seen hell and nothing in the states really scared them. The latter weren't necessarily brave; they were just naive without fear of consequences.

In both groups there were many who were raised along Florida's coast as water sportsmen. Luis knew that those with sea experience represented a workforce to choose from as potential players in the operation being planned. Offer some in the right place incentives plus a financial startup and you had your runners bringing bales of marijuana onshore.

Luis, David, and Juan flew back to Colombia the first week of February. They met with Julio and Jorge in Medellin. What they reported was basically the promise of a fortune to be made along with a method of minimal risk. The key was volume. From a transport ship, supply persons with small crafts in international waters beyond the lawful boundaries of the United States. Act as an offshore warehouse wholesaler and let buyers take the chances from ship to shore. Carefully pick your customers from the crowd of young Floridians who would welcome the rewards from such an opportunity. Maintain confidentiality and discrete communications with them and insist on loyalty. Juan would manage any breach of allegiance. Assistance would be limited to financial startups such as boats and a safehouse for storage. The messy business of distribution was their responsibility. And finally, all initial advancements made to them were to be repaid from profits.

Julio Restrepo enthusiastically approved the plan of action. David was officially appointed jefe of U.S. operations, but Julio insisted his son stay completely detached from any criminal liability. "David, you will have no personal contact with any of the smugglers Luis employs. Absolutely none. Protect the family name and run the restaurant as a legitimate business cover. Stay out of the day-to-day operations and provide directives to Luis and Juan only when necessary. If there's a need to communicate something important with me, fly home. Never talk about this business on the phone."

David shook his head in agreement. "Do all of these precautions apply to Jorge? What about you, Dad? Someone is bound to find out about all this sooner or later."

"Maybe," Julio replied. "But let me handle that. Comprender?"

Luis and Juan flew back to Florida three days later. On the first Thursday after arriving, they met with Bernie Claxton in his Miami office. Luis introduced both himself and Juan. Claxton returned his own introduction before saying, "Please gentlemen, come in and have a seat. I must apologize for the delay of this meeting. Purely because of court time you understand. So, how can I be of help?"

Luis answered straight away without hesitation. "Mr. Claxton, I am a lawyer with license to practice both here in Florida and in my country, Colombia. Attorney to attorney, what I am about to say here in your office is strictly confidential. If you agree, those are my only terms for this meeting."

"That's not a problem," Claxton replied. "Yes, I agree. Works both ways too. Whatever's discussed remains private."

Satisfied, Luis continued. "I represent a client who is making plans to export home grown marijuana into the United States. We are aware that you have a similar relationship with an individual currently importing the same product out of Santa Marta. His name is Raymond Stansel. At his earliest convenience, I want you to schedule us a meeting with him for the purpose of perhaps establishing mutual benefits. Can you do that?"

Now it was Claxton who spoke without hesitating. "Yes, Mr. Castillo. But it may take some time. Raymond is currently out of the country. He travels quite a bit. Is sometime next month okay with you?"

Luis gave a slightly disappointing nod. "I suppose that will have to do. Take my card and call my office when everything is set."

A little over a month passed before a consultation visit with Raymond Stansel was made. Captain Ray had a reputation as an incredible seafarer, so Luis and Juan had spent the previous five weeks mostly at sea trying to transition from amateurs to semi-professional mariners. They chartered fishing trips, paid their way as guests on shrimp boats, sailed on a schooner to the Bahamas and back, and crewed for three days on a Puerto Rican trawler. The latter was an experience Luis did not want to repeat. Juan loved it!

David Ochoa had a better part to play thanks to his father's instructions. He represented the family as part owner and manager of a successful restaurant, businessman, and foreign-born Florida playboy. He often visited Hialeah Park Racetrack, gambled, and purchased several thoroughbreds for his father's hacienda. He leased a beach side condominium in Miami for himself to stay removed from Luis and Juan. It was a precautionary privacy that also afforded him time with female companions. Other than Luis's occasional updates, there was nothing to connect him to the startup of a smuggling operation. David enjoyed his role as secret jefe.

Late that March, Luis and Juan took a redeye flight from Miami to Jacksonville. They rented a car at the airport and drove to a ranch home in South Georgia for an appointment with Raymond Stansel.

The place was remote and unpretentious. Apparently, no one noticed their arrival, so the two of them walked up on the porch and knocked. There was a bark from a small dog inside. They heard someone say "hush, Bo," before the door opened and a lady answered with a wide smile. "Good morning, gentlemen! You must be Luis and Juan. I'm Janet. Come on in. Ray is expecting you, but I think you're early. He and Mitch are working in the barn. Go sit down and I'll let him know you're here."

In a large family room, Luis and Juan seated themselves at either ends of a leather sofa. The room's ranch style decor reminded Luis of his home. Janet called Ray from a wall phone in the kitchen to announce that his guest had arrived. Half a minute later, she came out with a tray of glasses and a pitcher of iced tea. Without asking she poured both of them a full glass and politely said, "Ray is on his way. He'll be right with you."

It was a short wait before Ray Stansel stepped inside through a pair of sliding glass doors in the back of the house. They all exchanged customary greetings before he asked, "How was your trip? You can get lost trying to find this place. Did you have any trouble?"

"None at all," Luis replied. "Mr. Claxton's directions were very detailed."

"Bernie's my friend. Good lawyer as well. He checked you out before allowing this little encounter. In Colombia, you're known as one hell-of-good lawyer too. And now, starting a practice in Florida? Juan, what's your profession?"

Juan didn't hesitate or crack a smile when he answered. "I'm my jefe's bodyguard."

Rays' eyebrows were raised when he responded. "Ohooo! I see." Then he added with an approving nod. "There have been times when I needed someone with your abilities."

"Did Mr. Claxton explain the reason for this meeting?" Luis asked.

"Yes, best he could. You have a client in Colombia who wishes to start an export business and that we might establish mutual interests. Correct?"

"Hopefully? For the present, I simply need to discuss with you our plan of operations. Raymond, you have an unmatched reputation of seamanship when bringing marijuana into Florida. Because of your experience in this area, we would appreciate any advice you have to offer. The persons I represent in Colombia are extremely well connected both in business and politics. Helpful guidance or service from you will be considered a favor to be repaid."

"I don't deserve the compliment but thanks. Hell, some say I have saltwater running through my veins. A few months ago, I might not have been willing to comply with a request from competition. For reasons I'll explain later, my outlook has changed. How can I help?"

Luis sipped his tea before continuing. Just as he had done for Julio and Jorge weeks ago, he laid out a plan using international waters to provide Colombian marijuana on a wholesale basis along the eastern seaboard of Florida, Georgia, and the Carolinas. To manage the operation, they needed two registered fishing trawlers capable of sailing from Colombia to the U.S. while transporting huge quantities of marijuana. The ships would require experienced captains, be crewed by willing participants, and have a deck ability to offload at sea onto smaller craft. The emphasis would be on volume and quality. The idea was to remove themselves from the liabilities inherent in the process of smuggling from ship to shore and distribution. Luis ended saying,

"Now you see why we came to consult with you Raymond. What do you think of our plans?"

Raymond answered without pausing. "This will take some big bucks to start with, but if you have that kind of backing, I love the idea."

Ray explained why. "Maybe you're both too young to know, but this harks back to the days of prohibition. 'Mother Ships' running fifteen miles out and loaded with booze for fast boats to carry onshore. Like then, moving the stuff inshore is the dangerous part. I just spent the last month proving that. One of my shrimp boats carrying my biggest haul ever had engine failure near the Keys. Damn close call. Could have lost everything and be sitting in some jail instead of having tea with you two. That's why I'm quitting."

"Quitting?" Luis asked with a little hint of alarm.

"Yes. I've got two sons from a previous marriage to think about. Janet too! Made a lot of money and it would be stupid to carry on until caught. No more hauls for me but I have a lot of loose ends to tie up before retirement. By the end of this summer, I'll be just another beach bum tooling around islands in the Caribbean seas."

Luis looked slightly dismayed and asked, "Does this mean you can't help us?"

"Hell, Luis, not only can I assist you. I need to help. Since I'm moving on, your startup could not have come at a better time. I have assets in Honduras that are perfect for what your plan requires. Two fifty-five-foot shrimp boats in excellent condition that, with some healthy cash to boot, can be easily traded for fishing trawlers. Plenty of them are around in that neighborhood. Plus, I can make the exchanges for you along with a transfer of my captains and the crews. Top 'hands' that have experience in our business and want to stay employed. The pay is too good for them to just up and quit. All in all, I'd say you're in luck if we can agree on terms."

"Within reason, I'm sure we will."

"Me too, Luis, but I do have a stopping block for consideration that may be a problem for your clients."

"What's that?".

"I've been in the marijuana business for years. Smoked a lot of pot. It's a recreational thing. Lately, some suppliers have tried to have me bring in cocaine. I'm a family man. If your people are thinking about bringing in cocaine or heroin, I'm out. End of discussion."

"I promise you just marijuana. No hard drugs."

Raymond nodded in acknowledgment and raised his glass for a confirmation toast. "Great then!" Glasses clinked and they all sipped tea. Juan wished it was bourbon. This tea stuff wasn't to his liking.

The meeting carried on for another two hours. Details were discussed and accepted. Coordination was required to make the deal go through. In Honduras, Raymond Stansel's part would be to swap some cash and the shrimp boats for fishing trawlers. Once that was done, Juan and Luis would have to fly there to obtain ownership from Ray and employ his former crewmen. A large compensation was required. For Jorge's and Julio's approval, Luis would have to make sure David's communication with them accurately explained the advantages of the transaction. Months might be saved. Operations could commence before year's end if everything went smoothly.

Before they left the ranch, Raymond asked how he and Juan planned to find runners with fast boats willing to travel fifty miles out.

The answer was, "I'm not quite sure, Ray."

Luis went on to describe how they both had spent the past two months cruising the state's coastal waters with guides. "Don't laugh but I recently purchased a Bayliner. It's docked in the back of our house in Coral Gables. Juan and I hope to become fairly competent sailors while familiarizing ourselves with Florida's shoreline complexities. There's no shortage of good size fast boats running everywhere. Even so, we're new to this game when it comes to making the right associates. Any suggestions?"

"Maybe, but not on my part. I have a partner who knows a lot of marijuana dealers in Florida. Name's Mitch. Pretty secretive when it comes to business, so I may have to think of a way that both of you benefit from getting together. I'll let you know one way or the other."

Luis and Juan drove back to Jacksonville elated by the developments. In just a few hours they had made more progress than expected. Best part was Julio had arranged the meeting with Raymond Stansel. By the time they neared the airport, Luis had decided to make the trip back to Colombia with David. A lot of money was involved in this deal, and that required an in-person report.

David agreed it was a good idea for Luis to fly back to Colombia with him. The cost of purchasing two fishing trawlers came to a lot more than more than the restaurant he had just opened. If anything went wrong, Luis was responsible.

As it turned out, Julio had anticipated a smaller expense to get started. Still, he was pleased with the deal. Since he had found this Raymond Stansel, the credit was his. Julio instructed David and Luis to expedite the transaction and get to work on the ship to shore part of the operation.

A day after returning to Miami, Luis phoned Bernie Claxton. As Ray's lawyer, it would be his responsibility to draw up the paperwork. Bernie had already discussed the terms with his client and was halfway finished with the sales agreement. Title transfers would require an all-cash transaction made by separate but equal wire deposits to banks in Costa Rica, Honduras, and the Cayman Islands. Bernie's fee was modest, but enough that he offered to buy Luis and Juan dinner at an upscale restaurant just opened in Miami. "It's South American cuisine, so you'll enjoy the food and drinks." Luis laughed to himself and accepted.

Two nights later, Luis, Juan and Bernie met for dinner. Before looking at the menu, they ordered drinks. Once those were served, Bernie handed a contract to Luis, and they all toasted. A pleasant evening followed. Dinner was splendid. When everyone finished, Bernie requested the check. The hostess approached, thanked them for coming, and informed Bernie that everything was "on-the-house." Generous but strange, he thought somewhat surprised.

Accompanied by an attractive companion, David had watched them from a nearby table. He enjoyed every minute but never said a revealing word except for something he had whispered to the hostess.

Outside, while waiting for valet parking to bring their cars, Bernie handed Luis an envelope.

"What's this?"

"Another dinner invitation for the two of you. It's from Raymond's associate, Mitch. Came by courier yesterday along with a note to pass it on to you. Pretty unusual for Mitch to set up a meeting. He's very careful about who he works with. Matter of fact, we've never met!"

"Ray mentioned his partner might be able to assist us. I appreciate the quick response. Bernie don't hesitate to contact me if there are any delays in closing our contract. Otherwise, we'll meet again in Honduras."

The note from Mitch read dinner reservations for three Saturday at 8pm in the main dining room of Miami's Fontainebleau hotel. Semi casual dress attire required. Next day, Luis thought to ask David if he would like to attend in Juan's place.

"Sure would," David replied. "Heard about this hotel but never been there. Dad might not approve, but I'm not flying all the way to Colombia to ask him. Let's just say I'm checking out our restaurant's competition in Miami?"

David and Luis arrived at the entrance to the Fontainebleau shortly before eight. Driving inside, both commented on the sheer elegance of the grounds around the hotel. David mentioned it might be just the right kind of impressive accommodations for their own visitors in the future.

At the entrance to the restaurant, Luis gave their names and asked the hostess if their third-party, Mitch, had arrived.

"Yes sir, we're expecting you. Come with me, please."

The dining area was large and modestly extravagant. Tables were spaced well apart, candlelit, set with sterling silverware, and covered by embroidered white cloths. David observed and gave a low whistle. They followed the hostess to one placed against a window fronting a view of the ocean where an attractive and stylishly dressed lady was seated. Smiling as David and Luis approached, she stood and said, "Good evening, gentlemen. Nice of you to be so prompt for this appointment. I'm Michelle Linville. My friends call me Mitch. Have a seat and let's have some cocktails to get the night started."

Luis hid his astonishment. Not so for David. He was wide eyed, mouth parted, and staring. Luis saw his reaction and took the lead. "Mitch, I'm

Luis Castillo and my speechless friend here is David Ochoa. Forgive me for saying so but what a pleasant surprise you are."

"Thank you, Luis. It's by choice I keep my gender a secret. This meeting between us requires that I do not. Drinks and dinner first. Afterwards, I have a room in the hotel for us to have our business discussions privately."

"David, you're a young handsome fellow and a nice surprise too. I was expecting Luis's tall, black, and scary bodyguard. Glad you're here instead of his bruiser. No need for him tonight. You're both safe with me."

Dinner was quite enjoyable. The three of them took turns exchanging backgrounds. David kept from mentioning his last name or any family connections to their current objectives. Also, he chose to appear as a subordinate to Luis.

The hotel room Mitch had reserved for discussions was a top floor suite with a fully stocked bar. After they made drinks, and since it was a perfect Miami night, she suggested the balcony for their talks. Once there and everyone was seated, Mitch started the conversation. "I have a business proposal to offer to you tonight. It has to do with my current circumstances and what Raymond has shared with me about your plans. Ray and I have worked together as partners for several years. And now, as you know, he's shutting down. For good reason I might add! Ray is, or should I say was, the best coastal smuggler in all of Florida. Even so, he recently had a bad experience at sea with one of his best shrimp boats. He had to take risks that could have cost him dearly."

"Ray explained to us his reasons for quitting. Can't say it's not a smart move on his part, Mitch."

"Yes, but to clear out our inventory from this last big haul, he and I have several months of work ahead of us. Just no more trips in the Caribbean for Ray unless it's strictly for pleasure. All of this is why I decided to meet with you. My end of the partnership was temporary storage followed by distribution to dealers who could purchase substantial amounts at a time. No 'nickel and dime' stuff! A minimum transaction of four hundred kilos. I have other sources, but without Ray, I'll be unable to supply my people before the year is out. Then you came along."

"You need a new supplier?"

"I will soon enough, and you need to connect your trawlers with ship to shore smugglers. If my proposal is agreeable, I can definitely help with that part of the operation. It was something I made sure of before sending Bernie your invitation."

David interrupted before Luis could reply. "Forgive me, Mitch, but this sounds too good to be true. Is there a catch."

"Maybe if you consider providing an initial investment a 'catch'? Let me lay it out for you. I've already put together two teams of individuals willing to make the runs. Capable young men anxious for a chance to make some real money. What they will need is a safe shore facility to operate from and fast watercraft for trips out into international waters. Boats sizable enough to return with a heavy cargo of marijuana. We will have to set them up initially. That requires us to work together and provide the upfront cost. Recoverable with time, so I'm willing to split that with you."

David's interest was obvious. "This sounds pretty damn good, Luis, don't you think?"

Mitch spoke first. "Wait before you answer. I haven't finished. These men will work for me, not you! Communications for deliveries come to me and I arrange for their trips to the trawler. They are to be kept off your ship during loading and in the dark when it comes to any details of the operation. Any 'who, what, when, and where' will remain confidential between us. Can we agree on this?"

"Absolutely, Mitch," Luis replied. "Unless there is anything else to consider?"

"There is but I was saving both for last because you'll like them. To keep my dealers happy requires about four thousand kilos a month. My two teams of runners can handle that for me. Still though, I know you're not buying two big fishing trawlers to transport a measly few tons per month. Consider our little deal as just your way of getting started. Over time, you can add as many additional runners as you like apart from me. When you do and to stay competitive, I'll need a twenty-five percent discount over what they pay."

"Sounds fair to me, but just so you know, we've decided to buy only one trawler to start with. Damn ships are expensive. Raymond is okay with the change. If things work out, maybe we'll buy another from him next year. You said, 'saving both for last.' There's more?"

"Like Raymond is doing, I plan to retire in a couple of years. When I do, I'll turn my guys, equipment and facilities included, over to you free of charge. Probably join Ray and Janet for some pleasure cruises. Maybe even come to visit you sometime in Colombia, David?"

David smiled and quickly responded with an approval by raising his glass. "Let's toast to it. My hacienda in two years."

A 'hacienda,' Mitch thought to herself. Strange. David must be more than just someone helping Luis? Young, but Luis and I are about the same age. Maybe?

Because Juan and Luis stayed so busy during the next two months, time passed quickly. Working with Mitch, they set her teams up with the means and excuses to travel offshore. One was in Fernandina Beach and would run coastal excursions for tourists. The other was to operate out of Saint Augustine as a saltwater-fishing guide service. Both were licensed in Florida State as legitimate businesses. Mitch chose both places by explaining she wanted to be near the border with Georgia. The excuse went over well with Luis since her choices left most of the Florida coastline open for him to exploit.

Luis and Juan wasted no time finding additional help. Out of Big Pine Key, they convinced the nearly broke owner of a scuba diving business he could get rich as a marijuana smuggler. A few days later, they added some hungry surf boarders in West Palm Beach. Operations for all were to begin by October.

Every part of the plan was going smoothly. Early that May, Luis, Juan, and David met with Raymond Stansel in Honduras for a closing. Bernie was there with the papers ready for signatures once wire transfers were confirmed. The meeting took less than an hour.

They had purchased an almost new trawler named the *Paso Seguro* captained by Rene Perez and his crew transferred from one of Ray's former shrimp boats. Captain Rene was invited to the celebration dinner that evening to meet with his employer. After dinner, and with Ray's help, Luis, Juan, and the captain spent hours discussing procedures, compensations, and methods of communication. It was the first of several organizational discussions Luis held with Rene. A hell-of-a-lot of details had to be understood by everyone involved before mid-October. No later either because back home, Jorge and Julio had scheduled the last days of October for shipping sixty pallets of Colombian Gold from the shores of Santa Marta.

With the understanding it would be another four months before taking on their first cargo of marijuana, Captain Perez suggested he and his crew take the *Paso Seguro* for sea trials. He explained that if they were going to pretend to be fishermen rather than smugglers, some experience in the former might prove beneficial. Luis quickly agreed to the idea and added that the trip take place in Florida's Gulf Stream. To complete the disguise, they would fill the trawler's hole with whatever the nets caught. More importantly, use the time there to acquaint themselves not just with the area but also the manner and timing of U.S. Coast Guard patrols.

After business was concluded that night, Ray asked Luis if they might talk in private.

"Sure," Luis said and pointed. "Let's take the booth in the corner."

Once seated, Ray's mouth gave a wide grin. "I have a question to ask you. It's a private matter on behalf of my closest friend."

"I'm an attorney. Private conversations come with the job."

"Okay but this client may surprise you. My friend is Mitch. The two of you have worked well together these past two months. Luis, she wishes to get to know you better. Actually, I think much better."

"Ray! The feeling is mutual. I was taken by her the first time we met at the Fontainebleau, but all the while, I thought she was interested in David. Thanks for your assistants tonight and especially for the good news at this booth. Now I can't wait to get back to Florida. That's three or four days from now, but I'll call her first thing in the morning." Luis ended by giving Ray a hug.

The first possible problem with plans came by phone to Luis's Miami office the afternoon of June 7th. Juanita had answered. It was Bernie Claxton trying to reach Luis about something important.

"He's not in the office, Mr. Claxton, but I can have him call you back within the hour."

"I suppose that will have to do. Thank you."

Five minutes later, Luis returned Claxton's call. When he answered, Luis knew to ask, "Good news or bad Bernie?"

"Bad, I'm afraid. Raymond was arrested yesterday. He's in jail."

"Dammit! Well, get him the hell out."

"That will take some doing. They arrested him in Florida hours after they had raided the farm. Searched everywhere. There were twelve tons of marijuana in the barn. Making matters worse, his passport showed he had visited several foreign countries just in the past month. In his desk, they found corresponding bank deposit slips. At this morning's hearing, the prosecutor argued he was a flight risk."

"How much, Bernie?"

"One million. Absolutely no precedent for that amount but the judge shut me down with a gravel slam."

"Does he have that much?"

"Yes, and more but it's in those banks. Now the feds have the deposits and routing numbers. He can't touch it, and you can bet your ass they will try to take every penny. Shame too, because in a few months he would have been rich, free, and clear of this whole damn thing. Most likely his plans to retire was why he was spreading his cash around. Instead, there will probably be nothing left for Ray but a cell."

"Was Ray alone when he was arrested?"

"Just barely, thank goodness! He and Janet had stayed the night together in a hotel. She wanted to sleep late. Ray had some business matters to take care of and left her there for the morning."

Claxton paused to catch his breath, then continued. "Don't know if it was payments or collections. Twenty thousand dollars was lying in his car's front seat when they pulled him over on the highway. It's gone too!"

"Where's Janet?"

"She's here in my office with me. We both went to the hearing this morning. They have nothing on her."

"Bernie, I need to speak privately with Janet."

"Okay, but she's pretty upset right now. I'll turn the phone over to her and wait outside in my reception room."

"Thank you. We'll need to talk some more when I'm finished."

A few seconds passed before Janet spoke. "Luis, can you help us?"

"Yes, of course, but first I should tell you, Mitch was not at the farm when they raided it?"

"I know," Janet replied. "She had business to take care of in Fernandina Beach. I haven't been able to reach her. She and I are best friends, so I'm aware you two have been seeing one another. Mitch needs to be told something. At the hearing, Bernie talked with the FDLA officer in charge of Ray's arrest. I think his last name was Cummings. Said they had an arrest warrant out for Ray's partner. A woman named Michelle Linville. Caught Bernie by surprise because he didn't know Mitch was a lady."

"Damn! That's more bad news. How the hell did they know all this? The farm was a safehouse like no other, and Mitch was careful about her real identity."

"Simple answer. Only one person could be responsible. Ray's ex-wife! She knew about the farm, Mitch, and me. Especially me! Ray made the mistake of telling his oldest son that he was retiring soon, planning to marry me, and then sailed off into the sunset together. Once that news was passed on to her, she had nothing but hate left for him. Bitch just wanted to screw all of us up. Succeeded too, I guess?"

"There's always a rat somewhere in the barn, Janet. I know how to get in touch with Mitch. I'll do that as soon as this call ends. In the meantime, try to stay calm. It may take some time. Maybe even a couple of months, but rest assured, we will get Raymond out. Not only that, he will not be going to prison. I promise! Remember this. It's important. If you visit Ray, do so only with Bernie. If his lawyer is with you, they can't listen or record anything said. Understand?"

"Yes, but how can you help, Luis?"

"Don't ask! Let me speak with Bernie again."

Bernie Claxton came on the phone. "I'm back. Janet has started crying but says you can help us."

"I know it's the United States and not Colombia, but people everywhere have faults. I want you to send my assistant, Juanita, a summary of the hearing. Along with that, provide her the names and addresses of the judge and prosecutor."

"No problem. She'll have it by fax before five. Anything else?"

"When Janet goes to visit Ray, always accompany her. The authorities already have twelve tons of ammunition. Let's don't let her slip up and give them something more to work with."

"I follow you, Luis. Any messages to Ray you want to pass along? I've told him not to say a word except that he's innocent."

"Tell him to be patient. Getting him out may take some time. After we do, there are lots of options."

Mitch had called Luis the night before. She had left Fernandina Beach that afternoon for St. Augustine. Business there would be finished within a day or two. Afterwards, she was hoping he could join her for a long weekend of pure relaxation at the Casa Monica Hotel. Luis had eagerly agreed. Now he dialed the number she had left him. Desk answered and patched him through to her room. She answered on the first ring.

"Michelle, I've got some bad news"

"I heard just an hour ago. One of the young men we were working with here in St. Augustine left a message for a 'Mr. Mitch' at the desk. In short, it said the famous Captain Ray had been caught red handed. I tried to call your number, but the line was busy. When I spoke with Juanita, she said you and Bernie were talking. Can you fill me in?"

"Wish I didn't have to, Michelle. They raided the farm."

"Crap! The barn was still half full."

"They're claiming twelve tons of marijuana confiscated. They also found Ray's foreign banking information. Careless on his part."

"Good thing I was in Fernandina."

"Michelle, they have an APB out for you."

"No way! How could they make the connection? Ray would never tell!"

"According to Janet, he told his son he was getting out of the business and marrying her. She thinks Ray's 'X' found out and turned on him."

"More than just a possibility. She's been blackmailing Ray since they divorced, and I don't mean alimony. If he was cutting the purse string, the game was over. I warned him it was best to keep his plans quiet. Trusted his son I suppose. Ray's a good man but hard-headed to a fault."

"Most men with any backbone are stubborn. Makes no difference now. What's done is done. Keeping you safe is my priority now."

"I'll have to find a place to lie low for a while."

"Hiding out in the states is not an option. They'll eventually find you. But if I can get you to Colombia, you're home free. I and my associates have political connections very high up in the government. Problem is getting you here."

"I know someone that can help with that. Some recent friends of Raymond's. Marijuana smugglers too. Except for partnering with him on this last incredibly big haul, they bring smaller amounts in by airplanes. Damn good pilots too. One of them could fly me to Colombia. No one would even know I had left the country."

"Perfect! Can you call and set it up?"

"Yes, I think so. Skip's the main man. And if I know Skip, he'll agree to have me picked up here in St. Augustine. He owes Ray that and more for saving his ass twenty-five tons of Colombian Gold."

"Tell him David's father has an airstrip at his hacienda. I'll send you the coordinates. Land there and I'll meet you. Just let me know a day in advance of the departure."

"Thanks, honey. Give me time to make a phone call or two and then get back to you."

"With all this unpleasant news coming down, consider this. I need a couple of weeks' vacation. When you arrive, I'd like to show you around the better parts of my country. Should have told you this before but I have a small ranch."

"Luis, I'm going to make sure you never want me to leave. In the meantime, we'll need to post bail for Ray don't you think?"

"They set his bail at one million dollars. Do you have that much?"

"You've got to be kidding. He's no murderer. Just a marijuana smuggler. Can they do that to him?"

"Yes, Michelle, if they consider him a flight risk. The prosecutor used Ray's passport and bank records to prove that."

"I have enough money stashed away to help Ray, but it will have to wait until I get to Colombia. May take some time. This 'manhunt' they have out on me complicates access to things."

"Bernie will be asking Ray to be patient. In a short time, I'm confident the bail can be reduced. Juanita and Juan will be looking into that for Bernie. The Colombian way I might add."

Luis flew into Bogota June 10th. Michelle was flying into Colombia the next day by private plane and landing at Julio's airstrip. Jorge met Luis at customs and within two hours they had joined Julio at his hacienda. David was there and had already explained the circumstances of Michelle's visit. Since her assistance with getting them started in their enterprise had proven very useful, Julio was glad to return a favor. David also shared with him the new and serious relationship between Luis and Mitch. Julio's response was, after he quit laughing, "About time that boy fell in love with a woman. Now I'm anxious to meet her. Must be some great gal!"

Once Jorge and Luis arrived and all were together enjoying drinks in Julio's den, and after the three men had finished teasing Luis about his masculinity for nearly five minutes, Julio asked for a business update.

Luis was prepared with some good news. "Gentlemen, my lady friend is going to help us even more. She no longer has need of her dealers, but they still require their supplies. When Michelle arrives, she is bringing us a list of names, addresses, and manner of transfers. On top of that, the teams she set up in Fernandina and St. Augustine will now work directly with us. Mitch is out! It's a jumpstart to say the least. By October, we'll have eight different groups of smugglers ready to meet each week with the *Paso Seguro* in international waters."

Jorge, with pencil and pad, was working the figures. "How much can they carry ashore, Luis?"

"To maintain a high-speed capability safely, and while keeping their waterline exposed so that they don't look overloaded, eighty bales. That's eight hundred kilos per trip. Weather can slow transports down temporarily. That's especially a concern when hurricanes are in season, but they end by November. Storms happen, but in any given week, these guys can double down on runs to make up for loss trips."

"What does the *Paso Seguro* do when a bad storm is coming?" Julio asked. "Ride it out? I paid a lot of money for that ship. I would be very upset if she sank! Get my drift, Luis?"

She's a big fast trawler crewed by experienced seamen from Honduras. I spent considerable time with the captain. Best there is and he knows how this game works. The ship's max speed when loaded is fourteen knots, so she can make it to a safe harbor that's 350 miles away in one day. Or, with that kind of speed, another choice might be to move out of the storm's way. All they have to do to stay safe is follow advisories by the good old U.S. Coast Guard."

Both Jorge and Julio were firing questions now. Jorge asked. "Where do you find a safe harbor if you're sailing off the coast of Florida and loaded with tons of marijuana?"

"Freeport," Luis smiled and replied. "At little cost I might add. I lunched with the Bahamas' Consulate General in Miami. Very helpful fellow for a measly price. At any time of year, the *Paso Seguro* can anchor in Freeport without being boarded by customs. All she has to do is fly a yellow quarantine flag and keep her crew aboard. Captain Rene will go ashore and pay a $600 entry fee, no questions asked. I've advised him to mistakenly pay several times that amount should the occasion arrive."

David nodded and added. "Father, the Bahamas are right on the coast of Florida. Off and on during these past few months, I've spent time in Freeport and Nassau. Most of the government officials there can be helpful when provided with an incentive. Even more so than here in Colombia. It could be an advantage for us in the future if we start to make the right friends now."

"I like the idea," Julio replied. "David, continue your visits to Freeport. Introduce yourself to the local higher-up authorities as someone interested in finding business opportunities in the Bahamas. Mention the restaurant in Miami as an example. Offer gratuities for some assistance with any of the island's bureaucratic obstacles. Basically, identify and make friends with those willing to take a bribe in case we need them."

"My pleasure. I'll make a list of those willing to cooperate!"

Julio turned his attention back to Luis. "Everything seems to be progressing well. Anything else I need to know?"

"One problem with our progress. Though in a way, it's a good problem to have."

"Okay, let's hear it."

"There was no way we could have anticipated how fast this would all come together when we decided to delay purchasing the second fishing trawler. Come October in Santa Marta, we will be loading the *Paso Seguro* with your first sixty pallets of Colombia's finest marijuana. Thirty-six thousand kilos. Seven or eight days later we'll begin offloading to our runners. With just eight of them each making a trip every week, the hole of the *Paso Seguro* will be empty in just over a month."

Jorge interrupted. "Doesn't sound like a problem to me, Luis. That's a hell-of-a-lot of tonnage to move in a short time. What could be better?"

"An uninterrupted supply is your answer, Jorge. It takes eight days to sail back to Colombia. Add to that a few days of required trawler maintenance before loading the next shipment plus another eight days to get back on station off Florida's coast. Considering some probable weather delays, we can manage maybe six transports a year. Julio, if we don't want our runners sitting on their butts half the time waiting for us to show back up, we'll need another trawler and crew by October."

"Crap! I see your point. "I'll have to pony up for another ship. Take care of it right away, Luis."

Jorge could tell that the Don was concerned about the startup cost. It was running twice what the two of them had originally thought it would be. Decided he might ease his dad's worries with some math. "Father, on the streets of the U.S., a kilo of Colombian sells for a grand or more. We'll be wholesaling the stuff fifty miles offshore much cheaper than what it brings those dealers. Three, maybe even four hundred a kilo. Soon enough at that price, runners will be swarming to our ships. Gross income per shipment comes to between ten and twelve million. With that kind of money, you can buy a cruise liner and have change left over."

Julio thought for a moment and asked, "If it's that much, we can't be the only ones taking advantage of this. How much competition is out there?"

Luis knew the answer thanks to Juan's research. "Not as much as you might think, Julio. Mexico supplies most of the central and western states but it's crap. 'Panama Red' comes by way of the Gulf of Mexico into Louisiana and southeast Texas. Not bad marijuana and it's liked by some of the younger crowds. Still, compared to 'Colombian Gold', it's hamburger versus filet mignon. We're offering prime marijuana at basement prices. The only thing that equals our quality is Jamaican. It's called 'Lamb's Bread.' Jamaica's proximity to the Florida coast puts them at an advantage, but nobody is bringing it in like we plan to. Shear volume along with quality and priced low. Can't beat that combination. We stand to make tons of money without the risk of ever violating the territorial waters of the United States."

"So eventually we can pretty much control prices and the competition?" Jorge asked.

David and Luis both replied to his question with confident nods. Then, Luis said, "If you two can manage supply in addition to any problems that might arise here in Colombia, nothing stands in our way of dominating our country's whole damn marijuana market from Medellin."

Julio began to wonder if perhaps this new family business was working to his advantage. Didn't need the money. Any major smuggling operation in Colombia like what Luis had described was bound to be exposed sooner or later. That probability concerned him. Thinking about it, maybe he should remove himself from any direct connections to operations. Let the boys run things.

Early Wednesday morning, June 11th, Luis watch as a Lockheed 18-56 Lodestar made a picture-perfect landing on the dirt runway located a mile-and-half from Julio's home. While it was well within the hacienda boundaries, the airstrip's placement was chosen so as not to disturb the tranquility of Julio's home or the horses. His stables housed more than three hundred and included mostly thoroughbreds.

Four days had passed since Raymond's arrest. During that time, Mitch had secluded herself in a Saint Augustine apartment rented by two of her runners. Her friend, Skip had suggested they let a little dust settle before trying to make a run-for-it. It was an anxious few days for Luis, but now he realized the delay was worth the wait.

The twin engine Lockheed taxied to the hangar where Luis was standing. Engines stopped, the door near the rear of the aircraft opened with steps folding down, and first out with a big smile while waving was Michelle Linville. She was wearing a beige, floral print dress that flittered slightly in the breeze as did her shoulder length hair. In that picturesque style and with almost a showy air of confidence, she strolled the ten yards to Luis, placed her arms around his neck and delivered a gentle, long, and meaningful kiss to his lips. Luis melted, completely speechless.

Two men came out of the aircraft and walked over to the pair of love birds. Mitch introduced them. "Luis Castillo, I want you to meet my friends, Skip Steel and our pilot, Will Knox."

The men shook hands. "I'm grateful to both of you for the rescue of this wonderful lady. Understand it's a debt owed that if ever asked, I would be pleased to repay. Can you stay over today and enjoy the hospitality of Julio Restrepo?"

"Thanks for the invitation, but we have to decline. The timing of our trip here could not be better. We're combining business with the pleasure of saving your 'damsel-in-distress.' If Mr. Restrepo can spare us gas for our plane, we're expected in Jamaica before dark and back in Florida after that."

"I understand, Skip. Maybe another time. I'll have our tanker truck supply as much as you need. Will, you may want to supervise. Our guys may not be familiar with your aircraft."

"You bet," Will replied.

"In the meantime, Skip, join us in the hangar. There is something else in the works I hope you can help us with."

There was a small office at the far end of the hangar. Once inside, Luis offered refreshments. Both Mitch and Skip accepted. After the drinks were passed, Luis said, "Michelle and I have another favor to ask of you, Skip. Another rescue!"

"I expect this has something to do with Raymond?"

"Yes, but not right away. Just last night, Raymond signed a power of attorney over to his lawyer, Bernie Claxton. That move will enable us to purchase a fishing trawler in Honduras that Bernie will acquire by trading one of Ray's shrimp boats. We're closing the deal for a half million by September. Bernie will use the proceeds to post bail for Raymond."

Skip interrupted. "But I read in the *Miami Herald* the judge set the bail for twice that amount."

"That's correct, but we are working to have it reduced by fifty percent. Not so much as to attract the attention of the public. Although the government's prosecutors will be pissed, five hundred thousand is still a lot of money."

"So, how can Will and I help?"

"Arrange for another flight. This time to Honduras with Raymond as your passenger. Again though, not right away. The authorities will be watching after he's released. Allow for a few weeks of Ray following dull routines. With monotony, surveillance becomes careless. Once you set a time and place for departure, my people can easily help Ray elude his trackers and meet you for the flight. Janet will be waiting for him on arrival in Honduras."

"Why Honduras?"

"Ray has friends there as do we. I can guarantee his safety in Honduras, at least temporarily until he finds a permanent place to relocate. And I don't want to draw any attention to him having connections to Colombia when he escapes."

Skip considered the request thinking, if Luis has as much pull here in Colombia as he seems to, and as well, the ability to get Ray out from under one of the biggest drug busts ever in the states, best to tag along with him. Type of person who you might not want to turn down in our business. Better a friend than a foe.

"Luis. I'm totally ready to provide the flight for Raymond. How do we go about setting this up?"

"I'll work with Bernie Claxton. He will act as our go-between. To remain safe, you and he will only communicate on a lawyer-client basis. I have an office in Miami, but you and I will never meet in the states. Here in Colombia, it's not a problem."

Michelle gave Skip a hug. "Thanks again for your assistance. I'll make sure Janet knows all will be well soon. After this is over, you have a standing invitation to vacation with Luis and I here in Colombia. We promise you it will be an enjoyable and memorable stay."

"Mitch, I may take you up on that offer. Perhaps even bring my companion with me. She'd love it. Thanks!"

"Anything more to discuss, Luis? Hate to leave since we just got here but Will and I need to be on our way."

Luis nodded his understanding. "That pretty much covers it for now." With that settled, the four of them left the hangar office and walked towards the plane. Luis pointed at the aircraft. "Nice set of wings you're flying. Can I ask it's load capacity?"

Skip knowingly laughed at the question. "Not at all. Fully fueled, give or take about 1300 kilos. Will picked her out for that and reliability. She's powered by two 1200hp Wright Cyclone engines and can cruise over 2,000 miles at a speed of 200mph. Perfect for our business! If he has to, Will can set her down on a dime."

"Interesting." Luis responded. In fact, it's very interesting, he thought to himself.

Leading up to October's first shipment out of Santa Marta, Luis and Michelle were practically inseparable. Sometimes combining business with pleasure, they traveled in Colombia together. When working, Luis's office in Medellin was headquarters. Even then, their evenings included dining out in town, and afterwards spending quiet time at his ranch. In the early mornings there before breakfast, he and Michelle enjoyed horseback riding. They visited Bogota twice. On two separate weekends Julio invited them to be guests at his hacienda. All memorable times but

Luis had saved the best for last. Two weeks in and around Cartagena! Michelle's August 26 birthday surprise. The city's history proved both intriguing and pleasant, but Luis had reserved most of the first week for them to lay on white beaches and sail in the Caribbean while staying on Isla de Baru. Afterwards, it was from there by boat to Islas del Rosario for four days of snorkeling the incredibly beautiful coral reefs. Michelle never wanted to leave. They were in love!

Three days after they returned to Medellin, Luis received word from Bernie that Raymond Stansel's $500,000 bail had been posted by cashier's check. Once bailed out but having been imprisoned for three months, Ray was now begging for an early departure to Honduras to meet with Janet. With the help of Juan and Juanita, a manner of losing any sort of surveillance could be arranged. All that was required was Luis's approval and notifying Skip Steel where and when. Luis reluctantly gave in to Ray's request.

One week after being released, Raymond Stansel stepped off a plane in Honduras into the arms of Janet. The greeting was much the same as when Michelle had joined Luis three months earlier. Neither Ray nor Mitch could ever return to the United States. They never did!

October arrived. The *Paso Seguro* departed Santa Marta for the east coast of Florida. She was loaded with nearly forty tons of Colombian Gold. Forty million dollars in street value. A little over five weeks later with her hole almost empty, she traded places with a sister trawler, the *Gran Pretendiente*. That ship's name had been newly registered in Panama at the request of its owner. Few knew the reason for changing its name. It was done as a favor to one Raymond Stansel.

In Colombia, Michelle first tried to settle into a comfortable routine on the ranch but keeping a smooth transfer of cargo from the trawlers to runners now required that Luis stay on top of operations in Florida. Whenever possible, he would fly home even if it were only for a few days.

During Luis's absence, Michelle began traveling to Cartagena. She loved the city and its coastal resorts. After just six weeks, her interest there had grown to the point that she decided to buy a home. She found a beautiful place fronting the Caribbean. Money was no problem since past dealings had left her wealthy, especially by Colombian standards. Since he liked Cartagena as well, Luis supported the decision.

A ranch outside of Medellin complimented by a seaside home near Cartagena made the times Luis and Michelle spent together something like a dream-come-true. And just when it seemed life could not get any better, it did! After dining out in celebration of their second new-year's eve as a couple, Luis offered Michelle another glass of wine before leaving their table for home. She smiled. "Thank you, honey, but I better not." Michelle leaned close to Luis's cheek and whispered. "Honey, I'm pregnant." Remaining calm and collective to any surprising news was Luis's trademark characteristic. However, in this instance, he lost all control of himself with obvious and outward elation in a nearly full restaurant. Made for a memorable and happy scene!

By mid-spring 1975 the *Paso Seguro* and the *Gran Pretendiente* had each completed three shipments to the Florida coastal waters. Gross sales proceeds returned to Colombia totaled ninety million dollars. Expanding north to the shores of Georgia and the Carolinas were to be added the following year. A search in Honduras for another fishing trawler and crew was being considered. In general, operations at sea were carried on without any interruptions.

Communications were an important key to their success. Because she was smart as hell, and the method was somewhat complicated, Luis had recommended Juanita for the job of coordinating runners with the mother ships. She proved to be more than capable of the part after being trained by a hired instructor on the use of a single-sideband radio. To radiate properly, transmissions required a twenty-foot whip antenna, a tuner to match the antenna to desired frequencies, and a "ground plane" to reflect the antenna's radio waves. Prior to the *Paso Seguro's* first shipment, the radio unit's installation was completed beside the storage shop at the Coral Gables home.

Juanita never explained how she came up with a way of sending coded messages to the trawlers for delivery locations. An original idea or not, her procedures worked!

Both ship's radio rooms were located on the navigation bridge. Numerous maps were shelved there, but a particular one might have seemed oddly out of place for a fishing vessel. It was a map of the Miami Shores Country Club with its superb golf course. Printed next to each of its eighteen greens were latitudes and longitudes. As a precaution for ship to shore transmissions, Juanita would set her alarm clock for five or so minutes before one in the morning. Initial radio frequencies were preset for that time of day and the approximate distance to the trawler. Once contact was established, she provided the exact frequency she was transmitting from so that the ship's receiver could be tuned to the same and the audio would carry without distortion.

The Cuban cities of Mariel and Matanzas were chosen as aliases for the trawlers. Juanita's code name was "Sofia." Radio transmissions were kept purposely short and in Spanish. Once frequencies were set, Juanita would ask, "Mariel. ¿Estás recibiendo? Cambio!"

If anyone, including Ham radio operators were listening, it was highly unlikely they also understood Spanish. And so, the ship's captain might reply. "Fuerte y claro ahora Sofia. ¿Como está el clima? Cambió!"

Along the coast of the United States forecasts were transmitted continuously by VHF. Weather was always a consideration and Juanita would check prior to the call. If necessary and conditions allowed, she would occasionally double down on runners. "Perfecto para jugar a Mariel. Empecemos el Viernes a las 11 a.m. en el octavo T. Y el Sabado al mediodia en el Segundo T. Cambió!"

"Excelente, Sofia. Hasta entonces. Fuera!"

From the map of the country club's golf course, the trawler's captain would simply note the latitudes and longitudes printed by the second and eighth greens. Then he would subtract two hours from the times Juanita provided for the Friday and Saturday mornings. With that, a meeting at sea with the runners was set with a location and time. Offloading eighty bales of marijuana in good weather normally took less than ten minutes. Afterwards, the captain would sail twenty or thirty miles further out into the Gulf Stream and set an approximate course for the next group of smugglers.

Juanita's coordination with runners was simpler. Clocks were set for telephone calls to each team of runners and limited to fifteen second so as to prevent any trace. Brief conversations would confirm a breakfast time and day for 2,3, or 4 persons at a Waffle House, Denney's, or Dunkin Donut. The numbers matched a different latitude and longitude for each team. If weather was a problem, breakfast was canceled with the understanding of when another breakfast might be conveniently provided.

David was equally successful in establishing relations with influential Bahamians. Initially visits were just to Freeport for meetings with local officials there, but he soon learned that politicians in Nassau could turn out to be more effective friends in terms of the island's illegal drug trade. Two of the most important persons he managed to connect with were close acquaintances of Prime Minister Lynden Pindling. One was the minister's personal lawyer and the other was his long-time business crony. Through them, David raised the prospect of perhaps one day funding some of the administration's private endeavors. The suggestion seemed well received, and they even explained how the contributions could easily be accomplished through the country's strict bank secrecy laws. The word "bribery" was never mentioned, but when David reported back to Jorge and his father, both recognized exactly what it was and the significance of their support if ever needed. Julio approved a retainer for the lawyer and his friend in an amount that they would appreciate.

With the realization of becoming a father, Luis decided to arrange spending much more of his time with Michelle in Colombia. Being a family man, Julio understood his absence from Florida but decided it would require adding some support staff in Miami. Visas and passports were arranged for two Colombian nationals chosen from Julio's Hacienda staff. Lucia, a trilingual female office aide for Juanita. And Diego, one of Julio's experienced soldiers to assist Juan when needed. Diego also spoke English fluently. Both understood the importance of never betraying Don Julio Restrepo's trust but were glad to have been given the opportunity of substantial economic gains. Juan and Juanita welcomed the help. The marijuana operation was growing much faster than anticipated.

18.

THE GAME CHANGER

A year flew by. Luis and Michelle were now parents to a baby boy. At his ranch on an early May morning in 1976, Jorge phoned. Luis and Michelle were still asleep, but Luis woke and answered. "Hello."

"Sorry to wake you, Luis, but I need you to be at your office with me before ten today. Can you do that?"

"Sure. What's so important?"

"Someone requires your legal services. Insisting actually. We'll be meeting a Medellin local named Gustavo Gaviria. Do you know him by chance?"

"No, at least I don't think so."

"Well, apparently he's looking for the very best criminal defense lawyer in Colombia and thinks that's you. I'll explain some more when you arrive, but it has to do with the same line of work we're in. His call to me requesting your help made that clear. See you at ten. Okay?"

Luis looked at Michelle before replying. "Yes, I'll even try to make it before then. Will anyone else be there with us?"

"I've asked David to come. Just keeping my brother in the loop."

"What about Julio?"

"Absolutely not! Dad insisted on staying out of this."

Jorge's reply made Luis's curiosity race, but he thought better than to ask why? Hung up the phone, kissed Michelle and said, "Sorry darling, I've got to go to work."

With Juanita gone, Luis had hired a new receptionist for his office in Medellin. She was a pleasant lady in her late fifties whose primary qualifications were keeping all office dealings strictly confidential. First name was Emma, and she was not expecting Luis when he arrived.

"Good morning, Mr. Castillo. I would have had coffee ready if I'd known you were coming in today."

"I was not planning to, Emma, but something came up. Make coffee if you will and enough for several visitors. They'll be here by ten."

Jorge, David, and Gustavo Gaviria arrived together promptly at ten. David introduced Gaviria. After Emma brought coffee, she asked if there would be anything else, then left, closing the big double door behind her. Luis quietly inquired, "Mr. Gaviria, how can I be of service?"

My apologies, Mr. Castillo. Before I answer, I have to ask Jorge and David a delicate question." Gustavo turned toward the two brothers. "You are the sons of Don Restrepo. Last year a well-known Medellin drug boss was murdered. His name was Fabio Restrepo. Was he part of your family?"

Jorge immediately answered with an offensive tone. "No! No family relation at all! Purely coincidental! It's a common name in Colombia. Our father's first name is Fabio, and we have a younger brother named after the Don, but our ancestors date from the union between the Ochoa and Vasquez families. The man you spoke of was a low-life and even an opponent of ours. In retrospect, I think his death was deserved."

"I'm sorry for the rudeness of my question, Jorge, although I'm pleased with your response. Perhaps you'll understand when I explain that I'm not here for myself. I came to you, David, and your attorney, Mr. Castillo, on behalf of my cousin. He was arrested yesterday for smuggling cocaine paste from Ecuador."

David shrugged and said, "I'm sorry for your cousin, Mr. Gaviria, but why involve us with this problem."

"As I mentioned to Jorge when I called last night, we are aware of your recent purchases of Colombian marijuana, and in amounts that are very hard to keep secret, especially from us."

"Just who is this cousin of yours?" Jorge asked, expressing his question with obvious impatience.

"Pablo! Pablo Emilio Escobar Gaviria," Gustavo replied.

Placing a hand on his chin, Luis did his customary lean back. Both David and Jorge raised their eyes. The name was more than just familiar to all of them. After the drug boss, Fabio Restrepo, was killed following the "Medellin Massacre" last November, Pablo Escobar had reportedly taken control of the city's cocaine business.

Gustavo noticed everyone's somewhat surprised reaction and thought it was best if he continued. "Pablo's arrest is unfortunate, but the timing may prove to be advantageous. Because of your family's political influence here in Colombia and Mr. Castillo's reputation as your attorney, he had already considered that a mutually beneficial relationship might one day be established. If you can help Pablo with the authorities now, consider his gratitude as yours, and perhaps become better acquainted with him afterwards. I assure you some sort of arrangement with Pablo could prove to be substantially profitable."

David and Jorge were silent. The suggestion of getting into the cocaine business caught both men off-guard. Luis recognized their dilemma and answered for them. "Mr. Gaviria, an opportunity to work with Pablo Escobar is interesting, but it requires that we discuss the possibility privately among ourselves. You understand, I'm sure?"

"Yes, Mr. Castillo, I do. Can we be less formal? First names seem more appropriate now."

"I agree.".

"Good then." Gustavo replied. "Still though, we are getting ahead of ourselves. Any association has to come directly from Pablo. His current incarceration is still the primary reason for my visit. Gentlemen, can you help?"

Jorge responded more politely now to Gustavo's question. "It's true that our family has important friends in government. The connections are mostly compatriots proud to associate with our father. His prominence as an esteemed Colombian might be jeopardized if he were to ask favors on behalf of a known cocaine smuggler."

Gustavo's disappointment with Jorge's reply was evident, so again Luis intervened. "There may be another way we can handle this. Give me the rest of the morning to make some inquiries regarding the case against Mr. Escobar. I'll need to know who apprehended him, what he is charged with, the person handling the prosecution, and the judge or panel of judges appointed. My expertise in these situations might lead to a resolution."

Gustavo Gaviria stood and gave handshakes to David, Jorge, and Luis. "Then my visit with you is not wasted. Thank you and I hope your search proves to be of help, Luis. If it's convenient, I would like to return here later this afternoon for your report."

"Let's say we meet back here at 3 p.m.," David suggested. "We will take that time to consider if and how we may work together should Mr. Escobar be released."

After Gustavo left, Jorge politely asked Luis how Michelle was coming along? "She's a very happy mom!" Luis bragged, "My son is only ten months old but already trying to walk. I'll be taking some time away when he does."

"We're fine with that. For now, how long do you need to make your inquiries about Escobar's arrest?"

"Not more than two hours. It's not my first time in matters like this."

"I know, but before you start your calls, it's best that David and I bring you up to date on our business. It's a family matter and concerns Dad."

Luis naturally responded. "Is Julio okay?"

"Yes. Overweight but fine. As I said, it's family and should not be a problem for us. Started two months ago when our brother Fabio decided he wanted to join in the marijuana trade with David and I. We agreed but then Margot found out and she was not pleased with her youngest son's participation. He's only nineteen."

"Pretty mature for his age as I recall, Jorge, and only six years separate the two of you."

"David and I felt the same way."

"The family patriarch had to settle the question. Right?"

"Sure, he did. To keep the peace, Dad agreed to let Fabio partner with us but none of the rest of the kids. Also, partly to calm Margot worries, he decided he was ready to distance himself from the business."

"Wow! That certainly changes a lot of things. Leaves you and David in charge."

"Yes, and this is the way Dad reasoned it. He was responsible for financing the startup.

He already has a return three times what those cost amounted to, and our operations quickly became incredibly profitable without his backing. His reputation here in Colombia was another consideration."

"I'm beginning to see why you immediately excluded offering Julio's political influence to get Escobar out of trouble. It's exactly what the Don wishes to avoid."

"You understand perfectly," David added. "Father will stick with haciendas, his thoroughbred horses, and restaurants. We control things from here on out."

"Where do I fit in?"

"Same as before except you'll work exclusively for us. Not the whole family. Your representation and advice are crucial to operations."

"Thanks! If that's all, I'll get on with my calls. Can you both come back after lunch? Maybe a little before Gustavo arrives?"

It took Luis a little longer than he had anticipated to check out all the players in Escobar's troubles. Wasn't good information! He had barely finished before David and Jorge returned. He was prepared to review his findings with them, but Gustavo Gaviria arrived early and was obviously anxious.

Once they were all seated in his office, Luis came right to the point. "I wish I had better news for you, Gustavo. Pablo's arraignment and court case are being handled totally out of Bogota. They've already appointed a special prosecutor and assigned a 'tough-as-nails' judge that can't be approached. Both are formidable opponents if I have to face them. On the surface, it appears to be an 'open-and-shut' charge. He and his helpers were caught 'red-handed' importing cocaine paste from Ecuador in an amount that's significant if convicted. The two arresting officers detained him along with his friends for being in procession of eighteen kilos."

Before Gustavo could respond, David chuckled and said, "Hell, Luis! That's not much. Our trucks here in Colombia each haul two thousand kilos of marijuana."

"That's true, David, but in the states, two thousand kilos of Colombian Gold sell on the streets for about two million. Eighteen kilos of cocaine can bring twice as much. Even more if it's pure and sold in New York or Los Angeles. That's probably the reason Juan says some of our speedboat runners are asking if we can bring in coke as well as marijuana."

Gustavo with a quizzical expression said, "You can understand why the authorities are calling my cousin's arrest a big drug bust. But, Luis, did you say they caught him and his help with eighteen kilos?"

"Yes, I'm afraid so."

Gustavo stood, raised his hand high and asserted. "That's not right! I know for a fact he loaded his plane with twenty-four kilos in Ecuador. One hundred percent sure! What the hell's going on?"

Luis leaned back in his chair, smiled, and turned to Jorge. "Are you thinking what I'm thinking?"

"While returning his answer with an understanding grin, Jorge replied, "Unbelievable! What a break for Escobar."

Then, still smiling, Luis stood and walked over to Gustavo's side. "I have some more calls to make. Afterwards, I'm certain your cousin, Pablo Escobar, will be released without charges."

"Gustavo remained perplexed. "I still don't get it, Luis?"

"Happens sometimes here in Colombia, Gustavo. Crooked cops! Six kilos missing. Never turned in. Guess who?"

"Had to be the same two SOB's that arrested him. Right?"

"The temptation was just too great for two underpaid officers. It's unfortunate the case has notoriety. Someone has to be prosecuted. As a lawyer, I can contact them with a proposal they would be stupid to turn down. I'll suggest they made a mistake identifying Escobar as one of the smugglers. Just let his workers face the charges. Maybe add a little incentive money to boost. Accept the offer or guarantee their corruption will be exposed."

"How long will this take?"

"A day or two. No more."

"Excellent! I'm sure Pablo will want to thank all of you in person. Maybe we can become friends?"

"Perhaps," Jorge answered.

Gustavo Gaviria left the meeting with confidence that he had served his cousin well. Also, Luis thought maybe he deserved a small congratulation. "Compadres, the bars open. Shall we discuss today's events over drinks?"

David jumped at the idea. "You bet, and easy on the ice for me."

You could tell Jorge was in deep thought when he managed just a quiet "Okay." He took a hefty sip of his straight scotch, then looked at Luis inquisitively. "Do you remember the question my dad asked you about our competition in the marijuana trade? It was the day before Michelle arrived."

"I do. Believe the answer was Mexican, Panama Red, and Jamaican Lamb's Bread. Why?"

"You compared Colombian marijuana to Panama's. Said it was like choosing filet mignon instead of hamburger."

"Yes, but what's your point?"

"Learned something in this meeting this afternoon. Since October we've been patting our backside for all the money we've made. But think about it. In seven months, we've sold over 200,000 kilos of marijuana. After paying for the two trawlers and other overhead, cleared maybe thirty-five million. This Pablo Escobar is into a much higher stakes game. We're selling Panama hotdogs on the streets for 25 cents. He's selling Colombian filet mignon for forty times that. Our profits may have tripled if we had smuggled some cocaine along with the marijuana."

David and Luis both had concerned expressions. "I think I just heard my brother suggest we get into the cocaine trade, Luis?"

"Me too." Luis answered with a frown.

"Jorge spoke to both men. "An easy opportunity to do just that came to us today. Gustavo said as much in this morning's meeting. Before he was arrested, Escobar had been considering an arrangement with us. He knew we were smuggling large amounts of marijuana to the states. I think he may have wanted us to diversify our cargo by adding his cocaine to the shipments."

"Partly explains why we were asked to get him out of trouble," David said. "Our established marijuana trafficking along with the family's influence here in Colombia would make it a good deal for him."

Luis pointed out. "From a legal standpoint, I like the idea if we can maintain the cooperation almost anonymously. Sort of like being silent partners or innocent investors in an enterprise. Pablo Escobar is already considered Medellin's cocaine jefe. If we do business with him, let it stay that way. Escobar can have all the glory. If something goes wrong, he takes all the heat."

"That's our lawyer looking out for us," David agreed with a laugh.

"Well, sounds to me like we should go along with this if Escobar makes an offer," Jorge suggested. "Good timing too because if he does, it's our decision to accept or not. Dad is out of this!"

"Let's not forget, I have to get Escobar's ass free first," Luis reminded them. "When I do, he'll want to thank us in person. Use a private dining room at the family's restaurant for that. Set it up first class but make sure he comes to us with a proposition. Not the other way around."

David and Jorge nodded in agreement.

"Gentlemen if that's all, I have work to do on Escobar's behalf, and all before I can return home to my sweet, little family. I'll update you on my progress."

The charges against Pablo Escobar were dropped two days later. For reasons never explained, his release wasn't mentioned in any of Colombia's newspapers. A call from Gustavo Gaviria to Luis came the first morning after Escobar was freed. Pablo wished to thank everyone in person. Luis made dinner reservations for the next night and confirmed the date and time with Jorge.

Colombia has a tropical climate, but Medellin is about 1500 meters above sea level. Its warm season ends in March accompanied by frequent rains with temperatures in a Fahrenheit range of sixty to seventy degrees.

At Don Restrepo's restaurant on just such a rainy night in mid-May 1976, Luis, David, and Jorge met with Pablo Escobar and his brother, Roberto. On arrival, Gustavo Gaviria made the introductions.

After the maître d' had escorted everyone to a private dining room and departed, Pablo Escobar offered his hand for a second time to each of his host while explaining the gesture. "I'm in debt to you all. Please count me as your friend in Medellin. I understand the officers that arrested me required a payment to drop the charges. Roberto will reimburse all of your cost before we leave tonight."

Jorge raised both hands along with a negative head shake. "No offense, Pablo, but I would prefer our friendship begin with nothing owed. Besides, Gustavo said you were already considering contacting us. We're interested to learn what exactly you have in mind?"

"Partners," Pablo explained matter-of-factly. "Some details to be worked out but partnering with me in supplying cocaine to the east coast of the United States. We're going to expand our processing operations in Colombia. I have a two-story house in Comuna 13 that serves as a lab where we refine the paste to powdered coke. It's too confining for all the chemicals required not to mention cramping up the workers inside. Place attracts attention, and the most we can produce there is 50 kilos a week. The demand for cocaine is a hundred times that in the United States. Who knows, maybe more?"

"Fifty kilos every week is a lot of cocaine. How do you go about increasing production?" Jorge asked.

"Moving to the mountains." We've already started setting up an outdoor laboratory near the border with Venezuela. Remote as hell and plenty of farm labor available for recruitment. Add to that, I've flown over the location several times. The whole damn set-up will be practically undetectable from the air."

David shrugged his shoulders again. "Impressive, I have to say, Pablo, but what do you need us for? Sounds like you have your new location all worked out."

"I need your help more than you might imagine. Two important reasons for starters. Everyone knows that many of Colombia's politicians and authorities can be influenced for personal gains. As you all have just proven on my behalf, your experience in these areas can and will be extremely useful as partners. Especially yours, Luis."

Luis smiled appreciatively. "Thank you, Pablo, but I believe you said two reasons? The other must be more important than whatever I can contribute!"

"The answer is volume, gentlemen. Currently I move about 200 kilos a month mostly out of the Leeward Islands. Antique and Montserrat. Methods require using airline stewardesses, baggage handlers, and even some money hungry tourists. We place small amounts of cocaine hidden in the false bottoms of their suitcases. Five or six kilos at a time. No more! Pretty successful. Rarely does anyone get caught."

Jorge's brain for accounting was always adding and now it forced him to interrupt Escobar. "And this new laboratory in the forest will increase your production?"

Pablo Escobar relished Jorge's question. Without cracking a smile, he answered, "Three, maybe four thousand kilos per month."

Escobar waited for their reply. Nothing was spoken but the response was obvious. Wide eyes with a stare from Jorge and the same from David but with his mouth half opened. Luis leaned back in his chair with his right hand placed on his face. Sat silent but astonished.

Pablo waited just a few more seconds for his reply to sink in before calmly continuing. "Not at first, you understand. We'll have to hire workers, guards, arrange for transportation, and construct the facilities. Takes time. There's an endless supply of cocaine paste available from Bolivia, Peru, and Ecuador, but processing materials can be a problem. From start to finish, refining four thousand kilos a month will require tank loads of acid, ammonia, and solvents. Some of that will have to be imported to Colombia. I'm planning for operations to commence by next year. As partners, that's when and where you come into play."

Luis broke his silence. "You need our help to smuggle some of that cocaine?"

"Something you already have. A way of transporting and distributing drugs to the eastern shores of the U.S. and tons of it by weight."

"Marijuana but not cocaine," Jorge argued. "We freight with fishing trawlers out of Santa Marta. They sail in international waters off the coast of Florida and act as mother ships for loading fast speed boats. Each one of those can carry eight hundred kilos ashore every trip. Much heavier cargo by comparison to cocaine, but like your methods in the Leeward Islands, pretty damn safe! Almost risk free!"

"I'm not asking you to quit trading in marijuana. Instead, all you have to do is add cocaine to your cargo. The demand for it is incredible."

"To be honest, some of our runners have been asking for coke," David replied. We're selling marijuana wholesale to them fifty miles or more off the Florida coast. Our price leaves room for them to make a lot of money as the middlemen supplying dealers. Would an arrangement like that work for you?"

"In some ways, yes. A little different though. My cocaine cost $2,000 a kilo to produce. Here in Colombia, I sell to almost anyone willing to smuggle it for $30,000 per kilo. Like your marijuana, once inside the U.S., stuff goes for many times as much. Call it ambitious, but what I hope we can eventually achieve together is a single cooperative that includes production, transportation, and distribution."

Jorge decided it was the right moment to say something outright and honest. "We're interested in working with you Pablo. Can you spell out some terms for us to consider?"

"Like banker hours. An eight to five split after expenses. My side is greater for good reason. In Colombia, as much as possible, it's best if the details of our association remain confidential. Any direct ties might compromise your ability to help with the authorities or government officials should the need arise. However, that means here at home, I'm taking most of the risk. I'm out front in this game and you're watching from the sidelines."

Luis nodded affirmatively. "Have to say, Pablo, I advised David and Jorge of exactly that of type connection with you."

David agreed to the terms. "Under those circumstances, your division of profits is fair and acceptable."

Acknowledging David's comment, Escobar opened both his hands and placed them on the table. "A mutual trust is key to our friendship and success. Roberto is an accountant. If you agree, he will be responsible for record keeping. Split the net income after all our expenses are deducted. I personally guarantee his books!"

"That works for us," Jorge said. "We'll have some work to do setting up our side of this, but your new laboratory is still six or seven months from completion."

"Yes, you're right. But there's a way to start small right away and build from there. When will you next load one of your fishing trawlers in Santa Marta?"

"The *Gran Pretendiente* is six days from port," Jorge answered. "She'll be ready to sail with her cargo around the second week of June."

"I can have four hundred kilos ready by then. It's a way to begin supplying any of your runners interested in adding cocaine to their haul."

This time, David answered instead of his brother. Reached his hand out to Escobar confirming an agreement. "Okay, Pablo, let's do it!"

Escobar smiled for the first time, partly because of David's enthusiasm. He returned a handshake to both David and Jorge.

Luis thought perhaps everything was moving just a little too fast and suggested, "There will be more meetings in the coming months. We're trying to build an enterprise. This evening at our restaurant has been a great start. Let's set aside business for now, enjoy some refreshments and have dinner. Lots to digest afterwards besides the food and drinks."

The rest of the evening was mostly social. For someone with a violent reputation, Pablo Escobar was a pleasant surprise. Soft spoken, polite, and well-mannered during drinks and dinner. The conversations were friendly and made it seem as though the six men at the table had long known one another.

During talks, David mentioned his recent achievements in the Bahamas. He was pleased with himself for having made some influential acquaintances whose assistance might one day prove useful. Explained that Freeport was already serving as a safe haven for the trawlers. Escobar listened carefully. His interest was evident!

As they were leaving the restaurant, Pablo approached Luis with a question. "Do you think the two narcotics officers were adequately compensated for dropping the charges against me?"

"More than just adequate," Luis replied.

"By chance, did they offer to return my six kilos?"

"No! Sorry, but I didn't think to ask either."

Pablo turned towards Gustavo. "Cousin, visit with the two of them and request they give back what rightfully belongs to me."

"Right away Pablo. If they refuse?"

Pablo shrugged. "Then let little Pinina handle it. Instruct him to make a statement others will remember!"

David and Luis returned to Miami the second week of June in preparation of adding a new pursuit to their smuggling venture. Cocaine! In Luis's office the day after they arrived, he updated Juan and instructed him to inform any of the runners who had inquired about obtaining the drug that cocaine would be available by year's end.

Escobar had recommended a price of $50,000 per kilo to start with. Cash in U.S. dollars on delivery. At that price and obtainable just off the coast of Florida, Juan told Luis the demand would far exceed a mere 400 kilos. In Miami, there were middlemen buying and transporting to the major cities all along the east coast. Many were Cubans. New York alone was consuming twice that amount each month. Supply was a big problem. A kilo of pure cocaine would be cut, sold in grams, and ultimately bring $500,000.

Coming from Colombia, Luis was familiar with cocaine but not its recent and remarkable popularity. Street sales amounting to a half million per kilo seemed inconceivable. If by the next year they were to start shipping thousands of kilos, more than a few runners of marijuana in fast boats would be required. They would need to acquaint themselves with one or more of the cocaine traffickers in the United States. Doing so presented the problem of how to go about identifying those to safely work with. It involved a transfer of huge sums of money which could be inherently dangerous. It was this unfamiliar territory in the drug trade that Luis, David, and Juan began to discuss that morning in the office. As the official person in charge of communications, Juanita was also present.

"David suggested, "We could approach one or more of our runners who have expressed an interest in cocaine. Ask for the names of dealers to meet with."

Luis responded negatively to the idea. "Possibly but doing so would expose us to total strangers. Maybe even the authorities acting under cover. To avoid that, we need a major cocaine distributor and not some small-time middleman."

Juanita looked directly at Luis with sort of an amusing smile. "Why don't you ask the New York City police department for assistance. They serve nearly eight million people there, and a lot of them use coke."

"David with a sarcastic expression. "You're joking, Juanita. Ask the cops for help?"

"Of course, not directly, David, but I'm serious. Give me a moment to check my file cabinet. I'll be right back."

Juanita left for the file room and David gave Luis and Juan a long dubious stare.

Luis answered him with, "Don't underestimate her. Sometimes she's smarter than the rest of us put together. Let's wait and see what she's going to suggest."

Juanita returned with a copy of the *Miami Herald* and removed a supplemental insert printed in Spanish. The front page of the insert featured an article taken from the *New York Times* published in 1975. She placed the paper on the table where all could read below a headline she had underlined, *Top Drug Dealers Named by Police*. Thirteen names were listed: each with brief descriptions, histories, and some even with addresses. Halfway down the article, Juanita had highlighted four: Ramon Matos, Hugo Curbello, Lilia Parada, and Gustavo Restrepo. All obviously Hispanics and they all dealt strictly in cocaine. The names of Ramon and Gustavo were circled as well as highlighted. The supposedly top-secret list had been compiled by the Organized Crime Control Division of the NY City police department. *The Times* did not reveal its source.

Juanita had purposely circled two of the four for good reason. Ramon Matos and Gustavo Restrepo were accused of being the two biggest cocaine dealers in the city. Gustavo was a native Colombian but both men were reported to have direct links to that country's smugglers.

Luis placed an appreciative arm around Juanita's shoulder. "Girl! You're in for one big bonus if this works out."

David apologetically said, "It may be exactly the start we're looking for. New York City. We'll have to figure out how to get in touch with them?"

Juanita was enjoying the compliments and couldn't pass up the chance to prove her worth again. "Not so hard to do, David. You saw their addresses were provided thanks to the law enforcement officials. I checked! Those two are both listed in the city's phone book."

Luis wanted to say to David, I told she was smart. Nothing to be gained by that. Instead, he continued the discussion with instructions for his secretary. "Juanita, you're in charge of communications. Contact both Ramon and Gustavo. Explain that I am a lawyer and the legal representative of an important Medellin drug Jefe who wishes to work with them. Pablo Escobar. If they're connected to Colombia's drug trade as the police say, then the 'name drop' will definitely cause them to meet with us. Add that we have some of his cocaine for sale."

"Yes sir." Juanita nodded affirmatively. "But Luis, are we in the cocaine business with Pablo Escobar?"

"Yes, we are." Luis paused to clarify a bit. "Just here on the east coast of the states." Not the rest of the country."

A month later in calm seas sixty miles off the coast of South Carolina, a 58-foot Hatteras motor yacht tied against the starboard side of the *Gran Pretendiente*. The yacht was crewed by two young couples from New Jersey working for Gustavo Restrepo. Its captain exchanged $10,000,000 in cash to purchase 200 kilos of Pablo Escobar's cocaine. The transaction took ten minutes. The hired couples were a perfect disguise. Vacationers returning from the Bahamas after a summer cruise. Once lines were released, the Hatteras sailed due east to the South Edisto Inlet and connected four miles further inland to the Atlantic Intracoastal Waterway. Six days later her cargo was offloaded during the night at a dockside in Trenton, New Jersey. From there it was transported by van to New York City.

At that time in 1976 it was the largest single sale Escobar had made. A similar exchange from the *Paso Seguro* with Ramon Matos took place five weeks later. Once Escobar's field laboratory was completed, volumes sold were larger. Much larger in the years ahead and not just transit by ships. Escobar integrated aircraft.

Pablo Escobar was himself a pilot. He had experience smuggling from neighboring South American countries and knew well the advantages of flying drugs. Once airborne, you were safe. Places to take off and land were where the risk came into play. Even that could be significantly reduced by communications with well-placed observers on the ground.

It was an increase in the volume of cocaine refined at his new field laboratory together with a knowledge of air transport that drew Pablo's attention to two newcomers in the business. Like Escobar's initial method of smuggling coke, they had entered the trade late in 1976 as partners by using women to pose as tourists visiting Antigua. The young girls would return by way of Boston's Logan airport with several kilos of cocaine hidden in the false bottoms of suitcases. As a cover in Medellin, one of the men involved operated a car dealership. His name was Carlos Lehder. The other was a pilot with considerable flight experience gained by smuggling marijuana from Mexico to California. His name was George Jung. Mostly, it was Jung's connections to the west coast that interested Escobar. Los Angeles and San Francisco were areas of opportunity. All over California but especially in those cities, cocaine was becoming a favorite pastime with many of its citizens.

Just prior to the start of Colombia's 1977 spring season, Gustavo Gaviria casually walked into a Medellin car dealership. Inside, he approached Carlos Lehder who was seated at an office desk near the entrance.

As he was standing up, Carlos asked, "Can I help you?"

"Actually, I came here to help you," Gustavo replied. "Rather, I should say, you and your partner, George Jung."

The answer back was quick and sharply worded. "Who are you and just how do you propose to do that?"

Relax, friend. My name is Gustavo Gaviria. I'm here on behalf of my cousin, Pablo. He wishes to extend a dinner invitation to the two of you. At yours and George's earliest convenience."

A realization was already apparent when Carlos responded. "Is your cousin Pablo Escobar?"

"Yes."

"Lehder now spoke more respectfully. "We would be honored to dine with Mr. Escobar. But in a few days if that's okay with him. George is taking a break from work at his girlfriend's home in Massachusetts. I'll call and have him fly here right away."

"Perfectly okay." Gustavo handed his card to Carlos. "I'll explain that to Pablo. Call me when he arrives."

The first week in March 1977, at Don Restrepo's Medellin restaurant, Pablo Escobar, Jorge and David Ochoa, George Jung and Carlos Lehder all met together for the first time. Gustavo Gaviria, Fabio Ochoa, and Luis Castillo were there as well. The participants would ultimately achieve a notoriety none attending could have envisioned.

Over dinner, Pablo made an offer to Jung and Lehder. It was an incredible opportunity for them to become very wealthy. Using their own aircraft, Jung and Lehder would begin flying Pablo's cocaine from a ranch near Medellin to California and arrange for distribution. Return with the proceeds to Colombia. After the first successful flight and back, having then proven themselves, Escobar would start paying $2,000 per kilo for their efforts. At that time, Jung only had one single engine Cessna. With Carlos as a copilot, it could carry 250 kilos each trip. That came to $500,000 per flight for doing something they both enjoyed.

By mid-May 1977, Escobar began constructing his second cocaine processing lab. This one was located on the eastern slopes of the Colombian Andes. He also started "encouraging" many of the remote farming communities to grow coca plants. A local supply of the tropical shrub would simplify his operations.

In a good way, a second laboratory was problematic. The combined labs would be able to produce more pure cocaine than his current methods were capable of transporting. Jung had added pilots and planes to fly the west coast route, but they maxed out at 600 kilos per week. Every month in Santa Marta, the Ochoa brothers were loading another three thousand kilos aboard their trawlers. With his new lab coming into play, Escobar needed to almost double his transports.

To help resolve the issue, Escobar asked Jung and Lehder if they might add more aircraft for trafficking to California. Carlos suggested an alternative. "Pablo, these past few months, I've had the opportunity to spend time with your partner, David Ochoa. Great guy! Twice visited with him at his ranch. He's come to know some important people in Nassau. According to David, his connections might be willing to provide assistance for a price. I've given it some thought. If we could arrange a safe passage through the Bahamas for planes, it would provide an entire new avenue for your cocaine."

Escobar thought for a moment. Over a year had passed since their first meeting, but he still remembered David talking about his political connections in the Bahamas. On the Atlantic coast, transportation had been his partner's side of the company. As an integral part of that, Luis and David had maintained excellent relations with the Bahamian authorities. No interference whatsoever and for a pitiful sum of payments. Those islands were so close to Florida, a small plane could fly there in an hour or less. Lots of that type of traffic to mix with once inside Florida's airspace. And there were dozens of small runways all over the state to choose from. Lehder's idea wasn't necessarily original, but it was definitely worth exploring. "Carlos, let's phone David."

The next day, both David and Jorge responded to Pablo's call for a conference concerning the Bahamas. Carlos laid out his scheme to use the islands as a way station for planes transporting from Colombia.

Surprisingly, David thought the plan could be easily accomplished and shared his reasoning with the group. "Pablo, I'm pretty sure we can use Windsor Field for this. Landed there several times to meet with my friends. It's Nassau's International Airport with lots of coming and going.

Customs inspectors are totally controlled by higher officials."

Carlos tried to be polite but wanted more details. "Just say so if I shouldn't ask but who are these friends of yours?"

"No. Perfectly alright Carlos. One is an attorney. Luis has worked with him on an occasion or two. The other is a business acquaintance I've come to know well. Played golf with him several times. Point is these two men are already on a secret retainer with our family. Political donations in a way because both are connected to the very top people in government."

Carlos and Escobar sensed David's reluctance to specially identify who his "friends" were, so Escobar cut right to the chase with the next question. "What's their name and who at the very top of the government?"

Before answering, David looked at Jorge for a second and received his brother's nod of approval. "Lawyer's name is Nigel Bowie. He's the legal representative for the Prime Minister. Other one is Everette Bannister. He and the minister have business relations."

"The Prime Minister of the Bahamas?" Carlos asked, surprised.

"Yes, Lynden Pindling himself. With the help of the country's banking system, we have been able to financially assist with some of his investments. Indirectly, of course, by working almost exclusively with Nigel and Everette. In return, when needed, our trawlers have used Freeport for refueling and even as a storm shelter."

Escobar wanted to learn more. "You said, 'almost exclusively,' David?"

"A few payments down the ladder. Always a handout in Freeport where the authorities are involved. Much like here in Colombia."

"Let's be perfectly clear about this," Carlos insisted. "Your friends can arrange for instructions to come from the top government official in the Bahamas that will allow aircraft coming from Colombia to land and refuel at Winsor field without inspections."

"Almost positive they can, Carlos. But it's probably going to cost us a lot more than the donations we're making now. It's an international airport, so even with orders from the government to leave your planes alone, some local customs and law enforcement officers will be looking for compensation. Count on it."

Escobar nodded a sign of approval. "I don't believe the amount we will have to pay them will be a problem. Timing is more important to me. How long will it take to set up a trial run or two?"

"Not sure, Pablo. Two or three weeks at least. Luis and I will have to go there and meet with Nigel and Everette. Once we have their clearance, we'll still have to visit with those in charge at Winsor Field. Some advance payments will be required for cooperation. Cash only! A little complicated maybe, but once everything is agreed to and bribes paid, you can try this whole idea out."

"Okay, you and Luis get started." Escobar thought for a moment and added. "Since this is his idea, I want Carlos to go with you. Introduce him to your friends. Afterwards Carlos, it's your responsibility to make this work for us."

"Trust me, Pablo. If it's doable, I'll make it work." Carlos paused to think for a moment. "But about that 'trial run' once everything is ready. Last night, I discussed the possibility of using the Bahamas for a new route with George. Just wanted his thoughts. He has a pilot friend that has flown in and out of Nassau several times. George says for the right amount of money, we could convince him to make the first flight or two. If anything goes wrong, he goes down, not Jung or I."

"Who is he?" Pablo asked.

"An American. His name is Barry Kane. Even better. He has his own plane."

"Good! Use him if you can." After looking around the table, Pablo decided it was time for some courtesy. "How does all of this suit you, Jorge?"

The reply came with a slight hint of annoyance. "Thought you would never ask, Pablo! I'm on board with the plan, but I have two suggestions."

"The Bahamas are your backyard, Jorge, and this involves the east coast of the states where we're partners. I welcome your advice."

"Then, here are my thoughts on sending David, Carlos, and Luis to meet with the minister's lawyer and business associate. Don't let them show up empty handed. In the past, we've made deposits to their private banking accounts using corresponding routing numbers. If we want their cooperation, place an advance payment to them in an amount they're going to appreciate. Whet their appetite with an investment of maybe $100,000 each. Afterwards, my bet is our envoys will be received with open arms."

"Consider it done. What's the other suggestion?"

"Our brother Fabio is in Miami and already involved with the handling of your cocaine once some of our runners bring it ashore from the trawlers. Doing very well at it I might add. He recently arranged for some shipments to be flown from Florida to a private airstrip in South Carolina. It serves as a safe point of distribution with vans then transporting south to Atlanta and north to Chicago or Detroit. After this Barry Kane refuels in Nassau, let him continue to the Carolina field and land there."

Escobar shook his head in approval. "You'll get no argument from me on that. Completes my aims for an overall integration of our cocaine business. I eventually want to control everything from the South American fields to the cities in the U.S."

"Couldn't agree more, Pablo, but don't you think that may have to exclude Jose Rodriguez?"

After he had just practically insisted on control from beginning to end, it wasn't an easy question for Escobar to answer. Nicknamed "The Mexican," Jose Gonzalo Rodriguez Gacha had begun an association with Pablo Escobar a year earlier by offering to establish the cooperation of a Mexican drug lord to traffic cocaine through Mexico to Houston, Texas. As well, and partly for that purpose, he and Escobar were in the early planning stages of constructing a third processing laboratory in Colombia's jungles of Caquetá. The labs' location was very remote but its proximity to both Ecuador and Peru offered a plentiful and convenient supply of cocaine paste. For these reasons, Escobar carefully answered Jorge's question.

"Rather than exclude Jose Rodriquez, I think the appropriate way to consider him is as a partner. I have Jung and Lehder working the west coast, you and your brothers on the east coast, and soon Rodriquez right in the center. Once we get our cocaine to Mexico, he has an agreement with Miguel Gallardo. Locals there call him 'El Padrino.' Because of his *take*, I'm not particularly happy having to go through him. But this bastard controls most of the Mexico-United States border. We either work with Gallardo, or someone else will."

"I understand. Better to have Jose as a friend rather than a competitor. Even if we're able to use the Bahamas, three laboratories refining cocaine will require lots of avenues into the U.S. The Mexican border is an open door. If Rodriquez is successful, he'll make a productive partner in your enterprise."

Pablo waved an open palm around the group looking for anything more to discuss. "Everything's settled then. We'll meet again when you three return from Nassau."

With that comment, Pablo and Carlos left. Jorge asked David if he had eaten. When David replied he hadn't, Jorge suggested they have dinner at the Don's restaurant.

The request wasn't out of the ordinary, but David could tell his brother's invitation was not about dinner. "What's bothering you, Jorge?"

"Maybe nothing, but it can wait until we get to Dad's place."

Thirty minutes later they were seated in a private room at the restaurant with drinks in hand and meals already ordered. David looked straight at his brother. "What is it?"

"I'm not sure. Just adding up everything that's happened since we partnered with Escobar. The enter-circle started with just six. It's been barely over a year, and we've added Jung, Carlos, and now this Jose Rodriguez. Nine seated at the 'King's Round Table.' As more of his cocaine comes available, probably extra partners will be needed."

"By 'King', you mean Pablo Escobar?"

"With three big processing labs, he will definitely be the king of cocaine in Colombia. Keep reminding myself what we're doing is illegal. Even being silent partners with someone so unequaled in this criminal enterprise might bring you, Fabio and I unwanted attention."

"But we're raking in money by the truck load. What are you proposing we do?"

"Where's Luis?"

"He's spending a few days with his family in Cartagena."

"Have him come back to Medellin. I'd like his legal opinion on our future when it comes to dealing with cocaine on such a large scale. I think we should discuss the risk before you're all off to the Bahamas."

"I'll have him here by tomorrow afternoon."

"Better make sure Luis tells Mitch he will be away in the Bahamas for a week or so. He's a family man now."

The following evening, Jorge and David updated Luis on Escobar's recent changes to operations. The main topics discussed were the soon to be completed second large cocaine lab in Colombia and adding the Bahamas and Mexico as smuggling routes. The latter required Jose Rodriguez as a new member. Jorge made clear his concerns. Were they getting too big? Discernable partners! Did the rewards justify the risk?

Luis responded with his typical air of calm and confidence. "Looking ahead for potential problems before it's too late is always smart, Jorge. That was the precaution followed when we first joined with Escobar. Let him run the show, but he also takes the fall if the authorities come into play. The same applies to Jung, Lehder, Rodriguez and anyone else Pablo decides to work with. Currently you, your brothers, and I remain somewhat anonymous while enjoying unimaginable compensation along with almost no chance of legal complications here in Colombia."

"In Colombia?" Jorge quoted Luis as a question.

Luis nodded in acknowledgement. "Yes, here! But not nearly as much in the U.S. At home we have lots of political influence. Whatever other problems arise we usually can solve with currency. The states are a different game altogether. Raymond Stansel, for example."

"What advice are you giving exactly?"

"Escobar wants David and I to help Carlos with the Bahamas in order to establish a new smuggling route. Go ahead with that plan but let Carlos act as jefe of the operation. Like here in Colombia with Escobar, we can assist but stay in the background. The authorities always look for the drug kingpin. In the Bahamas, let that be Carlos Lehder."

"Okay, your insights into how we continue working with Escobar without overly exposing ourselves eases my concerns. Use Carlos as an obvious culprit running things in case of a bust. Once his cocaine is transported inland to our east coast operations, Fabio is in charge of it. That's the high money end of the business, and we'll reap the benefits there. Do you have anything more to add?"

"Actually, I do, Jorge. Couple of things. One in particular because of what you just said. Fabio has started moving cocaine to major dealers as far north as Chicago. With a lot more coming in from the Bahamas, he will be the main supplier for the east coast. Millions in cash involved with every transaction. Fabio is going to need protection, and I mean a lot more than Juan and Diego can provide."

"He's only twenty," David said. "Gutsy as hell too. Provide as many men guarding Fabio as it takes to keep him safe. Make it a show of force so nobody is stupid enough to fools with our brother."

"Okay, David. I'll have Juan see to it."

Again, Jorge thanked Luis for the insight, especially when it came to looking after young Fabio. "You said there were a couple of things. What else?"

"The other has to do with me. I'm a family man now and because of that, I'd like to be more careful with my future. We started with marijuana. When I first met Raymond Stansel, he asked me if we were going to smuggle cocaine. The truth then was no. Now, and just three years later, we've added coke. In the beginning, my primary responsibilities were to recruit runners, organize and coordinate, and serve you guys in legal matters. I'd like to keep it that way."

"Understandable," Jorge replied. "You're like family, Luis. In fact, Dad asked about you just the other day. You've proven yourself perfect as both counselor and personnel recruiter. Carry on as before except that now you'll have to start finding pilots as well as seamen. Work with Lehder in the Bahamas as best you feel comfortable doing, but report to me or David just as you've always done. Stick primarily with the marijuana trade from our trawlers. Leave the cocaine in the islands to Carlos and distribution of it in the states to Fabio. Under that scenario, if any problems come up, I'll resolve them for you. Does this sound agreeable?"

"Absolutely, and thanks," Luis responded with an affirmative head shake. He thought, Michelle will be thankful too!

19.

BREACH OF TRUST

In Nassau and just prior to the end of May, David introduced Carlos Lehder to Nigel Bowie and Everette Banister. The request for the uninhibited passage of small planes coming from Colombia and landing at Winsor field was agreeable. It could be easily arranged, possibly because both men had already received the bank deposits Jorge had suggested. Carlos explained that those down payments were just the beginning of a rewarding relationship for them and the appropriate government official they might associate with. No name was mentioned but there was an understanding. Nigel showed his willingness to cooperate even more by scheduling meetings for Carlos with the two individuals responsible for airport security and customs. Apparently, Nigel had worked with these officials in the past. This time, his personal recommendation for their assistance was added for collaboration.

On returning to Colombia, Lehder reported to Escobar. He was literally overwhelmed with enthusiasm for operating out of the Bahamas. Told Pablo it would take more incentives, but they were buying the damn Prime Minister, and whatever else they might want.

Pablo liked the fervent brief so much that he suggested Carlos find a place of his own in the Bahamas. "If this turns out as good as you're saying it will, Carlos, I want you there with hands on every part of it. Buy yourself a beach house to work from."

Carlos thought for a moment. He liked the suggestion. "Good idea, Pablo. I'll look around for something."

Flying a Cessna 175 Skylark fitted with two eighteen-gallon auxiliary fuel tanks for additional range, Barry Kane made his first trip from a ranch in Colombia to Nassau International Airport. After a three hour layover to refuel, he continued to a small regional airport in South Carolina. His cargo was 250 kilos of Escobar's cocaine. Barry repeated the same journey a week later with 300 kilos. His successful flights in June 1977 had tested the cooperation of several Bahamian parties. Kane never flew another trip. Even so, he was the aviation pioneer who made the Bahamas one of Pablo Escobar's primary smuggling routes.

Luis and Juan focused on supplying marijuana and cocaine from the trawlers to runners. Fabio received all of the cocaine transfers and coordinated with Carlos to handle a steadily increasing amount of the drug arriving by airplanes. With the help of George Jung, Luis found and employed an experienced pilot for the Bahamas. His name was Jack Reed. Afterwards, Reed assumed the role of pilot recruitment. He was good at it.

Ironically, it was marijuana and Juan's familiarity with competitors smuggling it into Florida that would ultimately turn an island in the Bahamas into a famous cocaine passage to the United States. Jack often laid over in Miami once a trip was completed. At times, he, Luis and Juan dined together. On one such occasion, and because he knew Jack was always on the lookout for flyers, Juan mentioned there was an independent pilot flying Jamaican marijuana into Florida from a small island in the Bahamas. Since the island was remote and had a small landing strip, this guy had made it a convenient home for himself and his wife. His name was Edward Ward. And the island, located just 50 miles southeast of Nassau, was Norman Cay. Jack conveyed this information to Carlos suggesting he would try and meet with Ward. Instead, Carlos decided he would go along and check out both the pilot and the island.

Late February 1978, Carlos and Jack flew a Piper PA-18 Super Cub from Nassau to Norman Cay. Carlos took control of the aircraft. The trip required less than half-an-hour and the Piper Cub could land in 400 feet, so the small airstrip was more than sufficient. Coincidently on arrival, they taxied and parked next to another Super Cub. Turned out, it belonged to Ward.

Although the island was less than 290 acres in size, its amenities included a small hotel and restaurant. Carlos immediately loved the place and insisted they stay overnight. Except for a single cancelation, the hotel's cottages would not have been able to accommodate them. Tourist season was at its peak even on Norman Cay.

Jack and Carlos spent the better part of the day just tooling around the island's small residential community which consisted mostly of scattered beach front villas. Besides the short airstrip, there was a marina that afforded access by boat. On two separate occasions they encountered locals. Carlos introduced himself as Joe Lehder, a real estate developer looking at properties.

That evening at MacDuff's Bar & Grill, Jack and Carlos met with and convinced Edward Ward to fly for them. It should have been an easy accomplishment since the amount he would earn for each trip was ten times greater for pretty much doing the same thing as before. Just cocaine instead of marijuana.

Initially, Ward was hesitant. Carlos convinced him with an assurance that he could continue to fly from Norman Cay, not Nassau. The comment was a surprise to Jack, but he thought best to discuss it with Carlos on the return trip.

Next morning, Carlos had barely lifted the Piper Cub off the island's runway when he turned to Jack and asked, "Where's Luis? No. Never mind where! How soon can he get to Nassau?"

"Not Sure, Carlos, but his secretary is always able to reach him. I'll call when we land. In any case, no later than tomorrow afternoon if that will do? Is there a problem?"

"Yeah, there's a problem, but I think we just found the solution. Norman Cay! It's gotten so every time one of our planes lands in Nassau, a crowd appears with hands out. Word of our cargo has spread all the way down to ground crews. I'm not making this crap up. We're paying off baggage handlers."

"So instead, you want to use this island to land and refuel?"

"Hell, Jack! More than that." Carlos was trying to fly the Piper and contain his excitement. "The place is perfect and not just to layover for refueling. I believe we can make Norman Cay our personal 'Hub' right off the coast of Florida. No customs, police, or anyone else to worry about. Just a few sun loving locals. We can buy that marina and some houses. Buy the airstrip. Get Luis to Nassau. If we have to, we'll buy the whole damn island."

At eight the following morning, Luis was on a flight from Miami to Nassau. Carlos met him at customs. Two hours later they landed the Piper Cub for a second time on Norman Cay. During the flight, Carlos had explained his plans for the island but wanted Luis to see it first-hand. Following a four-hour tour of the grounds, and while they were returning to Nassau, Luis offered his recommendations.

"Carlos, when David started working with officials in the Bahamas, we needed a front company for the transfer of funds, both to officials here and back to our family's accounts in Colombia. In Nassau, we in-corporated a business called International Dutch Resources. Operates under the insignia IDA. It has deposits with three separate financial institutions, two in Nassau and one in Freeport. Totally safe and private under this country's banking statutes."

"So, we can use your IDA to buy property in Norman Cay?" Carlos asked.

"Absolutely! During the purchase phase, your ownership can be kept secret from the local population and without the slightest interference out of Nassau."

"Pablo suggested I buy myself a place in the Bahamas. I've found the perfect house on this island. A small estate really and right on the beach."

"If it's for sale, IDA can buy it and you can live there as the company's representative, at least until the marina and airstrip are acquired. Just stay friendly with people on the island as a prosperous developer until you have the controls necessary for your imports and exports. This will take time and patience, but it can be accomplished.

Carlos approved of Luis's strategy. By the end of May, the marina and two villas had been purchased. Also, a closing date was set for the airstrip's acquisition. Offers were made for the beach front estate Carlos wanted for himself, but the homeowners were not interested. For reasons never explained to anyone, the owner and his wife suddenly changed their mind and sold. Strange? Shortly after the airstrip's title transfer to IDA, Carlos also took possession of the estate. In June, smuggling cocaine began with the first plane arriving from Colombia. Norman Cay was fully operational by summer's end.

Pablo Escobar dominated the cocaine market out of Colombia by 1980. He had succeeded in this with the help of Medellin's Ochoa brothers. Escobar had infiltrated the United States from both the Pacific and Atlantic coast and through Mexico by way of Central America.

Luis, Juan, and Juanita remained active in Florida, but as requested, they were primarily responsible for offshore drug transfers from the trawlers. If cocaine was involved, Fabio was in charge once it came ashore. In this capacity, Luis often assisted Carlos Lehder in legal matters and investments arising out of the Norman Cay operations. Whenever he was not busy in Florida or the Bahamas, he made regular trips home where periodically, he reported to his real jefe, Jorge Ochoa. And of course, on every occasion there, to his wife, Michelle.

Recruitment of new personnel was an endeavor constantly pursued. Luis considered his acquaintance with Trevor Dunbar as one of the most successful in that regard. He told Juanita the boy had lots of potential and might grow with the organization as a loyal friend.

Actual proof of Luis's judgement of Trevor came as the unfortunate consequence of one of their runner's indiscretions with his fiancée. Trevor was at his Lake Murray home with Leann Fox, his new girlfriend. She was nine years older but real attractive, smart, and terrific in bed. Easter was two weeks away. Spring break time at the beach with surfside parties at night. For that, Trevor had made reservations for a four night-night stay at the Sand Castle in Ocean Drive Beach followed by a flight to Las Vegas for another six days of fun. Shows were already booked for their stay there with plenty of spare time allowed for winning at the blackjack tables. Leann could barely contain her excitement. She made no secret about her feelings for Trevor. Soon after they met, she wanted to move in with him.

Link had left early Saturday morning for a quick run to Port St. Lucie and a return on Sunday. It would be Trevor's turn to follow up with another trip two days later. Almost back-to-back runs but demand for marijuana always increased dramatically during spring break!

Trevor and Leann spent a quiet fireside evening together. The next day, Trevor suggested, "Let's get ready for Link to come back. Surprise him. I'm barbecuing spareribs tonight. His favorite, so invite his latest partner to join us for a cookout."

"Sounds perfect," Leann replied. "For sides, I'll make 'deviled eggs' and a big, tossed salad."

Trevor removed overcooked ribs from the grill at eight that night. Link had not arrived. Link's date and Leann left at ten. There were some circumstances such as weather, that at times prevented transfers either from the trawlers or the marina. Delays occasionally happened. Trevor was concerned but only because Link had not called as he was supposed to do. Trevor spent a restless night.

Whenever Link was on the road, his cocaine habit was always something Trevor worried about. Link argued it kept him sharp and alert, but his usage was daily now. The dependency was obvious.

By ten on Monday morning Trevor was debating whether to start making calls. If Link had crashed on the highway, he could be lying in some hospital, or worse. A bad car accident most likely would have exposed his cargo. Then, much to Trevor's relief, his private phone with the unlisted number rang. Had to be Link calling but as always, Trevor answered with a simple "hello."

It wasn't Link. "Sorry to disturb you but I'm trying to reach Thomas Boyce. My name is Charles Whitfield, his attorney. Although we've never met, it's important I talk with him."

Trevor cautiously responded wondering how Whitfield came by his private phone number. "This is Thomas Boyce."

"Mr. Boyce, I'm afraid I have some bad news for you. It's about your brother. Richard has been arrested in Florida on drug charges."

"Damn! Where in Florida? Is he hurt?" Trevor was thinking it was a car crash for sure.

"Jacksonville. He's in jail, not a hospital. The information I have comes this morning from a young lawyer the authorities provided him. His last name was Calloway. Said Richard did not resist the police when he was apprehended, so he was not injured. This lawyer wanted to represent him, but Richard insisted Calloway call me instead."

"Mr. Whitfield, we've both memorized your phone number in case of emergencies like this. What do we do now?"

"Great question but call me Charles if you like. I'll explain where we are at this point. Afterwards, we can discuss what I think we should do going forward. From what Calloway told me, during interrogation yesterday, your brother remained completely silent. Even though he had asked for legal representation from the start, attempts to get him to talk without an attorney present lasted from 2 p.m. to after 8 p.m. that night."

Trevor asked, "Can they do that? What about his Miranda rights?"

"Legally not! But they have the advantage of denial. Just because they are the law doesn't mean they always follow it. To be honest, proving something like that would most likely boil down to Richard's word against theirs. Unfortunately, that's not uncommon in drug cases, especially with these DEA guys. Some of them think they're above it all. Fact is, in court sometimes, it seems they are. I've been there! Consequently, without an attorney to interfere, they are real good at threatening the seizure of everything you've ever owned and putting you away for 15 or 20 years. They can break a hardened criminal into turning on a next-of-kin. When caught by the DEA, most dealers spill everything they know."

"Not Richard, Mr. Whitfield."

"Apparently not. Kept his mouth shut, almost like he was trained. They ended by placing him in a holding cell overnight. Brought your brother back for more questioning this morning. Introduced this Calloway lawyer into the interrogation room to represent him. Richard must be smart as hell or well-rehearsed. Right off he asked for attorney-client privacy. Cops granted it probably thinking he was about to break. Instead, when there were just the two of them in the room, he gave my name and number to Calloway with instructions to call. Nothing more. Even this Calloway couldn't get anything else out of him. The attorney called and that's where it stands now. Any questions Thomas?"

"One for sure. If he was only brought in this morning, how did the lawyer know all that you just told me?"

"Remember the DEA guys brought this lawyer in. You never know who they have in their pockets. They could have caught Calloway smoking a joint in some bathroom. Convince him his license to practice was on the line unless he helped out occasionally. Crap like that happens. Before I phoned you, I took the liberty of contacting a good attorney in Jacksonville. Friend of mine. In the sixties, we were at USC law school together. His name is Robert Newsom. Goes by Bobby. I suggest we bring him in to replace Calloway right away."

"Okay, do it. What happens next? How do we get Richard out of jail?"

"He has to be arraigned within forty-eight hours of his arrest. No priors that I'm aware of which is good. Still however, if he was caught with a substantial amount of schedule one drugs, bail could be set pretty high. Often depends on the judge he appears before."

"What's the worst-case?"

"My friend in Jacksonville would know. I can ask him."

"No. Just give me a ballpark figure for now."

"Okay, then. Between ten and twenty-five thousand I'd guess. If Richard can offer some collateral, a bail bondsman only needs ten percent of that amount."

"No bondsman, Charles. Use the trust account we set up for you to draw your retainer. I'll place an extra fifty thousand more in that account today. Wire Mr. Newsom whatever he needs to get Richard released. Send a retainer for him as well. An amount that will gain his respect. Withdraw an equal amount for yourself. You've earned it."

"Mr. Boyce, I must say, it's a pleasure working for you."

"Thanks! When can I talk to my brother?"

"After paying bail, processing takes four to six hours. If they caught Richard while driving, they would have impounded his car. Bobby can take him to his office and have him call you from there. We can have a rental car waiting for him. I'm betting he'll be free by tomorrow afternoon."

"Okay, call me if there are any problems. Otherwise, I'll be waiting to hear from Richard. Once we've talked, I'll get back to you. One more question I need to know. Can he leave Florida?"

"I'll have an answer for you tomorrow after the arraignment. Depends on whether the court makes it a condition of the bond. In cases like this, they often will not allow the accused to leave the state."

After a trip to the bank where he transferred cash from savings to the Whitfield trust account, Trevor returned home and spent an anxious evening. Several drinks of Jack Daniels didn't seem to help. He convinced himself it was Link's coke habit that caused him to be caught. Overconfident, pulled over for speeding, and the officer could tell he was high on drugs. Made sense, so he wondered if he should call Russell. Why? Nothing they could do to help and there was no way to connect them because Link would never squeal. Sleepless night and up at 6am with coffee before finally deciding to hunker down and wait for Link to call.

Trevor's unlisted phone rang late that afternoon. He answered immediately with one word, "Link?"

"Yeah, man, it's me."

"You okay?"

"Lot better now, Trevor. I'm in a lawyer's office. Jacksonville. Guess you heard, huh?"

"Mr. Whitfield called yesterday. Said you were locked up in Jacksonville. Glad you're out. What the hell happened, Link? Bad luck?"

"I don't think 'luck' had any part in this. That's why I first need to know if you've talked to anyone except our lawyer?"

"Not a soul. Should I have?"

"No! Hell no! I've had nearly two days in a cell to think about this. We were ratted out. No doubt about it."

Trevor was still thinking the arrest was Link's fault. "How can you say that? No finks on our team. We're all tight friends."

"You'll believe me when I tell you how it went down. Twenty miles south of Jacksonville, I passed two sheriff cars sitting on my side of I 95. Wasn't speeding or nothing, but looking back in the mirror, I saw both of them taking off behind me like gangbusters. Next thing I saw were blue lights flashing about a mile ahead. Traffic in front of was waved through. When my turn came, I was stopped cold with damn guns pointed at me. Trevor, it was Sunday for Christ's sake!"

"Means they were waiting and watching for you."

"You think?" Link replied sarcastically. "There's more. Lots more. I was pulled out of the car headfirst and shoved to the pavement. Two cops sat on me. Another one twisted my arms back and snapped handcuffs on. Rough as hell too! They treated me like I was some kind of Al Capone."

"Why? Whitfield said you didn't resist."

"On the way to his office, I told this lawyer, Bobby, about it. He said in drug bust, they often do something like that on purpose to scare the hell out of you. He's right about that. They had my butt shaking."

"I had no idea what you went through."

"Not finished. Story gets better from here though. Puts a nail in the coffin about being ratted out."

"Let's have it. Everything, Link, so I'll know what to do here. I'm sitting at Lake Murray with 300 kilos under the boathouse along with a lot of our cash."

"Try this on for size. While I'm laying cuffed on the side of the interstate, they surround my car like a swarm of termites. Opened both rear doors, pulled back the mat, flipped the latches, and lifted the seat. A couple of them whistled. The rest laughed. Trevor, they never even looked in the trunk. They knew!"

"This story is getting worse, not better. Got me worried now."

"Maybe not, Partner. Give me a second and you'll see why, at least where you're concerned. Some of these guys weren't with the local law. Had on blue jackets with DEA on the back. You could tell they were the ones in charge, especially when two of them dragged me into the rear seat of a black sedan. Bumped the hell out of my head by throwing me inside. I still have a knot to prove it."

There was a short pause before Link continued. He was still stressed out. "We took off in this sedan. One sheriff car in front with lights flashing again. Followed him all the way to a big downtown building where I was booked and photographed."

Trevor tried to calm Link a little. "Must have thought you really were Al Capone. Have to get you a tommy gun when this is over."

"Sounds about right. I could have used one the way those DEA jerks rough me up. Listen up though. Not through yet because I'm coming to the important part. During that trip downtown they screwed up. One in front sitting shotgun reported on his radio. To his boss, I think. Overheard him saying, 'got one of them loaded for bear and we've put out an APB for his brother.' I knew right then and there to keep my mouth shut no matter what. They thought we were Thomas and Richard Boyce. Brothers. Go figure where they got that from. No clue who we really were."

"Crap!" Trevor complained. "Means it has to be one of Russell's gang."

"Think dammit! That's something I did sitting in a jail cell. If they took one of his team down, they got all four. Our friends in Port Saint Lucie turned on us, probably to save their own asses."

Trevor went silent. He thought, Russell too. Shit! Thank God none of them knew our real names. Or where we were from for that matter. Thinking back even more, except for Luis, I might have told them.

"You still there? Say something, Trevor!"

"Still here. Just pissed off. More than pissed off if I ever get to any of those bastards."

"Well, maybe someday we'll get even. Before I forget, there is one more thing this big man up front said to his boss. Must have thought I was stupid or deft. Went something like this. 'Yeah, everything's set for Saturday morning with the coast guard. We'll get them. Count on it. Besides, we'll have everyone else rounded up before then.' Trevor, I think Russell and crew spilled everything. I'm just the first one they busted."

"You're right. This DEA force is not through yet. They want everybody."

"Not finished with me for certain. Bobby says I'll have to go to trial, but the courts are busy, so it's set for six months from now. Any time before then, they may offer a plea bargain. Still have to go before a judge though. Court has to approve everything from now on."

"That'll be in Florida, so Whitfield can't help much. What did you tell Mr. Newsom?"

"The story we rehearsed a dozen times thanks to Kenneth. I'm Richard Boyce from Melbourne. Follow instructions I get by phone to drive cars back and forth from Florida to South Carolina. Suspect I'm hauling marijuana but never ask. Need the money."

"Did Mr. Newsom believe you?"

"Hell no! He's too smart for that, but he liked the whole thing and said to stick with it. Unless a prosecutor can prove otherwise, my trips made me a small naive player in the operation. The DEA is after the big fish, not taxi drivers. Bobby thinks a judge and jury might see it the same way."

"I remember that's how Kenneth saw it too. Miss him sometimes, like now. He was awfully sharp for a white man. Bet your sweet ass Link, nothing like this ever happened when we were driving for him."

"No, but that's wishful thinking now. Bobby says I can't leave Florida. Comes with my release on bail. The law took all the cash I was carrying, but he supplied me with plenty plus a rental car. Said the money came by wire from Whitfield."

"Yeah, Link. I took care of that for you. Fifty grand was added to our lawyer's trust account, but I'm glad he's on our side. What now?"

"Put up at a hotel tonight. Tomorrow morning, I have to go to the Duval County pound. They even locked my lab up. After I get him out, Newsom says go home. He thinks that's Melbourne. He wants me to stay there and keep out of trouble."

"For how long? You said the trial was six months from now."

"I guess I'm a Florida resident until then. No phone though. Newsom says I should make all calls from a public telephone booth. Both to him and anyone else. Especially you or Whitfield."

"Good advice."

"Think so too. I'm going to take it. Make it a vacation from work. Maybe spend a few weeks in the Keys. That counts as staying in Florida. Chase around some. I'll have to stay in touch with you for cash and news. I can get the money through Newsom again."

"Okay. I'll keep you informed on whatever goes down on this end. And Link, better watch that coke crap. If you're caught with a sniff of it, they could lock you up and throw the keys away. Stay straight. Call tomorrow when you get settled in Melbourne. Right now, I need to call someone myself."

Trevor debated who he should call next. Whitfield or Luis? Decided on Luis and dialed his Miami office number. A woman answered. "Bufete de abogados Castillo. Juanita hablando."

Trevor responded in English.

"Juanita, my name is Trevor Dunbar. I would like to speak to Mr. Castillo."

The reply came back in perfect English. "Mr. Dunbar, so nice to hear from you. May I tell Mr. Castillo the nature of your call?"

"Yes, please say it's important. Urgent in fact!"

"Very well, Mr. Dunbar. Unfortunately, he is out of the office at the moment. I can have him return your call if that is convenient?"

"Si, Gracias. As soon as possible, Juanita. Do you have my private number?"

"Si. No tomará mucho tiempo."

Trevor wished he had called Whitfield first. Thought dammit! Nothing to do now but wait. Have to keep the line free. His phone rang after only five minutes passed. This time he answered, "Thomas Boyce."

"Good afternoon, Trevor. This is Luis. My secretary says you need to speak with me?"

Yes sir, if you can spare a few minutes. Maybe more? I think it's important or I would not have bothered you."

"Perfectly alright. I have some time. What is it?"

As briefly as he could, Trevor began to recount the events of the past two days. He included in detail the stop and search of Link's car near Jacksonville. Next, he repeated what Link had overheard the DEA agent say over the radio while being transported to jail."

Up until that point, Luis had listened without interrupting. "Excuse me, Trevor! Are you sure Link heard the man say something to the effect that 'we'll get them with the guard Saturday morning?' Absolutely certain? The day before Easter?"

"Yes sir, I'm certain. But Luis, the officer's thought Link was Richard Boyce. Still do!" He was carrying all the proper identification for that. And, they have an APB out for Thomas Boyce."

"Mierda!" Luis responded. "They know you just by your fake names. Sorry to say we know where that had to have come from. Maldita sea! Esto es jodidamente malo."

The reaction surprised Trevor. Luis was speaking in English and cursing in Spanish. "Yes sir, I think we do. Link said nothing to the contrary. Actually, he's convinced they sold us out."

"I'm certain too. Where is your friend, Link, now?"

"Lawyered up yesterday and made bail this afternoon. Funny in a way. Even his attorney thinks he's Richard Boyce. Link is going back to our place in Melbourne and laying low. For months probably because his trial is set half-a-year from now. I'll be looking out for him and act as his only contact for a while. For talks, on the advice of his attorney, he can only use pay phones."

"And you. What's your plan?"

"Almost the same. Shutting down everything. Play it cool just in case. I have a 'safe house' not too far away. Completely fireproof. Move my inventory into storage there and enjoy an honest civilian life until this mess blows over. If that's okay with you, of course?"

"Definitely okay! Right thing to do. And Trevor, I want to thank you for keeping me informed. The part about Saturday morning is especially important. I'll have Juan look into the problem with our friends in Port Saint Lucie. You and Link stay out of it. Comprender?"

"Yes sir."

"If you need to get in touch, continue to do so through my secretary. She can contact me wherever I might be."

"I'm feeling better already, Luis. Just wish all this had not happened."

"Sorry for your troubles. Crap like this comes with the business we're in. Just two more things I want you to know. For sure now, you'll have to visit us in the Bahamas, but only after all this is over. That will take some time. I'll let you know when. Not sure about the other but we may be able to help Link with his legal problems."

"He would be grateful for any assistance, I'm betting. As for a visit with you after taking a hit like this, relaxing on a sunny beach alongside some bikini girls sounds like a winner."

Luis laughed. "Hasta entonces, amigo."

The conversation with Luis was exactly what Trevor needed. An assurance of help with what he now considered a betrayal by friends. Guess you never know, but he could not believe Russell was in on it too. Lesson learned.

One more call to make before five. Whitfield. Some catching up to do, so Trevor dialed the number. The secretary put him through immediately. He and Whitfield talked for about ten minutes. Newsom had kept his old classmate well informed, so most of the conversation dealt with a question Trevor asked. What Link might expect if he went to trial?

"Thomas, they have to prove Richard is more than just a driver. If that's all they have, he could wind up with a light sentence. Some jail time but short and followed by probation."

"That's an outcome I think Richard could live with, Charles." Trevor was thinking a few months in jail might be good for Link. Get him off the cocaine.

"One problem with that scenario, Thomas. Bobby has a source in the district's US attorney's office. Lady friend if you know what I mean. She tells him they're going to introduce witnesses against Richard. The purpose will be to convince a judge or jury that he was a major dealer of marijuana. If convicted as one, it could mean some serious time."

"Did Mr. Newsom say 'witnesses' like more than one?

"I asked that same question. The answer was in the affirmative. Several in fact."

"Several," Whitfield had said. Trevor wished he had known this before he talked with Luis. A final clue to include Russell and all the rest. Decided he would call Juanita and let her pass it along to Luis. No time to waste either. Needed to stay safe. Tomorrow morning, he would start moving everything to his cabin on Lake Wateree. Afterwards, he would let his dealers know "TB" was out of business. Explain that shutting down just when everything was great can't be helped. His source was busted. True enough when he thought about it.

"Anything else, Mr. Whitfield?"

"Not at this time. I'll be working closely with Bobby. Both of us are experienced in cases like this, so rest assured we'll do our best for your brother. We have months to prepare. Lots can change between now and then. I'll keep you posted."

"I'll count on that. Thank you. Call this number anytime. I have a message machine in case there's no answer. Also, if I'm going to be away, I'll provide that information to your office secretary."

Five uneventful days passed. Trevor was more or less at ease in his Lake Murray home since he had removed the marijuana and cash to his cabin. Kenneth had built a well-hidden storage compartment beneath the pump house concrete slab. Once everything was sealed inside, locked down and covered with an assortment of tools and fishing gear, it was secure as Fort Knox. The pump house itself was constructed of reinforced concrete blocks and a locked metal door. Kenneth had referred to it as "fireproof" in more ways than one. Trevor copied the reference.

It was a little past one in the afternoon and Trevor was returning from grocery shopping at the A&P. He was trying to resume a drug free normal life. Bringing home steaks, potatoes, and salad fixings to have with his date, Leann. Even though the relationship was just a few weeks old, they were becoming pretty tight. Easter holiday together at the beach and the trip to Las Vegas were still in the works.

Good too that Link was confined to Florida and could not join them in Vegas. He often traveled there. Along with coke, Link had gained an addiction to gambling and lost most of his income made from dealing the marijuana. He compensated for losing with an attitude that there was always more where that came from.

Plan for the night was to enjoy the lake view while cooking out on the patio. Afterwards, a slow cruise in his boat followed with wine and fireside time on the couch. Leann considered such occasions very special. In truth, it was a routine Trevor had used with several others. The shopping trip took a little less than an hour, but there were two phone messages waiting. Both were from Mr. Whitfield requesting a call back.

Trevor complied and the secretary answered. "Mr. Boyce, I'll put you right through. He's expecting your call."

Seconds later, "Thomas, sorry to bother you but I have some news I need to share."

"Good or bad, Mr. Whitfield?"

"Not good I'm afraid. Some

of this comes from the *Miami Herald*. The rest is from Bobby. According to his friend and news releases by the district attorney's office in Jacksonville, Richard's arrest was part of a much larger sting operation carried out over the past several days. Apparently, it was implemented as the result of a joint investigative effort by the AUSA, the FDLE, and the DEA. Several drug dealers have been arrested."

"Trevor lied. "Good grief! Link just drives a car. Had some marijuana in it. Not a big deal."

"This district attorney will be charging Richard as a major drug dealer. Besides your brother, they caught two guys supplying marijuana in Miami, another working the keys, and three more responsible for distribution in North Florida. They claimed the latter bunch concentrated sales in the universities."

"And they think Richard is a part of all that?"

"Yes."

"Can they prove it?"

"Probably, or this AUSA for the middle district would not be praising himself to the newspaper reporters. Bobby knows him. Says he's in his late thirties and ambitious as hell. Wants to be a governor or a US senator someday. Could be trying to use this as a political steppingstone."

"What the hell is an AUSA?"

"I'm sorry, Thomas. Stands for Assistant United States Attorney. He's a federal prosecutor."

"Does he have a name?"

"Albert Turner. He claims they have confessions from some of those arrested, and says they are willing to plead guilty along with testifying against the others. Almost certainly "plea deals,' if it's true. And there's one more thing to this prosecutor's story that supposedly connects them all together. The marijuana. All the same. 'Colombia Gold' was the term the paper used. Headline stuff. Story ran on the front page."

"Yeah, Charles. Sounds like he has a bunch of rats trying to save their own tails. Spill their guts if they have to. Will any of this change Richard's bail status?"

"No. He was lucky in a way. Richard was the first one arrested. The sting operation was just getting started, so they kept quiet about it during his arraignment. Bail was set at twenty thousand. He was released before all hell broke loose."

"Well, thank god for small favors. Is that all of this mess?"

"Almost, but not quite. May not be important. Bobby said they missed one."

"Me, you think? After all Richard and I are brothers."

Whitfield chuckled. "No, not you, Thomas. At least I don't think so unless the shoe fits. Missed the big fish! Word out was they never caught the main person running the whole thing. Bobby's source told him somebody or something very important sure as hell got away clean."

Trevor had taken notes of his conversation with Whitfield. Minutes after they hung up, he called Luis's office. In considerable detail, he passed on all the developments to Juanita. Took fifteen minutes because of all the questions she asked. When they finished, she politely thanked him. "Mr. Dunbar, Luis appreciates your help in these matters. Please call anytime and have a nice evening."

Out of work for the first time in years, Trevor could not remember having a more enjoyable Easter season. It was a religious holiday, but it came with Leann and the beach stay, their trip to Las Vegas, dining out, outdoor barbecues with neighborhood friends at Lake Murray, and sleeping with her most nights. Before bedtime, she liked to sniff a little coke. Didn't bother Trevor because afterwards, she was fantastic. Six months later, she moved in with him permanently.

20.

THE DEA

Shortly after retiring from a twenty-year career with the marine corps, Eric Stogner was employed as a U.S. government drug enforcement officer. His qualifications included three tours in Vietnam. The year was 1974. The organization he joined was brand new. It was the brainchild of Richard Nixon in an effort to stop substance abuse in the U.S.

Special agent Stogner spent four years working in the administration's New York Field Division before he was reassigned to a Miami based task force. Eric was to be part of a drug interdiction assignment code named "Operation Stopgap." Having joined the DEA when it was first formed, he was senior to the other agents there, and as such, reported directly to the Chief of Operations.

On the second day of March 1979, a Florida state parole officer identifying himself as Mark Timmons called asking to speak with someone in charge of drug enforcement. Eric took the call and listened to the officer's report of a possible smuggling operation being carried out on the coast of Florida. Coastal smuggling was nothing new, the task force was understaffed, overworked, and the information this guy was providing was not firsthand.

If not for the fact that Mr. Timmons was with the state's corrections department, Eric might have just thanked him for the call and lied that he would follow up on the story. Instead, and because Timmons was located in Miami, David requested his address and offered to visit with him the next day.

Mark Timmons was married to Amy Grayson Timmons. Amy's sister, Ruth, worked as a nurse in the Port Saint Lucie hospital. Her best friend was Tiffany who also was a nurse working in the same hospital. Tiffany was engaged to a young man named Eddie Hanson. The wedding was scheduled to take place in May. Ruth was to be maid of honor. It was considered a good union in the eyes of Tiffany's parents. Eddie was a mechanic specializing in watercraft motors, and he was also one of the partners in a highly successful marina located in Port Saint Lucie.

Eddie and Tiffany were recreational users of marijuana. They particularly enjoyed smoking some before and during sex. Eddie had debated if he should share a secret with his wife-to-be. The secret was he smuggled marijuana. One night after intimacy in bed, he decided it was best for her to know now rather than find out later. Tiffany, being somewhat naïve and maybe because she was a little stoned at the time, didn't seem too concerned. Said it was okay but just didn't want her parents to find out. Good enough Eddie thought. Glad he told her.

Of course, and only a few days later, Tiffany confided in her best friend. Ruth was apprehensive and later shared her worries with her sister. Amy asked her husband's advice. Mark was a sworn officer of the law. Consequently, he made a call to the DEA.

Eric sat in Mark Timmons' office the morning after he had called.

Took notes as Mark described the connections leading to his report. Eric tried to hide his male based skepticism. A chain of what appeared to be gossipy women were involved, and Mark's account wasn't firsthand. Christ, it was fourth hand. With all the stacks of work already piled on his desk, Eric wasn't sure he wanted to bring it up in his next meeting with his boss. On second thought a marina with offshore access was part of the story. Because the DEA had administrative subpoena authority, it would be easy to check out the bank records of Eddie Hanson. David decided to do that first. If something suspicious showed up, he would take it higher. Towards the end, it went much higher!

March 8th, the DEA rented a waterfront home on Manatee Pocket directly across from the St. Lucie Marina. Working eight hour shifts from inside the house, a two-man surveillance team using cameras fitted with telescopic lenses began recording all movements in and out of the marina. Surveillance continued for three weeks.

One of the DEA's favorite paths to catching a crook was simple. Follow the money! In Port Saint Lucie, Eddie Hanson had established savings and checking accounts in both TD Bank and Sunset Bank. In twelve months, he had made separate deposits into each of the four accounts. Added together, the deposits totaled $187,000. Both banks also had safety deposit boxes in Eddie's name which he had accessed half-a-dozen times each over the past year.

The DEA had search warrants issued for the St. Lucie Marina on April 2nd. Eric was the lead agent assigned to the case. From the weeks of photography, he already knew what serving the warrants would find. The marina was being used as a cover for smuggling marijuana.

Four individuals operated the marina. One was Eddie Hanson. The others were Ronald Hall, Steven Grigsby, and Russell McKinnon. All were young men still in their twenties. Bank records showed each of them were making a huge amount of money. The surveillance revealed these men made regular offshore trips in a 34-foot Bayliner and afterwards returned to the marina with a substantial cargo which they always off-loaded at night. By agents observing and counting, the weight of a single shipment was estimated to be two thousand pounds.

The bank deposits along with three weeks of observation records were sufficient for the search warrant, but there was more. On many evenings after the marina was locked and closed, cars and vans were allowed to enter and drive inside the warehouse. All of the cars had Florida plates enabling the DEA to identify its owner and trace each back to counties across the entire state.

Eric decided to have the warrant served during a time when these men were engaged with unloading a cargo. The opportunity occurred on April 4th. At 11:30 p.m. under the cover of night after cutting through the fence, eight heavily armed drug enforcement agents entered on the far- right side of the marina grounds. Two agents remained at the front of the warehouse. The rest divided and quietly walked on each side of the building towards its waterfront docks. Rounding the warehouse corner,

Eric watched as Ronnie pushed a loaded dolly through the rear door of the building. Three of the agents followed Ronnie but waited just outside for Eric's signal to enter. Russell was emerging from the Bayliner's cabin with both arms beneath two ten kilo bales of marijuana. Eric waved a "go" to all agents. He and two others simply walked out and approached Russell just as he was placing his twenty kilos onto another dolly. While holding out his badge in his left hand and his marine issued M1911 Colt 45 in his right, Eric calmly said. "Russell McKinnon, raise your hands and turn around. You're under arrest."

Inside, towards the back of the warehouse, agents had found Eddie and Steve stacking Ronnie's haul of marijuana behind a false wall. All three were placed under arrest without resistance. It was a classic takedown conducted solely by a well-trained DEA staff. Quiet and without fanfare for a reason. Several more arrests were anticipated. The four men were transported to the St. Lucie County Jail. Chief of operations for the DEA had prearranged for them to be held there for questioning in separate holding rooms. The DEA agents informed sheriff officers there that the men were advised of their Miranda rights when arrested. A bit odd because Russell was the only one who repeatedly requested a lawyer.

Consequently, Eddie first, then Steve and Ronnie broke down. By 6am the next morning, they had signed confessions and were charged with multiple violations of the "Comprehensive Drug Abuse, Prevention, And Control Substance Act." At 9 a.m. that morning, Russell was confronted with his friend's admissions of guilt and their accusations that he was the boss of operations. An attorney supplied to represent Russell advised him that a reduced sentence might be arranged if he was willing to cooperate with the authorities. Russell broke too.

About the same time Russell gave up, legal representation was brought in for Ronnie, Steve, and Eddie. With confessions in hand, plea deal discussions began. With signed confessions, the DEA was in complete control. For the group's referral, they had named the defendants "The Gang of Four."

Literally, having been caught in the act with so much marijuana, Russell and friends had very little in the way of options. Total cooperation meant the difference between recommended leniency for first offenders and serving three to five, or a more punitive sentence of fifteen years without the possibility of parole. Basically, a no-brainer! All they had to do was help the DEA catch everybody involved. Double cross everyone they had worked with, especially if the person or persons, whoever they might be, could be taken down as the drug Kingpins. In effect, in less than twelve hours, four young men had gone from very rich successful smugglers to poor stoolies for law enforcement. Even with that, all still faced hard time in prison. With the promise of reduced sentences for full cooperation, they were released on bail after being arraigned.

Saturday afternoon on April 8th, Link arrived at Russell's home for an overnight stay. He, Ronnie, and Russell had a late dinner at their favorite restaurant before driving to the marina warehouse. There they packed twelve bales of Colombian Gold under his rear seat compartment. Sunday morning at 8 a.m., Link started home on his usual I 95 route. Trevor was scheduled for the next run in another two days. Link's mind was focused on spending a week or more in Vegas. Girls and cards to enjoy, plenty of money to spend, and not a worry in the world.

Until the day before, the DEA plan was to allow Richard Boyce to travel back to his destination in South Carolina. With a detailed description of the car and its Florida plates, they had arranged for him to be followed by an unmarked police car once he crossed the Carolina state line. The DEA wanted to trace by who and where the marijuana was distributed. Transporting across state lines made Richard and associates a prime catch. In the interim, they had several more fish-to-fry and all of those in Florida.

Great plan. Unfortunately, leaks and politics prevented its execution. AUSA Albert Turner received a call from a court-appointed attorney in St. Lucie, Florida. The caller was Tony Mathis. He was more than just a friend. Much more! Albert was married with two kids, but the two men had enjoyed some good times while attending conventions in Tallahassee and Miami. And they were planning to spend some evenings together during the 1980's primaries. The relationship was extremely secretive considering Albert's family status and his political ambitions.

"Albert, this is Tony. How are you, my friend?"

"Very well, Tony, and you? A nice surprise to hear from you. Everything alright?"

"Couldn't be better. Have you got a moment? I have something to share with you."

"Sure, I always have time for you. Looking forward to those primaries next year. What is it?"

Tony explained how he was brought in to represent some young men accused of smuggling marijuana. Laughed because he arrived too late to help them. The DEA already had signed confessions from three. "Here's the part you may be interested in. It's a big operation covering all of Florida and then some. These guys have been nicknamed 'The Gang of Four' by the agents."

Turner laughed. "Attention getter. The title will make great headlines. Those drug agents love that kind of stuff."

"Yeah, but the DEA is keeping all of this quiet for the time being. They flipped these men with the promise of a plea deal. In the next few days, they're planning to use them to bust dealers from one end of the state to the other. Only then will they let it out to the papers."

Who's running the show for the DEA?"

"In Port Saint Lucie, special agent Eric Stogner. I met him at the jail. A former marine, Albert. Tough guy and the senior agent working out of the Miami office."

"Means he answers to the Chief of Operations there. That's Jason Sanders. He's a wimpy political appointee by Nixon. They put him in charge of something called 'Operation Stopgap' about a year ago. I can make one call to the district office in Miami. After that, he will answer to me."

"So, I was right, Albert. You're interested in becoming involved."

"The public exposure for a federal prosecutor in something this newsworthy could be exactly what I need Tony. Remember two years back what the newspapers made of the 'Night Train' seizure. Front page news for a week. This 'Gang of Four' has the same ring to it. If I can manage obtaining the prosecutor's role, you're in for my personal thanks during the primaries next year."

Tony gave a brief laugh. "Sounds really good, but that's a year away. I have to be in Jacksonville the first week of September. Criminal case. I'm defending the bad guy as usual. Trial starts Monday morning, so I'm arriving on Sunday and staying at the Hilton for at least a week or so. Maybe we could get together?"

"You bet! I'd like that. See you soon and thanks for this tip. I owe you one." The last part was Albert's favorite political goodbye.

Turner buzzed his secretary. "Lori, get me Helen Alston on the phone. Say it's important."

Minutes later, USDA for Florida's southern district called. "Good morning, Albert. What's so important?"

Turner explained the recent capture of some drug smugglers working out of St. Port Lucie with more arrests to come across the state. The charges were federal crimes, so he requested to be appointed lead prosecutor. To contain everything in Florida, Turner asked her to contact Jason Sanders for that purpose.

Since Albert Turner was central district AUSA and located in Jacksonville, Alston wondered how he came by so much information. Sometimes it was better not to ask. Besides, she loved the idea. "I'll have Sanders contact you before lunch time. He'll delegate final authority in this operation to you, Albert. As such, you will please keep me informed."

"Agreed and thank you Helen. I owe you one."

On April 7th, two days before Link was to return to South Carolina, DEA Chief of Operations phoned special agent Stogner with new instructions as to how future operations would be carried out. Richard Boyce was to be arrested prior to crossing into Georgia. His arrest and others were to be part of a joint operation between the US attorney's

Jacksonville office, the FDLE, and the DEA. As well, the Duval County sheriff's office would assist.

To no avail, Eric argued how the change might affect the scope of the marijuana's distribution network. Too many agencies in the takedowns and word would get out. Once the papers got involved, the game was over. Every dealer, at one end or the other, big or little, would either disappear or lawyer up. Jason Sanders interrupted him before he was finished with his protest.

"Sorry, Eric, but not my decision or yours. Orders come from above our grade. The USDA here in Miami and backed up by the Department of Justice in Atlanta. The federal prosecutor you'll be working under is AUSA Albert Turner. He's located in Jacksonville and expecting your call. Make it!"

In Eric's six years with the DEA, this was not the first-time political influence had interfered with drug investigations. Included hi-ups in both the Justice Department and the State Department. Reasoned it was like Vietnam in a way. Commanders sitting at their desk in some safe base of operations and sending out orders to marines in the fields. Often with tragic consequences. Idiocy, but Eric was trained as a marine. He followed orders and called Albert Turner.

At 6am April 9th, USCGC *Steadfast* was cruising counter drug patrol thirty miles southeast of Key West. Commander Winston Tyler was captain in command and on the bridge. Lieutenant Hal Timmons stepped inside, saluted, and handed a communication from the Command Master Chief Sector Miami, Captain Joseph Altman. Orders were to proceed to US Coast Guard Station Fort Lauderdale and remain docked there until further instructions.

Three days later, and hours prior to the *Steadfast* departing Station Fort Lauderdale, Eric Stogner, one other DEA agent, and two FDLE officers were taken aboard. The mission orders were to arrive at a lat/long location sixty miles east of Port St. Lucie on Saturday morning, April 15th. where they were to intercept the fishing trawler, *Paso Seguro*; board the ship and conduct a search and seizure operation. The interdiction was based on actionable intelligence that the *Paso Seguro* was a "mother vessel" trafficking large amounts of illicit drugs.

As the sun rose Saturday morning, Commander Tyler allowed Eric to come on the bridge. At 8 a.m. the *Paso Seguro* was sighted 4,000 meters to starboard. Perfect timing Eric thought watching with binoculars glued as they circled towards his prey. Appropriate way to think of the approach since the *Steadfast* was nicknamed "*El Tiburon Blanco.*" Spanish for "*The White Shark.*"

USCGC *Steadfast* closed and its crew prepared for a show of force. It's two M2HB 50 caliber machine guns were locked and loaded. Force wasn't needed. The trawler hauled in its nets, stopped engines, and prepared to be boarded. With a broad smile and a salute, Captain Rene Perez welcomed the guard's heavily armed boarding party. Eric, with his colt 45 holstered under the left shoulder, was last to climb on deck.

Nine hours later, Captain Perez's warm greetings were understandable. A thorough search covering every inch of his ship found no weapons, twenty-two cases of Dos Carreras beer, twelve 750 ml bottles of Aguardiente, eight 750ml bottles of rum and, in the captain's quarters, two boxes of Cohiba Maduro 5 cigars. In addition, the trawler's hole held ice covering an estimated 20,000 pounds of unsorted snapper, mackerel, red grouper, amberjack, and tuna.

That evening, Eric sat in the officer's mess of the *Steadfast* wishing he had confiscated one of those bottles of rum. Needed a stiff drink. Several maybe. Could not believe his "Gang of Four" had lied about their source. No way. They were too scared. More likely, and just like he had warned Jason, too damn many people got involved. All it took was one rotten apple in the barrel. Game over!

Onboard the *Paso Seguro*, Juan spoke to Captain Perez. "Gracias capitana por el cigarro Cubano. Necesito llamar a Luis por radio ahora. Todo fue bien."

Captain Perez saluted Juan and nodded in agreement. "Juan, por favor transmite mi agradecimiento a Luis y a nuestro patrón."

"Si, lo hare," Juan replied and returned the salute.

Eric had no idea it was his communication with Jason, while ferrying Link to jail, that let the cat out of the bag. When Trevor called Luis, the key words spoken were "brothers" and "Saturday morning." Only Russell knew to meet with the *Paso Seguro* Saturday morning. In fact, he had complained about the timing because it was the day before Easter. That, and because he still thought Link and Trevor were brothers. Too obvious. The DEA agent sitting shotgun in the car, with Link in the back seat, had to have flipped Russell. All his team as well.

Any mistakes made by Russell and crew were Luis's responsibility. He had recruited them. Jorge and David would easily write off the loss of the marijuana if it were dumped overboard. Came with the business. The cocaine was another problem altogether. The ship's hole held 3,000 kilos. To Escobar, that was worth nearly 90 million dollars. Damn that cocaine, Luis thought.

Luis had few choices. The *Paso Seguro* was in the early stages of a voyage along the U.S. coast. The reason its cargo hole was still full. Option one was to make a run for it and try to reach port back home where they could safely offload. But if the DEA knew about Saturday, they knew the ship's identity and that it was laden with drugs. Colombia was 1500 miles away. The ship would probably be spotted by their aircraft before it was past the keys.

Norman Cay was option two and only a few hundred miles. Didn't matter though. If the *Paso Seguro* headed there, it might still be spotted and stopped. Even if she made it to the island, the possibility of bringing attention to the place would piss Carlos off. That could prove to be a serious mistake.

Luis wondered if there might be another way. Hide the damn stuff somewhere. Lots of ships out there. Maybe there was a possibility that, under the cover of night, they could make an undetected offload of the cargo to another ship and then let the *Paso Seguro* stay on course. Tricky? One way to find out.

By radio to the *Paso Seguro*, Luis asked Captain Perez if his idea of a transfer of the drugs at sea was plausible.

"Not only can we do it, Patron, we passed by just the ship to make an exchange with a few hours ago. *Isabella*. I've known it's captain for years, but he just fishes. Family man out of Puerto Rico. Never has anything to do with our business, so I'm thinking it might be hard to convince him to help us."

Luis's reply to Captain Perez was something rehearsed. A quote from a movie he had watched twice. "Rene, 'I'll make him an offer he can't refuse!' We have associates in Puerto Rico."

Thursday morning at 4 a.m., Juan and three crewmen left Norman Cay, Bahamas in a 26-foot Sea Ray Sundancer. They powered it's 260HP engine up to 25 knots with a WNW heading. At 3 p.m. that day, roughly 120 miles east of Fort Pierce, Florida they made an arranged rendezvous with the fishing trawler *Isabella*. Juan and one other left the Sea Ray and went aboard.

Isabella's captain was Arturo Lopez. A commercial fisherman with thirty years of experience. His home port was Mayaguez, Puerto Rico, but the Gulf Stream along the Florida coast was a paradise for a mid-water stern fishing trawler. In just nine days the ship's catch was mostly snapper, but it included an assortment of other fish. 20,000 lbs in total weight Now, however, Isabella's nets were hauled in. Captain Lopez had been radioed instructions to follow. He and his crew were to come along-side the *Paso Seguro* that night and prepare to swap cargo. They would be rewarded for their assistance. Considerably more than the value of their fish. Noncompliance was not a choice. Any refusal and the captain and his family would suffer deadly consequences. That part of the radio communication was made crystal clear.

Thursday night, April 12th, between 8 and 10 p.m., the crew of the *Paso Seguro* lifted by crane from the hole of the ship to its deck eighteen pallets of marijuana and twenty-three crates of cocaine. Around midnight, Captain Perez positioned his trawler alongside *Isabella's* starboard. Once the two ships were securely moored, the crew of the *Isabella* transferred its cargo of fish to the hole of the *Paso Seguro*. Two hours later, Captain Perez's crew transferred their ship's marijuana and cocaine from its deck to the hole of the *Isabella*. As well, a cache of weapons was taken aboard along with four armed guards. By 4 a.m., securing lines were detached, the crews of both ships waved off, and the *Isabella* set course for the Bahamas. Juan stayed behind on the *Paso Seguro*. Captain Perez ordered engines ahead slow towards a lat/long point 60 miles from the coast of Florida. For a bit of humor and disguise, he had the crew lower nets and begin trawling. Lastly, he and Juan radioed to Luis, "mission complete."

Jason Sanders phoned Albert Turner's home at 6pm Saturday night. He gave the assigned prosecutor some bad news. They had not interdicted a "mother ship" as planned. Instead, they had searched the fishing trawler suspected of being one and found nothing but fish.

AUSA Turner did not hide his disappointment. He spoke harshly back to Sanders criticizing the DEA's incompetence and abruptly hung up the phone. Turner had already prepared a news release that now would have to be scrapped. Still, he had the "Gang of Four" plus a half dozen other marijuana dealers across the state. Lots of court appearances and news interviews to come. He thought. Damn right! This was still his chance to move well up into the political world.

The *Isabella* arrived off the coast of Norman Cay four hours before sunup Monday morning. The day before, the crew had celebrated an Easter feast in the ship's galley. Their conversation was one of anticipation. What would they be rewarded for helping the *Paso Seguro*?

A barge towed from Norman Cay's marina was used to transfer *Isabella's* new cargo. When its crane was lifting the last 480 kilo pallet of marijuana to the barge, an armed gunman handed Captain Lopez a duffel bag. With a very serious tone while looking directly into Arturo's eyes, he said. "Un pequeño agradecimiento de mi jefe. Por supuesto capitán, tú y tus hombres saben que esto nunca sucedió."

Arturo nodded. "Si, entiendo amigo."

Two hours after daybreak, Captain Lopez set course for Puerto Rico. At noon, he and crew gathered on the bridge of the *Isabella*. Arturo opened the duffel bag. With wide eyes, they counted $400,000 US dollars. All in $100 bills. An hour of laughter and back slaps followed along with passing bottles of Aguardiente and smoking Cohiba Maduro cigars. Last-minute gifts from Captain Perez.

It was an unbelievable good fortune for fishermen only familiar with extremely low wages. For whatever it was worth, and before they were allowed to leave the bridge, Captain Lopez repeated to each of his crew the warning of the gunman who delivered the money. "Toda esta maldita cosa nunca sucedió. Comprender?" Each nodded obediently.

Beautiful weather on Norman Cay the next day. At breakfast, Luis received a request to come for a poolside visit with Carlos. Polite instructions to arrive at 3 p.m. Luis knew the reason he was wanted, so he came prepared to explain events of the past two weeks. Essentially everything that forced the recovery and transport of *Paso Seguro's* cargo to Norman Cay.

Carlos Lehder was an intelligent, generally well mannered, thirty-year-old man.

He considered himself handsome and a lady charmer. Recently however, his addiction to cocaine began to interfere with not only his natural gifts but his judgements as well. Increasingly, Carlos proved to be too ambitious and authoritarian. When those two traits were mixed in with an abuse of cocaine, he became intolerant.

Surprisingly, Luis's explanation of how the *Paso Seguro* was betrayed by some young smugglers he had recruited went over well with Carlos. He agreed Escobar would have been very upset to lose such a large amount of cocaine at once. None was but the close call reinforced Lehder's belief that sea going ships may be an appropriate way to transport marijuana into the states, but not cocaine. Marijuana was bulky and the same weight of cocaine was sixty times more valuable. Small planes carrying three hundred kilos at a time were much safer. Especially now that he had a secure island only 250 miles off Florida's coast.

Basically, Lehder thought using aircraft from his very own island was revolutionary to the business. He made this point clear to Luis suggesting using the trawlers only for marijuana.

Luis acknowledged the instructions. "I understand, Carlos. I'm scheduled back in Colombia Friday. I'll discuss your recommendations with Pablo and Jorge."

Because Luis's conversation with Carlos was going much better than expected, he took the opportunity to mention his appreciation of the information provided by two loyal runners. Luis referred to both of them by their real names. Trever Dunbar and Link Rollins. "Carlos, their information may have saved the *Paso Seguro*, it's cargo, and the crew. They did this even when one was arrested with a substantial amount of marijuana and the other was forced to close down to remain safe."

"You want to repay their loyalty?" Carlos asked.

"Yes, but not with money. Something else."

"What then?"

"I would like for Juan to assist with preventing the one called Link from going to court. Remove the threat of him having to face a judge and possibly serving time in prison."

Carlos knew what type of assistance Luis was referring to. "You don't need my permission for this. Have Juan see to it. If he needs help, get them from my guards here. Repaying Link's loyalty is a good thing. What about the other?"

"The one named Trevor is an American black, very smart, and speaks Spanish fluently. He invented an interesting method of remaining practically invisible while transporting and selling large amounts of marijuana. I think, with our encouragement, he would be willing to forget the 'bulky' stuff and become an asset to your cocaine shipments into the states."

Carlos thought for a moment. "Perhaps I should meet Trevor. I don't suppose he can fly?"

"No, I don't think so, but no doubt he would be a fast learner."

"Let things settle down a little, Luis. Best we do not draw attention to ourselves. Wait a few months and then invite him for a stay here with us. Use your recruiting skills to make sure he enjoys the more pleasurable rewards of joining my organization."

Luis smiled at those commands. Exactly what he was leading Carlos to say. Replied as if ordered. "Consider it done. I'll keep you informed with Juan's assignment. We have time on our side, so not right away. But rest assured those who turned on us will pay dearly."

"We always repay disloyalty, Luis. Harshly! No exceptions."

Three weeks passed before Luis returned from Colombia to Norman Cay. Spent the time in Cartagena with Michelle and his son. The day after he arrived back on Norman Cay, Juan came from Miami. That same afternoon Luis drove a new Land Rover Santana to the island's airstrip. Juan followed behind in an identical Land Rover. They were there to welcome and ferry guests arriving from Colombia.

Fernando Arenas, Lehder's personal pilot, easily landed his Cessna Citation ll with 400 feet to spare. The airstrip had been extended to 3,300 feet. Fernando's passengers were six young attractive girls. All Colombians. Early on, Lehder had used his home for polite social gatherings, often including a Bahamian official or two. Regularly now however, his island paradise 'parties' were becoming well known for sexual entertainment. Tonight was just such an occasion and particularly because of certain guests. They included the deputy to Bahamas' governor general, two senate cabinet ministers, and the public relations assistant to the Bahamas' prime minister. Carlos kept several ladies on the island for the occasional visitor, but these new arrivals were trained professionals brought in for the special entertainment of exceptional guests. Carlos considered the girls a business expense. It was an enjoyable part of maintaining his secure base of operations.

21.

JUDICIAL INFLUENCE

Albert Turner could not be more pleased with himself. The *Miami Herald* had front paged his role in the capture of "The Gang of Four" and all subsequent arrests. Ten defendants in total. As lead prosecutor, his name and picture were often part of the paper's story. Still, a little over two months passed before Turner was able to persuade a federal judge to allow a deposition from one of the accused. Russell McKinnon. It was a conditional examination of a defendant in the case of a serious felony. The judge granted it only after being convinced Mr. McKinnon was also a material witness whose life might be in danger.

July 12th at 9 a.m. AUSA Albert Turner, lawyer for the accused, Tony Mathis, Miami DEA Chief of Operations, Jason Sanders, a court appointed administrator and a court reporter all gathered in Port St. Lucie's courthouse. A conference room on the second floor was made available for a deposition in the case of *United States* v. *Russell McKinnon Et Al.* The meeting was canceled at 10:30 a.m. Russell McKinnon did not appear as subpoenaed. An arrest warrant was issued that afternoon.

At 6 p.m. the same day, two US marshals, Eric Stogner, and two FDLA officers arrived at Russell's home in Port Salerno. Overkill for sure, Eric thought. Two cars were parked outside. One of the marshals knocked, then loudly announced himself at the door. No response from inside, so he repeated his presence adding, "Russell McKinnon, we have a warrant for your arrest. Open up!"

Not five seconds later, the two marshals went shoulder to shoulder and busted through the front door. Within minutes, with guns drawn and all of the law officers searching together room by room, they confirmed the house was empty. Obviously missing were some clothes, shoes, dresser items, and so forth. Apparently, Russell had packed and left. Convincing evidence of that was the Santa Cruz 28 Express was not at his dock.

Eric radioed the report to Jason Sanders. By 7:30 p.m., an all-points bulletin had been issued for Russell. As well, the coast guard was asked to search for the 28-foot watercraft.

An hour later, Eric and another DEA agent followed up Russell's disappearance by going to the bayside condo Steve and Eddie shared. There was no answer at the door, but it wasn't locked. Once inside, it was obvious to both agents the place was empty. Like Russell, the occupants had packed and left.

Eric found the same story at Ronnie's home. A check of plates showed that one of the cars parked in Russell's driveway belonged to Ronnie. The DEA's "Gang of Four" was missing. They had evidently left together by sea. So much for a judge imposing house arrest as their condition of bail. They didn't skip town in a boat. They probably skipped the country in one!

Eric passed what was now very bad news to his boss. Early the next morning, Jason phoned Albert Turner. He forced himself to listen to the AUSA scream minutes of profanity laced accusations. Jason tried to convince Turner the fugitives would be found. In return, he received more cursing with an assurance that his position with the DEA depended on exactly that outcome.

With Turner's threat, Sanders decided to remind the bastard that days ago, the *Herald* ran an article about Russell McKinnon's upcoming deposition. "Supposedly came from an anonymous source in your office, Mr. prosecutor. In the drug business, leaks like that make someone about to testify very nervous. Put yourself in their shoes and maybe you might think twice about staying around?"

Turner abruptly ended the conversation with a discourteous, "I'll try to forget you said that, Sanders. Goodbye!" Afterwards, he sat in his office agonizing over the developments. Of course, he could blame incompetence on the authorities, but through claims to the papers, he had made himself a part of that group. Instead, as prosecutor, he had to figure a way to play an escape by "The Gang of Four" to his advantage.

Turner still had six defendants to parade in front of reporters. Plus, because of all the time required to go to court, busting these drug dealers had moved to short articles in the back pages of the papers. Maybe? Just maybe play up this big escape! Front page news again. A movie he liked gave him an idea. Make the "Gang Of Four" into another *Bonnie and Clyde*. Use his friend with the *Miami Herald* for the story and make himself into Texas Ranger Frank Hammer. Legend material that the public would love. Damn right. Turner phoned his friend at the *Herald*.

There was a not so small problem with the prosecutor's theatrical plan. The analogy wouldn't work. His Bonnie and Clyde were already dead!

Two days prior to Russell's deposition, a 1975 Dodge Tradesman Van pulled up in front of Eddie's and Steve's condo. It was 1 a.m. Juan, Diego, and two Colombian nationals from Norman Cay stepped out. The Van's driver left with instructions to return in half an hour. Juan and the others quietly went to the front entrance. A minute later, one had picked the door's deadbolt.

Eddie and Steve were asleep in separate bedrooms on the second floor. After ascending the stairs, the four men separated into pairs. Juan and Diego crept up next to Eddie. He was snoring in a sound sleep. With efficiency, Juan slipped a garrote fashioned with wooden handles attached to a short length of piano wire around Eddie's neck. A brief but almost silent struggle followed. Juan was incredibly strong. In twenty seconds, Eddie was dead. The two Colombians in the other bedroom duplicated the procedure on Steve.

Both bodies were rolled in heavy plastic sheets and carried downstairs. For another fifteen minutes, Juan supervised the packing of clothing and other personal items until he was satisfied the pair appeared to have left for a trip. The van returned and backed to within a few yards of the condo. Quiet, dark night, and not a soul in sight. The driver signaled an "all clear." Eddie and Steve along with luggage were loaded through the van's side door. Juan checked to make sure there was not a hint of foul play. He was last to leave and purposely left the front door unlocked.

At 2:15 a.m. the van pulled to the front of Ronnie's home. Three men got out this time and again the van's driver left with instructions to return in half an hour. Inside, the house lights were on and music was playing. Juan stood on the porch and looked through a window. Ronnie was sitting at a counter bar stool listening, having a drink, and apparently smoking a joint. Juan gave a soft knock. Ronnie, perhaps because he was stoned, not thinking about the time, carelessly answered by opening the door. The three men pushed him back inside with Juan pointing a pistol in Ronnie's face. Diego calmly asked if anyone else was there. Ronnie's eyes teared as he nodded. "No sir, just me. Please Juan, don't shoot!"

Diego knew exactly what to say. "Don't worry, Ronnie. Cooperate and we won't hurt you. But listen carefully. You have to get out of town. Tonight! Do you understand?"

Ronnie's hand wiped a tear before he nodded again.

Thirty minutes passed. All of them came out of the house just as the van returned. Diego and one of the Colombians held Ronnie under each arm. Both carried some of his luggage. In a fairly rough manner, they pushed Ronnie into the back seat of his own car. Diego sat beside him while the other placed Ronnie's luggage in the trunk. Juan went to the side window of the van and spoke to the driver. "Siguenos amigo pero no muy de cerca, retrocede cien metros."

The driver replied "Si, Jefe."

Juan entered the driver side of Ronnie's car. As he was starting it, Diego decided to assure his scared hostage once more that he would be fine. "Amigo, you and your friends are going on a long vacation. Getting away from all this mess you're in. You're all packed. We'll meet with Luis after we pick up Russell. Relax and trust us."

Like clockwork ten minutes later, Ronnie's car slowly entered Russell's driveway. Juan purposely parked it directly in front. Including Ronnie, four men got out. The house was dark, but the porchlight was on. One man walked to the back of the house while Juan and Diego went to the front door with Ronnie. They lean on either side while Ronnie stood in front of the peephole ringing the doorbell. Waited and rang it again before lights came on with the sound of footsteps inside. Once at the door, Russell yelled, "Who the hell is it?"

"It's me, man. Open up! Gotta talk to you."

Russell knew the voice but looked through the peephole to make sure. Saw Ronnie and recognized his car, then unlocked the deadbolt and opened the door. End of story.

At 4:30 that morning well before daybreak, Russell's 28-foot Express Cruiser passed through the Saint Lucie Inlet. Juan was at the helm with Diego and two Colombians as crew. Inside, lying on the cabin floor were "The Gang of Four." All were dead. As the sun cleared the horizon two hours later, the cruiser met with a familiar 26-foot Sea Ray Sundancer. Two men aboard the Sea Ray were busy chumming the waters. Sharks were everywhere in a feeding frenzy. Russell first, then Ronnie, Steve and Eddie were lifted overboard. The pace of the sharks churning the water increased dramatically. Lasted five or six minutes before it was over.

One of the men on the Sea Ray passed Juan a chainsaw. Two pulls and it cranked. Juan sliced through the hull of the cruiser twice. Water came pouring in as he, Diego, and the rest climbed aboard the Sundancer and watched the other boat sink. The assignment was complete.

The Sea Ray's bow was aligned SSE. Its engine was revved to a speed of 25 knots. Five hours and a little over one hundred miles later, Juan, Diego, and the four Colombians from Norman Cay were seated at a bar in Freeport. All were laughing and drinking. Juan took time from the celebration to call Luis and report how well the mission went. Luis reported their success to Carlos. Luis still wasn't finished. There was more to come, the Colombian way.

Private detective Jerry Anderson worked out of a four-story office building near the upper east side of Miami. There he occupied a bottom floor space of 320 square feet consisting of a small reception area without a receptionist and a door to his equally small private office in the rear. Not the best part of town for certain but all he could afford. Generally, he was hired by family law firms, which accounted for most of his working time being spent proving spousal infidelity. He was damn good at it after twenty plus years in the business. Even so, Jerry made a living and nothing more.

Jerry's circumstances changed on July 22, 1979, when an attractive middle-aged Spanish woman walked into his office unannounced. She introduced herself as Juanita Aguero. Unknown to Jerry, her real sur-name was Juanita Macarro. Ms. Aguero explained herself as the assistant to an attorney who specialized in sensitive cases on behalf of very wealthy clients. Her visit today involved just such a situation. "Mr. Anderson, if you're available, I'm prepared to offer you an exclusive retainer."

Jerry hid the fact that he was more than just available. Office rent was past due, no customers, and he was running short of funds. Tried to play it cool while hoping the retainer she spoke of would cover his debts. "Ms. Aguero, I may be able to accommodate your attorney by setting aside a few things, but of course I'll have to know a few details before I can accept."

"Very well, Mr. Anderson. This job requires surveillance of a high-pro-file individual. A public figure in fact. The purpose of watching him is straight forward. We will need documentation of improprieties that are extremely damaging to his reputation and can be used in court if necessary."

Holy cow, Jerry thought. The woman knows her business. Be careful. "Sounds as though this case has political overtones, Ms. Aguero, and may I call you Juanita?"

"Yes, is the answer to both your questions. But this also ties back into married with family as well."

"Family man," Jerry said with a slight smile knowing the answer to his next question. "What sort of documentation do you require?"

Juanita returned his smile. "Photographs, Jerry. The very embarrass-ing kind. I checked. You have the equipment and a reputation for this sort of thing."

"So, you're looking for dirt on a public figure. Does this person have a reputation of misbehaving with women outside of his marriage?"

"I have no idea, but he's a young man and travels a lot. If nothing turns up, offering him those temptations might be required. The very young irresistible type. I can provide that if necessary. I have nothing more to add, Mr. Anderson. Do you want the job or not?"

"Yes! But can I ask for an advance, please."

Juanita removed two thick manilla envelopes from her tote. "Two things, Jerry. My employer requires complete anonymity, so payments and reimbursements will be in cash. To your advantage, nothing will be reported to the IRS."

With his eyes focused on the envelopes, Jerry answered with anticipation. "I'm good with that. What else?"

"Before you accept this retainer, understand when my employer buys your services, he is the sole owner of your findings. No copies for yourself or anyone else. Total confidentiality. Do not, under any circumstances, break that trust. For your sake, I hope that's clear if you agree?"

"Yes, absolutely! Jerry was tempted to reach for the envelopes. Thankfully, he did not have to. Juanita handed both across the desk and waited for him to open the first. Lifting an unsealed tab, Jerry looked inside at $100 bills, then whistled out loud asking, "How much is this?"

"Twelve thousand, five hundred in each envelope. And Jerry, his name is Albert Turner. Florida's middle district AUSA, Albert Turner. He's stationed in Jacksonville. Is that a problem?"

Jerry knew who Albert Turner was. Pictures of him along with his name had been in all the papers. Did not care one bit. For twenty-five thousand, he would have spied on President Carter in bed. Simple answer back. "No, not in the least."

Juanita continued with instructions. "Pack plenty of clothes and start tomorrow. You will be working in Jacksonville for as long as this takes. A hotel room at the Hilton will have been booked in your name. All expenses while you're there will be fully reimbursed."

"How do I stay in touch, Juanita? Can I have your phone number?"

"No! I'll phone you at the hotel for reports. Once a week on Sundays at 6 a.m. The retainer is yours to keep. Produce what we want, and I'll double that amount. I have to go. I'll call you this next Sunday in Jacksonville. Be available at 6 a.m."

Juanita stood, shook hands, and left. Jerry was shouting inside himself. Thought, "Mother of God!" All these years in the business busting my butt to barely break even. Finally, an angel walks in and lays $25,000 on my old worn-out desk. Whatever it takes, I'll make this client happy.

Mid July, Trevor returned home from a two-week stay at an oceanfront house in Cherry Grove, South Carolina. The first week included the 4th along with the usual holiday crowd. Leann enjoyed every minute, even though there was only a sprinkling of their race on the beach. But times were changing. Some late-night parties made the experience exceptional, and inaugural plans were being made for a large "Black Bike Rally" the next year. Trevor was thinking of buying a canal home there for more regular visits. Do a little ocean fishing plus join in the rally.

There were three messages on the recorder. All were from Whitfield the previous day. Trevor phoned the attorney's office. As always, his secretary answered. Like a recording each time, "Mr. Boyce, he's expecting your call. I'll put you right through."

"Thomas, glad you phoned me back. I have some news from Bobby to share. Good news for a change I believe."

"Great! Let's hear it."

"As you know your brother's trial is still two months away. Bobby has been preparing one hell of a defense for Richard. Yesterday's Florida papers headlined what he described as a blow to the prosecution's case. Ready for this?"

"Hell yeah. Fire away. I'm all ears."

"Looks like their witnesses skipped out on them. Maybe even left the country. The so-called "Gang of Four' is on the lam! According to the paper, they cruised right by the Port St. Lucie coast guard station and out to sea in one of their boats."

Trevor laughed out loud. Knew better to comment but couldn't resist sharing something with his attorney. "Mr. Whitfield, they left in a Santa Cruz 28 Express Cruiser. I know it well. By now, they're probably somewhere in the Bahamas. Refuel there and they can island hop all the way to South America."

"Well and good for Richard if they're not caught. They still have him in 'possession,' but without witnesses to the contrary, his story of just being an innocent driver trying to make a living might play well in a trial. The prosecution will object to each of Bobby's choices, but he's determined to have some of Richard's own race on the jury."

"I'll pass all of this on to Richard. He's catching some rays in Key West. Getting blacker by the day. Got himself a local squeeze too."

"Staying clean, I hope." Whitfield added.

"Me too, Charles. Keep me in the loop if anything changes."

Jerry Anderson arrived at the Hilton in Jacksonville July 24th. Ran a day late because of loose ends in Miami. Some of the equipment he needed for this job was in hock to a pawn shop. Retrieved everything!

Besides two cases and a duffel bag, the desk clerk noticed Jerry's cameras and video equipment. Ask if he was a reporter.

"Yes, for a magazine, not the papers," Jerry lied. "I'll be on assignment here in Jacksonville for a while. Trying to do a story about your city."

As it turned out, there was some truth in Jerry's lie to the clerk. The part about being there for a while. Since he was on expenses, he had leased a late model Ford LTD for two weeks. When the lease expired, he had to extend it for another four weeks.

This Albert Turner was a tough assignment. He reported as much to Juanita each time she checked in. Jerry established the man's routines the first few days of surveillance. Eight to six on weekdays at the office. Lunched with associates but never with his secretary or any of the other feminine assistants. Plenty of good-looking ones around his office too.

Albert spent weekends with his wife and kids. Softball and soccer with the latter. Over the period of not quite a month, he observed one night of dining out with his wife and a couple of movies with her. Guy went to church every Sunday with his family, kept the home's yard immaculate, and walked the dog every evening. After some time, watching him on weekends was a waste of Jerry's time. He decided that Sundays were when he could take a day to himself. Daylight hours at least. Needed the rest but all he could think about was losing the bonus Juanita promised.

Jerry had exposed rolls of camera film. Nothing to show for it. This AUSA was a model spouse. Five weeks had passed, and he began to wonder if even the last resort Juanita had suggested would work on this angel of a husband. There were kids but now maybe he was impotent? Thought it was time to ask Juanita for help. If that didn't work, nothing would. It was Sunday and he could tell she was not pleased with his report that morning.

Later the same day, Jerry's luck took a huge turn for the better. In the mid-afternoon, he was relaxing in the hotel lobby reading something on page three of the *Herald* about a Miami store robbery. He happened to look up as two men passed by. They were going to the elevators. Caught completely off guard, Jerry thought, what-the-hell? One of the men was Albert Turner. As they entered the elevator, they looked at each other, then reached out and held hands. The realization of what he had observed was like being struck by lightning. Explained everything!

Twenty plus years of experience kicked into high gear. Jerry watched the elevator lights. Stopped on the third floor. He took the stairs. Two cleaning carts were in the hallway with housekeepers in adjoining rooms. Walked to his left all the way to the end of the hall. A couple of lunch trays outside of rooms but otherwise nothing stirring. Jerry turned around. Halfway down past the elevators, there was a doorknob with a "Do Not Disturb" tagged on it. Room 307. Looking back to make sure all was clear, Jerry knelt beside the door pretending to tie his shoe. Could not discern what they were saying but two men were talking to each other. A half minute later, it was quiet. Muffle sounds began. Jerry recognized the noises.

Jerry left and went to his room on the first floor where he retrieved his camera and VHS camcorder. Carried both to his car in the parking lot. Looked around the lot until he recognized Turner's black Lincoln near the front entrance of the hotel. Thinking for a few seconds on how to obtain the best view, he drove his LTD to an open space across the lot where he could park at an angle to the Lincoln. He positioned the lens of the camcorder in his ford's window and raised the glass tight to hole it in place. Next, he fixed a mid-size telescopic lens to his camera. He waited about forty-five minutes.

Turner and his friend came out the front entrance together. Jerry started recording and then photographing. He figured they were probably going to dinner or something. He was wrong. Both went to the driver's side of the Lincoln. Turner unlocked its door and sat down. His friend looked over both shoulders, then turned back, leaned inside and kissed AUSA Albert Turner. The show of affection left no doubt about the relationship.

Anderson had a week before he reported to Juanita again. He wanted a lot more than a kiss. Not nearly enough! Tarnish Turner's reputation a little but Juanita also wanted something she might use in court.

Jerry had always been amazed how easily a twenty-dollar bill would persuade a low-level hotel desk clerk. The man's name in room 307 was Tony Mathis. He had arrived that afternoon from Port St. Lucie and had reservations for a week. Perfect, Jerry thought. Complaining about his parking lot view from the first floor, and with the help of another twenty, the desk clerk changed Jerry to room 309. He made the move an hour later.

There was no guarantee Turner and Mathis would meet again over the next week. If they did, it would most likely be at the Hilton. Jerry had stayed there over a month. Except for the top floor, all the rooms were the same. On entering, two queen size beds with headboards and end tables were always placed on the left side so that they were not against the same wall in the adjoining room. Obvious reason for that. Opposite the beds, rooms were furnished with an entertainment center holding a television in the middle and shelving on either side and below. Nothing else but a small coffee table next to the window with two chairs.

The detective had requested room 309 for a good reason. Mostly from experience gained in motels, he was an expert at installing cameras from an adjoining room. His duffle bag held the tools and equipment for accomplishing that. It was a simple procedure, but when done properly it required some effort on his part.

Jerry rose early the next morning and waited for Mathis to leave. Afterwards, he still had to wait for housekeeping to come and clean. When they finished and left, he used a tape measure to determine the exact spacing of the entertainment center from both ends of his room. Its placement in the adjoining room would measure the same except for being on the opposite side. Next, he pulled his bed with the attached headboard from the wall. With a lead pencil, he marked where each end of the entertainment center would be in the adjoining room. Then, using a "stud finder," he located and marked the interior studs behind the sheetrock.

Jerry double checked every measurement. When satisfied with its accuracy, he was ready to cut and drill. With a saber saw, he sliced out a ten-inch square of sheetrock from where the headboard had been. On the opposite side, where sheetrock was facing the adjoining room, he used his drill fitted with a "hole saw" to cut a perfect one and half inch circular hole. Once through that side of sheetrock, he continued to drill through the thin wooden rear of the entertainment center. Peeping through into Mathis's room, his measurements proved to be accurate. His entrance hole was in the back and just to the left-center of an open shelf beneath the television set. It offered a perfect view of the room's beds and then some.

One last step and he was finished. Jerry removed a 10inch by10 inch wood framed container from his duffel. Both its front and back ends were left open allowing him to place his Pentax camera neatly inside its corked padded interior. The camera had a three-foot cable for a shutter release switch attached. He slid the container through the square he had cut in the sheet rock. With that square cut to the same size as the container, the fit was firm and stable. He knew it would be. Done this before, just not in a Hilton. Finally, Jerry adjusted the lens of the Pentax to slip slightly inside the hole cut through the back of the entertainment center. The shutter release cable-switch hung outside with two feet to spare.

His work was complete. With the press of a button on the cable switch, Jerry could very quietly photograph any activities in the adjoining room.

He pushed his bed and headboard back against the wall. There was not a sign of the damage exposed.

All Jerry had to do now was hope and wait for a little cooperation from Tony Mathis and Albert Turner. The rest of that Monday and then Tuesday went by. Tony had only entertained himself in his room. On the following Wednesday, Albert left his office in the early afternoon. Did the same thing on Friday. Both times he met with Tony at the Hilton. Jerry, with his thumb on the shudder switch, tried to pace himself but eventually used two rolls of 24.

Saturday morning, Tony checked out of the Hilton about 10am. Jerry had everything he needed but decided to leave the next day after Juanita phoned. Her call to his room came promptly at 6 a.m. He answered, "Good morning! Jerry Anderson speaking."

Juanita gave a short laugh. It was exactly 6 a.m. Jerry had to know who was calling. She decided to return his humor. "Jerry, this is Juanita Aguero calling. Any news for me?"

"Yes, I'm returning to Miami today. My work here is finished. I'm sure your superior will be pleased with my findings."

"That's good to hear. Strange though. I sensed from my call last week you were becoming discouraged. Something has changed?"

Jerry was in an excellent mood. Thinking about his bonus and since last Wednesday, he had planned a reply. "Ms. Aguero, consider me your fairy godfather with magical powers. Your dreams are about to come true." Jerry chuckled to himself thinking, a wet dream in fact!

Juanita's response was a return to business. "When can I see the results?"

"If I work tonight, would tomorrow afternoon in my office be convenient?"

"Fine then. Work tonight and I'll see you at 1 p.m. sharp."

Jerry arrived home around three that afternoon. He ate, rested, and enjoyed some well-earned refreshments until after 8 p.m. Because of the type of photographs he often took, he had long since processed his own film. He finished in his darkroom after midnight and prepared two identical packages for Ms. Aguero. There were twelve of the best pictures in each. Normally, for insurance, he would have kept a set for himself. Decided not to after giving it some thought. He had been warned. Plus, anyone who walks into your office and hands you $25,000 in hundreds may not be a person to mess with. In reality, he had no idea how right he was!

The office meeting at one took five minutes. Juanita walked in, they shook hands and without either sitting, Jerry handed her two 9X12 manila envelopes and a small plastic bag containing two rolls of film. "Both packages are the same, Juanita. I prepared two sets for you."

Without speaking, Juanita opened one of the envelopes and removed the photos. Looking just at the first two pictures, she turned back to Jerry with a wide grin of disbelief. She thumbed through the rest, placed them back in the envelope, and reached for her tote. Jerry was rubbing his chin in anticipation, but this time she removed a large single package wrapped in brown paper and bound with string.

When Juanita placed it on the desk, Jerry wanted to tear the paper off immediately but knew it was in his interest to remain polite. With a courteous nod, Jerry said, "Thank you, Juanita. By the way, the twelve photographs selected were what I considered to be the best. Each roll of film has twenty-four. Lots more to look at if you so choose. One more thing. The name of Mr. Turner's companion is Tony Mathis. He checked into the Hilton as a lawyer from Port St. Lucie."

Almost a formal reply now by Juanita. All business! "Very well, Mr. Anderson. If we require your services in the future, I know how to reach you. Otherwise, and for your sake, we never met! Comprender?"

Jerry nodded for the second time. Then she just turned and left.

Still resisting, Jerry didn't open the package right off. Walked to his office door and locked it. Came back around his desk, sat down and opened the right-side drawer. He took out a glass and a half full bottle of scotch whiskey. He filled the glass, then placed the bottle beside the package Juanita had left there.

In well over twenty years, nothing even close to this had ever happened to Jerry. He was determined to make it a moment to remember. He swallowed a large part of the scotch, picked up the package and hefted it up. Damn he thought. It's heavy. He swallowed the rest of the scotch and removed the paper from the package. On top, there was an envelope titled "$6,000 For Expenses." Beneath were ten bank wrapped stacks of hundred-dollar bills. The face of each wrapper read $5,000. Jerry let out a long breath, reached for the scotch and poured another full glass. This time he sipped the scotch and stared at all the money. Thought with a smile. Move over Buffet. *Margaritaville*, here I come!

Back at her office, Juanita briefed Luis by phone describing the photographs in detail. Luis was both surprised and elated. Purposely, Juanita had saved the best part of her report for last. "Mr. Castillo, our private detective provided us with the identity and hometown of the AUSA's sex partner. Does the name Tony Mathis sound familiar?"

"You've got to be kidding, Juanita! His name was mentioned several times in the papers. Russell McKinnon's lawyer.

That nails it for sure. Turner's toast!"

Instructions followed. "Juanita, I want you to put one set of the prints in our office safe. Tomorrow, go to our bank and put the other set and the film in the safety deposit box. I'm coming to Miami in three days. Got to see these for myself. Afterwards, I plan to let Albert Turner know his sweet little ass belongs to me! Not Tony Mathis."

"I'll go to the bank first thing in the morning. Anything else, Mr. Castillo?"

"Stay up to date with the state news. Keep me advised as always. Thanks to you, that has paid off for us."

"You can count on me. I love to sit and read in the office. Makes my workday shorter."

Juanita was much more than a secretary. Luis's assistant and a team player. His mention of "paid off" was a reference to a July article in the *Herald*. They ran a story about one member in the "Gang of Four" to be deposed in Port St. Lucie. Russell McKinnon. He was to be represented by a court appointed lawyer. Tony Mathis. A deposition could be used in court even if he didn't appear. Smart move on the part of the prosecution. Not smart that it was released early to the press.

By phone, Juanita had passed the news of Russell's pending deposition to Luis. During the call, he had requested she read the entire story from the paper and then politely responded, "Thanks, I'll have Juan look into this in a timely manner."

Someone in the prosecutor's office was leaking information to the press. For the "Gang of Four", this particular leak turned out to be fatal!

On September 6th, Luis was in his Miami office studying the photographs. Ended his review of the prints with a look of disapproval. Afterwards, he dictated a letter to Juanita followed with instructions. "I think it's appropriate to send this message by courier right away. With it, enclose a set of the photos to our newfound friend, Albert Turner. Also, have Mr. Anderson make us another set. I can't wait to show these to Carlos and Jorge. Never hurts to have a federal prosecutor serving you in our business."

"Mr. Anderson delivered more than what we asked for, Luis. Perhaps we can have him work for us in the future. It can't hurt having important officials protecting us, especially in the Bahamas. He might prove useful there at one of Carlos' parties."

"Did you compensate Anderson in the amounts we discussed?"

"Yes, and I might add he was a happy camper. We made his day with the payments."

Link's trial was scheduled to begin September 25th. With the absence of witnesses appearing against Link, Bobby had advised him to be tried separately from others arrested in the sting. Had to actually. Most had already confessed to dealing marijuana. Not Link. Bobby was hopeful some on the jury might buy the "naive driver" story. Plan was to put Link on the stand and testify. For that, Bobby would provide him with hours of coaching. Needed because the attorney for the prosecution, Albert Turner, was damn good at cross examinations.

Two weeks before Link's trial, AUSA Albert Turner returned from having lunch with US District Attorney, Helen Alston. She had praised him for the way he was conducting such a prominent case. Even hinted at recommending Albert as her replacement since she would be retiring soon. Ms. Alston had no idea Turner's ambitions were much higher.

Back at his office, Albert's secretary had placed on his desk a 9x12 manilla envelope addressed "Strictly Confidential, AUSA Albert Turner, Jacksonville, Florida." No postage, so it must have been delivered by courier. Albert received lots of useless crap from the public complaining about everything from used car dealers to utility bills. Unbelievable stupid people out there. Initial thoughts were here we go again but there was a letter also attached to the package titled in bold italics, *United States* v. *Richard Boyce*. That got his attention, so he opened the letter first.

In two paragraphs, the letter read. "To the Honorable AUSA Albert Turner: In the matter of United States v. Boyce, I bring to your attention the accused, Richard Boyce, on April 8, 1979, was arrested and held for interrogation in the sheriff's facilities of Duval County, Florida. During questioning by federal authorities with the Drug Enforcement Administration, Mr. Boyce repeatedly requested and was denied legal representation. This constitutes a flagrant violation of the defendant's rights under the Miranda Act."

Next paragraph. "Attached, you will find relevant materials sufficient to convince you that this injustice be resolved. All charges must be dismissed! Rest assured, with your timely cooperation to bring about the resolution requested, the materials provided herein will remain secure and confidential."

On a scale of 1 to 10, Albert's skepticism of what he had read was 10 plus. Spoke out loud to himself. "What a bunch of bull. Always some low-level wannabe trying to make a name for himself."

He removed the scotch tape from the top folds of the package and slid out the contents. Seconds later uttered an audible gasp. He was holding a handful of 8X10 glossy black and white explicit photos of he and Tony engaged in oral and anal sex. Albert stared at the photos for a short moment completely stunned, then slowly lowered his head to the desk and wept.

September 14th, Trevor received a call from Link. Initially he heard something like a mischievous laugh followed by, "Hey, man. What's happening?"

Surprised by the gleeful greeting, especially when in a week or two Link might be going to prison, Trevor immediately decided that his partner was calling stoned silly. "Not much, Link. Just hanging. How about you?"

"Like in the movie, Trevor. 'I'm on top of the world' and still climbing. You're not going to believe what just went down."

"Are you stoned or something worse? What's going on with you?"

"Nothing wrong, Trevor. Just the opposite. Man, I'm free! Free as a bird."

"Yeah, Link. Least you're flying like one, and real high with that coke up your nose. Come on, man. What the hell are you talking about?"

"No! You're way off base. I'm cool! Hell, I'm calling from my lawyer's office. You know, Bobby. Came to Jacksonville yesterday. I was learning how to take the stand and testify. He's a good teacher. We were working on that this morning when someone in the district attorney's office called. They dropped all the charges, Trevor. All of them. Caller told Bobby it had something to do with my Miranda rights."

"Link. You were caught with 260 pounds of marijuana and now you're just walking away? Whitfield said those rights about having counsel during questioning were often ignored in drug cases. I guess maybe he was wrong?"

"Could be, but honestly, I believe somebody high up got involved. Like I always say, 'think about it.' First, all the witnesses against me skip out. Now this! Bobby is surprised more than I am. Says I'm one lucky drug runner."

Trevor remembered something Russell had told him a couple of years back. Luis was the person you wanted watching your back. "Link, not sure but just maybe I know who may have helped you. We can talk about that later. When are you coming home?"

"Tomorrow. No need to go back to Melbourne. Packed for almost a month's stay here in Jacksonville. I had to plan time with Bobby and then maybe a long jury trial. Nothing to keep me here now. I'm coming home, but you may not recognize me. Months in the Key's sunshine and I'm black as soot. Look like I just stepped off a slave ship from Africa with not one drop of a white man's blood in me."

Trevor had to laugh. Same old Link. "Looking forward to seeing you again. Hell. It's been six months. Leann and I will plan a special celebration dinner for you. She can have one of her friends join us for a cookout. Some comfort company for you tomorrow night if you're lucky?"

"No need. I'll be bringing somebody with me. We met in Key West and stick together like glue now. We'll be there tomorrow afternoon. See you then."

Trevor debated who to call next with the news. Luis or Charles. He decided on Luis to see if he had something to do with this. If so, lots more than a "thank you" was needed. Hesitated too long. Phone rang. It was Whitfield.

"Mr. Boyce, my friend, Bobby called me with the news. Said you've already talked to Richard. I'm just calling to congratulate you and your brother. Stroke of luck to have this mess cleared up."

Trevor and Whitfield talked a minute or two longer. The conversation ended with Whitfield's assurance that he was always available to help followed by a cordial goodbye. Trevor then dialed Luis's office. "Bufete de abogados Castillo. Juanita hablando."

Trevor thought if he ever had a secretary, it had to be one like her. "Buenos dias, Juanita. Este es Trevor. Puedo hablar con Luis?"

"And a very good morning to you, Trevor. My apologies but Mr. Castillo is not in the office at the moment. Should I have him return your call?"

"Yes, please but at his convenience. The matter is not urgent, but I am looking forward to sharing some good news with him."

Juanita reply reverted back to Spanish. "Maravillosa! Entiendo. Que tengas un buen dia."

Trevor's unlisted phone woke him at eight the following morning. Luis was calling and polite as ever. "Trevor, I hope I'm not disturbing you so early in the day, but I was anxious to let you know how pleased we are with the way Link's problems were resolved. The news was on a back page of the Miami Herald this morning. Just shows that with a little patience, things have a way of working out. Tu entiendes?"

Trevor sensed humor in Luis's tone with the question. He replied similarly with a hint of comprehending without actually saying so. "Yes,

Mr. Castillo, they certainly do. Especially when you have a good attorney on your side."

With that reply, Luis recognized the inference made to his part in helping Link but decided not to comment. Figured Trevor might be fishing for answers. Instead, he said, "Glad for both of you. Let me add that the people I work with appreciated your loyalty throughout these troubles. As a show of that, one person there would like to make your acquaintance."

"Sure, Mr. Castillo. Nothing would please me more. At his convenience, I'm available. More or less unemployed at the moment with time to spare."

"Good then. I'll make the arrangements but not right away. He keeps a busy schedule, and this stormy period still needs to clear a bit. Not yours to worry about. When it's appropriate, I'll be in touch."

"Yes sir. That's all fine with me. I can wait. And Mr. Castillo, thank you. Thank you very much!"

22.

COCAINE

Link arrived mid-afternoon with his girlfriend. Half an hour after they came, Trevor and Leann had already decided she was someone they would avoid whenever possible. Summed her up as pretty much a slut which must have appealed to Link. Her name was Dicey Adkins. The first name described her perfectly.

That evening, Trevor grilled steaks on the patio. Late dinner deliberately. For an hour before serving, they all got stoned. Devoured the steaks and sides as though it were a Roman feast.

Link's stay in Florida did nothing to improve his cocaine habit. Far from it! The suntan, as he liked to call it, was not the only noticeable change. There was very little work to do since they were out of business. Still, Link didn't come around much at all. He was staying home most of the time and always seemed to have a reason to decline Trevor's invites to a movie or ballgame.

A couple of months passed with no improvements in Link's behavior. Trevor was concerned enough about his long-time friend that one morning he decided to pay a surprise visit. Get him out of his apartment for lunch and tool around some like they used to. Maybe talk about girls, sports, whatever?

Dicey answered the door wearing a tank top, no bra, and hot pants. Exclaimed, "Trevor." Said his name loud enough to hear a block away.

Welcomed him in with an opened arms hug making sure both her sili-cone boobs pressed. "Honey, Link is still asleep. I'll wake him. Stay right here. It'll only take a moment."

Dicey went into the bedroom, closing the door behind. She seemed nervous and Trevor could hear whispers even with the door shut. Dicey stayed inside but Link stepped out a minute later in just undershorts. Says, "Hey, Trevor. What brings you around so early in the morning?"

"Not so early. It's nearly eleven. Thought we might have some lunch or something. Honest truth. Haven't seen you in a couple of weeks and got worried."

Link's reply was accusing. "Why you coming here checking up on me?" Turned away and walked into the kitchen, opened the refrigerator door, and stared inside.

Trevor followed and lied. "No way, man! I was in the neighborhood and thought maybe we could go for burgers and fries like old times. Talk some. Been a while."

"Don't think so. Under the weather if you know what I mean. I'll drop by your place tonight when I'm feeling better. We can have a drink and talk. Okay with you?"

The refrigerator light was on with Link's right arm holding the door. With a clear view, Trevor saw that the arm's underside was covered with small pock marks. Obvious as hell even with the dark skin. Thought to himself. Dammit Link! Your cocaine habit has changed from inhaling to shooting up crack. Worse than heroin. Nothing to be gained by saying anything, especially with his bitch there, so better play it cool for now and see how a visit later plays out. "Sounds good to me, Link. See you around seven."

Trevor started to leave but there was a noise from the bedroom oppo-site Links. Someone flushed a toilet. Curious, so he asked Link politely, "Hey, man. I'm sorry. Didn't know you had company?"

Apparently, Dicey had been listening all along. Came out, knocked on the other bedroom's door and yelled, "Laverne, you wake? Come out here and meet somebody."

Someone replied, "Yeah, give me a second to get some pants on."

Link closed the refrigerator door and answered Trevor's quizzical expression. "Dicey's brother. He came from Miami, Florida a few days ago. Met him and Dicey in the Keys. I'm letting him stay with us until he finds a place of his own. He's checking out South Carolina for a new home state because his sister moved here."

A short, skinny black dude came out of the bedroom. Dicey introduced him. "Trevor, meet my wonderful brother, Laverne."

With one look, alarms sounded in Trevor's mind. Reluctantly shook hands and lied for a second time. "Nice to meet you, Laverne. Welcome to South Carolina."

Back at Lake Murray, Trevor had lunch with Leann. He asked her to prepare a guest snack for Link and Dicey since they were coming to visit that evening. Because she liked recreational use of cocaine, he decided not to mention Link's pock marks.

Link, Dicey, and Laverne showed up together. Dicey explained that her brother joined them because he was anxious to see the lake house. Trevor graciously complied and provided a brief tour. Before finishing their first drink, Link was apologizing for not being able to stay longer. Left after an hour and barely touched the snacks. Not much of a visit.

Later that night, Trevor asked Leann what she thought of Link and his new acquaintances. Not an appropriate timing for the question. They had just gone to bed.

"Sweetie." Her nickname for Trevor. "Except for his first night back, I've hardly seen him. I know he's your best friend and that's good enough for me. Link's okay. I like him."

Her answer soothed Trevor's concerns a little. Still, he pressed her for more. "Anything else?"

"Watch out what you ask for, sweetie. They were only here an hour, but Link seemed a little confused at times."

"I noticed," Trevor replied.

"As for Dicey and her brother, they're bad news in my opinion. Trash! While you were showing the place to Laverne, we talked. She's much younger than me. Never know it the way she looks. Another thing. Dicey doesn't exactly light up the Christmas tree. Neither she nor Laverne finished the ninth grade. Said she and Link met in a Key West bar. Hit it right off together and had sex the same night. So much for playing hard to get like I did. For the life of me, I can't see what Link sees in her."

Trevor laughed. "Link's not thinking with his brain where she's concerned. Talk about loose screws though, Dicey's the smart one between the two. Laverne's on the looney side. Told me he joined the army at eighteen. Went to Nam but six months later he was discharged under Section 8."

"What's that?" Leann asked.

"Somebody judged mentally unfit for service. Best we keep some distance from him. Guy's completely off his rocker. Dangerous maybe!"

Trevor fell asleep that night still thinking about Link. Decided a friend was a friend, good times and bad. Unlike Russell and his crew, Link didn't try to save himself and turn informant when arrested. Clammed up! Besides, the man had started him in the business by introducing Kenneth. He had made a lot of money and he owed Link some payback for that. Have to stick with him now even if he's a crackhead.

Two weeks before Christmas, Leann had finished deep cleaning Trevor's house for the upcoming holidays. She had moved in with him. Totally in love and then some. Confirmation of her feelings came that evening when she and Trevor were high from a shared joint. Trevor never seemed to work like he did when they first met. Leann asked if his and Link's Florida real estate business was in trouble. Pretended to wonder if it was her fault because they spent so much time together?

With the marijuana they had just smoked and because Leann liked cocaine as well, Trevor responded with several seconds of laughing. Finally, "Leann, can you keep a secret?"

The THC was working on Leann too. Laughing back and almost as long, she replied. "Till death do us part, sweetie."

Trevor told her what his true profession had been up until six months ago. Left out the part of Link's arrest and why they had quit. Ended his confession saying, "I made a pile of money. Link did too, but he's wasted most of his share in Las Vegas. Truth is, I'm pretty well off."

When someone you care about tells you he had been a drug dealer, perhaps it's best to be stoned on pot. Her "truth" was she had suspected there was more to his success than just being a realtor. Appreciated the honesty now and it made zero difference how she felt about Trevor. He was already the most exciting man she had ever known.

Link paid an unannounced visit the next day. Leann was out shopping. "Trevor, we need to talk."

"Great!" Trevor responded. "Got nothing but time, man. What about?"

"Here's how it is. It's been eight months since we shut down. Made no money since then, and I've had some bad luck at the tables lately. Need some dough."

"Not a problem. You and I have around $120,000 in the safehouse. There was almost twice that, but I paid out quite a bit for your legal expenses plus the money I sent you through Bobby while you were in Florida. What say we ride over to the cabin and get you back on track."

"Thanks, Trevor. That'll be a big help. Let's go. You drive, okay?"

It was nearly a two-hour drive from Trevor's home on Lake Murray to his cabin on Lake Wateree. Trever spent the best part of the trip telling Link about his plans to buy a beach home. Explained how he loved the salt water now and was thinking about learning how to fish offshore. Link listened but seemed distracted. The reason for that came after they reached the cabin and raised the concrete slab in the floor of the pump house.

Link looked inside at the stash of tightly bound bales of Colombian Gold. "Have to tell you this looks good to me. Damn lifesaver."

Trevor assumed Link was referring to the clear Sterilite storage container sitting on top of the Marijuana. It was half full of cash. "My favorite color too, Link. How much do you need?"

"My half, Trevor, but I wasn't just talking about the money."

"Damn, Link! That's a nice chunk of 'change' you're taking. Why all at once and what else are you talking about? You've got to come clean with me."

I told you I had some bad luck at the tables. I owe some dudes. Bad ass dudes"

"Christ! How much?"

"With interest, about $50,000. Sorry, but it's not out of your pocket, is it? It won't happen again. I learned my lesson not to play when I'm high. Promise. But I was talking about my half of the marijuana too."

"Tell me you're not going out there pushing on the streets again?"

"Don't have to. I told Dicey about this. Her brother, Laverne, has already lined up a sale with a big-time dealer in Charleston. A onetime purchase at six hundred a key. That'll make me whole again."

"That's not the way we were taught, Link. You're asking for trouble. Sorry to say this, but I don't trust that bitch of yours, much less her skinny ass brother."

"Got no choice. Have to keep my word. Already said I'd do the deal. As for Dicey and Laverne, I'll bust both their butts if they get out of line. Told them so."

"It's your call, Link, but you're making a big mistake. We don't have our cars anymore. How do you plan to move 150 kilos out of here? And when?"

"My van when the time comes, but I need my cash now. Our deal for the marijuana is set for some time in January. Hoping you can help me load. I'll make the trip to Charleston with Laverne."

"I'll help but this place is top secret. Don't tell that SOB about it. I need your promise on that." Link promised!

Great Christmas holidays with Leann. They spent serious time with both of their families. Leann loved Trevor's mom. Trevor's success had carried over into his family. His mom and grandparents still lived in Elgin together, but thanks to Trevor, in a much nicer three-bedroom, two and a half bath home.

At Leann's insistence that Trevor meet her best friend, they made a one-day trip to Darlington, South Carolina. The back seat of the car was crammed with Christmas presents Leann wanted to deliver. Only a couple were for her friend, Mary Talbert. Most were for Mary's nearly grown teenage son, Jessie. Leann told Trever she was the boy's godmother.

Trevor treated everyone to a favorite Darlington restaurant. Turned out he and Jessie had something in common. Football! Like Trevor during his high school days, Jessie played defensive and offensive line-man for the Darlington Blue Devils. He and Trevor shared some football stories.

One week into the new year, a cold front pushed deep into the south-east. Overnight, four inches of snow fell in Colombia. Beautiful view of the grounds and Lake Murray from the windows in Trevor's home.

Early that morning, the home phone rang. Trevor answered with a simple "Hello." The caller introduced himself as Darlington High's school counselor. He needed to speak with Leann Fox if she were avail-able. Trevor said, "certainly," and passed the phone to Leann while ex-plaining who the call was from.

Leann's lifelong friend, Mary, had been killed in a car accident. Leann knelt to the floor in tears. She couldn't speak. Trevor took the phone and the rest of the conversation from the counselor. He ended by asking him for his phone number and explaining that Leann would call back when she recovered.

Twenty minutes passed before Leann managed to get a grip on herself and return the call. She learned the details of Mary's accident and how Jessie was taking the tragedy. The counselor's answer was, "not too well, I'm afraid."

Leann packed and left before noon to be with her godchild. Mary's funeral was two days later. She was buried in the Black Creek Baptist Cemetery beside her mother's grave. Trevor came and attended the service as well as the church's reception afterwards.

It was nearly dark before Trevor and Leann returned together to Columbia. She had left her car for Jessie since Mary's was totaled by the accident. Halfway back, with hands folded and tears coming from her eyes, Leann turned to Trevor with a request. "Sweetie, it's a lot to ask of you but I have no choice. Jessie has no family to go to. There's only me. Can he come and stay with us?"

Because of her tears, Trevor replied softly with a question. "Perma-nently, Leann?"

"He's a senior with only a few months before he finishes high school. Then maybe off to college. Please. Will you think about it?"

"I don't have to think about it. I like the boy and there's plenty of room for him at the lake house. Let's call him tomorrow and see what he has to say about the move?"

Leann wiped the tears away and gripped Trevor's shoulder. "Thanks, sweetie. I love you. When we get home, I'm going to prove that all night."

Leann was true to her word. It was a long and enjoyable evening for Trevor. Consequently, they slept late. The private phone rang at 10 a.m. Had to be Link but Trevor answered with just a hello.

"Buenos dias, Trevor. Esta es Juanita."

Trevor felt an adrenaline rush, but Leann was there and even she didn't know he could speak Spanish. He replied in English. "Good morning, Juanita. Hope you're enjoying the holidays. Your call makes mine complete. How are you and Luis?"

"Busy as always. Luis would like for you to come and visit. An extended visit in fact. Spend some time together and meet someone he mentioned a few months ago. It's a chance to acquaint you with some business opportunities."

Trevor understood the "someone" part. The added referral of "business opportunities" was a pleasant surprise. "Juanita, it's snowing and cold here in South Carolina, so the chance of warming up on a beach sounds perfect. Just tell me where and when."

"Day after tomorrow for starters. I made reservations for you on a 12:10 p.m. Delta flight from Columbia to Jacksonville. I'm sorry but you'll have to change planes there for a flight to Miami. I'll meet you at the gate on arrival."

Damn short notice, Trevor thought. Reservations already made before she called. Luis's invitation was more like instructions. No matter. The man had saved Link's tail. Questioning the timing of his invite might not go down well. "That's great, Juanita. I can come. But we've never met. How will I know you?"

Juanita laughed. "Not to worry, I'll recognize you. Just in case though, look for an incredibly beautiful lady in a blue dress. And Trevor, I mentioned an extended stay. This may turn into an employment offer. Should you accept, Luis suggested you make arrangements to be away for several weeks. Pack accordingly and for warm weather."

Trevor apologetically told Leann he had to go away for a while. Weeks perhaps. It was an incredible business opportunity in Florida he would be a fool to refuse. Tried to be honest with Leann without any specific details. But the timing was perfect if her godchild came. A man in the house during his absence.

With Trevor scheduled to leave in two days, Leann was depressed for the rest of the morning. Then there was a call on the home phone. The same Darlington school counselor as before. Driving her car, Jessie had been arrested for speeding and DWI the night before. Considered as an adult at eighteen, he had spent the night in a county lock up facility. Sober now, but they were holding him there until bail was set and posted.

That afternoon, Trevor went with Leann to Darlington. Before leaving, Trevor phoned Whitfield for assistance. The lawyer assured him a call to his good friend with SLED, Spot Mozingo's son, Billy, and Jessie would be released by the time they reached Darlington. He was!

With Jessie out of jail and home, Leann offered him the opportunity to come and live with them in Columbia. In a few short months, he could finish high school there and maybe go on to a university. Most of that time, it would be just him and Aunt Leann. Trevor had business out of state. Jessie hugged Leann but wanted to think about it. Then said, "I'm sorry for last night, Aunt Leann. When you left so soon after the church reception, I thought you didn't care that much. Should have known better."

Trevor said goodbye to Jessie and a longer, more affectionate one to Leann. He needed to prepare to be away for a period of time. Leann would stay behind with Jessie and make all the required physical and legal arrangements for his move.

Back in Columbia, Trevor brought Link up to date with his plans to meet with Luis. "Not exactly sure, Link but I think he wants me to work for his organization. Hope it works out and maybe you can join too. Has to be some real money in this if you're interested?"

"I'm interested, but my deal in Charleston goes down next week. After that, Laverne and I have some plans."

"Be careful, Link. I don't trust the guy! I'll leave the keys to the cabin's gate and pump house in my boat's glove compartment here at Lake Murray. Go alone to my cabin. Remember the promise you made. That's my safehouse and only you know about it."

Trevor checked two suitcases before boarding in Columbia. He walked out of gate 12A in MIA at 5 p.m. Even with the change of planes, the trip took less than five hours. A Hispanic lady was waiting and somehow recognized him immediately. Offered her right hand while introducing herself. "Hi, Trevor, I'm Juanita. Come. We'll retrieve your luggage and be on our way. I have a car waiting for us."

Trevor followed, thinking to himself she's not one to waste time. Frank and right to the point. Nice looking middle-aged lady. And wearing a blue dress too.

The car waiting was a limousine with a suited driver. Juanita sat inside to Trevor's left. "You're probably ready to relax after your trip. Would you care for a refreshment?"

"Yes. Thank you, I would. Nice of you to go out of your way to meet me at the airport. This is a great ride, but I could have taken a taxi."

She smiled. Took two glasses and a crystal decanter from a cabinet attached to the back of the driver's seat. Pour both glasses half full asking him if whiskey straight up was okay?

"Perfect."

"About a taxi. Luis insists on much better treatment for his guest. Much better! Unfortunately, I have some personal matters to take care of, so I'll be dropping you at your hotel. Since I have to leave, I've arranged to have an attendant meet you there. More of an escort really and I've reserved a table for the two of you in the hotel's restaurant. Their grilled snapper is divine if you enjoy seafood."

"I do and I missed lunch, so dinner tonight sounds great." Trevor had barely finished his drink when Juanita announced they were arriving. He watched as they passed through a gated sign reading, "Fontainebleau."

Describing the scene inside as "nice" would have been an understatement. Place was Beautiful. "Enjoy your evening, Trevor. Your driver will pick you up in front tomorrow at one o'clock. Have your luggage with you."

"I'll be there. May I ask where I'm going?"

"Of course. I thought you knew. The Bahamas!"

Trevor gave his name at the front desk. Clerk checked her registrar, handed him two sets of keys, smiled, and welcomed him to the Fontainebleau. She motioned to a bellhop. "Your luggage will be up shortly, Mr. Dunbar."

Trevor rode an elevator to the top floor. His room was a suite with a large living area, complete bar, balcony, and a sizable master bedroom. He gave a soft whistle. Place was impressive. And probably very expensive.

There was a knock at the door followed by a woman's voice saying, "Your luggage sir."

Damn quick, Trevor mused. "Yes, bring it in please."

A very attractive white girl, smartly dressed in business attire, entered followed by the bellhop. She extended her hand saying, "Mr. Dunbar, I'm Rachel, your hotel hostess for this evening."

Beautiful woman and Trevor didn't quite recover from that before she had pointed the bellhop towards the bedroom. He acknowledged obediently and carried the luggage there. Trevor reached for his wallet thinking a tip was required. Rachel smiled and waved her right forefinger negatively. "That won't be necessary, Mr. Dunbar. Everything is complimentary for you."

Again, Trevor was lost for a response. She was damn gorgeous! Finally managed to say, "Thank you, Rachel. My apologies but I was not expecting someone so attractive. Please, call me Trevor."

"I will and thank you for the compliment. We have dinner reservations at eight, so there's time for you to freshen up. Our table is in the executive dining room but it's Florida, so the dress code is semi casual. I can meet you at the oceanfront bar for a cocktail before then if you like?"

Trevor had collected his composure now. He glanced at his watch. Plenty of time for a quick shower. "I'd like that. Let's say about seven."

Trevor had packed two summer suits. He chose Leann's favorite. It was tan colored and worn with an open collar, white silk shirt and complemented with a gold chain and cross. The latter was a gift from his mother. Just before seven, he looked himself over in the mirror. Liked what he saw. A nice attire for a successful black man in a very fancy white man's hotel dining room. Impressive, he hoped in Rachel's eyes.

After taking the elevator to the lobby, he followed hallway postings to the ocean front bar. He was greeted at the entrance by a hostess.

"Mr. Dunbar, Rachel is waiting for you. She arrived early. Follow me please."

Rachel stood as he approached. She was wearing a black cocktail dress fitted to a perfect body. Nice cleavage showing with flowing blond hair to her shoulders. Trevor made a useless attempt not to be awed by her appearance. Slightly leaned his head against the shoulder, smiled with his mouth closed, then graciously said, "You look nice, Rachel," but thinking, I sure hope I don't wake up.

"And you as well, Trevor," she replied. "Come. Sit with me. I've ordered martinis for us. Okay?"

They finished two drinks apiece before leaving for dinner. Trevor needed a meal after two martinis. Still, they complimented a seafood feast with a bottle of wine. Excellent food accompanied by interesting conversation.

Two hours passed like ten minutes. Trevor hated that he was leaving the next day. He had consciously behaved as a polite gentleman all evening and wished there were a few more days to be with Rachel. Get to know her. Really get to know her!

He thought. "Best not to offend a lady here. Good looking white girl with a black man at an exclusive hotel had probably caused enough heads to turn."

Rachel was exceptionally smart. She detected a sense of uncertainty in Trevor's composure and softly remarked, "It's getting late, Trevor."

Dammit, she was right. All or nothing now. Had to push his luck. "Rachel, where are you staying tonight?"

"With you Trevor, I hope, she answered without pause." Smiled and added. "That part of our evening together is still young."

Trevor was ten minutes early for the limousine. Thankful that it was not scheduled sooner. He woke very late that morning beside the body of what must have been Playboy's *Playmate of the Year*. Reflected for a moment laying there and realized he was just a black country boy from Elgin, South Carolina. Trying hard to play it cool with Rachel the evening before when this whole thing had to have been arranged. The plane trip flying first class, a limousine with a bar, suite in an elegant hotel, executive dining, and most of all, Rachel. Asked himself. What the hell is this all about?

The limousine arrived. Driver stepped out and opened the door for him. Trevor shook his head thinking, no doubt, I'm definitely being set up for something.

A short time later, they arrived at one damn big airport. Entrance sign read OPA-LOCKA. The driver continued inside until he came to the rear of a large hanger. Pulled up next to a corporate like twin engine jet, stopped, came around and opened Trevor's door. A casual looking Hispanic walked from the plane and held out a handshake. "Good afternoon, Trevor. I'm your pilot, Fernando. Welcome aboard."

After a brief taxi, they were in the air and over water. Trevor was the only passenger. Fernando was the only pilot. There was also a pretty flight attendant. Apparently Spanish. While they were still in a steep climb, she came beside his seat and asked, "Would you like a drink or something else, Mr. Dunbar? Anything at all!"

The way she put the last part of her question hinted that she really meant "anything at all." Trevor was recovering from a long night. He answered politely, "Just a bourbon on the rocks, darling. Thank you." A few minutes later, she returned. Leaned a little over him and placed a drink on his fold down. Whispered, "Here you go. Enjoy and let me know if you change your mind."

The flight lasted about forty minutes. Fernando circled low over what seemed to Trevor as a narrow strip of land surrounded by water as far as you could see. Flight attendant came for what was now an empty glass. "Welcome to paradise, Mr. Dunbar."

"Where exactly are we?"

"The Bahamas. Norman Cay," She replied.

Trevor looked again through his cabin window as they were ending the circle. Low now and coming around to a very short runway on this tiny patch of land. "Is he trying to land there?"

She noticed the nervousness of his question. Took advantage of it and with a big grin replied, "Yes, honey, but don't worry. Most of the time he makes it down by the second or third try."

Trevor buckled up, closed his eyes, gripped the arm rest. He experienced a white knuckled touchdown helped along by a sudden reversed engine thrust. It was a short smooth landing.

Flight attendant was still laughing while she opened the aircraft's exit door for Trevor. This time in not quite a whisper leaned close to him and said, "Maybe the next time, honey?"

Trevor replied yes with just a nod. His attention was focused on a white Land Rover. Luis stepped from the driver's seat with both arms waving. Walked up and shook Trevor's hand. "Bienvenido, amigo! Me allegro de verte."

Trevor returned the handshake while halfway looking back at the short runway and said, "Del mismo modo, compadre."

The two men made a three-minute ride from the runway to a beachside villa. They went inside with both carrying a piece of luggage. It was not a large place but nicely furnished and included a spectacular view from a porch fronting the ocean. Luis commented, "I'm sure these accommodations will suit you. Carlos acquired this place recently from a friend who used to work for him."

It was a baited statement by Luis and Trevor bit. Looked around for a second and responded, "Damn fantastic place. Can't believe his friend sold it. Did he have to move?"

Luis was watching for Trevor's reaction when he answered. "Yes, forcefully in fact. This past September he was arrested during a raid by the Bahamian authorities. They carried him and his wife off to Nassau."

Trevor sensed he was being tested but played along. "Tough break. What did they get him for?"

Luis grinned because it was obvious Trevor already knew the answer. "Smuggling drugs"

Trevor returned the grin. "Nice break for the new owner. Carlos, you said?"

Luis turned to leave. Stopped at the door. "His name is Carlos Lehder, and he wants to meet you. I took the liberty of telling him most of our history together. Someone will pick you up at six. We're having drinks with him."

"Sounds good. Looking forward to it. If it's just drinks, how should I dress for the meeting?"

"It's the Bahamas. Very casual. Anything you like." With a second thought, Luis laughed. "Sometimes when Carlos is entertaining guests, the servers wear nothing at all."

Luis's comment made Trevor remember something the flight attendant had said, "Welcome to paradise!"

Another but different white Land Rover pulled up front at six. Tinted windows were up as Trevor hopped in the front seat. Immediately he noticed his driver was a young Hispanic girl, maybe twenty, very pretty, and wearing only a bikini bottom. No top!

Driving off with both hands on the steering wheel, she gave Trevor a brief look. "Hi, I'm Susana. Sorry about the windows, but even here in the Bahamas, evenings get chilly this time of year."

Trevor purposely stared at her plentiful chest and responded. "Yes, it most certainly does!" Her personal headlights were on bright. Susana recognized the compliment and acknowledged it with a smile.

They arrived at a gated driveway with armed guards on either side. Susana lowered the windows and waved as they passed through. Luis and a bearded man maybe in his thirties were standing out front of an attractive and spacious tropical style villa. Once the Rover stopped, a guard peeked inside at Trevor and Susana. Satisfied, he opened Trevor's door.

Trevor stepped out having already decided, in the face of all this heavy-duty security, it might be impressive if he took a noticeable initiative. He assumed the bearded man standing with Luis was Carlos. "Good afternoon, sir. Trevor Dunbar."

The response was friendly. Carlos placed a left hand on Trevor's shoulder and extended his right for a handshake. "Carlos Rivas. Come inside. We have refreshments waiting for your arrival. Luis has told me quite a bit about you. Perhaps we also can get to know each other."

The meeting with Carlos lasted the better part of an hour. With obvious pride, he had shown Trevor his home before they settled at an ocean side patio table. The villa was built on an irregular fifteen-foot cliff of beach rock that allowed an elevated view of the water below. It was undoubtedly the nicest home on the island, but Carlos seemed apologetic for it not being larger. He waved back at the villa from the patio. "It's only 3,600 sq. ft. I need more room because I enjoy entertaining guests. Parties can get a little crowded."

Carlos Lehder Rivas was very well mannered. Almost as though it were an inborn trait for Hispanics in Trevor's mind. Once seated at the patio table, an attractive girl served drinks. Afterwards, the conversation was pretty much like when Trevor met Luis. An interview.

Wanting to learn as much about Trevor as a short time allowed, Carlos's questions were right to the point. Trevor gave a historical account of himself and how he came to be in the marijuana business. Carlos was most interested in the volume traded, how he transported it, and explaining his way of keeping anonymity during distribution. Especially the part of the conversation that was nearly a repeat of when he first met Luis. At times, they spoke in Spanish. Carlos expressed his appreciation of Trevor's fluency in his native language.

Everything went well Trevor figured. The meeting ended with one of the guards coming to the table. "Patron, Fernando is waiting. There's some weather in the Caribbean. He says to make your appointment with Pablo tomorrow, it's time to leave."

Carlos stood as an acknowledgement the meeting was over. "Trevor, I'm sorry. I have to go. Business! Luis will handle everything with you while I'm away. Please enjoy your stay on my island. I'm sure we will become good friends." Carlos extended a handshake to Trevor and then turned to Luis nodding an approval. Luis returned the nod indicating his understanding.

Once Carlos had left, Luis said, "I think you impressed el jefe. We have much to discuss."

Luis and Trevor spent the next part of the evening at a rustic little island restaurant. Menu offered contemporary food. After drinks, Trevor opted for his first conch burger. Luis joked it was the only place on the island to eat out. Consequently, popular with their associates. Pointed out one with a particular purpose. A middle-aged guy seated with a much younger companion. "Good time as any to make his acquaintance, Trevor. Come with me. The kitchen here is a little slow."

They approached their table and Luis made the introduction. "Jack, meet Trevor Dunbar. The young man we talked about."

Without standing, Jack reached across the table to shake hands. "Jack Reed. Good to meet you, Trevor. Did Carlos approve of your idea Luis?"

"Yes, the meeting went well. I haven't discussed our plans with Trevor yet. Maybe do that after dinner. Assuming he likes the offer, can we visit with you sometime tomorrow?"

"Make it early. Say by eight. I'm taking off a couple of hours after lunch. Some weather is headed our way."

"Fernando mentioned a weather problem to Carlos. They've already left. We'll see you at eight Jack."

"I'll have coffee brewing for us."

Trevor's curiosity was in high gear but decided to let Luis carry the ball to wherever the goal was. Besides, he was hungry. The burger with fries had arrived and required his attention.

While eating, a conversation about inconsequential things went along with good food and the pleasant surroundings. Luis paid the check and suggested they return to Trevor's villa. Once they were there, Luis explained a more private venue than the restaurant was needed for what he wanted to talk about. He went to the bar and poured two glasses of bourbon. Handed one to Trevor and asked with an unmistakable tone of seriousness. "Trevor, I need to know how you feel about the loss of your friends in Port Salerno?"

Trevor had anticipated the question from Luis. "We were supposed to be friends. You don't 'rat' on friends! Believe me when I say that someday, Link and I will catch up with the bastards, wherever they're hiding. Make them regret being born when we do. I cracked a guy's jaw once with an uppercut. Russell has that and a lot more coming."

Luis leaned back then forward on his bar stool. The jester was reminiscent of when Trevor had confessed he spoke Spanish. Luis sipped his bourbon just for a moment before replying, "Alright, Trevor. I'm glad you feel strongly about them. Today you met Carlos. You're here because he and I appreciated your loyalty. It's the one thing our organization insists on. Substantial rewards come with allegiance."

"You and Carlos can depend on me. I'll always be honest to a fault, and I'm no damn 'rat.' Neither is Link."

"You would not be here today if we thought otherwise. But a busted jaw is not the way we settle disloyalty. The penalty for betrayal is severe. Always! You will never see Russell and friends again. They're permanently gone."

Trevor immediately caught the meaning of what Luis had said. He felt a strange rush of adrenaline, and in the same instance, a sense of power.

Provided a response like one he thought Luis wanted. An approving nod of comprehension before adding, "They had it coming, Luis. Backstabbers deserve what they get. Wish I could have been there."

Luis raised his glass for a toast. "Here's to getting that little episode out of the way." Glasses clinked followed with each man taking a swallow. Not a sip! "Now, we can move on to the more fruitful part of our purpose here today. What do you know about cocaine?"

"Never tried it. It's around just about everywhere, but I'm not inclined to use it. Satisfied with just smoking pot occasionally. Link's a heavy user though. At times he gets really messed up on the stuff."

"I stay clear of it as well. Wish Carlos did too! I like to be able to think straight. Always. But you misunderstood me. I wasn't asking about how coke fit in with your personal life. What do you know about the whole enterprise? In other words, how cocaine gets from the fields all the way to someone like your friend, Link?"

"Not so much, Luis, but I'm a fast learner if that's where you're going with this. Sort of like marijuana, I figure. Smuggle the stuff into the states where it sells it on the streets."

"There are considerable differences. The biggest being your price on the streets where a kilo of marijuana can cost maybe a thousand. A kilo of quality cocaine brings forty or fifty times as much. Here on Norman

Cay, our organization is in the cocaine business. Marijuana is peanuts by comparison."

Best not to argue that he had made a lot of money selling those "peanuts." Instead, Trevor said, "I want in if you'll have me?"

"That was decided by Carlos this evening. At my suggestion, we're bringing you in as a rookie. Payback for staying loyal. After training, your end will be transportation. Down the road you might add distribution."

"I have experience in both from dealing marijuana for years."

"We know. That's in an area of the east coast we wish to grow. The Carolinas."

"A coincidence you say that, Luis. It's been nine months since I shut down, but there were times when my dealers asked if I could lay my hands on some coke. I worked with you through Russell, and it was strictly marijuana. No complaints though. It was a great ride until the 'Gang of Four' turned on us."

"Trevor, years ago I promised a friend to only smuggle marijuana. He's long gone, and I've changed with the times. You asked to be let in our operations here. For that, my friend, you're about to make a major change. Not just from pot to coke either. The real change will be in the way you transport."

Trevor joked. "Sounds like *Thunder Road*, here I come."

"Not even close to the movie. Starting tomorrow with Jack, you're going to train how to fly. On Norman Cay, that's our means of transportation. It's the part of the operations here you have to learn."

Trevor couldn't hide his surprise followed by an already answered question. "You're going to make me a pilot?"

"To begin with, yes. Consider it a learning curve. We have extended our transportation as far as your home state. Joey, the pilot you will be replacing, currently flies that route. Your familiarity with South Carolina is one of the reasons Carlos and I are bringing you on board."

"Have to say, Luis, damn sure wasn't expecting something like this. I won't sleep a wink tonight thinking about it."

Luis chuckled. "Here on Norman Cay, we always make sure a guest has a good night's rest. Susana is coming over to keep you company. See you in the morning around eight. Enjoy the evening but don't stay up too late. You have to be very sharp tomorrow. Jack's expecting an exceptional student."

Trevor was up, showered, and dressed before eight. Luis was punctual. Driving over to Jack's, Luis knowingly asked if he slept well. Trevor replied, "Must have, I think? Susana said I snored. I appreciate the entertainment you've arranged for my stay here and in Miami. Two nights in a row now. Can't get any better than this!"

"Don't be too sure. You haven't been to one of Carlos's parties. They can get pretty wild."

Jack welcomed them at the door. You could smell the coffee he promised. Another beachside villa like the one where Trevor was staying. After coffee cups were filled during small talk, they strolled to an outside deck table. Nice, pleasant morning but Luis stayed only a few minutes. Excused himself for business reasons. Once Luis left, Trevor asked a question he had pondered since he woke that morning. "Jack, is it hard to learn to fly?"

Jack nodded negatively with a grin. "Nope, not at all. Flying a plane is easy. Stick and rudder stuff." Then he laughed. "Landing and taking off are the tricky parts that kill you."

Trevor tried to think of a reply. Couldn't come up with one, so he took a swig of coffee instead. Wished it was something stronger.

Jack noticed the expression of anxiety. "Honestly, Trevor, if you're willing to work at it, I'll have you flying solo in three or four weeks." Jack reached over to a side table set with a stack of books. Handed the top one to Trevor. "One condition though. I'm good at training, but you'll have to study like hell too."

The title of the book read, *Basics of Flying*. Trevor looked at the rest of the stack. "Those too?"

"Yep, those too. After this first one I've handed you, read and study the rest in the order they're stacked. Luis said you were smart. Let's see how long it takes you to finish all of them."

Jack handed the other books one by one to Trevor. Their titles were *Stick and Rudder*, *Student Pilot Guide*, *Flying in Weather*, and *Airplane Flying Handbook*. The last was thick.

Trevor could see that Jack was watching for his reaction. Provided him a reassuring comment. "Thanks, Jack. None of these should be a problem for me. If I have questions, and I'm sure there will be a lot, I'll come to you for answers if that's okay?"

"I'm expecting that. If there is nothing else at the moment, I'll take you back to your villa. I have some preparations ahead of our flight today. In the meantime, spend your morning on *Basics of Flying*."

"Will do boss, but you said, 'our flight,' Jack?"

"Yep! Reminds me. How much do you weigh?"

"180 lbs. Where to?"

"Your first flying lesson and more. Florida! You'll find a 'carry-on' in the closet beside my front door. Take it and pack light but for an overnight or two. I'll pick you up at one. Be ready."

Jack was right on time. On the way to the airstrip, Trevor commented. "This island is sort of small. We could have walked."

"It's about 280 acres give or take depending on the tides. Carlos owns most of it. Tell me, how are your reading lessons coming along?"

"I finished *Basics of Flying* this morning, but there are several parts I need to go back over and study. Maybe memorize some of the important stuff. I packed it along with *Stick and Rudder* for the trip."

"Impressive! Nice going. Luis said you were smart. Have to be if you're filling in for Ward."

"Who's Ward?"

"Sorry. Since you're staying at what was his villa, I assumed Luis had told you. Edward Ward."

"Guess maybe he did, Jack, but didn't mention a name. Just said the previous owner was arrested for smuggling."

"Yep! Bad piece of luck for Ed, but it works out well for you."

"How's that?"

"Ward was an island resident even before I moved here. Occasionally he would fly a load of Jamaican marijuana to Florida. His own small but independent deal. About a year ago, he started working with Carlos. Losing a good pilot puts a strain on the rest of us. That's when Luis came up with the idea of you becoming one of our pilots."

"Wow! I owe Luis big time and not for just helping me to join up with the flying part. Still though, there must have been plenty of pilots around who would have gladly taken Ward's place?"

"It's not just a question of finding pilots, Trevor. Catch to it is finding ones you can trust. I know because it's part of my job. From what Luis has told me, you've already achieved that."

"Jack. I've been in the business of smuggling dope since high school. I know how to keep quiet no matter what goes down."

"Hope you never have that problem," Jack said as they arrived at the runway. "Looks like my ground crew has us fueled and loaded. Come on. I'll introduce you to flying."

Trevor followed Jack to a single engine plane with a couple of guys standing next to it. Another two men with rifles were watching from the hanger doorway. Jack seemed to ignore them in favor of speaking for a minute or two with the ground crew. Doors were open on both sides of the plane. Jack climbed in on the left side and motioned for Trevor to do the same on the right side. Jack buckled his seat belt. Trevor did the same without asking.

"Glad you finished reading the basics of the game, Trevor. Now it's time to 'play-ball.' You ready?"

"Probably not, but let's go," Trevor replied, slightly nervous.

Jack handed Trevor a clipboard. Attached were paper instructions. The first was titled with the heading, *Cessna U206G Stationair Checklist*. Trevor took a deep breath. He was staring at page one of two, but there were four columns of small print on each.

Jack said, "Don't let all that stuff scare you. After a while, fifty percent of what's listed there comes naturally, and by then, you can pretty much ignore the other half. We've got thirty minutes before we have to get airborne. Look over the 'Preflight' and 'Engine Start' columns. Ask me questions as they come to you. We have two hours of flying once we've taken off and get underway. Gives us lots of time to talk about the 'Flying' and 'Landing' parts of the checklist."

Trevor followed orders. Having at least read the first book on flying helped, but he must have asked Jack fifty questions before taking off and another fifty once they were in the air. Turned out Jack was a great pilot and a terrific instructor. Twice he reassured Trevor it was just his first flight lesson. Everything would be learned with time and practice.

An hour and half into the flight, Jack suggested they take a break from what was almost becoming an inquisition by Trevor. He pointed out Freeport to their right side. "Trevor, the international airport in Freeport is privately owned. Before Norman Cay, Carlos had arranged for his pilots to use it and Nassau International for refueling. Very costly having to work with customs, law enforcement, and local politicians. Lots of palms to grease. That's why Norman Cay came into play. Now we can avoid those airports when transporting cargo. Carlos still pays for the government's cooperation, but everything is much safer and cheaper now."

Until that time, Trevor had paid little attention to the rear of the plane. There were several tarps covering something in the seating area. He knew but thumbed his finger to the back anyway. "Cargo, Jack?"

"Yep! Not just a flying lesson today." Jack replied with a grin. "You're smuggling your first load of cocaine to Florida."

Trevor turned again to take a second look. "Looks like a lot?"

"Actually, we're short eighty kilos. The Cessna 206 is a workhorse. Like a Land Rover in the sky with a fuel capacity of 550lbs. On a normal flight, I take off with 350 kilos. Because of you and playing safe, we're carrying about 270."

"Glad you're not taking chances with me sitting here."

"Consider this. Eighty kilos less to compensate for your seat. The value of your one-way ticket to Florida is three million dollars."

"No way, Jack! How can teaching me to fly be worth that much?"

"I guess we'll see. Luis seems to think so."

"I won't let Luis or you down. Count on that."

"Not just the two of us counting on you. Keep in mind, we're not alone in this operation. Carlos has partners in Colombia. Fernando flew him there yesterday for a meeting with them. I'm sure your name will be mentioned. You're going to be part of a huge organization that covers everything from start to finish. To be clear, that means from a farmer's seed in the ground to someone putting the fruits of his labor up their nose. In between, lots of people and coordination are required."

"Hell, Jack. I'm glad to be joining the team. By the way, where in Florida are we going?"

"Vero Beach."

"What about customs? We're coming from the Bahamas."

"Good question but the answer is there aren't any customs inspectors where we're going. We're landing at a city owned regional airport. It's open to the public but not international traffic. Damn busy place because Piper Aircraft has a plant there. No customs to worry about because we fit in as a domestic flight out of Flagler Beach."

"Flagler Beach! How do you manage that?"

"Disguise. From what Luis told me about the way you ran marijuana, you're pretty good at that. Guess what? Disguises work for us too. In fact, we're almost to our rendezvous point. Hang on. I'm going low. Watch the horizon after I level off."

Jack did finally level off and begin to circle at what Trevor considered much too near the water below. Coming around on the second turn, they spotted a speck out front at about the same altitude. Jack smiled and pointed. "That's Shannon ahead. She's one of our pilots."

Within a minute, both planes had turned on a parallel southwest course and were flying side by side. They were not more than a hundred feet apart. It was another Cessna 206 identical to there's including the registration number. Shannon waved and Jack returned the greeting with a salute. Jack stayed on course while climbing. Shannon stayed low, made a 180-degree turn, and straightened out in the direction of Freeport.

Trevor was getting used to asking questions he already knew the answer to. "Did we just switch places with her?"

"Yep, and all below anyone's radar. We're forty miles northeast of Vero Beach. It's optional when you're flying Visual Flight Rules, but Shannon purposely filed a flight plan from Flagler County Airport to Vero Beach Regional. Same registration number, so now we're impersonating her."

"Nice Disguise. We're just a short domestic flight out of Flagler Beach and enjoying clear skies and good weather."

"Better than that," Jack explained. "One of about four or five hundred non-commercial flights a day in South Florida. Nothing suspicious and no customs inspections. Even so, as a precaution, we have ground personnel at the airport ready to radio me if they spot something wrong."

Trevor remembered his favorite two words in the business. Appropriate time to extend a compliment by sharing the thought. "Damn near full proof, Jack."

"Thanks, but this wasn't my idea. Luis came up with it when we first started. I have to say, it works like a dream."

Trevor started to relax, looking out the windshield at what appeared to be land on the horizon. Jack reminded him it was time to start training again. "Go to 'Before and During Landing' in the checklist. Watch and pay attention to what I'm doing. Ask questions as they come to you"

"Roger that captain."

Jack landed on the shortest of three runways Vero Beach Regional offered. Pretty uneventful except for Trevor's constant questions all the way until the aircraft landed. After taxiing the Cessna to the front of a hangar, Jack verbally went through the "After Landing" procedures. When he turned off the engine, a two-man ground crew approached his side of the plane. Jack stepped out and spoke with the nearest one. Pointed to Trevor twice while talking to the guy who, each time, looked towards the cockpit and nodded an understanding.

Next, Jack walked completely around the Cessna hands on and apparently looked the craft over. Following his one-minute inspection, he motioned a forward wave to Trevor. "Let's go. These guys take it from here. A driver is waiting to ferry us to a hotel. Almost dinner time, so once there, we can clean up and talk about our flight over drinks and a meal."

"Sounds good to me," Trevor said. "I skipped lunch."

At the hotel, Jack checked them both into adjoining rooms. In his, Trevor took a mini bottle of Jack Daniels from a cabinet fridge and showered while he sipped it. Tasted great and the combination of whiskey and a hot shower seemed to bring his thoughts into perspective. One revelation was starting to dawn on him. This was one great big organization he was getting into. No telling how many people were involved. Hundreds at least. Hell no, more! Maybe two or three thousand, if like Jack said, from a tiny seed to some stupid nose. And headquartered in Colombia. Made for another thought. Trevor was not even sure where Colombia was. Someplace in South America. Going to look it up on a map. Come to think about it, maybe visit Luis there. The way things were working out, he could fly himself to the country someday.

Trevor considered calling Leann but decided to wait. He had only been away three days. Even so, she would have tons of questions including, when are you coming home? He had no idea of when. Something else too. If he had learned anything at all these last few days, there were plenty of girls available in this new line of work. One, in particular, he planned to see again. Rachel. It was going to be damn hard to remain very faithful with so many temptations floating around.

Jack knocked. "Dinners on me. I'm ready if you are?"

Trevor opened the door trying to be funny. "If your butt's waiting on me, your tail's dragging. I could eat a horse."

Jack shook his head compliantly. "I'll ask if it's on the menu, but the steaks here are hard to beat."

Seated at a table in the restaurant, Jack ordered for both. Drinks first and then New York Strips. Once the drinks came, he volunteered to answer any questions Trevor might have regarding his new occupation.

"I have plenty, Jack. In case it's something I shouldn't know, just say so."

"No problem. Have at it!"

"Two right off. How often do you fly from Norman Cay to Florida, and how many pilots are there like you and Shannon?"

"Before we lost Ed, there were six pilots each flying a load every other week. Spaced that way so none of us drew attention. Early on, you will get to know all the flyers. The other three are Reginald Barnes, Alexander

Smith, and Joseph Parnell. No need for you to remember the real names. All go by their nicknames. Reggie, Alex, and Joey. By the way, me too. My first name is Jackson."

"Only two fights a month carrying cocaine. Another two coming back empty. Easy enough schedule. Link and I used to take turns running back and forth to Port Salerno every week. Long hours on the road but the money was worth it."

"Sometimes, Trevor, one of us has to double up because of our missing wingman. Also, like today, an extra flight at times because of weather moving in. Once you start filling in for Ward, we'll return to normal trips. Not a lot of airtime per person but think about it. Six pilots where each fly 350 kilos a trip. Adds up to over 4,000 kilos of cocaine each month. After our cost, expenses, and delivered at a wholesale price of $60,000 per kilo, the company still nets a hundred million. That's more than General Motors, and Luis says we're growing!"

"Lots of money when you break it down. Luis told me as much. Said coke was worth fifty times the value of marijuana. But if you fly just twice a month, how much are you paid?"

"Wondered when you would get around to that question? Pilots receive hazardous duty compensation. We're paid by the kilo. $1,000 per!"

Even after being told what his ride along cost today, Trevor was not remotely prepared for figures like a thousand grand per kilo. He was getting used to taking hefty gulps of whiskey. This time he took two while multiplying in his head. "Damn, Jack, caught me off guard with that one. I had no idea. Tell you what though! I'm going to be the best student pilot you've ever trained. Incredible money plus the work hours leave plenty of recreational time in between."

Trevor finished his drink with another swallow. Jack wasn't holding back anything so far as he could tell. On a roll, so why not continue? "Have another question for you. Curiosity you might say. The way we flew into Vero Beach today with cargo and all was amazing. Whole damn thing went off smooth as silk. Like I said, 'foolproof!' That makes me wonder how this fellow, Ward, got himself busted?"

Jack took a sip of his drink as a way of hesitating before answering. "Keep this one to yourself, Trevor. I can only tell you what I think happened. It's not a subject you should bring up again. His name was Edward Ward Hayes. We had known each other for the better part of a year. Ed was a friend and a good pilot."

"Almost the reason I had to ask. You're a good pilot, but he got caught. Doesn't make sense with the way this operation works."

"Exactly, and Ward followed all the rules. His handicap was his stupid wife, Lassie. Can't say anything nice about her. Arrogant bitch."

"I still don't get it. What difference did it make if he had a bitch for a wife?"

"That's an easy one to answer. What we do on Carlos's private island is totally secret. A lesson for you to remember. Don't share it in bed with some honey, no matter how much you trust her. Keep everything to yourself if you want to stay safe from both sides."

"Both sides of what?"

"We're an important part of this organization, Trevor. Right smack dab in the middle of it and probably know too much for our own damn good. Remember, I called it 'hazardous duty' pay. There's law enforcement out for us on one end, but more importantly, the Colombians are on the other. Don't screw up. Your friends in Port Salerno for example."

"No details, but Luis has already told me the consequences of their actions, so I can understand your advice. Still though, how did it all come down on Ward?"

"With all the money Ed was bringing home, Lassie started traveling to Nassau almost every week. Carelessly spent a lot of his cash there and partied with friends. She often bragged, and apparently to the wrong people, about how much he was making. Word was her big mouth put the Bahamian officials Carlos worked with in a bind. They had to do something to save appearances."

"How could they pull that off without compromising everything?"

"Simple really but shutting down operations in the middle of it cost Carlos one hell-of-a-lot of money. A staged raid by the Bahamian authorities a couple of months ago and carried out at the crack of dawn.

Go figure. Except for me and Ed, all the other pilots were temporarily grounded in Florida. Carlos, Luis, and I happened to be in Nassau, and by chance, the island guards were on a fishing trip. House staff were the only ones present on Norman Cay. Only ones except Ward and Lassie, that is. Nothing at all was found at Carlos's place, but after Ed and his wife were pulled from their villa, a short search turned up twenty kilos of cocaine and bales of marijuana."

Trevor cocked his head with a nod of amazement. "I see! Carlos and Luis have influential friends in the Bahamas. They needed a fall guy, and Ward was a perfect fit."

"Not just Ed. They arrested both him and Lassie. Hauled them off in handcuffs to Nassau. The bust made the front page of the Bahamas Post and the Freeport News."

"So, it didn't work out for the two of them. Still, I'm going to be flying from a safe haven island in the Bahamas and landing in the states, supposedly as a short flight from some nearby city. And the job comes with the benefits of a lot of money and pretty girls."

Jack nodded. "Yeah, but remember your lessons, Trevor. I don't mean the flying kind. Stay careful on both fronts! We work for the Colombians. They don't forgive or forget mistakes. On the other side, we're smuggling cocaine into the states right under the nose of the DEA. They go by different rules, but the results can be nearly as bad."

23.

REVENGE

For eight weeks Trevor trained, but he was flying solo in and around Norman Cay after just three. Practiced lots of takeoffs and landings there, and sometimes at Jack's insistence, when winds and weather were not favorable. Most of his flight instructions came from Jack, but he met and flew trips with each of the other pilots as a way of learning all the routes.

Alexander Smith had temporarily taken over Joey's flights to South Carolina. Since flying to that location was to be Trevor's, he had accompanied Alex twice before. The Cessna 206G Stationair was apparently everyone's favorite aircraft. Carlos provided a total of seven. Cruising at 150mph, the flight time from Norman Cay to South Carolina required five hours give or take a little depending on conditions.

Alex flew north 37 degrees west from Norman Cay. Four hours later and sixty miles off the US coast, a low altitude switch was made with another Cessna flown by Reginal Barnes out of Savannah, Georgia. After trading places, Reggie changed course for the Bahamas. Alex continued in the same direction as before coming in forty minutes later over Edisto Beach some 35 miles south of Charleston.

Reggie had filed a flight plan from Savannah to a city owned airport in South Carolina. The Lowcountry Regional Airport in Walterboro. It was fifty miles inland and a left-over Army Air Force base from World War II. Serving a city with a population of about 6,000, it had three runways, a small but recently built terminal, and several old hangars. Once they landed, Alex pulled inside one of the hangers. Just like in Vero Beach, a two-man ground crew was waiting to take over.

With multiple trips as a co-pilot in training, Trevor became acquainted with all the others flying for Carlos. Sharing conversations about their business was a normal part of the airtime hours. He eventually learned it was a Colombian located in Miami who was in charge of arranging for the arrival of cocaine from Colombia via the Bahamas. First name was Fabio. None of the pilots either knew or would say his last name. Maybe for a reason? Apparently, Fabio was one of the organization's top bosses and not a person to talk about without consequences.

Once their company's cocaine came ashore, whether by air or sea, not only was Fabio responsible for overall security; he also managed its gross sales and distribution in the eastern U.S. Trevor figured Fabio must be a very wealthy man. He had no idea just how right he was!

Pilot's job was finished until they would make a return trip three or four days later, reversing roles this time as the decoy for an incoming flight from Norman Cay.

Twice before when he had layovers in Walterboro, Trevor rented a car and made the brief 100-mile drive home. Thrilled Leann with surprised visits.

Jessie seemed to have easily adjusted to his new home and its lakeside advantages. He expressed his appreciation to Trevor. He and his aunt Leann had enjoyed evening boat rides and cookouts together. Jessie had transferred to nearby Lexington High and was expecting to graduate mid-May. Trevor thanked him for his attention to the place. Front and back yards were nicely kept plus a lot of fallen debris in the surrounding three acres had been piled and burned. Both cars and the boat were clean as new. Everything was working out for the good.

On his second visit, Trevor had asked Leann about Link. "Sweetie, I haven't seen 'hide nor hair' of Link since you left. Maybe you should check on him." Before leaving the next day, Trevor called Link. Phone rang for a minute with no answer. Trevor decided the next time he returned, he would make sure to see his old friend. Never happened!

On March 22nd, Trevor made his first solo flight to Walterboro with 300 kilos of cocaine as cargo. He landed at 1pm. The trip included a three-day layover and made for his first payday since he started training back in January. Not even a remote problem. His compensation for the flight was $300,000 in cash. Jack and Alex were helpful in telling him how to go about hiding it all. Banks in the Bahamas were extremely cooperative. For a substantial fee, cash deposits could be wire transferred record free to other banks and brokerages outside the country. Washed clean!

Trevor was planning to celebrate his good fortune. He phoned Leann from a payphone in the Walterboro terminal expecting a warm greeting. Instead, she answered with a quivering voice. Between that and the crying, Trevor couldn't understand a word. Practically yelled, "Leann! What the hell's wrong?"

There was a muffled sound, then Jessie. "Bad news, Mr. Dunbar. Real bad! It was in *The State* newspaper this morning. Your friend, Lincoln Rollins, is dead."

The word "dead" hit Trevor like a ton-of-bricks. Leaned heavily against the wall, took a deep breath thinking once more of a car wreck before asking, "What happened to him, Jessie?"

"All we know is what we read in this morning's paper. Murdered! Police were called to his apartment by a neighbor complaining of the smell. Report said he had been dead for at least a week."

Trevor glanced around the terminal. There was a paper stand by the exit. "I'm in Walterboro, Jessie. Be home in two hours. Is Leann okay?"

"She was just upset until the phone rang, Mr. Dunbar. Must have known it was you calling and completely broke down trying to answer."

"Tell her I'm on my way."

"Yes sir, I will."

Trevor hung up the phone and walked to the news stand.

Realized he had used his last quarter for the phone call. Came back to the stand after finding change for a buck.

The article describing Link's death began at the bottom corner of the front page. Link's time of death was yet to be determined, but the body's decomposition suggested a week or more. He had been shot twice in the head while lying in bed. An investigating officer said it may have been a robbery since his wallet and some other items were missing along with his navy blue 1977 Chevrolet "Hop Cap" Van. Police were searching for it and person or persons of interest.

Trevor thought about all the possibilities for Link's murder while driving home. Gambling debt maybe. Link had said he owed $50,000 to some ready bad dudes. Didn't make sense though. After killing you, bad dudes don't steal your wallet and stuff or your van. Smarter than that! "Person or persons of interest," on the other hand, had to be Dicey and Laverne. Not a mention of their names in the paper. So, where were they? One thing for sure. He was going to find out!

Trevor arrived a little after three that afternoon. Leann was much better now that he was there. Even so, he still had to console her for nearly an hour. Afterwards, Trevor decided he would have to personally solve the mystery of Link's death. He figured the cops never would.

Trevor placed a call to Charles Whitfield. As usual, the secretary put him right through.

"Mr. Boyce, nice to hear from you. Did everything work out for your young friend in Darlington?" The question was a bit rhetorical because Whitfield knew the answer would be yes.

"Released without charges, Charles. Thanks for your help. This time, I'm calling for your assistance again on something much more serious. A friend of mine has been murdered. His name was Lincoln Rollins."

Whitfield replied, "Read about it in the paper this morning, Thomas. Not a good friend I hope?"

"In fact, he was. I want to find out who's responsible. The paper said the cops were looking for persons of interest. I think I know who they're searching for. A brother and sister from Florida and they've disappeared."

"Do you know their names?"

"Laverne and Dicey Adkins. I think they may be in Miami. Also, they may be driving Link's van. Can you help?"

299

"Easy enough, Thomas. If they're involved in a murder in South Carolina and crossed state lines into Florida, SLED comes into play. I'll have Billy check them out with his FLDE counterpart. Same law that helped bust Richard. That Van was mentioned in the paper. Pretty distinctive model. With South Carolina plates, it'll stand out like a red flag."

"How long will it take, Charles? I have to leave here in three days."

"If either has a criminal record on files in Florida, tomorrow afternoon at the latest."

"Thanks. As soon as you have something, let me know."

Early the next morning, Trevor drove to his cabin at Lake Wateree. Worried all the way. He was relieved to find the gate locked. That lasted no more than a minute. The pump house door was wide open and the concrete slab that covered the hidden storage compartment was shoved to the side. Everything below was gone! No marijuana. No Money. Dammit, Link! You promised.

Trevor replaced the heavy slab, covered it with tools and fishing gear, then closed and locked the metal door. To check further, he went inside the cabin. At least there, everything was in order. Still early in the morning but Trevor took a beer from the fridge and settled down with it at the kitchen table. Figured he needed to think. Five minutes later, Trevor knew what he had to do.

Trevor returned to Lake Murray. Only Leann was at the house. Jessie had wanted to stay but she made him go to school. She and Trevor had lunch together. The private phone rang just as he finished. "Mr. Boyce, can you hold for Mr. Whitfield?" asked his secretary.

"Yes, I'll hold."

Whitfield came on the phone. "Thomas, I have good and bad news. Miami police with the help of the fire department had found Mr. Rollins' van about 1am in a Winn-Dixie parking lot the night before last. Unfortunately, by the time they put the fire out, it was burnt to a shell."

Trevor knew in that moment who had killed Link, even if Whitfield had nothing else to say. "Anything else, Charles?" There was much more!

"Yes! Lavern and Dicey Adkins have arrest records. Small stuff mostly but Lavern served some time for robbery. Here's the kicker that will blow your mind. They're not brother and sister, Thomas. They're husband and wife!"

Trevor's mind sailed into high gear. They were married? What the hell?

Whitfield continued. "There's a couple of more things you need to know. It must have taken hours, but Mr. Rollin's apartment had been wiped clean. Not a fingerprint anywhere including his. Topping that off, the police found several bales of marijuana in a closet. Billy said it was kept from the papers on purpose. If they ever caught whoever shot him, only that person would know about the dope."

It was a final clue. Trevor quickly put all the pieces of the puzzle together. Thought, those sons-of-bitches! They had to have planned the whole thing from the time they first met Link. Plot to kill a drug dealer and steal his money. Make it look like a sale gone bad. Happens to dealers sometimes and the cops mostly write it off as serves-them-right.

The pause in the conversation confused Whitfield. "Thomas, are you still listening?"

"What else does Florida's law enforcement know about the two of them, Charles?"

"There's a last known address. Probably useless though. Billy says unless my client has positive proof of their part in the murder, the case stays in South Carolina. Drug crimes in Miami are becoming commonplace. Police in the city can't keep up with their own homicides, much less investigate something that took place 600 miles away."

Trevor liked that explanation. He didn't want the cops involved in this. There was no way to know how much Dicey or Lavern knew about his and Link's dealings in marijuana. Lavern was the one who arranged for a big one-time sale in Charleston. Obviously, Link had told him about the cabin stash. And the damn money too! Both were taken. If either Dicey or Laverne were caught, they would spill everything they knew to save their own asses. He had decided earlier that day at the cabin how this was going to be resolved. The same way Luis had dealt with Russell and friends.

"Mr. Whitfield, you've been a great help, but I need a little more. If possible, your friend with SLED might have FDLE provide him with motor vehicle information on the pair of suspects. Photographs would be great too. Bound to be 'mug-shots' that go along with a criminal history."

"Billy and I often trade small favors. It may take a few days, but I'm sure we can supply that. Is there anything else?"

"No. Please though. For this and your services a few months ago in the Darlington matter, withdraw twice your normal fee from the escrow account."

"Well, thank you, Thomas. It's always a pleasure working with you. When I have the rest of the information you've requested, I'll phone."

"I may be away on business. If so, leave a message."

Link's death was personal. Trevor planned to keep it that way. He had made his first solo flight for Carlos with more to follow. Lots of money to be made. Best not to let his new employer get involved. Still though, he needed some help if he was going to find the bastards. He made a call to Juanita.

"Bufete de abogados Castillo. Juanita Hablano."

Trevor wondered. Does Juanita ever leave that office? Leann was home and she still didn't know he spoke Spanish. Replied in English.

"Juanita, this is Trevor."

"Good afternoon, Trevor. Congratulations. I understand you're a pilot now. Wonderful news! Luis is out of the office now. Can I take a message?"

"No but thank you. I'm flying back to the Bahamas in a few days. Luis will be there when I arrive. He and I plan to celebrate my maiden flight."

"Wish I could join you. There must be a reason you called. Can I help?"

"Possibly. For personal reasons, I need a good Miami private detective. Could you recommend someone?"

Juanita laughed softly at the irony of his question. "As a matter of fact, I can. He has worked for me in the past. Very reliable. His name is Jerry Anderson. One problem, however. When I've used him, I go by the name Juanita Aguero. I remain anonymous. Of course, you understand why?"

"Yes, I do. Can I have his number?"

"Certainly! And Trevor, tell him Ms. Aguero suggested you call. Nothing more though. He does not have my phone number. Keep me and our office confidential please. You might consider doing the same."

302

The rest of Trevor's afternoon and evening was spent with Leann. Her recovery during the day from the trauma of Link's murder was mostly attributable to an overindulgence of cocaine. Trevor's absence for nearly three months had not helped her dependency. Noticeable change in Leann's behavior included mood swings from depression to anxiety. In strict confidence, Luis had mentioned the same signs, and more were becoming a regular part of Carlos's conduct on Norman Cay.

For Trevor, transporting kilos of cocaine into the states was not his concern. Like cigarettes, alcohol, and even marijuana, it could be easily abused. One thing for sure though, he would never put the stuff up his nose. He knew what it did to Link, and now maybe Leann was well on her way too. Best to stick with a glass or two in the evenings of bourbon-on-the-rocks. And sometimes smoke a joint with it. Hard to beat that combination.

After breakfast the next morning, Trevor called Link's parents in Lugoff. Both were grieving the loss of a son but heavily relying on their devout Christian beliefs to compensate. It was a short conversation of offering his condolences for which they were thankful. A memorial service would be arranged later. Link's body was badly decomposed. Once the coroner's office released it, a cremation would follow.

With the number Juanita had provided, Trevor placed a call to Jerry Anderson. No answer but Trevor left a message that he was calling at the recommendation of Ms. Aguero, and he would phone again at one that afternoon. When he did, Jerry picked up on the first ring.

Perfect timing to talk. Trevor had requested stuffed pork chops for the evening's dinner. Leann left after lunch to go grocery shopping. He wanted to keep this conversation private.

"Good afternoon. Detective Jerry Anderson speaking."

"Mr. Anderson, my name is Thomas Boyce. My friend, Juanita Aguero has high regards for your professional abilities. I need your services."

"I'm delighted with her opinion of me. How can I help you?"

"A very simple task, I think. Find someone for me. Sorry, I should have said, find two people for me."

"Are they locals, Mr. Boyce? If so, it will not be a problem at all."

"A married couple and they were residents of Miami until about six months ago. Their names are Lavern and Dicey Adkins. Now they are missing, but there is recent evidence the two are still somewhere in South Florida."

"I'd like whatever information on them you can provide. Once I have it, my work for you will be a priority."

"Along with your number, Juanita gave me your office address. I expect to have photographs and vehicle information within a week. I'll send that to your office by express mail."

"Mr. Boyce, how do I get in touch with you?"

"I prefer to contact you for updates, Jerry. Your office Monday mornings at 9 a.m. if that's convenient? In the event you're away, leave a number on your answering machine for me to call."

"What instructions do you have for me once I locate these two people?"

"As I said, detective. Simple job. Search, find, and report. Nothing more unless asked for. Are we clear?"

"Clear as day. Please give my best to Juanita."

The Lake Murray home had formal living and dining rooms, but everyone's favorite was the day room. Trevor enjoyed the use of a comfortable leather chair facing his patio through a set of French doors. Nice relaxing view. The side table was where he kept his private phone with an unlisted number. The kitchen adjoined the day room behind him. Jessie had arrived early from school and entered through the garage and into the kitchen just as Trevor made his call to private detective Jerry Anderson. Trevor apparently did not hear him come inside. The door from the kitchen to the day room was a quarter open. Jessie heard everything Trevor said.

When Trevor hung up the phone, Jessie walked into the day room and next to where Trevor was seated. Trevor's look showed he was taken by surprise at his presents. "Mr. Dunbar, I'm sorry. I don't think you heard me come home. Because you were on the phone, I thought it was best not to disturb you."

"Did you overhear the conversation, Jessie?"

"Yes sir, I did. At least everything on your side of it. You told him your name was Thomas Boyce. Mr. Dunbar, you've hired a detective in Miami to find Link's killers for you. Lavern and Dicey."

Trevor's reaction unconsciously mimicked Luis. Leaned back in the chair with a hand on his chin and his head tilted towards the shoulder. An expression of deep thought. "Jessie, let's stop with 'Mr. Dunbar.' I'm just eight years older than you. Might say your aunt Leann robbed the cradle when it comes to me. As for the conversation with the detective, it was private but my fault for not keeping it that way. I'm asking that you don't share any of what you heard with Leann. Keep it between you and I."

"Mr. Dunbar. Oh, I'm sorry. Forgot, Trevor. You have nothing to worry about. I can keep my mouth shut. Weird though. You told the detective Dicey and Laverne were married. Link and Dicey were very tight. I think Laverne was her brother."

"I thought the same until this morning. And Link too unfortunately. Fact is Dicey was Lavern's wife."

"Sort of makes them prime suspects."

"There are several other things that I can't tell you, but Dicey and Lavern are not suspects. They murdered Link!"

"You're positive?"

"Damn sure!"

"I have personal reasons for asking, but what happens when you find them?" .

"Link was my best friend. No way they get a free pass for this. Let's just say I believe in an eye-for-an-eye and leave it at that. But what do you mean by personal reasons?"

"I graduate in May. This summer I plan to kill somebody. Actually, two somebodies."

Trevor felt the same quick adrenaline rush he experienced when Luis explained the fate of Russell's team. Took a deep breath and said, "Suppose we have a drink together on the patio? Nice day and Leann won't be back for an hour or more. With what you just told me; I think we need to get to know one another a little better."

Once settled in chairs on the patio, Jessie sensed he needed to explain his declaration. "Trevor, has Leann ever told you what happened to my father?"

Even before he met Leann, Trevor knew how Stumble had died. Also, who killed him. Hell, everyone in Stumble's neighborhood knew. Even so, he thought it was better to let Jessie carry his story to conclusion. "Yes. She said he was shot a couple of years ago."

"Not just shot. Blown to pieces on the streets by a shotgun. Have you ever heard of two men called Higgs and Topcoat?"

"They're drug dealers in Columbia.

Why?" Trevor really didn't have to ask. He even knew they were brothers.

"They killed my dad. More than just a father. My best friend too. He was a marine. He fought in Nam."

"You're planning to avenge him?"

"I've been planning to kill the sons-of-bitches for two years now. No offence, but it was one of the reasons I came to live here in Colombia with you and Aunt Leann."

"Have you told anyone else, Jessie, and I mean anyone?"

"Remember what I said. I know how to keep my mouth shut. Trevor, you're looking for payback just like me. Those two men don't get a 'free pass' either."

"I asked if anyone else knew what you told me for your own safety. If Higgs or Topcoat were to find out your plans, you'd be a dead man."

"Nobody else but you, now. Do you know their real names?"

"Yes. It's my business to know about people like them. Those two are really bad drug bosses. They live here in Columbia. Abraham and Isaac Higgins. Brothers. Two very dangerous men!"

"Are you telling me to stand down?"

"No. Hell no, Jessie! I never knew my father. Raised poor in Elgin by my mother. Like your dad, she sacrificed for me. If someone were to harm a hair-on-her-head, I'd be in your shoes. What I'm trying to say is be careful. You have to figure out a way to kill both of them at the same time and still walk away clean."

"Yeah, but I've got time on my side to come up with a way to do that. Maybe start watching them. Find out their routines. Can I count on you for advice?"

"I can give you more than just advice. Some help if you're determined to go through with this. Tell me, do you know anything about guns?"

"I did some dove hunting with friends around Darlington. Pretty good shot too!"

"Good enough! Besides some pistols, there's a 12 gauge Browning semi-automatic in my bedroom closet. The barrel length has been shortened to18 inches. Legal but deadly at close range. Jessie, suppose you and I visit a local firing range during the times I'm home these next few months.? A little practice might come in handy."

"I already owe you a lot, Trevor. Taking care of Aunt Leann and bringing me here. Now this! Too much to ask I think?"

"Let's call it a fresh start. Go from here. Okay?"

"You bet it's okay. My glass is empty. I'll go fix us another if you want.?"

"Make it a short one. Best not for your aunt to come home and find us both looped."

As Jessie stepped inside, Trevor tried to comprehend this new relationship. Had to admit, he liked the young man. They had both endured some hard knocks in life. Maybe that was it. Another thing. Without Link, he had no close friends in Columbia. Strange, but for no reason at all, he felt he could trust Jessie. Not all at once though. Give it some time and see how the cards fall. Hope for a pair of aces.

Jessie returned with drinks and a question. "I've asked Leann what you do for a living. She just says you're into Florida real estate."

"True enough as far as you're concerned. I work for a very large organization. Strict confidentiality is an important part of my employer's requirements. You'll have to be satisfied with that and nothing more for now. Understand?"

"Guess so? None of my business anyway. I was sort of curious because of Aunt Leann. Wish you were here with her more."

"Yeah, me too. Can't be helped. What's bothering you?"

"Aunt Leann uses cocaine. Found out right after I moved here. You probably knew already?"

"I did, and I've talked to her about it. We both like to share an occasional joint together, but I personally don't care for coke. Does she know you found out?"

"Yes, and not long ago, I tried to warn her about the crap. I wasn't born yesterday! I've seen a few guys my age at school get hung up on coke. Screws them up sometimes."

"What did Leann say?"

"Claims she has it under control. Not to worry. Says she only does it on occasions when she's depressed or something. Like missing you for instance. But you're gone a lot."

"This new job of mind required quite a bit of training. Finished with that, so the good news is I will be coming home more often now. Like this time, I'll be staying for a few days and nights before going back to work. Maybe that will help her?"

"Hope so. Are you leaving tomorrow?"

"Have to, and a day earlier than planned. I think I hear Leann coming down the drive. Finish that drink or you may get me in trouble."

At 7 a.m. and halfway back to Walterboro the next morning, Trevor thought of something he needed to do. From the same payphone as before in the terminal, he phoned Whitfield. Secretary claimed he was lucky to have called early because her boss had court and was about to leave.

Whitfield picked up and asked as usual, "What can I do for you, Thomas?"

"Charles, I'll leave your secretary the office address of Jerry Anderson in Miami Florida. When you have the information we discussed, forward it to him by express mail. He's a private detective I've hired. Withdraw $5,000 from the escrow account and include it in the package as a retainer. I'll touch base with you in a week or two."

"Not a problem, Thomas. Call if there is anything else."

Trever left Lowcountry Regional at 9 a.m. after filing a flight plan for Flagler Beach, Florida. Due east of that destination and sixty miles

308

off the Florida coast, he made a low-level switch with Shannon coming from Norman Cay. Trevor climbed and changed course for the Bahamas.

Shannon was carrying 300 kilos of cocaine. The Flagler County Airfield was similar to Waterboro's. Lots of old hangers as military leftovers from the war and all donated to the county after it ended. The airport was open to the public and busy from use as a practice field for students learning to fly. It served as a convenient point of entry for Carlos's delivery of cocaine to Fabio. Like Vero Beach and Walterboro, no customs and the location was just a few miles off I-95.

That night in Norman Cay, Luis invited Jack and Alex to join him and Trevor for dinner at his villa. Men only. No girls. Probably why Carlos, who was invited, didn't show. Still, it was a great cookout with congratulations and back pats to Trevor for his membership in the flying team. Since it was a celebration party, the 'guest-of-honor' had decided not to tell his host about Link's death until Jack and Alex left.

Luis had refrained from a question as well and beat him to the punch. "Juanita tells me you need a Miami private detective, Trevor. Is it something you can share with me?"

"Yes, it is. I was waiting for the right time to do that. Hated to spoil the party with bad news. Link's dead. Murdered!"

"Mierda! Que paso?"

It was only the second time he had heard Luis curse. Without too many of the details, Trevor tried to explain the sequence of events leading up to Link's death. Told how Link had hooked up with a slut in the keys during his stay in Florida, and when he returned to Columbia last September, she came with him. Shortly afterwards, her "brother" joined them. Added that the three of them had become heavy users of "crack."

"Dicey Adkins was her name, Luis. The brother's name was Laverne. I tried like hell to talk some sense into Link. No use. Said he had everything under control. Never did as it turned out. They completely fooled him. Me too. Dicey and Lavern were plotting to kill Link all along. Weren't brother and sister. They were married!"

"Why, Trevor?" Luis asked. "Why kill him? Why pretend to be siblings? What kind of scam were they trying to pull off?"

"Remember the safehouse I told you about when Link was arrested. Out of caution, I shut our operations down and moved 300 kilos of Colombian there for storage. Whole box full of cash too. Thing was that half belonged to Link. He must have said something to her when his veins were full of coke."

"You're telling me your best friend, Link, who spilled absolutely nothing to the DEA when they questioned him for hours, told everything to this damn whore?"

"Appears that way. Took time though. And, like I said, it had to be because of all the 'crack' he shot up. Link came to me a couple of weeks before Christmas saying he had gambling debts to pay off. When I offered half of the cash stored in the safehouse, he wanted his half of the marijuana too. The story was that Lavern had arranged a one-time sale in Charleston sometime in January."

"You let him have it?"

"Only his part. He gave me his word that the rest was safe. Link and I trusted one another like kin. Hell, I had to help him out of his mess. At least that's what I thought I was doing. Thing was, right after the new year started, I came to work here on Norman Cay. Lost touch with Link and what happened afterwards."

"When did you find out he was killed?"

"Four days ago, right after I landed in Walterboro. Front page of 'The State' newspaper. They shot my best friend in the head twice while he was lying in bed. Left him there to rot for days. Stole Link's wallet where he kept his false identification papers. Stole the money and marijuana from my safehouse too."

As troubling as Trevor's story was, the part about Link's cocaine abuse caused more than an equal concern to Luis. Carlos's coke habit seemed to be getting progressively worse. Almost crazy sometimes. It would have to be an important part of his next report to Jorge and David. Returned his attention back to Trevor. "You've hired a detective? What happens if he finds them for you?"

"Something you taught me in this business. We don't forgive or forget. I'm going to kill them!"

310

The statement didn't seem to faze Luis. Instead, he replied, "If the time comes for that, you will let Juan and Diego assist. Comprender?"

Whenever Luis ended instructions with that word, Trevor knew without asking. It was a command. Not a request!

Although he only had names to work with, Jerry Anderson spent most the week following Thomas Boyce's request to locate this Adkins couple. Because of an old listing in Miami's telephone book, he guessed wrongly they had to be somewhere in the city. Questioned the neighbors of their former address and checked every bar and hangout within miles of it. Six days passed with nothing to show for his efforts.

Jerry's first break in the case came by express mail from a Columbia, South Carolina law office. The package included photographs, arrest records, a vehicle registration with assigned license plates, and $5,000 in an envelope labeled, "Retainer." The second break came Monday morning at 9am on his office phone. It was Thomas Boyce calling.

"Good morning, Mr. Anderson. Any luck yet?"

"No sir unless you can describe eliminating possibilities. I've searched around most of the area where they once lived, but with just their names, I had very little to go by. Miami's a big city, so it was like looking for a needle-in-a-haystack. I expect better results now, Mr. Boyce. Yesterday's mail came. What you've sent will be a big help. And by the way, thanks for the retainer too."

"I have a suggestion, Jerry. Somewhere around the middle part of last year, they spent time in Key West. Met a friend of mine there. Maybe it's where you should try. Take as long as you need to. Expenses on me."

"In my younger days, Key West was my old stomping grounds. Changed a lot since then but I still love the place. If they are there, it won't take long to find them. Meantime, if you need to contact me, I'll stay at the Crown Plaza off Duval Street."

"Thanks, and good hunting. Consider this as an incentive. Find them for me within the next week or two and I'll triple the retainer you received."

"Okay, I'm on my way out the door before we hang up." Jerry Anderson couldn't believe his second good fortune. If this worked out, he might retire. Better yet maybe offer to work for one special client. Juanita Aguero! He thought. Dream on Jerry. Before heading home to pack, he phoned the Crowne Plaza and booked a room. By 6 o'clock that evening, private detective Anderson was enjoying dinner at his favorite restaurant in Key West.

Jerry's search began early the next morning and continued for four days and three nights without success. During daylight hours, he drove slowly in and around parking lots bordering beaches and hangouts looking for a tan colored 1976 Jeep Cherokee with Florida plates 302 ZST. Evenings and nights were spent in bars. It was something Key West offered an endless number of, but a large proportion were located in the historic district. The Crowne Plaza sat right in the middle of them, so he could leave his hotel and walk from one drinking hole to another in 'pursuit of his prey,' as he liked to think.

On the evening of the fourth day, Jerry hung around Mallory Square until the sun set, left there for a drink at Captain Tony's Saloon followed by another at The Bull. Each time before in those bars and others, he had shown photos of Dicey and Lavern to the bar managers. Explained he was staying at the Crowne Plaza and passed over twenty-dollar bills along with the promise of a C-note if either she or him was spotted.

Four days of this left Jerry thinking perhaps he needed to expand into new territory. Nice night out, so he walked northwest on Caroline Street and turned left towards the wharf. The Schooner Wharf Bar was the oldest attraction facing the historic seaport. Why not, he thought?

Inside, Jerry looked over the patrons, sat on a bar side stool, and waited to be served. Head bartender came up with the usual question. "What's your pleasure?"

Jerry figured what the hell, I'm on expenses. Slipped a twenty over the counter and said, "Chivas Regal on the rocks."

Bartender surprised him by pouring a double. When he passed the drink, Jerry had the photos and another twenty ready for trade. "I'm looking for this lady and her friend. Private reasons for that but if you come across either, I'm staying at the Crowne Plaza. There's a C-note in it for you."

Bartender looked at the photos. Then he surprised Jerry a second time. "I can help you out. Cost you two hundred though."

It was detective Jerry Anderson's first hint of a sighting since he had arrived in Key West. Didn't hesitate to reply. "Deal! You deliver, I'll pay."

Bartender smiled wide and said, "Well, hand it over!" He pointed across Jerry's right shoulder. "Don't know about the guy, but the gal in this picture is sitting with another fellow at that corner table on the deck."

Jerry turned and looked. Schooners was an open-air-bar. Dicey was sitting at its railing with an older man. Both were looking out over the harbor while holding hands. Jerry turned back around, took two hundred-dollar bills from a pocket role. He handed one to a still smiling bartender. Asked, "How long have they been here?"

"Couple hours. I just tallied their bar tab. They're waiting for the check to come."

Jerry took a large swallow of the scotch before explaining, "I haven't been here?"

Bartender replied, "Never seen you in my life."

Jerry forked over the other bill and left. Outside were three or four taxis waiting in line for fairs. Jerry got into the back seat of the furthest one. Handed two $20 bills across the front seat to the driver and said, "I want you to follow someone when they leave here. You okay with that?"

Taxi driver laughed. "Sure am. In Key West, happens all the time with PI's. This place is not where you should go to mess around. Know what I mean?"

"I do but look! Here they come." He and the taxi driver watched as Dicey and her bar friend walked to a dark green Mustang convertible in the parking lot. The rear bumper sported two U.S. Navy stickers. Dicey waited with an expecting look for him to open her door. When he did, she turned, placed a hand on his crotch and gave the sucker a long kiss.

Jerry couldn't help but wonder if he had found and now was going to trail someone a little dangerous. Best to be careful in any case. This bitch was married to a convicted felon and obviously up to no good with this poor slob.

It's not hard to follow someone in the keys. US 1 is the only highway in and out. The taxi driver stayed one car behind the Mustang as they left Key West. They cross over Stock Island and just pass the Naval Air Station before making a right turn on 941 Boca Chica Road towards Geiger Key. They drove a mile further before parking in front of a single wide manufactured home on one of the key's cut canals. Both the driver and Dicey got out and went inside. Jerry took notes of the address number on the mailbox and those of the Mustang's plates even though he knew he didn't need to. Just to the left side of the home was a 76 Jeep Cherokee, Florida plates 302 ZST. Jerry had located Dicey and Lavern Adkins.

Saturday afternoon, March 29th, Trevor completed his second solo flight to Walterboro. He had doubled down for Alex who wanted some vacation time. His schedule called for a return to Norman Cay on Tuesday. The three-night, two-day layover was perfect for relaxing at Lake Murray. Crappie season was at its peak. He planned to have a fish fry Sunday evening. His mom was still in good health, only fifty, and had recently acquired a "boyfriend." They were invited.

Jessie accompanied Trevor early Sunday morning in the john boat. Using lightweight spinning reels with jigs, they landed a dozen nice size crappie within an hour. Back at the dock's cleaning station while filleting their catch, Jessie's curiosity forced a question. "Pardon me for asking Trevor, but did the detective you hired turn anything up?"

"Not yet. At least I don't think so. I'll talk with him tomorrow morning. He's looking around Key West for them."

The fish fry was an amazing success. His mom brought deviled eggs to go with Leann's potato salad and sliced tomatoes. With a lemon meringue pie served as desert, everyone stuffed themselves.

Next morning at 9 a.m. sharp, Trevor phoned Jerry Anderson's office. He had expected to either have to leave a message on the recorder or call the Crowne Plaza for an update. Instead, Jerry answered on the first ring. "Good morning, Mr. Boyce."

"Good morning, Jerry. Any luck?"

"Yes, I found them! Not Key West though. Geiger Key about six miles to the north." Detective Anderson spent another few minutes providing the details of his search. He made sure to describe the part about Dicey's new acquaintance.

"He drives a dark green Mustang convertible with Florida plates and navy stickers on the back bumper. I followed them from a Key West bar to a manufactured home in Geiger Key. The two love birds went inside. He must have stayed all night because when I came back early the next morning, the Mustang was still there. So was Lavern, I think. His Jeep Cherokee was still parked next to the house. Pretty wild behavior for a married couple!"

The Adkins' new street address was 25 Boca Chica Road, Geiger Key, Florida. From Jerry's description of how Dicey behaved outside the bar, Trevor figured the navy fellow was their next target. This time, they wouldn't succeed. "Mr. Anderson, I think your work for me is finished. A package with the $15,000 promised will arrive at your office in a few days. Another $3,000 for expenses too. If Juanita or I need anything more, we'll contact you. One last very important thing. You've never heard of me, Juanita, or this Adkins couple. For your sake, I hope you understand."

"I understand, Mr. Boyce. Completely!" Jerry knew it was a warning. Same one Juanita had ended with.

Luis had asked Trevor to keep him informed of any progress the detective made. Trevor called the Miami office planning to forward a message. Two lucky calls in a row. Luis answered instead of Juanita. Trevor explained that Link's killers had been located just south of Key West. He included most of the details Anderson had provided.

Trevor was scheduled to return to Norman Cay late in the afternoon on April Fool's Day. Luis had a suggestion. "Trevor, after the switch with Shannon, fly to Miami-Opa Locka. Since you're determined to go through with this, I'll have Juan and Diego there to meet you. They will know what to do. But I'm giving you fair warning, once they get involved, there will be no backing out on your part. You won't be going along as an observer. Comprender?"

Trevor felt the adrenaline rush! Simply replied, "Si, y gracias."

Flight time to Miami Opa-Locka was two hours shorter than Norman Cay. Trever had flown there with Reggie Barnes only once. He taxied to the same terminal as before. Juan and Diego were waiting with transportation.

At eight that night, they pulled into the front driveway of 25 Boca Chica Road. Lights were on inside and a Jeep Cherokee was parked to the right of the home. Trevor was told to remain in the car. Juan and Diego walked up the front steps, quietly opened the screen door and knocked. Both had handguns held behind their backs. Diego carried a small satchel on his left shoulder.

Lavern opened the house door without asking who was there. Juan raised the forefinger of his left hand to his lips, and with the right hand, placed his pistol against Lavern's forehead. Juan and Diego backed Lavern inside almost as though they were being received as visitors. Trevor thought he heard a woman's voice say something, but it was inaudible. Seven or eight minutes passed. Seemed like an hour. Juan came out onto the stoop and motioned for Trevor to come inside.

Lavern and Dicey were sitting in chairs at a kitchen table. Both had their hands bound from behind with duct tape and both were gagged with it. Lavern was bleeding from his right ear. Dicey had a bad bruise on her face. Her eyes swelled wide when she saw Trevor. Tears were streaming down her cheeks.

Diego pointed with a bloody pencil to an opened cardboard box on the floor stuffed with money and said, "I believe that belongs to you, Trevor. At least that's what he told us after we shoved this in his ear." He raised the pencil and grinned. "The box of money was under their bed."

Trevor leaned forward towards Dicey and asked, "Which of you killed Link?"

Dicey quickly turned her head in Lavern's direction and nodded an accusation. In return, Lavern let out a muffled scream and fell from his chair when he tried to kick her.

Diego said, "It's time to go, Trevor. Luis instructed us to let you have the honors of taking care of whichever one killed your friend."

316

Trevor nodded his understanding and held out a hand for Juan's pistol.

Juan smiled while shaking his head. Next, Diego explained. "Not that way. Too loud and messy." He reached into the satchel. "Watch and I'll show you·how with this bitch."

Diego took two clear plastic bags from his satchel. He handed one to Juan and the other to Trevor. Both had a cup or more of powdered cocaine in them. From behind her, Juan slipped the bag over Dicey's head. With two quick wounds of duct tape, Diego wrapped the bottom of the bag around the neck and then held her to the chair. With an expression of incredible fear, Lavern watched as Dicey struggled. In vain, she tried not to breathe. Dicey died with her eyes bulging.

Trevor watched but showed no emotion. His heart was racing, but the adrenaline rush wasn't there. Weird, he thought. No matter. With an acknowledgment of the instructions, he repeated to Lavern what Juan had done to Dicey. Diego wrapped the tape. It was over a minute later. Trevor looked at both of his accomplices. Nodded his appreciation and said, "Juan. Diego. Link y te doy las gracias!"

They arrived back in Miami a little after 1am. Before leaving the crime scene, Juan and Diego removed the duct tape and plastic bags from the bodies. They carried both corpses into a bedroom and stuffed them inside a closet. Juan scattered twenty or more little baggies of cocaine on the floor. Back in the kitchen, Juan wiped off everything with a wet cloth. Finally, Diego scribbled some writing on a piece of paper. As they left, he locked the front door and stuck whatever he had written against it with duct tape.

Trevor was tired from rising early that morning for his flight. He was looking forward to some rest. As they drove through Miami, he was pleased to see a gate and front entrance sign to the Fontainebleau. Questioned Diego, "Are we staying here?"

"Just you, Trevor. Courtesy of Luis. We're leaving you and going home."

Trevor smiled obligingly. "I'll have to remember and thank Luis for the accommodations. There's a girl that works for the hotel." Added jokingly. "I think I'm madly in love with her. Names Rachel."

Juan and Diego both laughed. Diego said, "Take that box of money with you. You'll need every penny. She's a whore, Trevor. A $4,000 a night prostitute but still a whore."

Somewhat disillusioned with his masculinity, Trevor checked in but did not inquire about Rachel.

The bedside phone woke him at a little past ten. Luis was calling. "Good morning, Trevor. Did I wake you?"

"Afraid so. Late night but well worth it."

"Juan informed me of your successful trip early this morning. Hope you can put Link's loss behind you now?"

"I can, thanks to you, Luis."

"I only have a few minutes to spare. I'm calling from Miami International, and my plane is starting to board. Going home to be with the family over the holidays. My wife would never forgive me if I wasn't there for Easter."

"Family means everything, Luis. Enjoy yourself."

"Actually, the reason I'm calling is to change your schedule. It will allow you to do the same. Leave from Opa-Locka and return to Norman Cay this afternoon as planned. But instead of flying back to Walterboro Saturday, you'll be going there tomorrow. Fully loaded I might add. Ground crew is expecting about 3 p.m. This change will give you nearly two weeks in Columbia with your family. You'll even be home for Good Friday."

"That's great, Luis. Thanks!"

"Glad to do it but had to. Nearly everybody is taking off. Easter is the greatest celebration in the Catholic church. I won't be back in Miami until April 25th. Juanita will be gone too. Her assistant, Lucia, will be filling in for her if you need to get in touch."

"Got it. Have a safe flight." Trevor didn't have time to reflect on yesterday's events. A two-hour flight to Norman Cay was sufficient for that. Still though, lots to think about. Regardless of whether they deserved it, with Juan's and Diego's help, he had killed two people.

24.

"CIRCLE THE WAGONS"

Michelle and son, Daniel, met Luis on arrival at LANSA Airfield International just outside of Cartagena. The holiday plan was to spend the upcoming week at her oceanside home. The ancient city's festivities during Semana Santa were spectacular. The following two weeks they would stay at Luis's ranch. Hopefully relax there in an entirely different countryside setting. Michelle loved horseback riding and little Daniel at nearly five, would accompany her on his Shetland pony. Luis also needed to be close by to Medellin so as to attend conference meetings with David, Jorge, and Fabio. One of his concerns required a report.

The family patriarch Don Fabio Ochoa Restrepo always insisted his children and grandchildren join together during the holiday for a stay at the Del Ochoa Hacienda. It was a magnificent ranch. A necessity since the Don had fathered twelve daughters and sons. It was a substantial reunion of siblings, all very loyal to their father. The Don's youngest son, "Fabito" was nearly the guest of honor. His work in Florida made for rare visits home to Colombia.

Two weeks into April 1980, Luis, David, Jorge, and Fabio met to discuss their drug business. Except for Luis, Jorge had instructed that immediate family only were to be allowed. He explained why once everyone was seated at a table with drinks. "Our father is worried about us. We talked at the reunion. I think all of us know how well he is kept informed by his circle of influence in Colombia. Especially if family is involved. Rumors have it that we are closely tied in with Pablo Escobar's drug organization."

Fabio shrugged. "Everything we do with Pablo is centered around our base here in Medellin. Word of our association was bound to get out. So what? I have a much bigger problem! How to hide millions and millions in cash every week? Can we talk about that instead?"

Jorge raised an open hand. "Calm down, Fabito. Let me finish. The Don knows we're all becoming very wealthy. He's troubled by the larger picture of drugs here in Colombia. Specifically, how and who controls cocaine in the country. There's Pablo Escobar here in Medellin, but there's another group that's started in Cali. Others too but on a smaller scale. With so much money involved, competition could turn violent."

Fabio held his hands up in a gesture of conciliation. "Nothing much new to Colombia, Jorge. Gangs everywhere, FARC, M-19 in the jungles, and government soldiers with patrols almost as bad. Hell! We drug dealers are peace loving by comparison."

"Perhaps we at this table are Fabito. Pablo is a different story. In Florida, you're removed from the way he controls operations. Even a show of disrespect for Escobar can get a person killed. It's only April. David, tell our little brother how many so far this year."

David answered. "Six that we know of, Fabito. Probably more?"

Now it was Fabio who changed his expression to disturbed. "That many? This bothers me. Did any of you know that Pablo recently added someone to help with my management in Miami?"

Jorge and David looked at one another quizzically. David answered. "No, Fabito. That's news to us. What's his name?

"He's a she. Real ugly woman. Her name is Griselda. Griselda Blanco."

Luis had remained quiet until alarmed now. It was obvious to him that he was the only one in the room familiar with the name. This was probably because he was a lawyer. Griselda Blanco had a criminal record in New York for dealing drugs. Some said she had even murdered a husband there plus another in Colombia. Luis asked, "When you say help with your management, Fabio, exactly what part do you mean?"

In the agreement with Escobar, distribution along the east coast of the U.S. was their responsibility. Along with production in Colombia, Escobar was only to manage that part of operations along the west coast of the country and in its central regions. Fabio explained, "Nothing has changed, Luis. I'm in charge of sales and distribution if that's what you're worried about. She's kind of a personnel director in my organization. Supposedly came to help with relations when it comes to our competition."

Jorge could tell Luis's questions were leading somewhere. "Do you know her, Luis?"

"By reputation only. Let me put it this way. Her management skills in terms of relations with others in our business may be a lot like Escobar's."

David was the compromiser of the four men. "Maybe we should talk to Pablo. No doubt, he should have told us about this Blanco woman. With all that's going on, it could have just skipped his mind. What do you think, Luis?"

"I think very little skips Pablo's mind. When he puts someone into the organization, you can bet there's a reason. If you want my opinion, she's like a bad apple in the barrel."

Jorge had heard enough. "We will say nothing to Pablo concerning Griselda Blanco. If she's been planted in Fabio's operations for reasons, keep what we know about a rat-in-the-henhouse to ourselves. Let's wait and see what she's up to in Miami. If she screws up, we'll have something to get pissed off about. Then go to Pablo. All agree?"

Luis partially agreed. "Yes, of course, but Fabio is the one at risk. He has to watch his back with Blanco. You and David are safe here in Colombia and I have Juan and Diego for protection. Let's quietly get Fabio even more added security."

"Consider it done." Jorge placed his arm over Fabio's shoulders. "Our father would never forgive us if anything happened to our little brother here."

David asked, "Besides this Griselda crap, is there anything else we should discuss about how things are going in Florida?"

"Maybe." Fabio replied. "You all remember about a year ago when Carlos wanted to use airplanes exclusively for cocaine."

"Remember it well." David said. "We nixed that idea because it would have given him total control over your supply. Why bring it up?"

"I wanted to make sure you all knew ours was the right decision. Currently, his pilots transport 1,200 kilos a week to four different locations along the southeast coast. Without problems, I might add, thanks to Luis's method of changing where the planes are coming from."

"Thanks, but it was not entirely my doing." Luis acknowledged. "A few years ago, a marijuana smuggler taught me the benefits of disguising transportation. What's your point?"

"Boats! We had our local teams making runs inshore after meeting with our trawlers. To that, I've added a couple of Cubans coming into the keys from Bimini. They speed across in racing boats that can outrun anything on the water. When you add them all together, it beats what Carlos's planes carry. His and our methods combined make us the largest cocaine importer to the east coast of the U.S."

"Never hurts to diversify." Jorge admitted.

Luis decided this was the opportunity he had waited for to report circumstances in Norman Cay. "Jorge, one of my duties to you and family is to assure that we don't draw the attention of U.S. authorities. I need to warn you this may be happening."

"How's that?" Jorge asked.

"To his credit, Carlos's decision to use Norman Cay as a hub for flights out of Colombia was brilliant. Unfortunately, it's my opinion he is blowing the whole damn idea up his nose. I mean that literally too! Carlos turns crazy on coke. Entertainment parties include women, lots of our product, and Bahamian officials on the take but too stupid to keep their mouth shut. Word is getting out. Sooner or later his bubble will burst."

"He's Pablo's man, not ours, Luis. Any suggestions?"

"Not at this time. Keeping you informed is all. We're in the drug business. Mistakes can cost. Carlos is making lots of them."

"Okay, then. I think this is something we can bring to Pablo's attention. I'll speak to him. Make sure he's aware of Carlos's behavior. Let it be on his back if something goes wrong."

The meeting ended with an understanding that in case private evenings together might draw Escobar's attention, just the four of them would avoid meeting again like this. Rather, they would keep each other informed and the appearance of total cooperation in the organization.

Michelle looked forward to every time Luis came home. A stay lasting three weeks was unusual, but they were still a family devoted to one another. This time, Luis hinted he was thinking of returning to Colombia permanently within a year or two. He had become a very rich man in a short period of time and saw no reason to push his luck in the U.S. He had mentioned this to Jorge. Together, they decided he should remain at least another year with an office in Miami. Continue there as a legal representative for the organization. Jorge's primary concern was because Fabio was there!

Luis arrived back on a late flight to Miami April 25th. Juanita had returned two days earlier. On his office desk the next morning alongside his coffee, she had set an eight-day old copy of the *Miami Herald* turned two page two with an article circled in red ink.

In what police described as an apparent drug deal gone bad, the bodies of a married couple had been discovered in their Geiger Key residence. An acquaintance of the deceased, Petty Officer First Class Erwin Brant had reported a suspicious odor emitted at the front door. A note attached there suggested the couple had departed two weeks earlier due to a family emergency in Miami. Police were requesting the public's help in their investigation.

Juanita rarely, if ever, failed to make sure her jefe was not informed of events affecting their operations. She had waited for Luis to finish reading about the murder of Dicey and Lavern before placing a current copy of the *Herald* on his desk. "Luis, study more than just the front page. There are several related stories in section one. When you're ready, we should talk about how this may be a problem for us."

Luis settled back in his chair with coffee. The entire front page was devoted to what was headlined as, *The Mariel Boatlift*. Ten days earlier, Fidel Castro had offered the port in Mariel, Cuba to any citizens wishing to leave the country. The first overloaded boat of forty refugees arrived in Key West on April 21st. Yesterday, April 25th, an estimated 300 boats arrived. All were overloaded. By offering an open-door policy, President Jimmy Carter had welcomed the emigrants to the United States.

In the outer office, Lucia sat at reception. Juanita came into Luis's office and closed the door behind. Sat with a notepad ready if needed. "I was not so worried until yesterday, Mr. Castillo. It's a zoo of motor craft and rafts in the waters of south Florida. Both by air and sea, the place is swarming with the U.S. Coast Guard and the Navy. Anything that floats and is not carrying Cubans stands out like a sore thumb."

"What changes in scheduling did you make, Juanita."

She had anticipated that would be his first question. "I had the *Gran Pretendiente* sail north and lay 100 miles off the coast of Titusville. She's to wait there for further instructions. Until this flood of immigrants ends, I think only our runners out of St. Augustine and Fernandina should operate in Florida. Georgia is okay too."

"I need to call Fabio," Luis replied. "Get him on the phone for me." As Juanita was about to leave his office, Luis remembered something else. "Almost forgot. Thanks for saving the week-old *Herald* for me. That was an interesting story about some bad drug dealers in the keys."

"Don't thank me for that. While I was gone, I had Lucia read the daily paper. She saved that one for us."

Luis spent another minute or two waiting to speak with Fabio. He thought an interruption in the supply chain to Florida could not be avoided unless additional flights out of Norman Cay were made. Hopefully, this Cuban thing would end as quickly as it started, and everything could return to normal.

Juanita buzzed his intercom. "I have Fabio on line one."

"Good morning, Fabio. You can guess why I'm calling."

"Yes, it's a real mess out there. Never would have believed something like this would happen to the U.S. Do you remember I mentioned my powerboat duo bringing in large loads from Bimini?"

"Yeah, I remember. Augusto and Gustavo. Both Cuban Americans."

"Well, they called from Bimini last night to explain a no-show yesterday morning. Said when they came within twenty miles of the keys, it was like 'bumper cars" in an amusement park. Hundreds of damn boats crowded with men, women, and kids. The Coast Guard was too busy to bother with them, but out of caution, they turned back to Bimini. Two boats with 600 kilos each, dammit!"

I've got more bad news. Our trawler, *Grand Pretendiente*, had to change its route to northern Florida only. We'll be short of runners in the south. Just too much law enforcement in the area to risk it."

"And it might get worse, Luis. I heard the governor was considering adding the national guard to help out. Does Pablo or Jorge know about this?"

"Doubt it. I flew in last night and only just found out this morning." Let's don't break the rules though. No calls from Miami to Colombia. I'm flying to Nassau tomorrow. I'll contact Jorge from there before flying to Norman Cay. I'm afraid Carlos will see this fiasco as an opportunity to increase his flights from his island."

"We've got a good thing going. Let's don't double-up with Carlos if we can help it. This whole Cuban thing will blow over."

"I agree. Still, we need Jorge's opinion. Judges never allow bugging an attorney's phone. I'll communicate what I learn to Juanita in my law office. She will pass everything on to you as my client."

Jack was waiting at customs when Luis arrived at Nassau International. Luis needed to wire transfer some funds to a bank in Port au Prince, Haiti. Jack didn't have to ask why. An old friend and his bitch had taken refuge there after skipping bail in the Bahamas. Ed and Lassie.

Luis wasn't sure how much Jack knew when it came to Ward. On the way to the bank, he volunteered to explain a few details of the arrangement. "Jack, I remember Ward was a friend of yours. Maybe it's important you know he's being taken care of. Shortly after he and Lassie made bail, some of the officials we work with here in the Bahamas suggested they would prefer the two of them disappear rather than stand trial."

"Understandable, but how exactly?"

Luis amused himself with the opportunity to use his favorite movie quote. "We made him an offer he couldn't refuse."

Jack had seen *The Godfather* and no further explanation was needed but Luis continued. "He accepted our offer to set him and Lassie up in Haiti for a couple of years. At least stay there and out of sight until the authorities in the Bahamas lose interest in him. Perhaps he might even fly for us again when the smoke clears."

"I'm surprised Ed didn't prefer taking off to the far east or someplace. He made a lot of money flying for Carlos."

"Not a choice. Ed invested everything back in the states. The mistake he made was not paying a single dime to the Internal Revenue Service. The moment he was arrested, those IRS boys placed claims on everything he had stateside. Ward and Lassie couldn't touch a penny of it."

"I suppose in Haiti, they depend on us for support?"

"More than just support. It's a poor country. We send $30,000 every quarter. They have a home that comes with servants in Petion-Ville where all the wealthy Haitians reside along with other rich foreigners. Not a bad deal for two drug felons."

"I've heard of it. Tourists go there. Pretty exclusive community."

Before leaving the bank, Luis phoned Jorge in Colombia. Bad news travels fast in the drug business. Jorge was already aware of the sudden influx of Cubans arriving in South Florida. Luis's update on how it was affecting their cocaine imports wasn't a total surprise. Jorge and Pablo were planning to meet that evening to discuss the situation.

Flight time to Norman Cay was short. Halfway there, Jack asked Luis if he knew about the DC-6.

"What DC-6?" Luis replied.

"Carlos bought one. Fernando's idea, I think."

"What the hell for? Can't use them on Norman Cay, can we? Sometimes I worry about the Cessna getting off the ground there."

"On our short runway, I'm sure someone like Pan Am or Delta would opt out but not us. It's a DC-6B, Luis. With a range of 2,500 miles, it can fly non-stop from Colombia with 20,000 kilos of cargo. By the time it reaches Norman Cay, the fuel tanks are three quarters empty. It's much lighter and can land there with three or four hundred feet to spare. To depart, it's the weight of an aircraft that determines the amount of runway required. With all that cocaine unloaded and without refueling, Norman Cay's is long enough for the DC-6 to take-off and then land at Nassau International or Freeport. Layover for a day or two before refueling for a return to Colombia."

Luis remarked, "Over twenty tons of cocaine flown aboard a single plane. Fernando's a smart pilot. Carlos probably loved the change from smaller aircraft." In fact, so did Pablo Escobar!

Small inconspicuous planes flying into Florida's airspace had proven to be a safe method of importing cocaine. Norman Cay was the perfect point for arrivals from Colombia and departures for the U.S. Huge amounts of money can affect judgements. The old saying, "if it's not broken, don't fix it" applied to the island. Unfortunately, with the DC-6, Carlos was capable of tripling incoming supplies. Naturally, he wanted an accommodated adjustment to exports. As the month of May passed, even Fabio was supportive of the initiative because of the Mariel boatlift interruption.

Luis wrongly assumed that the flotilla with Cubans would be short lived. Refugees continued to risk their lives making it to US shores. With no status change in May, Carlos and Fabio tasked him with either doubling up some trips out of Norman Cay with the existing crew or finding new routes and pilots to fly them. Neither were easy to accomplish safely, but by the end of July, Shannon and Alex had volunteered to help with extra flights. To that, Luis had recruited two brothers to the air team. Clarence and Dempsey Lawhorn. Both were good pilots, but they had struggled financially to manage a crop-dusting business in central Georgia. The two siblings practically welcomed the opportunity to become drug smugglers. A no brainer when they could receive unbelievable payments for flying cocaine rather than pesticides.

Glynco Jetport outside of Brunswick Georgia was selected for their port of entry. Again, it was a former military base and recently turned to Glynn County for operations. Even though it had only one long runway, it was suitable because traffic was 95% general aviation. And you could throw a stone to I-95.

Despite Carlos and Fabio still insisting he somehow had to increase air exports into the US, Luis managed regular visits home to his family. After the Georgia route was completed, he used one of those trips to meet with Jorge. In a manner of speaking, he reiterated his concerns about the Norman Cay operation. "Jorge, last April, I cautioned you and your brothers about Carlos's behavior. It's getting worse every day."

Jorge replied, "I spoke to Pablo. Made it sound like it was something only I had noticed on the occasions when Carlos was here in Medellin for meetings. Escobar is a very observant person. He knows."

"Then Pablo and you need to consider the whole picture. I've had to add routes and people to meet demand. Things are getting sloppy. We need to prepare for a total shutdown in Norman Cay."

"I sure hope you're wrong, Luis. It's been one hell-of-a-ride so far. In any case, you should know Pablo and I are exploring other means of exports. Some just-in-case scenarios."

"Can you tell me any details of what you're considering?"

"I suppose so but understand, your ears only and certainly not Carlos. Operating sort of as an independent, George Jung still works for Pablo with flights to Panama and then to Mexico. Jung even banks his money in Panama. He managed to have a high-up friend introduce Escobar to an important government official there. I should say a very important official. There's the possibility of establishing a completely protected way of transporting as much as we like though Panama to Mexico. Lots of hands out with that path, so some negotiations have to be worked out. Remember though, we're decidedly in the wholesale part of this. Who cares what the end cost might be?"

"When did this all-start, Jorge?"

"Last April right after I brought up the Carlos addiction business to Pablo. There's another organization in Cali that just changed from marijuana to cocaine. They're using the Dominican Republic much like we use Norman Cay. Pablo has Gaviria looking into substituting that country for your planes."

"I feel like a fool. Please accept my apologies for suggesting you and Pablo were not looking at the whole picture. It's just me. I've been too long in Miami and the Bahamas. Out of touch with operations here."

"Not so. You're needed in Miami for Fabito's sake. You have responsibilities there, but my little brother is your most important. Also, you needn't have to add additional pilots to Norman Cay in the future. In place of our planes with small cargos, the DC-6 is flying 20,000 kilos each trip. Plus, we now have a surplus of pilots here. Colombian nationals but Pablo has all of them in English classes. Rest easy. I think we have all the bases covered."

On June 3rd, Jessie Talbert received a congratulations letter from the University of South Carolina awarding him a football scholarship. A written acceptance was required to be addressed to head coach, Jim Carlin. Summer camp would begin August 5th. Leann was beside herself with pride. Gamecock stickers were placed on car bumpers and rear windshields. At the front driveway, a crew installed a twenty-foot flagpole flying USC's Gamecock flag beneath the Stars and Stripes.

Meanwhile, Trevor was enjoying the best of all worlds. Two or three days at home every week with the rest spent on Norman Cay. He had Leann in South Carolina and Susana in the Bahamas. The side benefits of flying for Lehder came with an enormous amount of money. Twice he had attended parties held by Carlos. There were lots of girls and practically no rules. Pretty wild but Luis and Jack had cautioned him not to get too involved. If it had not been for Susana, resisting the island's entertainment would have been difficult.

While home in Columbia, Trevor and Jessie spent considerable periods with just the two of them together. Often there were intervals of boating, fishing, and private talks during evenings on the patio. Leann was pleased for the most part. Sometimes, she was almost jealous. A friendship became obvious between Trevor and Jessie. Slowly but surely a man-to-man trust evolved. A test of that was inevitable. It came with Jessie's obsession to avenge his father and later with a place called Cherry Grove.

Trevor had decided a year in the past to buy a beach home. He had chosen North Myrtle Beach during an Easter vacation there with Leann. Because he wanted boating access to the ocean, the distal end of the city that incorporated Cherry Grove was the only option. Early in July, with Leann and Jessie in tow as advisors and a real estate agent to assist, they toured four choices on House Creek. Trevor picked the very largest and best of the four located less than a half mile from the waterway's inlet. And by far the most expensive in Cherry Grove. Without trying to negotiate the price, Trevor surprised the realtor with his offer. "We'll take this one. Tell the seller it's a cash transaction. No mortgage loan will be necessary." Trevor used his alias, Thomas Boyce, for the purchase.

An hour later, after signing buy-sale agreement papers and placing a $5,000 good faith deposit with the seller's agency, they drove back to Lake Murray. With a late arrival there, Leann complained she was tired and went to bed. Trevor and Jessie both knew the real reason for excusing herself was needing a fix.

As soon as Leann left, they made drinks and relaxed on the patio. Trevor commented he wished he didn't have to leave the next morning. Jessie decided it was past time for the moment of truth between them. "Trevor, you're not in the real estate business, are you?"

Trevor performed the Luis move. Lean back in his chair, then carefully raised his glass to sip his jack-on-the-rocks while looking directly at Jessie. Lowered his drink and said, "No! I'm not."

"If it's out of line for asking, say so and I'll shut up. Are you a drug dealer?"

"No. At least not anymore, Jessie. I used to be before I met your aunt Leann. Link and I ran a wholesale marijuana business. That ended a year back when he was arrested in Florida with a large load of the stuff in his car."

"A large load! How could he have avoided jail time?"

"With the help of good lawyers and some other friends, the charges were dropped."

"The same way you had my charges dismissed, I bet."

Trevor smiled and sipped his drink again before replying, "It was a little more complicated than a DWI arrest in Darlington County, Jessie. Same results though."

"So, you and Link used to bring marijuana from Florida to South Carolina and sell it to dealers?"

"Yes."

"Is that what got Link killed?"

"Yes and no. Several things contributed to his murder. A large stash of marijuana was one, but his cocaine addiction is the actual reason he died. Link was shooting up crack. Every day, I think? He lost his ability to make good judgement calls. For instance, hooking up with Dicey and Lavern. Obviously, they were bad company."

"They killed him just for some marijuana?"

"For that and some cash."

"What some people will do for a little dope or money is pathetic. Higgs and Topcoat for example. Believe me when I say I haven't changed my mind about those two. Did your detective ever locate Dicey or Lavern?"

Trevor remembered Luis's way of explaining the consequences of Russell's betrayal. He answered Jessie's question nearly word for word. "Detective Anderson found them in the keys. You will never see either of them again. They're permanently gone!"

Jessie sat silent for a moment. The realization of what he heard had to sink in. Finally, he said, "Trevor, who the hell are you?"

I told you last March I work for a very large organization, and the relationship is confidential. Any breach of that can put me in hot water, so you'll have to be content with not knowing everything about me for the time being."

"Can I ask if it's the mafia?"

Trevor grinned. "It's not the mafia. Much bigger than a few Italian crooks. Besides, we're black, remember? Wop's least favorite color. But like the mafia, what we do is not exactly legal. That's it! Enough about me. What about you and the Gamecocks?"

"Preseason bootcamp starts in August. With my height and all, Carlin wants me to try out for the defensive end position. Coach says even as a freshman, I may make first string."

"I'm looking forward to a regular season watching you play in the 'Cockpit'. With your body, you're made for football, Jessie. One thing for sure, Leann will be at every home game."

"Thanks, but before practice starts, I have some business I promised myself to finish. Remember. No free passes!"

"You're still hellbent on killing both of them?"

"Owe it to my dad, Trevor. You'd do the same. Already proven that! I just haven't figured out how yet."

"Maybe you need someone with a little experience to help you, Jessie. If we can come to an agreement, my assistance will be useful. Tell me, have you been practicing on the firing range?"

"Yeah, and I've used up most of the ammo from your closet. Love that damn Browning. Awesome weapon!"

"I'll buy more ammunition my next time back."

"What sort of agreement did you have in mind?"

"Listen up. I'll lay it out for you. You're going to need your own wheels. It was going to be a surprise, so act that way when it happens. Your aunt Leann convinced me to reward you for receiving a Carolina scholarship. She picked something out from your magazines and ordered it before we left for Cherry Grove."

"I can't let you do that for me. Way too much!"

"Not really. My company pays well. Besides, I'm tired of you using my car every time I'm away on business. The point is, to accomplish this dirty deed of yours first requires some surveillance. The Higgins brothers have protection. Guards and hired guns that do as instructed. Consider this. To keep their operation running, Higgs and Topcoat must have a routine to follow. The stuff they market isn't free. Someplace there is a supplier to meet on a scheduled basis, and you can bet they don't store their goods at home. Too risky. They probably have a safehouse. From there comes everything they provide to the street dealers."

"You think I should tail them."

"Very carefully. They're not amateurs. Stay so far back you can't possibly draw any suspicions. You've got time on your side if you should lose them. Never try to catch up because there will always be another day. Eventually you'll know every move they make. Someplace in the chain, there's a weak point where the two of them together are vulnerable. Find it! Once you do, that's where we can kill both the son-of-a-bitches."

"How soon, Trevor? I start training for the Gamecocks in four weeks. But did you say "we?"'

"Yeah. It'll take both of us to make this work. But that's why I need an agreement from you. In Florida, I'm doing something that can't be interrupted, especially now with all the Cubans coming in. To do this right and walk away clean, we'll have to take our time along with lots of planning. The answer as to 'when' is after football season ends. Maybe even sometime next year."

Around seven the next morning, Trevor left for Walterboro. The evening before, Jessie had reluctantly agreed to bide his time with the Higgins brothers. Sealed the deal by shaking hands. The two-hour drive to and from the airport served Trevor as reflection periods for events. His willingness to help Jessie with the demise of Topcoat and Higgs was certainly something to think about. Wondered why, to himself. Nothing to be gained. Introspective thinking but Trevor gradually began to realize he wanted to get involved. Like Dicey and Lavern, these brothers were the bad guys. They had killed Jessie's Dad and really deserved to die. Making that happen was something he aimed to do. Strange! He enjoyed the feeling of power it gave him. Maybe that explained the adrenaline rush?

Jessie spent the latter part of his next morning at the firing range. Besides the Browning shotgun, Trevor allowed him to practice with the Kimber 1911 forty-five. Loud but what a pistol. On the way home, he stopped at the newly opened Target. Its first store in Columbia. He purchased a pair of binoculars and a polaroid camera along with film. Trevor had said Leann would soon surprise him with a car. Once he had it, watching the two Higgins brothers would be at the top of his priorities. Study their movements and find their weak spot as Trevor had instructed.

When he arrived home, there was an obvious gift in the driveway. A car of course but shrouded in a car cover with a huge red bow on top.

Leann was waiting by its side holding a bottle of champagne and grinning. "Surprise," she yelled as he stepped towards her.

Because of Trevor the night before, he was prepared to provide his aunt with appreciative hugs and astonishment. Having accomplished that, Jessie pulled off the big red bow. As he began to remove the cover and before he had it half off, he gasped with almost a shocked expression. The firebird decal extended from the hood to the front fenders. After the most important stock car race in history, the 1979 Daytona 500, the dream of every sports car enthusiast in America was that event's pace-car. The 1979 Firebird Trans Am.

Jessie finished taking off the cover. Now his very genuine look of surprise excited Leann to the point that she had to brag on herself a little. "It's a limited-edition! Hard to find one, especially a year old but still brand new and never driven. Came all the way from a factory lot in Michigan."

An explanation of this model wasn't needed. Jessie had studied it several times in editions of *Car Craft Magazine*. A last of its kind because of emission standards, it came with a "four-on-the-floor" manual transmission and was powered by a high output 6.6liter 280HP V8. This one was an all hi gloss black exterior color with burgundy leather seats inside. Absolutely beautiful.

Two hours passed with Jessie and Leann cruising first the back roads around Lake Murray and then the streets of Columbia. Downtown, both noticed and then began to look for and enjoy the envious stares of the passersby. Jessie slowly realized something from watching their reaction. As proud as he was to have these great wheels, his Firebird stood out like a flashing red light. There was no way to tail the Higgins pair in this car without being noticed.

It had been six months since Mary's accident. It had taken Jessie nearly all of that time for the pain of losing his mother to soften. Constant thoughts of her, especially at night, gradually stopped. In place, his love for Aunt Leann seemed to have grown even stronger, and Trevor had become more than just a best friend. They were his family now!

On Trevor's next return home, Jessie graciously thanked him for the Trans Am. He knew a car like that had to have been Trevor's idea. Leann could never have imagined it. Later that night, and again after Leann had excused herself, Jessie brought up the problem of using the Firebird during surveillance of the two Higgins.

Troubled Trevor for a second that he had not considered this complication until Jessie mentioned it. "You're right. That car draws attention even in the best of neighborhoods. It would be like waving a flag in some of the places you might tail Topcoat or Higgs. Glad you thought of this because it's easy to solve."

"Easy! How so?"

"Leann still drives that seven-year-old Ford Maverick. What say we take your sweet aunt to a dealership tomorrow and let her pick out whatever she likes."

"You're thinking we keep the Maverick as a way of watching the Higgins brothers. With all the dents and scrapes she's put on that car; it should fit right in with the poor segregated parts of Columbia."

"Yeah, sure should. I'm ready to have one more before we hit the rack. Won't be long before you have to give up having drinks with me on this patio. Better enjoy while you still can. Let's talk about football for a change."

Trevor's nightcap on the patio, while talking football, turned out to be the year's understatement. Preseason training lasted just over three weeks. Jessie spent hours each day on the practice field, workouts in the athlete's weight room, and overnights sleeping in the "Gamecock House." Visits home were short but full of anticipation that he would qualify as a first-string player. When those brief stays overlapped with Trevor's, the conversations focused on football. On August 24th coach Carlin personally congratulated Jessie as one of USC's starting defensive ends.

Leann and Trevor instantly became hard core fans of USC's football team. His flight schedule to Walterboro on Fridays and departures on Mondays was perfect for weekend games at home. Trevor purchased fifty-yard line, front row, season tickets.

The first two games were played in Brice Stadium against California's Pacific Tigers and the Wichita State Shockers. The Gamecocks won both with blowouts. The next seven games were equally impressive with losses only to the University of Southern California Trojans and the Georgia Bulldogs. Acceptable in a way because those two teams were ranked numbers 3 and 4 nationally. Not so terrible either for Jessie's very vocal home game supporters, Leann and Trevor, because both losses were away.

Jessie was a star defensive end, a recognition diminished somewhat by Carolina's outstanding running back, George Rodgers. By the end of October, the team's record was seven and two. Even as a freshman and with only three games left to play, Jessie was already being watched as professional football material. He was so consumed with the stardom of playing, Trevor wondered if maybe his business with the Higgins might be forgotten.

Perhaps Jessie would have if not for an at home, tenth game of the season against Wake Forest. Carolina squeaked a win out to clinch the Gator Bowl, winning by one point, 39 to 38. In the final minutes of the fourth quarter, Jessie Talbert had stopped a screen pass play that would have otherwise gone for a touchdown. He was hurt making the tackle. Two players holding both sides of his shoulders helped him from the field. Jessie sustained a severely torn anterior cruciate ligament. The ACL injury ended his football career. You never know, but maybe because of Jessie's absence, the Gamecocks lost their next game to archrival Clemson followed in December by a Gator Bowl loss to Pittsburgh.

Almost anyone familiar with the intense reliance on cocaine once addicted to the drug would argue that a user rarely stopped without substantial help. Leann almost became an exception. Jessie's amazing success in football was the contributing factor. Apparently for three months beginning in September, she consistently began substituting the delights of watching him practice and play for the highs from coke. By December, Leann was nearly "clean," a description sometimes used by addicts that implies a complete recovery from drugs or alcohol.

Trevor and Jessie could not help but notice the improvements in Leann's behavior. Unfortunately, depression came fast and hard with Jessie's injury. She escaped by returning to cocaine. Upset Trevor lots. Even though he would rarely refuse sexual relations with other women, Susana in particular, his feelings for Leann were real. He despised what the drug had done to Link. Leann's abuse was taking a similar path. Trevor knew his hypocrisy was inexcusable. Monthly, he flew 1,300 pounds of cocaine into South Carolina. He was getting filthy rich doing it. Bad part was he imagined some of what he smuggled was going up Leann's nose.

During the month of December, Trevor twice doubled flights for Jack so he could have the Christmas holidays at home. Jack was happy with the accommodation because his home was Norman Cay anyway.

The Cherry Grove beach house had barely been used during the preceding months because of Carolina football. Trevor convinced Leann and Jessie they should spend Christmas there instead of Lake Murray. It turned out to be a great choice. "O.D." bars with dancing the shag, evening walks on the beach where Jessie met a special girlfriend, endless restaurants to try, celebration fireworks displayed over a calm ocean, and even a North Myrtle Beach parade with a Santa Clause. Topping that off, the House Creek was full of speckle trout waiting for a hook. Such a fantastic two weeks there, they regretted having to leave.

Returning to work in January, Trevor found nothing had changed over the holidays. Since the Cuban boatlift had ended that October, Carlos's planes were once again flying normal schedules. Initially, Trevor had figured on flying just a year or so for Carlos. Nothing but pure "greed" was forcing him to reconsider. Thanks to advice provided by Jack and Luis, he had transferred over $6,000,000 in the past nine months from the Bahamas to the Swiss Bank Corporation. Swiss banks served both as a tax haven and a safe depository for cross border assets. The country's bank secrecy laws considered disclosing client information a criminal offense. Trevor imagined amassing $50,000,000. Then retiring!

The old saying, "when it rains, it pores," could not have been more appropriate for Luis and company throughout the year of 1981. The beginning of troubles came on Friday morning January 23rd with a phone call to his Miami law office. Juanita answered but the caller only spoke French.

Lucia was fluent in the language, so Juanita passed the phone to her. The caller identified himself as Frantz Medard, Minister of Interior, Haiti. It was very important for him to speak with Mr. Castillo. Luis was in Miami and expected to be in the office sometime that morning, so Lucia assured Frantz her boss would call back shortly.

In Haiti, the Minister of Interior serves one year. Luis had placed the previous two and now Frantz Medard on a retainer. Their only responsibility in return for this financial support was to inform him if Edward Hayes Ward or his wife left Haiti. When he arrived at the office, Luis called back with Lucia as interpreter. Frantz told Lucia that both Wards were arrested at the Francois Duvalier International Airport yesterday. Following their detention, they had been immediately deported to the United States. Lucia translated the message to Luis.

In return for support and protection, Ed and Lassie had agreed to remain in Haiti for a few years at least. Since both were arrested at the Port au Prince airport, it's likely they were breaking that arrangement. Odd though, that they would be "immediately deported." That would have required substantial cooperation between the Haitian authorities and the U.S. federal government. Probably the DEA.

From the very start, Ward had flown for Carlos. He knew everything about Norman Cay and most of the people working there. Even though Luis was an attorney, Ed's knowledge of operations also included him because of his involvement in recruiting pilots and designing the method of disguising flights from Norman Cay. It was absolutely necessary to find out if Ed or Lassie were cooperating with the DEA.

Luis asked Juanita to come into his office. After going over the situation with her, he said, "I want you to make a call to Albert Turner in Jacksonville. If federal authorities arrested Ward and brought him to Florida, the United States Attorney's office will know. He needs to provide us with information on this matter for the same reasons he helped out once before. Please inform this AUSA that our confidentiality agreement will remain if he cooperates."

Juanita knew it would be unwise to phone the workplace of someone with federal law enforcement from her office. A trace was unlikely but possible.

There was a corner telephone booth a short distance away that she had used before for the same reason. She placed a long-distance call using that pay-phone to a number listed for Albert Turner taken from her rolodex.

The secretary for the Assistant United States Attorney, Middle District, Jacksonville, answered. Moments later, she buzzed Albert Turner on the office intercom. "Mr. Turner, I have a call for you from Ms. Juanita Aguero regarding a case involving Tony Mathis."

With a brief feeling of apprehension, Albert thanked his secretary and answered. "This is Albert Turner, Ms. Aguero. I take it you are an acquaintance of Tony?"

"No, Mr. Turner, I'm not. I'm a legal assistant, but I work for a different lawyer. I'm calling you at his request. There is a current matter he would like your help with."

"I'm very busy, Ms. Aguero. I see no reason to interrupt my schedule for a stranger even if we have a mutual friend. Who are you representing?"

"He prefers to remain anonymous, but you're not strangers. You've assisted my employer once before with a client he represented in exchange for keeping some of your personal life confidential. I'm sure you recall *The United States of America* v. *Richard Boyce*."

Albert Turner's recollection of the case, in every detail, was 100%. It had changed his life. He decided to try and argue. "Yes, I remember, but we had a confidentiality agreement. Has your boss forgotten our arrangement?"

"Absolutely not, Mr. Turner. Rest assured, so long as he might occasionally impose on you for a small favor, those photographs will never see the light of day."

Her mention of photographs was all it took. The AUSA accepted defeat with his next reply. "What does he want this time?"

"Very little really. Some information that might affect persons he represents. Edward Hayes Ward and his wife were arrested in Haiti yesterday and deported to the US. The arrest of a high-profile individual like Mr. Ward will draw the attention of the papers for sure. My employer would be able to advise the principals that retain his legal services much better if you would provide him with certain information. And before all the details of the arrest are released to the public."

"I'm the AUSA here in Jacksonville, Ms. Aguero, so I'm familiar with the indictment of the defendants and their subsequent apprehension by the DEA. The Wards are being detained here in Jacksonville along with five others arrested in Haiti and another two here in Florida. I will not be the prosecutor in this case, but I can tell you what I know since it will be made public very shortly."

"Please continue, Mr. Turner. I'm taking notes," Juanita lied. Actually, she was recording the conversation.

"An arraignment is set for Tuesday before U.S. magistrate Schlesinger. He is one tough federal judge, I might add. If bail is set for the Wards, it will be substantial. There are three fugitives still to be arrested, and the DEA is going to announce that additional indictments will be obtained."

"How can they be so sure?" Juanita asked.

"Again, I am not the prosecutor handling this, but it is common knowledge in our office here that Edward and Lassie Ward are cooperating fully. In return, they have been offered a plea bargain along with the witness protection program should they opt for it."

"Anything more, Mr. Turner?"

"No! I've told you everything I know. Can I be sure that my previous arrangement with your employer stays as before?"

"I can speak for him. You have his word the confidentiality agreement remains. Thank you and have a nice day."

Juanita wasted no time returning to the office. Once there, she played for Luis the taped conversation with Albert Turner. Luis leaned back, took a deep breath, then said, "Get Fabio on the phone for me."

Fabio picked up on the first ring. Juanita patched him through to Luis. After explaining the urgency of the call, Luis played the tape for him over the phone, then asked, "Was that clear enough for you?"

"I understood every word, Luis. You must have something bad on this attorney. Sounded like he was almost begging. Since it's obvious this pilot of Carlos's has turned on us, how do you propose we handle this? Normal way, I take it?"

"If he's placed in the witness protection program, there is very little we can do to eliminate the threat. Makes him virtually untouchable. We will have to make the adjustments on our end. Most of my pilots will be compromised. Probably already have been. Shannon, Jack, Joey, Reggie, and Alex will all need to retire and get lost."

"Not lost in Haiti this time. We paid those bastards a lot to keep this from happening. Maybe Colombia."

"I agree. With all the money they've made, Colombia can be like paradise. I'll introduce them to Cartagena."

Fabio laughed but then Luis continued. "Unfortunately, that's not the end of the damage. Ward also knew our method of switching planes offshore and making them into domestic flights. You heard the tape. He and Lassie are 'fully cooperating.' Almost certain Ward has spilled our disguise to his DEA buddies. Leaves us with no choice, Fabio. Our flights from Norman Cay will have to stop."

"You're right, Luis. At least for a while until Carlos can come up with something to replace them."

"You forget I'm a lawyer. Ward will name Carlos as jefe of operations in the Bahamas. The DEA will come after him in Norman Cay as soon as they can have him indicted. I'll be flying there tomorrow just to bring Carlos in on this. That's definitely something I'm not looking forward to doing."

"How long does Carlos have left?"

"Takes time to gather the evidence and put all the pieces together for a grand jury, but for sure before the year is over."

"Are you saying we will lose Norman Cay completely, Luis?"

"Yes! I'll have Juanita contact our pilots with instructions to fly their Cessna's to Norman Cay. I can meet with them there. Each will have to plan what to do next. You need to do the same with your ground crews here in Florida, Georgia, and South Carolina. No exceptions, Fabio. Perhaps later, we can work something out with the two brothers in Georgia and Trevor in South Carolina. Ward never knew them. He was gone before they joined our team."

"Carlos is not going to go along with this. With the amount of money he's making, he'll insist that keeping flights from the island are worth the risks."

"You're probably right. I believe Carlos has started thinking with his nose full of coke rather than his brain. Continuing operations as before from Norman Cay will be a poor choice if he makes it. Not with our pilots though. Escobar has a number of replacement pilots standing by if needed. All Colombians but schooled in English. Carlos can bring them to Norman Cay as substitutes."

"No offence, but I hope he does. Two or three more years working the east coast from here in Florida and I'll be able to return to Colombia as the richest man in the country."

Luis had a lot on his plate now, so he opted not to argue with Fabio about remaining in Florida. Instead, he asked, "Can you arrange a conference meeting in Colombia next Thursday? Pablo and his people along with you and your brothers. We'll know a lot more about the damage Ward has caused after his arraignment."

"I'll set it up," Fabio replied. "Leave tomorrow for Medellin. If there's nothing else, I'll see you there."

Damage control. That was now Luis's priority. His familiarity with judges made him thankful for the weekend ahead. Federal employees enjoyed five-day workweeks. It explained why Ward's arraignment was scheduled for Tuesday. Most likely it was the earliest time available for this U.S. magistrate to hear the case. Three days was enough time to take the precautionary measures required. Luis pressed his intercom. "Juanita, could you come in please."

Juanita was anticipating her summons. Stepped inside Luis's office seconds later. Sat in front of his desk with her notepad and pencil ready. "Mr. Castillo, how bad is this?"

"Not good, but it's hard to say exactly how much damage Ward and Lassie will cause. I want you to contact all our pilots. Shut the flights from Norman Cay down. Except for Trevor, have the ones that are stateside fly their planes to the island Saturday. If any object, tell them it's a command, not a request. Emphasize that if necessary."

"Consider it done. What then?"

"Prepare to shut our office down. Burn anything that might be used against us. If there is something we need to keep, send it by FedEx to our office in Medellin. Ward knows my part in the operations. We may have to leave the United States."

Juanita nodded, then commented, "If we have to leave, it's worse than I thought. When do you think this will happen?"

Luis answered her by raising his shoulders while holding both hands opened and nodding negatively. "Can't say! The same question Fabio asked. Don't worry. We have some time on our side."

"Does this affect our trawlers or any of the runners they supply?

"I hope not, Juanita. Turner said besides the Wards, another five in Haiti and two in Florida were arrested. He added there were outstanding warrants for more. We won't know if some of ours are caught up in this mess until after the arraignment."

"Okay, but keep me in the loop, Luis. There are lots of calls to make if our coastal operations are in jeopardy. Do you think our Freeport beach house will become our new base?"

"As soon as the details of those arrested are available, I'll let you know. Meantime, I'm flying to Nassau tonight. I'll call Carlos from there. He'll need to understand why all of his planes are coming at once. Tell Trevor to pick me up in Nassau as early as he can tomorrow. He'll fly me to Norman Cay."

Trevor had landed in Walterboro Friday morning. Arrived home in Columbia two hours later. There was a message on his recorder from Juanita asking him to call back as soon as possible. When he did, the instructions were to fly to Nassau early the next day and meet Luis at the airport. Juanita would not provide an explanation.

Trevor knew better than to protest the loss of a long weekend with family. At eleven Saturday morning, he met Luis in Nassau. After refueling, they departed for Norman Cay. By the time they were about to land, Luis had given him a full report of events. The part about an arraignment scheduled on Tuesday for those arrested reminded Trevor of Link's bond hearing. "I have a suggestion, Luis."

"I'm open to anything at this point. What is it?"

"Let me run an idea by you. Maybe give us a way to stay on top of this even though we're 600 miles from the action. When Link was arrested in Jacksonville, I had a good lawyer represent him. Robert Newsom, but he goes by Bobby. He was worth every penny we paid him. I can contact him through my attorney in Columbia and have him attend the arraignment. Bobby can report back to us everything about the prosecutor's case. Take notes of all the names involved, charges, and whatever else is laid out before the judge."

Bothered Luis he had not thought of doing that. Slipping in his old age maybe. "I like your idea. How soon can you set this up?"

"By Monday morning if I return to Columbia tomorrow."

"Perfect. Have this lawyer phone his findings directly to Juanita. She'll pass the information onto me. And Trevor, thanks for coming up with this. Damn smart advice."

"I owe you lots more than advice, Luis. Might make it hard paying you back for everything since it looks like the Norman Cay flying team will be moving into the ranks of the unemployed."

"Forget about paying anything back, but in your case, unemployment is not something I'm contemplating. Except for you and the Lawhorn brothers, I'm going to suggest the rest visit Colombia. Stay there for a while out of harm's way."

"Why not me, Luis?"

"You're still an anonymous player. You joined up after Ed and Lassie were arrested. They never knew you. Consider yourself on a nice long vacation. Similar to the one when Link was busted. I'll put you back to work when all is safe. Okay with that?"

"Yes, of course, but how about you?"

"Different story. Like most everyone else on this damn island, I'm probably on the list of those exposed. The Wards will name me as part of this operation right along with Carlos and the other pilots. Pretty soon, I'll have to return home for good."

Of all the inopportune times for Lehder to be having one of his house parties, this weekend was it. Luis already suspected the problem before he and Trevor arrived. When he had called from Nassau, Carlos was too busy to talk. A meeting with him would have to wait until all his guests and the entertainment girls left.

In hindsight, Carlos's absence that evening may have worked out for the better. They met at Jack's place. Every pilot was there. All were disappointed with the news. Pending the outcome of Ed's and Lassie's arraignment, Luis offered his country and Cartagena as a place for any of them to retreat.

Reggie accepted right off. Shannon and Joseph were second to respond. It turned out to be a pleasant response. "Luis, we're so very sorry about all this, but the truth is both Shannon and I were planning to resign after the next few flights. We started seeing each other last year and now we're engaged. Shannon's pregnant. We're going to have a baby this summer."

There were rounds of congratulation before Luis asked, "Where will you go, especially now that there are three of you?"

Shannon and Joey both smiled. "We had already made our plans because of the child. It's a big place, and we can easily get lost there. It's called Europe."

Jack was next to speak. "I understand your concerns, Luis, but Ed and I were awfully good friends. He won't turn on me!"

"The DEA is mighty good when it comes to obtaining confessions. Jack. The information we have is that he is fully cooperating. We'll know for sure Tuesday, but I might remind you Lassie was detained as well. You and she got along like cats and dogs. I'm sure she wouldn't hesitate to sell you out if it saved her ass."

Jack acknowledged affirmatively. "You're right. Plus, I've got to think about my wife, Sheldon. I'll tell her to start packing. Cartagena, here we come."

"For now, that leaves just you Alex. What have you decided?"

"I'm not pregnant, Luis, but there is one more revelation to be shared with you and my friends here this evening. Time for me to come clean."

Eyebrows were lifted by all there. Especially Trevor's. He and Alex had spent lots of time flying together. Luis leaned back waiting for an explanation before saying, "Come clean! How so?"

"Did you all really believe my name was Alex Smith? Not very original if you think about it. When we met in Miami, that was the phony name I used to fly a little marijuana from Jamaica. I didn't know you then, Luis, so I decided to remain incognito. Still do too if none of you mind? Ward thinks that's who I am, so even when he's flipped, the DEA guys will be looking for someone that doesn't exist after today."

Trevor grinned. "Sounds like the Thomas and Richard Boyce story to me, Luis."

Luis shook his head in agreement with Trevor, but he thought it was best not to explain any more aliases to the rest of the guys. Instead, he turned back to Alex. "Just to be clear, you're not coming to Colombia with Jack and I?"

"No. I have a real passport and all the proper identification to go with it. A stay in Cartagena with a view of the Caribbean is tempting, but I'm headed for the Mediterranean. Maybe someday, I'll bump into one of you there. It's incredibly beautiful."

Jack picked up on what Luis had just said to Alex. "Pardon me for asking, Luis, but did I understand you to say you're going back to Colombia with me?"

"If yours truly is placed on the list by Ed or Lassie, I'll have no choice. I've already instructed my secretary to prepare for departure from Miami. There's always a chance some of our names won't be mentioned, but I'm pretty sure Carlos and I are not going to be so lucky."

Somebody in the group of cocaine smugglers decided the bar was open. Only Shannon abstained. Several rounds were passed. The meeting ended with the characteristics shared by a group having their final class reunion.

Sunday morning, Trevor flew back to Walterboro. The Cessna was empty. Once back in Columbia, his mission was to contact Whitfield with instructions to have Robert Newsom take notes at Ward's arraignment. When it was over, Bobby would report everything to a number provided for the secretary of a law office in Miami. Mission accomplished except that Trevor decided to have the same report made to Whitfield's office. Curiosity got the better of him. Besides, there was a slight chance that he might be exposed along with all the rest. Trevor wanted firsthand knowledge of the court proceedings.

Luis only allowed Trevor and the Lawhorn brothers to fly from Norman Cay back to their respective states. Supposedly safe because they were pilots Ward never knew. However, Trevor's route to South Carolina was known to Ward before the Bahamians busted him in the raid on Norman Cay. It had happened well back in the past but still a concern.

If Ed spilled everything he knew, the Lowcountry Regional Airport in Walterboro might be on a DEA watch list.

Luis had to wait until late Sunday evening to go over current events with Carlos. The delay was necessary. El jefe was in very bad shape from the previous night of drugs and debauchery.

Everything considered, Carlos took the developments in stride, partly because Luis assured him Pablo could quickly replace the pilots at one tenth their predecessor's compensation. Carlos liked that part. Regardless, he swore that Edward Ward and his bitch were as good as dead. He insisted Luis put a price on their heads as soon as he returned to Miami. Luis didn't mention it but returning to Miami was unlikely.

Fernando had flown in several of Carlos's weekend guests. Luis instructed Fernando to take him and the remaining pilots to Nassau Monday morning. Once there, Alex, Shannon, and Joseph took commercial flights back to Florida. All three would leave for Europe within days. Fernando refueled in Nassau and flew to Colombia with Jack, Reggie, and Luis as passengers.

Fabio had successfully arranged for a conference meeting at the downtown Medellin Las Margaritas hotel. He reserved the penthouse. Pablo and his brother, Roberto, arrived early. Luis, Fabio, David and Jorge were right on time. Gustavo Gaviria came shortly afterwards. Carlos Lehder was the only member missing. Still, sixty percent of the cocaine entering the United States was controlled by the men in attendance. It was 1981.The figure would increase!

Attorney Newsom's report to Juanita had been thorough. As Luis anticipated, he, Carlos, Jack, and Alex were named by the Wards as co-conspirators in a drug smuggling enterprise out of the Bahamas. For reasons never explained, Reggie, Shannon, and Joseph weren't mentioned. The only bit of good news from the hearing was that none of the nine others arrested in the DEA sting, or the three still at large, were part of Luis's and Juanita's offshore runners. The *Paso Seguro* and The *Gran Pretendiente* could continue coastal operations.

The hotel's penthouse featured a dining room with a large, marble top table and comfortable chairs. It may have been a little presumptive, but once everyone was seated, Luis assumed the role as the group's counselor and legal advisor. He articulately explained the circumstances for calling all of them together. He made it clear that his pilots would probably soon become fugitives. Also, the routes and methods they had used to smuggle were compromised. Carlos's island operations had ended Saturday.

Questions were asked and answered. In summation, Luis assured the group a grand jury would render indictments against Carlos and all the others within a year. Probably, himself included! Norman Cay, consequently, would be closed permanently. Preparations needed to be made now if this part of the organization's activities along the east coast of the U.S. were to continue.

Pablo Escobar thanked Luis for the presentation. Hesitated thinking, then shrugged his shoulders and said, "Let's solve the immediate problem first. I can have six, maybe eight pilots on the next DC-6 to Norman Cay. More than enough to replace yours, Luis. They trained in Cessnas, and all speak English. We'll have Carlos back up and running."

Luis partially agreed. "That will work if we can figure out a place for them to land someplace undetected."

Escobar looked across the table at Fabio. "Florida's your backyard, amigo. Can you arrange three or four private fields for new landing sites? Dirt runways work fine for the pilots I'm supplying."

Fabio nodded affirmatively. "I have two already. They're remote and not nearly as convenient to I-95, but we've used them before as alternative sites when anything appeared suspicious at the regional airports. There are hundreds of possibilities in the three-state area we fly to. I can add more within a few weeks."

"Does this sound like a resolution to you, Luis?" Escobar asked.

"Definitely, but only temporarily out of Norman Cay, Pablo. After it's shut down, what then?"

"I have counterparts in Cali anxious to work with us. Only a small bunch and just getting started in the business, but they have connections in Santo Domingo. All I have to do is ask and they'll share. Meantime, step up your offshore runs to the trawlers. Make up for some lost time."

348

Until now, Jorge and David had simply listened. "Carlos isn't here, Pablo. If you can speak for him, how does he fit into Santo Domingo?"

Pablo Escobar habitually gave direct answers so there were no misunderstandings. This time he avoided doing that. Simply replied, "In the event Norman Cay is lost, he and I will have to work something else out." Escobar was purposely vague, but the implication was to let him handle Carlos.

Luis felt the meeting had been successful. No arguments among the two entities attending. "We can leave now gentlemen if there's nothing else to discuss?"

"Not quite yet!" Gustavo Gaviria said. "All of us know what the consequences are for betrayal. No exceptions, especially when our operations are jeopardized. Fabio, you have Griselda Blanco working with you in Florida. Very capable for a woman and she's responsible for maintaining our worker's loyalty. Pablo and I would like for you to let her eliminate Edward Ward and his wife. Make an example of them so that this does not happen again."

Normally, a request such as the one Gustavo had offered would need to be approved by all of the Ochoa brothers. The east coast was their territory. Luis saw that Fabio was looking at David and Jorge for support before answering. He interrupted by applying his role as legal counselor for the group.

"Gustavo is right. The offence warrants the death penalty for Edward and Lassie Ward. Unfortunately, the damage is done. Their arrest and arraignment are headline news in all the Florida papers. Also, both have been placed under the protection of federal authorities. Even if we could, killing the two of them now would draw uncontainable attention to Carlos, all those named as co-conspirators including myself, and ultimately our organization in Colombia. My point is, we have to delay any punitive response for now."

Pablo Escobar didn't wait for Gustavo to respond. Instead, he answered for him. "The U.S. government still thinks marijuana is their nation's number one drug problem. Not cocaine or us! Doing anything to change that perspective, like killing these two rats, would not be to our advantage. Let's wait. Someday, they will receive an appropriate reward from us. My word on that!"

When the meeting adjourned, the Ochoa brothers and Luis left the hotel together. Jorge suggested they all spend the evening having dinner at their father's restaurant. It was something they had agreed not to do again, but Jorge wanted family privacy. Once everyone settled in with drinks and before ordering meals, he asked Luis if there was anything more of concern that wasn't discussed with Escobar.

"There is Jorge but clue me in on something. Some time back when I explained my worries to you about Carlos, Cali was mentioned. Today, Pablo did the same. We have complete control here in Medellin. Who the hell are we talking about doing business with 300 kilometers to our south?"

"This was Escobar's doing, not mind Luis. A pair of brothers in the marijuana trade out of Cali approached Pablo last March. Upper class types. Their names were Miguel and Gilberto Orejula. Got started in the business with a family friend named Jose Lodono. Snobby bunch in my opinion. Can you believe the three together refer to themselves as 'Los Caballeros de Cali?' They wanted to transition into smuggling cocaine instead of marijuana and offered to purchase it directly from Pablo's "tranquilandia" lab. At the time, the laboratory was producing more supply than our combined distributions were capable of smuggling, so he accepted the proposal. David and I figured they deserved watching, but it shouldn't affect us since these so-called 'gentlemen' were only a small start-up operation."

"Wish you or David had told me about this before now. I could have checked them out. Let me remind you their story sounds a lot like you and your brothers only a few years ago when Pablo came to us. Look at yourselves now. You especially, Fabio. An organization smuggling cocaine can grow quickly."

"We'll be careful here in Colombia, Luis, but something else is bothering you."

"In the meeting today, as respectfully as possible I tried to warn of pending indictments brought against most, if not all of those the Wards named in their hearing. If you wait until that takes place, it's too late. I need to come home, Jorge. Permanently!"

Fabio asked, "Do you mean leaving Miami right away? After today's meeting with Escobar, it's clear that we'll soon continue the flights from Norman Cay. Can't you wait until Carlos has to shut down?"

"I'd rather not. There's my family to consider if I'm indicted while still in Florida. Better safe than sorry."

Fabio argued politely. "Luis, you're an important part of our east coast business. Replacing you would be difficult."

"Thanks for the compliment. Consider this, all of you. I can continue to provide legal assistance from Colombia. However, an alternative to Miami is required if we're to keep everything running smoothly with our offshore operations plus scheduling flights from Norman Cay. For that, I've come up with a contingency plan for communications out of Freeport."

David interrupted. "This is news to us. Interesting too! When did you come up with this idea?"

"Actually, after I met with Jorge last July. I was worried that Carlos's behavior might cause Norman Cay's demise. Your brother and Escobar had already planned ahead just in case it happened. I decided perhaps we should do the same."

David nodded an approval. "Nothing wrong with forward thinking Luis. Keeps us out of trouble on occasions. Carry on!"

"We have excellent relations with officials in Freeport. Juanita and I spent a weekend house hunting there. Found a perfect waterfront place for moving our communication equipment to. Closed on it in August."

"How long will it take to set up communications?" Jorge asked.

"The time it takes Juanita and Lucia to fly to Freeport from Miami. We've had a half dozen phones hooked up to a nearby rented apartment. They're traceable from the U.S. only back to the Bahamas and it's 200,000 inhabitants. For ship to shore from the house, a single sideband radio with a 26-foot antenna was installed. This time with an even better tuner to match frequencies than the one we used in Coral Gables."

"Excellent!" Fabio complimented. "Please somebody give Luis a gold star. Lawyers like him are rare."

"Thanks again, but I had lots of help. Juanita, Juan, Diego, and even our new gal, Lucia, made this happen."

David stood and placed an appreciative arm around Luis's shoulder. "I'm not sure we can stand any more of these surprises before dinner."

"Better sit back down then. I'm not finished just yet. Understand what might be the most important thing I'll say today. One of my primary legal responsibilities is to keep all of us safe. That's much easier to do if we're all working from Colombia. When those indictments are eventually handed down, the DEA will come after Carlos and all his associates. They'll offer plea deals to anyone willing to turn on a kingpin. In Florida, that's you Fabio!"

"I can't leave Miami in the middle of these changes, if that's what you're suggesting?"

"Listen to my advice, Fabio. Just promise me you'll prepare to leave at a moment's notice. Keep your bags packed. You know I have a contact with the U.S. Justice Department's criminal division in Jacksonville. I'll make sure he gives me advance notice if and when a grand jury indictment is imminent. Once they start arresting defendants, their pleas for leniency will put you in the DEA's crosshairs."

Both David and Jorge took Luis's side in the discussion that followed. They felt responsible for Fabio. Bringing him into the organization at a very young age may have been irresponsible on their part. Any chance that he might be arrested in Florida had to be avoided.

Fabio was raking in money by the truckload. Fairly understandable that he resisted being told to maybe leave Florida and quit making a fortune. If it were not for the pressure from both of his brother's and Luis, there was no way he would have consented to return permanently to Colombia, even if Carlos and crew were indicted. He reluctantly had to agree with their instructions.

Luis commended and affirmed the decision with a handshake and another one of his movie quotes. "Sometimes, Fabio, it's time to 'Circle the Wagons.' You just have to know when."

That evening at his ranch with Michelle, Luis surprised her with the probability of him returning to Colombia for good. The Ochoa brothers had all agreed it was the right thing for him to do under the circumstances. Michelle was pleased to say the least. Some tasks needed to be completed to accomplish the move of communications to Freeport but nothing very complicated. Thanks to foresight, almost everything was already set to go.

Since they were closing the office in Miami, Luis had broken his rule about never phoning there from Colombia or vice versa. Juanita was instructed to leave little or no trace of the years they spent in the city. Afterwards, she and the rest of the team would gather everything they could carry or ship and move to Freeport. It was not quite as simple to do as Luis had told Jorge. Juanita estimated three or four days were required to clean up business in Miami before all might fly to Freeport. Luis was glad to hear of the delay. He wanted a few days with Mitch and Daniel before leaving for the Bahamas.

That night alone with Michelle, Luis shared a secret with her. Something he could not say outright to the Ochoa's or Escobar. He was actually glad the Wards had bargained with the DEA. Finally, he could come home where he was safe!

25.

RETRIBUTION

Isaac Higgins had turned forty-five on December 23rd, 1980. Along with just two friends, he and his younger brother Abraham celebrated the birthday at a home the two shared. It was located in the historic area of Columbia called Heathwood. Neither were married. They were black and Isaac was "gay." It was an increasingly familiar term used by homosexuals at the time to describe their sexual orientation.

In the early eighties the combination of two men, both black, one single and the other gay, residing in the upscale neighborhood of Heathwood was unique. There were only two other families of color and being gay still carried negative connotations among most, if not all, of the other residents. But the Higgins brothers were very private individuals who kept to themselves. Prejudices were probably set aside because of their seclusion, and because Isaac and Abraham were obviously wealthy. They employed a full-time maid, security guards, and a part time gardener. Both men also rode around in brand new cars. Abraham sported a BMW and Isaac a Cadillac, most times with a chauffeur.

Rumors among nearby residents were that these two neighborhood black men were South Africans who had once owned a diamond mine before immigrating to America. Just gossip speculations and nothing could have been further from the truth. They were South Carolina drug bosses born and raised in Florence, a city about 70 miles east of Columbia.

In the predominantly segregated parts of Greenville, Spartanburg, Charleston, and Columbia, the two men controlled distributions and sales of heroin and cocaine. Blacks in those communities knew well they weren't foreigners. Even there however, Abraham and Isaac were known by nicknames only. Higgs and Topcoat. Both owned a reputation as being ruthless to the point of murder. Something they had earned while building a drug domain.

The Higgins brothers moved from Florence to the state's capital in 1965. Early after arriving in the city, they began to supply street dealers with heroin. By the late sixties, they had become the supplier of hard drugs in most of South Carolina's black neighborhoods. Together, Abraham and Isaac had to overcome the difficulties of safely getting the drug from producer to consumer. It required a well-organized method of purchase, transport, and distribution without being caught by police or killed by competitors. With time, they carefully solved the legality problem by sharing a portion of profits with certain command authorities. Removing the opposition, instead of being removed, fixed the latter. That too took time and doing so gained the two of them the brutal reputation.

Heroin was the drug of choice for heavy abusers in the fifties and early sixties. The Middle East, Southeast Asia, Turkey, and Mexico were the principal sources. Along the southwest border with the U.S., the preferred method used by Mexican traffickers to smuggle were privately owned vehicles and semi-trucks at legal points of entry. Brown powdered and black tar heroin was hidden inside car seats, tires, doors, and gas tanks. Semis hid much larger loads stored among packed crates of fruits or vegetables. U.S. Customs was ill equipped during the sixties and seventies. As well, they mainly focused on the cross-border flow of marijuana.

Estimates are that 15% of veterans returning from Vietnam had become users of illicit opioids and cocaine. Starting in the late sixties, producers in South American countries began supplying Mexico's drug lords with cocaine. The popularity of coke increased dramatically in the U.S. over the next decade. By the 1980s, its profitability exceeded heroin.

Mexico's smugglers pretty much confined their activities to transit. They acted as volume distributors and rarely involved themselves with street level distribution. For that part, relationships were established with U.S. gang leaders. By comparison with some of those in New York, Chicago, or Los Angeles, Higgs and Topcoat were "bush-league." During the 1970's in the United States, that reality would have been difficult to comprehend when the two men's annual income was several million.

In earlier years, maintaining a prosperous dealership in drugs had required Higgs' and Topcoat's regular presence among most of those they employed. Disobedience wasn't tolerated. Both men committed atrocities during that period, often together and entirely against their own race. Occasionally, cruel acts of violence were applied purposefully to earn fear and respect in the black communities they controlled.

By the late seventies, a chain of command was in place such that in person contact was limited to about a dozen supervisors and henchmen. The two Higgins reminded residents of their area control by sometimes driving the streets with these gang members caravan style in three or four cars. Higgs and Topcoat were always chauffeured in a middle car and at times waved or nodded to observers. The practice was their visible display of power, and something anyone with good sense acknowledged.

There was one part of operations that could not be left to underlings. Transfers of heroin and cocaine from Mexican suppliers and payments to the same required strict secrecy. Only two of the brother's most trusted bodyguards accompanied the Higgins during deliveries. Cash amounts handed over during these transactions averaged between one and two million. Once cut, bagged, and distributed, the street value of the drugs purchased was several times that.

The American taxpayer's addition of the Interstate Highway System made possible a convenient method of transporting drugs. Semi-trailer trucks used the roads extensively. The U.S. was a major importer of Mexican fruits, especially tomatoes and avocados in route to major cities across the country. The food products were refrigerated and stored from front to back making it virtually impossible to search for two particular contrabands. Heroin and cocaine.

The favored route to eastern states utilized Juarez-El Paso as a legal point of entry. From there, I-10 east for 150 miles intersected with I-20 which ended 1600 hundred miles later in Florence, South Carolina. As young men, Abraham and Isaac had worked as shift labor in the farmer's market located on the outskirts of the city. By accident one dark night made worse by fog, they unpacked the wrong trailer of tomatoes. Working alone without supervision, they found halfway back a few crates packed tightly with kilos of heroin.

In later years, Abe and Isaac would remind themselves of the experience and the smartest move in their lives. They had repacked the crates of tomatoes, closed the doors, and left everything inside as if it had not been disturbed.

Abraham, Isaac, and one assistant manager were the only ones working the "graveyard shift." It was the manager's instructions that had led to the wrong trailer. They woke him from an inebriated sleep in his small warehouse office. Clearly drunk and upset, his reaction to their discovery was evidence he knew the drugs were in the trailer. Swore them to secrecy and didn't even thank them for repacking it. Passing over a few dollars to both men would have been an appropriate response.

A week later and this time working a day shift, the brothers were summoned to the same warehouse office. Inside, the plant manager introduced them to Nicolas Estrada. Although obviously Hispanic, his English was perfect. For several minutes, Estrada questioned the pair about their personal history. He asked if they were familiar with drugs. Learning that neither Isaac nor Abraham were substance abusers, he wanted to know how they felt about heroin. More importantly, why they had kept quiet about the trailer experience. Abraham answered the last question perfectly. They had hoped to be rewarded something for their efforts. A small expression of the shift supervisor's gratitude would have been nice.

Apparently, Estrada must have reached a satisfactory conclusion from the interview. In appreciation of their cooperation and silence regarding the drug incident, he offered Abraham and Isaac a lucrative career change. Work through him and become drug dealers. For two almost always broke black men with no real future, an opportunity to possibly become wealthy was readily accepted. Whatever risks were involved were meaningless!

Estrada's offer was generous but came with one non-negotiable provision. Isaac and Abraham could not work in their hometown. Anywhere but Florence! The city was kept relatively clean for a reason. The farmers market there was being used by Nicolas and his associates to distribute heroin wholesale to dealers as far away as Philadelphia. Anything that might draw the attention of federal or state authorities to that city was prohibited. Hypocrisy in a way. One of the most drug free cities on the east coast was unintentionally engaged in polluting many others.

For starters, Abraham and Isaac were provided with front money and four kilos of heroin. Estrada's instructions were made with a clear threat. Return to him $200,000 within three months and receive new supplies. Failure would not be excused. If either the drugs or the money was lost somehow, they would be held responsible. As an example of his seriousness, Estrada reminded the brothers of an unfortunate accidental drowning that had occurred just days ago. After apparently falling out of his john boat while fishing, a shift supervisor for the farmer's market had been found floating face down in the Great Pee Dee River.

During the sixties, the wholesale price of a single gram of heroin averaged forty dollars. Prices were even higher in the northernmost cities. Its value doubled when sold on the streets. For Abraham and Isaac, Colombia, South Carolina was a convenient place for starting their business. It included plenty of heroin users among their race, and blacks were mostly segregated to an inner part of the city. There was one other advantage. When they required fresh supplies, Florence's farmer's market was only seventy miles away.

In the beginning, local street dealers were reluctant to work with them. There was a major problem from competition in the city. One person controlled all the heroin sales to blacks in Columbia. His name was Victor Sowell. As a supplier, he had started out in Charleston where he was raised. By 1960, he had expanded distribution to Columbia. Sowell quickly learned of two newcomers in Columbia trying to convince some of his street dealers to, instead, work with them.

This was not Victor's first experience with rivalry. His method of removing any threat to business was simple, effective, and well known. First, provide a convincing warning. If not heeded, kill the idiot, or idiots if there were more than one. Problem solved and remembered.

One week following the move into Columbia, Isaac and Abraham were cruising a neighborhood favored by drug users. They were shopping for potential recruits. Isaac was driving. Just before coming to a stop light, they were passed by a solid black 1960 Lincoln Continental Mark V convertible with two black men staring across from the front seat. Ironically, Isaac waved, and Abraham commented. "Nice car!"

Ahead the light was green, but instead of continuing, the driver of the Lincoln stopped and waited for it to turn red. Next, the two occupants stepped out and walked back to either side of Abe's and Isaac's car. Both brandished pistols and motion for the windows to come down. Isaac and Abraham were caught completely off guard. Left without any choice, they complied with the order and lowered the car windows. Victor Sowell placed his Colt 38 revolver against Isaac's temple, cocked the hammer and asked, "Do you know who I am?"

A weak answer came from one scared as hell Isaac. "No sir, I don't. Please don't shoot me. Take whatever you want."

"Victor is my name. His name is Ali. Ask anybody! This is our territory you stupid piece of shit. If you or that jerk beside you ever set foot around here again, we'll blow your brains out. Understand?"

Isaac nodded yes with a wide-eyed comprehension. Abraham had sat silent without moving a mussel. Ali to his right also had a gun pointed directly in his face. Abraham raised both hands and nodded his agreement as well. To make his point, Sowell held the pistol's hammer with his thumb and squeezed the trigger. Then he let Isaac watch as he purposely lowered the hammer quickly. Just not down fast enough to fire the cartridge.

Victor and his henchman walked back to their convertible and drove away. As they did, Abraham noticed the two smiled at each other. Neither realized the mistake they had made. A short time later both very briefly would.

With a gun held against his head, Isaac still had lied. He and Abraham did know who Victor Sowell was. More than one of the dealers they tried to recruit had warned they were messing with this really bad ass of a man. The consensus among those on the streets was these boys are about to get themselves very dead.

There are times when life decisions are made from few choices. The Higgins brothers had received a warning from Estrada along with his money and heroin. While driving back to their rented apartment, they discussed options.

Abraham argued, "No going back to Florence. Dead meat if we do."

"Yeah, but just as dead if we stay in Columbia, Abe. I really thought he was going to pull that trigger. Maybe we should try Greenville instead. We're only two weeks into this. Plenty of time to go somewhere else."

"If there is business to be had in another city, Isaac, you can bet your sweet ass there will be another one around like Victor Sowell protecting his turf. Maybe even worse. We've already made some progress here. At least a lot of the dealers recognize us. I think we should stay!"

"Whatever it takes, little brother, I'll go along with you, but there's no question about it. Staying means kill or be killed. Are you up for that?"

"Those SOB's stuck guns in our face and said they would blow our brains out. You damn right I'm up for this!"

"Then let's show them they screwed with the wrong brothers. All we'll need is a plan to take them out."

Abraham and Isaac were only a week into the heroin trade before they had committed themselves to murder an opponent. A rapid and significant change for two men who just prior were simply poorly paid black shift labor. The year was 1960. Neither knew at the time but this action would not be a one-time-event.

Victor Sowell lived in Charleston. Whenever business required him in Columbia, he stayed at a home right smack in the middle of a neighborhood he controlled. It was a single-story upscale house for the area and no secret to locals who the place belongs to. Also, the same guy that held a gun to Abraham's face was a permanent occupant.

It occurred to Isaac and Abe that perhaps they had an advantage because of this house Victor owned in Columbia. They knew where he stayed whenever in town. Abe suggested using it as a location to strike. Hide someplace and bushwhack the bastard. Trouble was not knowing when he would visit.

Isaac had an idea. Use the threat Sowell had made that day. "Abe, we've been told never to set foot in his territory again. Tomorrow afternoon around five to seven, let's rub our feet in his face. Ride around and tell every dealer we see that there's a new boss in town. Us! Say we're taking over his operations. Word will get back to Charleston pretty quick. If Victor Sowell lives halfway up to his reputation, he'll come for us right away. We can be waiting at his house. Catch him off guard just like we were."

"Risky, but I like your plan. Everyone recognizes our car including Victor and that bodyguard, Ali. Use it tomorrow when spreading the word, but then let's get a rental car. There's plenty of street parking in Sowell's neighborhood. Drive the rental tomorrow morning so no one recognizes us. Watch for him to come. If we see an opportunity to make the hit, we'll take it!"

The following evening word spread like wildfire. The dealers knew all hell would break loose when Victor Sowell heard what these two newcomers were telling them. Their attitude was wait and see, but most figured these two young men's blood and guts would be all over the streets by the same time the next day.

At six in the morning, Abraham and Isaac parked their rental car across the street and sixty yards down from Sowell's home. There was a gentle rain, but the location gave them a clear view of the front door and a two-car garage attached to the side of the house. They didn't have to wait long. About a half past seven, the garage door raised, and a car backed out. It was Ali driving. He was alone. Staying well back with a car or two between, Isaac followed behind. Two miles later, Ali pulled into a small shopping center and entered a grocery store.

Isaac asked, "What now, Abe? Do we just sit and wait for this man to shop?"

Abraham thought for a few seconds. "Hell no! His was the only car in that garage. The house is probably empty now, and he's buying groceries to bring back home. Come on! Let's get going and wait for him there. This may be the chance we were hoping for."

The rain was coming down harder by the time they had returned. Some lighting off in the distance. Abraham and Isaac parked on the street the same as before but left their car and walked fifty or so yards to Sowell's house. Both carried fully loaded 12-gauge shotguns wrapped in blankets. The garage had a side door on the part not attached to the house. Wasn't locked. There was an eight-foot by four-foot tool room against the back wall. Abraham suggested they wait and hide inside.

Maybe fifteen minutes passed before the garage door raised. Ali pulled in until the car's rear bumper cleared and lowered the door down with a remote before getting out of his car. He was holding a large paper bag filled with groceries. Abraham and Isaac quickly walked out of the tool room towards him with guns raised. Neither said a word. Almost simultaneously, both fired from less than ten feet away into Ali's chest.

For a moment or two, they stood silently surprised by all the blood from Ali's body spreading across the concrete floor. Isaac said, "Did we just do what I think we did?"

"Believe so, Big Brother. I'll check outside and see if the noise got anybody's attention."

Abraham looked around the front of the house and down the street, then came back. "Quiet as a mouse, Isaac. The storm probably helped. How the hell do we clean this mess up before Sowell gets here?"

Isaac had already decided what to do. He walked into the rear tool room and came out with a shovel. "We don't need to clean it up, Abe." He made three hard swings with the shovel against the overhead garage door opener. Busted it to pieces.

Abraham watched and asked, "You have a better idea?"

"Yeah! It's raining. Lock that side door. If Victor pulls into the drive and the garage door won't go up, he'll have to come in the house though the front. When he does, we'll let him have it!"

From the attached garage, you entered the house through the kitchen. There was a hallway to a large living area and then, slightly off to the right, another short hallway with a coat closet leading to the front door. Isaac and Abraham took seats in the living room with a window view of the outside driveway. They waited. Not long!

A little past 10 a.m. and almost like waving a flag announcing an arrival, a shiny black Lincoln Continental convertible pulled into the driveway. Top was up because now rain was pouring. Two men were in the front seat. The driver was pointing to the garage with a remote in apparent frustration and talking. "Boss, the damn thing won't open. Maybe the battery's dead."

Victor griped, "Wouldn't you know, Sal? Raining like hell too. Blow the damn horn. Let's hope Ali will hear it."

Sal obeyed with several honks. "Nothing boss. We'll have to make a run for it."

Inside Abraham and Isaac experienced a short panic. Abraham whispered loudly. "Dammit, there's two of them! If either get away, we're screwed. No choice though. Can't run for it now, Isaac."

"Why not, Abe? This is our first try. Come back in a week or two. Pick another time and place. This bastard isn't going anywhere. I think maybe we should slip out the back while we have a chance."

Abraham took command. He saw his brother was losing some of his nerves. "Got to do this now, Isaac. Remember what's laying on the floor in the garage. Can't run away from that. Listen, they're going to have to come in through the front. I'll hide in the coat closet. You get yourself behind the refrigerator in the kitchen. Once they're halfway between the two of us, we'll have their asses in a crossfire. Step out shooting. I'll do the same. Okay?"

Isaac agreed with Abe's suggestion but changed it for the better. "If they're between us, you'll have their backs. You shoot first. When I hear your first shot, I'll come out blasting."

"You got it! Let's finish what we started. Hey, looks like they're getting out. Hide."

When it's raining like hell, you might think twice about hiding in a coat closet. Damn dark inside with the door closed but Abraham realized the mistake and readied the shotgun. Not ten seconds after leaving their car, Sal opened the front door. He and Victor came in. Victor had covered himself and his travel bag with a raincoat before making a run from the Lincoln. While taking off the coat, he instructed Sal. "Find out where the hell Ali is. Dammit, I'm soaked! Tell him the garage door is stuck. You two fix it! If it's batteries, get some!"

"Will do boss." Sal turned and started down the hallway leading to the kitchen. Victor set his travel bag on the floor and opened the closet to hang up his coat. Abraham shot him just below the chin. Very close range. Two feet at most, so the buckshot never spread, but they exited through the back of his neck severing the vertebra just below the skull. Victor fell backwards against the wall having instantly become a quadriplegic.

With the noise of the shot, Sal instinctively turned back in the hallway while reaching with his right hand for a shoulder holstered pistol under his left arm. In that turn maneuver to defend his boss, he never saw Isaac step out from behind the refrigerator. Isaac's first shot from 20 feet away struck Victor's bodyguard in his lower right side causing him to fall face down on the floor. A split second later, Isaac fired again with better aim. This time the buckshot raked Sal's body across the upper back and head. A third shot was aimed but never fired. Sal was obviously dead!

Abraham yelled from the closet. "Isaac, you okay?"

"Yeah! Come on out. The coast is clear."

"Okay, but don't shoot me. Coming out." Abraham left the closet having to step over Victor's

legs spanning the width of the hallway floor. Isaac joined his brother but instead circled around Sal's body. Both men looked down at Victor Sowell laying there with his eyes and mouth wide open. Abraham asked, "Does he look dead to you? Can you tell?"

"Maybe. What's that gurgling noise he's making?"

364

"Hell, Isaac. I don't know. He's done for though. Let's get out of here. Been lucky so far. Better not to push it."

With a successful murder of both men and the danger passed, Isaac had regained his nerves and composure. "Wait, Abe. We're not through yet. You and I went around yesterday telling all those dealers about us taking over. They all thought we were crazy. Dead men for sure because they were scared to death of this piece of crap lying here."

"Yeah, sure they did. What's your point? We've done all of those dealers a big favor, but I doubt they're going to thank us for it."

"Thank us! Hell, Abe, I want them to be just as afraid of us as they were him. Watch this!" Isaac raised his 12 gauge Remington a yard above Victor's face and fired.

The action caught Abraham by surprise. "Shit, Isaac! Look at the mess you've made. I think he was dead already except for that bubbly sound. You just making sure or what?"

"I am making sure in a way. Leaving him like this to give anyone we might deal heroin with something to remember us by. A reason not to fool with us, or they'll wind up looking like this thing."

Abraham looked down at a very dead Victor Sowell. Unrecognizable now. "I think you've made your case Big Bro! Can we go now?"

"Not yet. Like we did in the garage, let's be safe and pick up our shell casings. Do that while I check out what he was carrying in the travel bag"

Abraham quickly found the four spent shell casings fired from the shotguns. Came back to Isaac and asked, "What was in the case?"

"Remember the big gun he shoved against my head? It's in here."

Abe grinned. "Well, he sure as hell won't be needing that anymore. Is that all?"

"Not quite!" Now it was Isaac grinning and much broader. He held the travel case open towards Abraham. It was packed with banked bound $20 bills. Shook his head at Abraham and said, "Now we can leave."

The case weighed a little over twenty pounds. After counting it twice once they were safely back in their apartment, Isaac placed a hand on his brother's shoulder. "$200,000, Abe. You gotta admit, not bad for a morning's work. I think I like this drug business!"

A few days after coming into their fortune, they purchased new cars. A solid black Oldsmobile 88 for Abraham and a solid white Chevrolet Impala for Isaac. Both automobiles contrasted with others in the areas of Columbia where they had been trying to recruit dealers. Even so, it wasn't just the showy new cars that drew attention to them.

Word of Victor Sowell's death and that of his two guards shocked the black neighborhoods. The condition of his body had spread and had been quickly exaggerated. Isaac had achieved far more than expected with his disfigurement of Sowell's face. It brought with it a reward of instance recognition, fear, and respect. Within a week, they had inherited Sowell's heroin business in Columbia. Shortly afterwards, a dealer from Charleston approached them. Victor's passing had caused a shortage of heroin to dealers there. Addicts can become quite desperate when availability runs low. Literally overnight, Abraham and Isaac became relied on within South Carolina's two largest cities for supplying heroin to street dealers. Consequently, they were anointed the title of drug boss. In that role, it was the locals in those communities they worked who soon nicknamed Abraham a simple abbreviation of his last name. "Higgs." Isaac frequently wore an overcoat. Hence, "Topcoat."

Nicolas Estrada was not surprised when the manager of the farmer's market informed him of a scheduled pickup and delivery by his two newest employees. A little less than a month had passed, but the newspapers had carried the story of Victor Sowell's brutal demise. Estrada had heard who had replaced one of his organization's competitors. To show an appreciation of their service, he made plans to be present when Abraham and Isaac arrived at the market.

Normal weekday hours for Florence's farmers market were 7 to 5. After closing, Abraham and Isaac arrived as scheduled at 8 p.m. in the new Olds 88. The manager opened the gate for them and waved them towards his office. Nicolas Estrada was there waiting to greet them.

Abe and Isaac entered carrying a military style duffle bag between them weighing eighty pounds. It contained $200,000 for Estrada. Half of it was in $5 and $10 bills. The other half in $20 bills. Broad smiles and outreached hands by the pair of brothers were made with an air of confidence that betrayed the bag's contents. It was obvious to Estrada a transformation had occurred. The two men handing over that money were a far cry from what had been ordinary shift workers just four weeks ago. Both men looked successful. Abraham was well dressed, and Isaac was wearing an expensive new London Fog overcoat.

The conversation with Nicolas was more cordial than the first. He took the duffel bag without even looking inside and congratulated Abraham and Isaac for their accomplishments in a much shorter period than expected. Nicolas also knew their payment meant they had exhausted supplies. His assumption of that circumstance came with some advice to both men. "Abe. Isaac. I and my associates are pleased with your success. However, for reasons of keeping our market here safe from exposure, we prefer to resupply you no more often than monthly. Otherwise, the traffic might be noticed."

"I understand," Abe replied. "But to comply, we will need quite a bit more to keep our streets happy. We've already expanded into Charleston. Can you spare ten, or even better, twelve kilos this time?"

Estrada granted the request with an affirmative shake of his head. "Charleston too, already? Makes sense when I think about it. The city was Victor Sowell's territory as well as Columbia."

The mention of Sowell's name caught Isaac off guard. His expression showed an alarm. "Maybe we should have asked, Nicolas. I hope he was not a friend of yours?"

"I can promise you he was no friend. A competitor and a ruthless one. You and Abe were not the first to try moving our goods into Columbia. Others that tried were warned away or found dead in some alley. You've done us a favor."

Isaac's relief was obvious. "I suppose you read about it in the news-papers?"

"Front page news in *The State*. Afterwards, the word around Colum-bia was two guys named Higgs and Topcoat took over. I knew it had to have been you two. Still though, what made you decide to take on an opponent like Sowell? In Vegas, the odds against you would have been forty to one."

Abraham's honest and humorous answer made Nicolas Estrada laugh with recognition. "Truth is, Nicolas, we considered our options and decided that neither of us wanted to go fishing in the Pee Dee River."

Isaac was relieved by Estrada's reaction. Even so, he wasn't absolutely sure that Abe's response to the question was okay. He added to his brother's explanation. "Sowell and one of his thugs stuck pistols in our face and threatened to blow our brains out. Then they walked away smiling. Big mistake! We had no choice but to take them out."

Estrada prided himself on an ability to judge people. Abe and Isaac had impressed him during their initial interview, else he would not have offered either an opportunity to trade heroin. Now that he was certain of them, sharing some details of how his group fit into the business was appropriate.

"Well, Isaac. From the paper's description of the crime scene, you and your brother did that and more. Hopefully your style of managing similar problems won't be required too often. Honestly though, we're in a rough and competitive business. There are times when actions like the ones you took will be necessary."

"We learned that lesson in our first week, Mr. Estrada."

"And you handled it alone. Impressive, but in the future if you face bad odds, let me know. Like I said, you did our organization a favor. We repay favors."

"Good to know," Abraham said. "We can manage the small stuff. Anything outside of that and one of us will call for help."

With that understanding, Nicolas next assumed the role of teacher. "When we met a month ago, I asked what either of you knew about the heroin trade. No offence, but your lack of knowledge was evidenced by honest but naive answers. There's no substitute for experience. You've gained some of that and proven yourselves worthy of becoming members of our organization if interested?"

To Estrada's offer, Abraham and Isaac Higgins replied, "Yes, absolutely," and they agreed to it with appreciative handshakes. As subordinates, the brothers had that evening unconsciously joined a small but organized crime group composed mostly of Mexicans.

Nicolas Estrada spent the next hour schooling his new members in the heroin business. Considering the amount of money Abe and Isaac had made in less than a month, it came as a surprise to them that Mexico was a minor player in the multibillion-dollar enterprise. Also, for two men raised as under-privileged blacks in Florence, South Carolina, titles like *The Golden Triangle* and *The Golden Crescent* were as foreign as the countries they were assigned to. Imports of their heroin into the U.S. were primarily controlled by organized crime syndicates. The Cosa Nostra and the Mafia operated the eastern and central parts of the country. Often, lines were drawn to prevent one group's interference with another.

Entrepreneurial individuals working out of Mexico like Estrada and his associates were permitted by the syndicates but mostly restricted to the southern parts of the country and California's Tongs. Since the eighteen hundreds, opium poppies had been grown in Mexico's sovereign state of Sinaloa. The trade in opium there was tolerated because it was exported.

Abraham's and Isaac's education into the broader aspects of dealing in hard drugs began that night with Estrada. However, there were many changes over the next ten to fifteen years. Heroin sales out of Mexico prospered thanks to enforcement efforts by the United States and several European countries. Throughout the seventies, governments worked to dismantle the smuggling rings importing the drug from Asia and the Middle East. Major interdictions occurred, but in the U.S., Mexico quickly replaced shortages. And in the U.S., cocaine became increasingly popular with the return of soldiers from the Vietnam War.

Accordingly, by the mid-seventies, the Higgins brothers working with Estrada had added it to their sales.

The relationship between Nicolas, Abraham, and Isaac benefited with time and profits. South Carolina was ultimately declared a territory reserved for the brothers. Enforcement of those territorial rights was occasionally required.

Nicolas Estrada's position in the drug business changed as a consequence of consolidations in Mexico. Rather than fight competition, independent groups began to merge and become stronger. Estrada and his associates were no exception. Ultimately, a few central figures began to take control of drug operations in all of Mexico. The earliest and largest came about in the late seventies. The Guadalajara Cartel headed by the "Jefe de Jefes," Miguel Angel Felix Gallardo. Estrada and party joined the cartel in 1979. His status in the organization's hierarchy was significant.

Early in their drug career, Abe and Isaac purchased an Open-Air Vegetable Market on the outskirts of Columbia. They added another in Charleston six months later. The businesses were a well disguised excuse for a produce truck to make regular trips to the farmers market in Florence. The idea was suggested by Estrada and copied his own methods of trailering from Mexico. Kilos of heroin were concealed inside crates beneath stacks of others containing vegetables. When the brothers expanded trades to Greenville and Spartanburg, "A&I Vegetable Markets" were added in those cities. Unprofitable but useful entities!

By February 1981, Abe and Isaac had spent sixteen years dealing drugs in South Carolina. They were the state's established bosses of heroin and cocaine dealers. Supplies continued to traffic through Florence's farmers market, but that operation was now tied back to Mexico's Guadalajara Cartel.

Abe nor Isaac ever used their product. In fact, they were only periodically in close contact with it. Their company was organized like any legitimate business. Subordinates managed distribution and sales to dealers. Collection of receipts were made to one of two accountants who were responsible for general expenses, payments to some local authorities, and dividing an appropriate portion to staff. A substantial amount remained for Abe and Isaac. They personally oversaw returns to Nicolas.

Out of necessity, the Higgins brothers held regular conference meetings with their management personnel. Problems came with the business they were in. Money from drugs! But, by the late seventies, neither had to carry out the punitive acts of violence sometimes required to

maintain control or respect. As bosses, those could be assigned to a second or third in the command structure. Henchmen assumed the role of assassins in Higgs' and Topcoat's name. Consequently, Abe's last murder was a poor slob of a street dealer named Stumble who had cheated on sales revenue. A year later, Isaac had slain a young man with whom he had shared a sexual relationship. The unfortunate and naïve kid wanted a lot of money and had threatened to blackmail Isaac.

On a regular monthly basis, Abe and Isaac made trips to Florence. The sale of heroin and cocaine came with predictable sums of cash. As always, business trips were conducted after the farmers market closed to the public. A&I produce trucks distributed drugs from there.

On a Saturday evening the first week of March 1981, Abe and Isaac left their home in Heathwood. They rode together in Abraham's new BMW. The trip to the farmers market took slightly less than two hours. The arrival time was coordinated with an A&I produce truck. Almost simultaneously, both drove through the market's guarded gate at 8pm. Once inside, the truck's driver followed Abe's car to a back-office building. They were greeted there by one man with whom a brief transaction took place. Four vegetable crates were taken from the produce truck and carried inside the office. Abe and Isaac went inside but left a minute or two later and drove back to Columbia. The produce truck and it's two occupants remained at the market. Fully loaded and still hours before dawn the next morning, they drove the truck to the Higgins brother's Open Air Vegetable Market in Charleston. Arriving there just after daylight, the drivers delivered to an armed manager thirty-five crates of assorted produce, six kilos of heroin and fourteen kilos of cocaine.

The routine of transferring cash to suppliers and receiving new shipments of drugs had varied little over the years. Sometimes due to major storms and weather conditions across the southeast, occasional interruptions occurred, but not once had supplies been intercepted at the Mexican border. The procedures Abe and Isaac practiced that March morning were normal and without a trace of problems. They were totally unaware of being followed from Columbia to Florence by two men in a Ford Maverick.

In Leann's old car, Trevor and Jessie had for several mornings watched and waited at Heathwood's main entrance for either Topcoat or Higgs to leave their subdivision. On almost every occasion, they had followed one or the other brothers around Columbia. Jessie drove and Trevor took notes. Neither Abraham nor Isaac realized they were being stalked, even when they rode together.

Trevor was keeping a promise he had made to Jessie that past summer on his patio. Two very bad men had murdered Jessie's father. Massacred him in fact. For that they deserved to die. He hated to admit it but something else was part of the effort. Maybe the "thrill-of-the-hunt!"

Parked on the side of Lucas Road a little over a hundred yards from the Pee Dee State Farmers Market, Trevor and Jessie used binoculars to watch Higgs and Topcoat escort four heavy crates inside a small office building. Jessie, obviously puzzled, shook his head. "What the hell's going on Trevor? This is weird."

From experience, Trevor had to laugh a little before answering. "Not really, Jessie. I learned a long time ago that disguise pays big time if you're trying to hide something. You can bet your sweet ass those crates aren't full of tomatoes. You think an armed guard at a locked gate and five men at that little office were needed to carry in four boxes of vegetables. We've found their source of heroin and coke. Better yet, we just witnessed a payment."

"You're telling me those wooden boxes were full of money? Damn, Trevor! They looked heavy from here."

"Yeah," with a nod. "Tens and twenties from the street dealers probably. I bet sixty pounds in each of them. Uh-oh, Higgs and Topcoat are coming out. I've seen enough. Better leave before somebody spots us sitting here."

Driving back to Columbia Jessie's impatience began to come into the conversation. "Trevor, you and I have been watching them every morning for days. And before that, I followed both of their butts around town for over a month. We pretty much know their movements now, so what's the plan?"

"I came up with one last week before we started surveillance together. Just personally making sure it might work. You gave me the idea by trailing Isaac."

"For Christ's sake! You've waited until now to let me in on it?"

"Only because you're too anxious to get this done, Jessie. Remember, I said to do this dirty deed we needed to make a clean getaway. Otherwise, we're toast. Takes time to figure something like that out. We've got an hour on the road. Listen up. I'll lay it out for you."

"Sorry, Trevor. Can't help wanting to kill those two! Every time I see them and think of my dad lying dead in the street, my blood boils. I'm ready, so get on with it."

Alright, but there's something you should know first. Word back when it happened was Higgs shot your father that morning after Topcoat accused your dad of cheating."

"Both still deserve to die!"

"That's true but I'm saving Higgs for you. I'll take care of Topcoat. Here's my plan. The bar you followed Isaac to on Friday nights is known for its gay patrons."

"Yeah, and the man's gay for sure. Leaves there with a new guy most times. His chauffeur drives them back to his place in Heathwood. Whoever he picks up doesn't leave until the next morning. Are you thinking of making the hit in a bar? It won't work if you are. He always has that driver watching after him."

"No! Too messy, public, and his chauffeur is really an armed bodyguard. This has to be done quietly and in private. Like in a bedroom with a knife sliced across his throat. Next Friday, I'm going into that bar pretending to be a homosexual looking for company. Isaac's company."

"Sorry, but look at yourself. No way you can pass for one."

"Maybe not normally, but then you haven't heard about the 'liberation movement.' It's brought a lot of men out of the closet. Nowadays, some even dress to advertise their preference."

"Risky, Trevor, but it might work." Jessie decided he should add some humor to the scheme. "Suppose I do it? I'm younger and much prettier than you!"

"Answer's no! You made quite a name for yourself playing USC football. Someone might recognize you and the game's over. Has to be me. Comprender?"

Bars were always active on Friday nights in Columbia. Workdays had ended plus classes at the colleges and universities were finished until the following Monday. Young and old celebrated the start of a weekend. Isaac was a creature of that habit. To meet a potential partner, most Friday evenings around nine he frequented his favorite lounge. Generally, he left with someone.

Trevor had waited with Jessie in the Maverick parked down the street from the lounge. As sure as rain, Isaac arrived chauffeured in his light blue Cadillac right on time. Purposely to be noticed, Trevor entered the bar just feet ahead of Isaac and his bodyguard driver. For the occasion, Trevor wore snug Levi's with an opened plaid shirt complimented by suede cowboy boots and a gold chain around his neck. It was an overtly obvious attire.

Jessie watched impatiently for two hours. Finally, the chauffeur came out, looked side to side, then waved for Isaac and his new acquaintance to exit. It was Trevor!

Jessie started the Ford Maverick and left. There was no need to follow. He knew from previous times the home in Heathwood was their destination. He parked fifty yards down and across the street from the Higgins' house. Trevor wanted him armed with the Browning and nearby as backup in case things didn't go as planned. Jessie waited locked and loaded for three minutes. The Cadillac pulled to the front entrance and stopped. All three occupants went inside. Unless he heard gunfire, Jessie's instructions were to stay put until Trevor signaled an all clear to come in.

After having drinks and getting acquainted at the lounge, Trevor had accepted a frank but warm invitation to spend the rest of the night with Isaac. Even with his motive there, Trevor was impressed when he entered the home. The brothers had a beautiful place with an extravagantly furnished interior. At the base of a circular stairway, the bodyguard spoke politely to Isaac. "Sir, will there be anything else before you retire? If not, I'll be downstairs should you need me."

Isaac smiled and answered his guard. "Thank you, Glenn, but I believe we will be just fine. He turned towards Trevor and apologized. "I'm sorry, Thomas. Impolite of me. Would you like a nightcap?"

"No. I had more than enough at the bar. Your place is amazing."

"Glad you like it. My brother and I have enjoyed it here for nearly eleven years."

Trevor nodded with approval and grinned a come on while looking towards the stairs. Then said, "Can't wait to see more of it."

Isaac and Trevor ascended the stairs holding hands. Going up, Isaac cautioned him to speak softly so as not to disturb his brother. Higgs' room was at the opposite end of a long hallway. Perfect Trevor had thought. I'll be as quiet as possible when I kill you.

The bedroom was large and spacious. Isaac closed the door and approached Trevor but was waved off with opened hands. "Do you mind if I use your bathroom first? Just one drink too many at the lounge."

"Of course, please do." Isaac replied. "It's just there to your left."

Trevor closed the bath door, unbuckled his belt, and pulled his pants down. He had taped his Kimber 45 to the highest part of his right thigh. After removing it, he gave a deep breath of relief. The gun had been quite uncomfortable even though its position in his jeans had advertised a false manhood. Plus, he felt much safer now with its protection available.

Once he had his pants up and fastened, Trevor removed his suede cowboy boots. In one he had concealed an extra clip for the 45 and a flatten roll of duct tape. In the other, a Browning Spring Assisted Folding Knife with a razor sharp five-inch blade. Trevor unbuttoned his plaid shirt, tucked the 45 behind his back, put the extra clip in a left rear pocket, the knife in the right and replaced the tape in his boot. He flushed the commode for sound effects, then checked himself in the mirror above the sink. With an open shirt, his chest exposed and adorned with a gold chain, he mused slightly intimidated by his own appearance. Christ, I look gay!

In the bedroom, lights were turned low, and Isaac had proceeded to undress. When Trevor came out of the bathroom, he was standing beside his bed in just socks and underwear. Isaac motioned for Trevor to join him. Trevor faked an agreeable compliance and walked to the side of a man expecting an entirely different experience.

Isaac turned to pull covers from the bed. A fatal mistake! Trevor had practiced his next maneuver. Using his strength to an advantage, he wrapped a left arm around Isaac's head with the hand fully covering the mouth. In the same instance, the spring assisted knife clicked open in his right hand and went to the left side of Isaac's throat. The slashing cut across was excessively deep severing both the exterior and anterior jugular veins and the carotid artery. Isaac had muffled an attempted shout, but the noise was barely discernible and could have been confused with his intended activities.

Adrenaline was flowing full force in Trevor's veins. He would never admit it, but again that "rush" was something he had been looking forward to. Isaac's legs gave way and Trevor slowly lowered him to the floor. For about ten seconds, he stared at what was now his unconscious victim pouring blood. Isaac died in that space of time.

Trevor went to the door and listened. Not a sound. Still one to go though. Figured he should take a little time before phase two, so he cleaned off blood stains from Isaac in the bathroom and checked himself in the mirror again. Something didn't look quite right for what he had to do next. Trevor knew what it was. He pulled his jeans off leaving just his open plaid shirt and tight red underpants. The pants were purposely suggested by an amused Jessie to be worn for the occasion. He slipped the 45 in the back of his shorts so that it was concealed by the shirt. Now Trevor was ready because he looked the part he was playing. Isaac's body was lying on what had become a blood-soaked floor but hidden by a king size bed from the entrance to the room. To be sure of that, Trevor covered him with the bed's comforter. Trevor sat on the edge of the bed and waited another anxious twenty minutes.

Finally, thinking enough time had passed, Trevor went out to the top of the stairway. Glenn looked up curiously. "Sir, Mr. Isaac wishes to speak with you." The bodyguard came up the stairs grinning and obviously overconfident from the way Trevor was standing there partially exposed in red underpants.

At an opened door to Isaac's bedroom, Glenn realized his mistake when Trevor placed a Kimber 45 against the side of his head and menacingly whispered. "Make a sound. Even a peep and I'll blow your damn brains out. Lie face down on the floor, do as I say, and you'll live. Say even a word and I'm pulling this trigger."

The threatening manner in which Trevor spoke was convincing. With his hands out front, Glenn bent one knee and then the other to the floor. Laid flat down. Trevor closed the bedroom door and sat on the guards back. "I'm going to tie you up. Resist and I'll kill you. Cooperate and you'll be fine until morning. Comprender?"

Thinking he would someday find this faggot and personally beat him to death; Glenn spoke one word. "Yeah."

That opportunity would never come. Trevor had no intention of letting him live. Once the bodyguard's hands and feet were bound and hogtied together with duct tape, Trevor silenced him by pushing a washcloth inside his mouth secured with the tape. Satisfied Glenn was completely helpless, Trevor opened his knife and repeated what he had done to Isaac. He thought. Two down according to plan and one to go.

Trevor returned to the bathroom and dressed. Before leaving it and the bedroom he took a towel and wiped off every place he might have touched. With his gun now held in case Higgs came out, Trevor went downstairs, eased open the front door, and waved for Jessie. An hour had passed since Trevor had entered the home with Isaac and the guard. Jessie was practically thrilled with relief to see him at the home's entrance. Thirty seconds later, he walked inside carrying the Browning shotgun in one hand and a billy club in the other. The club was Trevor's idea.

Upstairs, Trevor turned off the hall lights and pointed Jessie towards Higgs' room. They listened at the door. Higgs was snoring and the door wasn't locked. Higgs was laying sound asleep on his back. Jessie crept up next to him and swung the billy club hard against the forehead.

Higgs was no longer sleeping but knocked out cold as a fish. He came around five minutes later after Trevor had splashed a glass of water in his face. Dazed and puzzled at first because he was unable to move. Understandable expression. He was completely hogtied with duct tape. Also, his mouth was stuffed with a washcloth and taped.

Trevor held his knife to Higgs' right eye and threatened, "If you want to keep this eye, tell us where you hide the money. Otherwise, your eyes will just be the first thing I take." Trevor moved the knife to Higgs' crotch to signal his next place of surgery. Higgs nodded he understood. Not much of a choice and he was so rich, money was of little consequence.

All along, Trevor's intention was to make their crime look like a robbery gone bad. The Higgins brothers were drug dealers and wealthy. Possibly, some fool might be tempted to score big. If no money was found, then he and Jessie would still steal anything there of value.

An interesting coincidence occurred that night. Many years back, Abraham and Isaac had murdered a drug boss and two of his bodyguards. After killing them, they had lucked into a travel bag filled with cash. Fate perhaps but to save his body parts this night, Abraham had given up where he kept a large stash of money in his home. There was a sizable wall safe behind his bedroom Chester drawer. He provided Trevor with the combination. It contained $1,278,000 in one-hundred-dollar bills. Bank wrapped!

Trevor left the safe open with a few thousand in scattered bills. Jessie turned his attention to Higgs. He sat on top of him, replaced the gag, and asked a simple question. "Do you know who I am?"

Higgs shook his head back and forth.

"My name is Jessie. My father's name was Lamar. Lamar Talbert. Remember him?"

Again, Higgs had shaken a negative answer. His reply enraged Jessie to the point of tears. The son-of-a-bitch didn't even know his dad's name. He held his hand open and back. Trevor knew it was a request and complied with his knife. Jessie flicked it open and asked one last question, "Maybe you knew him by a different name. How about Stumble?"

Higgs' sudden expression of recognition was not the final one in his life. His last was the look of grimacing in pain. Jessie stared directly into Higgs' face and inserted the blade deep into the right side of his neck. Then Jessie slowly drew it all the way across to the left side. Years of wanting revenge for his dad had finally come to an end.

It was past 3 a.m. when Jessie and Trevor arrived at the Lake Murray home. As usual from her nightcap of cocaine, Leann was asleep. After changing clothes and bagging for disposal those they had worn earlier, both men went back out to the Maverick. Its trunk contained a large bundle of cash wrapped up in a bedspread. Trevor carried the money to his boathouse and placed it in what had been the secret marijuana cellar. Next, he and Jessie made a short night cruise out to deep water, tied three concrete blocks to a bag of clothes stained with blood, and dumped them overboard. Back home on the outdoor patio, what now were two assassins relaxed with a drink and went over the events. The discussion made sure nothing was left by mistake that might tie them back to the crime scene. In that regard, the cash taken from the safe had to be considered.

"You know half that money is yours, Jessie. Even so, you can't start flashing one-hundred-dollar bills all around unless you want to spend the rest of your days in prison."

"Don't worry. Not stupid. How much do you figure my share is?"

"Half million. Maybe more?"

"Damn! I've never even dreamed of being that rich."

Trevor thought for a moment before responding. Days before it had occurred to him that if they were successful in their endeavor, South Carolina's two biggest drug dealers would be quickly missed on the streets.

Users live for their next high. Tomorrow, with the Higgins brothers permanently gone, he decided to arrange for that scarcity to multiply. Create an opportunity for himself. Maybe Jessie too?

"Tell me something, Jessie? Easy question for you. How would you like to become twenty times richer than you are now?"

"If you're serious, sure! Who do I have to kill next?"

Trevor smiled at the remark. "Nobody, I hope."

"Good! It's something I'd rather not make into a habit."

Another smile now from both men. Although he knew the answer to his next question, Trevor asked out of politeness, "Have you ever been to the Bahamas?"

"Other than North Carolina and Georgia, I'd hardly been anywhere until I played home-away games with USC's Gamecocks."

"We should take a trip together. I'll have to make some calls in the morning. If they prove productive, we'll fly to Miami tomorrow afternoon and maybe to the Bahamas the next day. You up for a visit south?"

Jessie raised both arms and said, "After what we've just been through, you've got to be kidding. If you're waiting on me, your tail's dragging. Of course, I'm up for it. Hell, lets pack and go."

Trevor climbed out of bed at eight the next morning. Leann had taken the newspaper from the driveway and placed it on the kitchen table. Trevor quickly glanced over the first few pages. There was no mention of the Higgins brothers, so he poured coffee and clicked the TV onto channel 10. News reporters and cameras were all over the street in front of Higgs' and Isaac's home. They were covering the brutal murder of three men in the upscale neighborhood of Heathwood. Abraham Higgins, Isaac Higgins, and a security guard. The maid had discovered the bodies. Police were everywhere. Some were questioning neighbors. Others had taped off the home and were searching for clues. The speculation among reporters suggested it was a robbery. Made sense because the two residents were so wealthy, they employed private security.

Leann was watching from the kitchen. She commented. "Friday the 13th is when stuff like that happens. Terrible! Change the channel or even turn it off, sweetie. Let have some peace and quiet with our coffee."

Trevor grinned in agreement and turned the switch to "off." While having coffee with Leann on the patio, he told her about some travel plans. "I need to touch base with some business friends. If I can arrange it, Jessie and I may take a trip together."

"Where?" Leann asked.

"Florida. Maybe the Bahamas too. Be gone for two or three days."

"Can I come with you?"

"Not this time, sugar. It's all business. I want to introduce Jessie to some associates that I work with."

"Okay, so long as it has nothing to do with marijuana. He's my godchild, remember?"

Trevor answered her question truthfully. "I promise you, Leann. It has absolutely nothing to do with marijuana." Thought to himself. But everything to do with cocaine.

Right at 9 a.m., Trevor phoned Whitfield's office. Whitfield answered seconds after his secretary patched him through. "Morning, Thomas. A pleasure to hear from you, even if it's not a business call."

"In a way, the nature of my call is about business, Charles."

"Okay, how I can help? I always enjoy working with you."

"I have to ask a serious question first because it involves your friend with SLED. Is he completely trustworthy? Totally honest and dedicated to law enforcement?"

Somewhat alarmed by the inquiry, Whitfield responded forcefully. "The answer to both questions is hell yes! Let me add that I would never ask him to do anything more than the small favors he has helped us with before. They don't come any better than Billy Mozingo."

"I was hoping for exactly that type of lawman, Charles. I have some information for you to give him. It involves very large amounts of heroin and cocaine being imported into South Carolina. Worse of all, the smugglers are using a state facility to accomplish it. Interested?"

"You damn right, I'm interested. Billy even more so, I guarantee!"

Trevor provided Whitfield the details of how the farmers market in Florence had become a hub for narcotics coming from Mexico. It was a perfect place to receive drugs concealed in simi trucks shipping vegetables from there. After closing hours, heroin and cocaine were distributed from the market throughout South Carolina by carriers disguised as produce trucks. Transfers involved large amounts of cash payments made at night under the protection of armed guards.

Charles Whitfield was astounded by the information. Still, Thomas was a client and he had to make sure a lawyer's confidentiality wasn't broken. "My god, Thomas. You're telling me to pass this on to Billy?"

"I am and immediate action is needed by SLED. Check out the news on channel 10. It's why I'm calling. Two of this state's biggest drug dealers were murdered last night. Their names were Abraham and Isaac Higgins, but in the world of street dealers they were known as Higgs and Topcoat. They bought their heroin and cocaine from Florence's farmers market. With their deaths, people running operations there might get nervous and close shop for a while. Your friend in SLED should strike while the iron's hot."

"I'll make the call after we hang up. Anything else?"

"Yes, two things. I'll be paying you a substantial fee for your services in this case. Withdraw $50,000 from the trust fund and place it in your personal account.

Whitfield let out an audible whistle over the phone. "What's the other thing? I sure like the first."

"The source of this information has to remain anonymous. If asked, decline to answer on attorney-client privilege. It is imperative you follow this instruction. My life might depend on it."

"You can count on me, Thomas."

Trevor had a new contact number for Luis. To avoid complications brought about by Ed Ward's arrest, Luis had moved out of his Miami office. Out of the U.S. actually, to Freeport in the Bahamas.

Trevor made the long-distance call from his secure phone. After a short delay, Juanita answered. The customary cordial greetings were followed by Trevor asking if Luis was available. Juanita replied as if hesitant. "No, Trevor, I'm so sorry. He left early this morning for Colombia. A family emergency and he was needed immediately."

"Is it Mitch?" Then before Juanita could answer, Trevor said, "I hope not his child for Christ's sake."

"Neither. I mislead you. Luis represents a family of very important people in Colombia. Their daughter has been kidnapped. I'm sure Luis is needed to negotiate her return."

"A kidnapping! That means your boss will be absent for some time. Is Juan running things in Freeport?"

Slightly annoyed, Juanita replied, "No, I am! How can I help you?"

"I can't explain over the phone. Perhaps I could fly in this evening and meet with you?"

"Sorry Trevor, but with this unfortunate development in Colombia, tomorrow afternoon will be better. I assume you'll be flying yourself here, so schedule your arrival for about 2 p.m. I'll have Juan waiting for you at customs."

"Thank you, Juanita. A friend will be coming with me. We've started working together. Rest assured he can be totally trusted."

"That responsibility is yours, Trevor. You know the rules and the consequences if something goes wrong. Your 'friends' in Port Saint Lucie for example."

"Yes, I remember them well! See you tomorrow."

26.

THE GRADUATE

Leaving Lake Murray early that afternoon, Trevor connected with I-26 three miles north of Columbia's Metropolitan Airport. Minutes later his right front seat passenger, Jessie, glanced at the exit sign and said, "Better slow down, Trevor. You're going to miss it."

"We're flying out of Walterboro, not Columbia."

"I didn't know that little town had an airport. Where to and what airline?"

Trevor amused himself with a ruse. "Miami, but just for tonight. Freeport in the Bahamas tomorrow. The airline is called TLD Express. It's a small private carrier."

"Must be? I've never heard of it."

Two hours later, Trevor was still laughing to himself as they arrived at Walterboro's Lowcountry Regional Airport. He had phoned ahead for his Cessna to be fueled and ready. When they continued driving past the terminal towards one of the old hangers, Jessie's curiosity couldn't be helped. "What's going on, Trevor?"

"See that Cessna Skyhawk sitting beside the hanger? It's our TLD flight to Miami. My plane, Jessie. 'Trevor Lamont Dunbar Express' airlines."

"You can fly planes?"

Trevor remembered Jack Reed's favorite answer to the question. "Sure! Flying is easy. Taking off and landing the damn thing is the part I have trouble with."

Once airborne, their flight to Miami-Opa Locka took four hours. After taking off, Jessie seemed to relax while they were in the air but closed his eyes for the landing. Reminded Trevor of his first trip to Norman Cay.

For the night, Trevor had made room and dinner reservations at the Fontainebleau. He opted out of entertainment with Rachel.

During dinner, Trevor figured it was time to discuss with Jessie what he hoped to achieve in Freeport. "Jessie, here in Florida and later in the Bahamas, I've worked for an organization headquartered in Colombia, South America. From an island in the Bahamas, we smuggled cocaine into the states using planes like the one we flew here. It was very profitable, and I'm pretty rich."

"You've been home for nearly three months. Did you quit?"

"Not exactly. Our methods were compromised by an informant. There were other pilots like me, and on the advice of our boss, we all sort of disappeared."

"Are you thinking about starting back to work? Count me in if you are!"

You wouldn't be here with me if I wasn't counting you in. But the game plan has changed. You and I took out two of the major drug dealers in South Carolina. To make supply matters worse, this morning I provided our states' law enforcement with Higgs' and Isaac's source."

"The farmers market?"

"Exactly! Within a couple of weeks, cocaine addicts will be screaming for the junk. A kilo of coke wholesale will go for $60,000. Maybe a lot more."

"Damn, Trevor, if we can get our hands on maybe ten kilos, just imagine what it'll sell for. Over half a million, I bet."

Years ago, Trevor had made an almost identical statement to Link saying, "if only he could get his hands on 10 pounds of marijuana." Now it was his chance to paraphrase an old friend's reply. "Jessie, we're not flying all the way to the Bahamas for a measly 10 kilos."

Jessie's eyes widened and a hand partially covered an opened mouth that only managed to say, "Oh!"

Trevor waited at the hotel until 9am the next morning so he could make a prearranged call to Whitfield's office. It was Sunday but Charles answered. Trevor barely finished saying good morning before his seemingly excited lawyer exclaimed. "I guess you heard the news this morning. Some are saying it was the biggest bust in the state's history."

"No, I'm completely out of touch, Charles. Out of town on business. Can you give me some details of what happened?"

"Absolutely, and I can tell you more than what the TV has reported. It was a state-owned facility, so no search warrant was required. In all there were about twenty SLED and DEA agents involved. They went into the market last night at about 10pm."

Whitfield paused to catch his breath and continued. "It turned out to be a grand slam, Thomas. Caught them red handed right in the middle of moving their drugs. They were unloading the stuff from a big simi into an Airstream travel trailer. Apparently, you were right. They were clearing out the place. Shutting down!"

"Smart move on SLED's part not to wait. Otherwise, all they would have found would have been a lot of vegetables."

"I still haven't come to the best part. It's not released yet, so keep it to yourself. Including the market's manager, assistant manager, guards, drivers, and shift labor, nine people were arrested. Some were armed to the teeth too. Here's the icing on the cake. Billy said they found somewhere around 100 kilos of heroin, over 400 kilos of cocaine, and get this! They're still trying to count all the money but at least six million in currency. Billy says my client and I are heroes."

"I hope you're staying anonymous, Charles. These are some bad people. If they find out the information came from your office, you could get hurt."

"Understood. Don't worry. Billy is keeping his source totally secret. I trust him completely."

"Thanks for your help as always. Don't forget your fee. You've earned it."

"Call any time, Thomas. Makes my day!"

They landed in Freeport early Sunday afternoon. Passing through customs, Jessie used his six-month-old passport for the first time. Trevor had cautioned him to be exceptionally respectful of those he would soon meet. His first was while at the airport. They were met by a large and well-built man named Juan. Showing him respect was easy.

Another surprise came right away. Juan had greeted Trevor in Spanish. Trevor replied back fluently, and the two men carried on a conversation in the language as if both were comfortable with it. Jessie watched them quietly and thought. What the hell else is my partner going to amaze me with?

Luis's new office was a Freeport beach house. A really nice beach house! Diego answered the door. Inside, Juanita gave Trevor a hug and a handshake to Jessie with his introduction. Coffee was served on an oceanside patio where Juanita skipped the casual formalities and went right to the point. "Trevor, it's nice of you to visit with us. A surprise actually! You and your friend must have a reason for coming all this way. What is it?"

A frank and honest answer with Juanita, Juan, and especially Luis was always best. With that in mind, Trevor decided not to "beat-around-the-bush" and replied, "Cocaine, Juanita. For starters, I need a couple of hundred kilos of it."

Juanita leaned her head forward, hesitated, then smiled and said, "Really! What for?"

"To distribute wholesale in South Carolina. The state has always been a weak link in your organization. Luis has mentioned that often. An opportunity for change has just happened." Trevor described the recent demise of two South Carolina drug bosses responsible for most of the hard drugs traded in the state. As well, a subsequent DEA raid had busted their source. Heroin and cocaine brought in from Mexico. South Carolina had suddenly become an open market waiting for a new supplier.

Juanita was impressed. Trevor was right about South Carolina. It was their organization's weak link in the southern chain. Luis had thought from the beginning that bringing in someone familiar with the state might one day solve the problem. Partly for that reason, he had recruited Trevor. Now, Trevor's description of events made it seemed an opportunity was available. Answers were needed to a couple of questions though.

"Let's suppose you had 200 kilos, Trevor. What then?"

"It's been two years since I closed my marijuana shop, but my alias, Thomas Boyce, still has his connections. Not all but some would jump at the chance to supply coke to street dealers. Even at wholesale prices, cocaine is way the hell more profitable. With this supply shortage coming, the addicts will be begging for it. I could be up and running by the end of this month."

Juanita cut straight to the chase. "You're asking for us to front you 200 kilos? That's six million worth. A lot to be responsible for if something goes wrong."

"I know. Let's hope I don't have to, but I can cover the cost of a total loss from my Swiss bank savings. Otherwise, if everything goes as planned, payback from sales can be made in three months."

Jessie was listening but had kept his mouth shut. He was getting used to Trevor's revelations. His best friend was a pilot, fluent in Spanish, and had $6,000,000 in a Swiss bank. He thought once more, what's next?

"You understand Luis will have to approve this. It's above my pay grade. Even if he does, how do you plan to transport 200 kilos to South Carolina?"

"Like I've done before. Fly to Norman Cay, load up, and fly back to Walterboro. I checked as we left. The place looks normal."

Juanita shook her head. "Can't let you do it that way. Walterboro may be safe, but since Ed turned informant, Norman Cay has been on the DEA's watch list. Carlos is still there and using Colombian pilots to make flights, but it's risky as hell. If Luis goes along with this scheme of yours, I'm going to suggest something else. Do you have a nice boat?"

"Sure do. One at my Lake Murray home and a skiff for fishing the saltwater creek at my house in Cherry Grove." A second after he had answered, Trevor realized what Juanita was leading to. "Sorry, you meant one capable of cruising offshore?"

"Yes! Where is 'Cherry Grove?' Is it near the ocean?"

"It's a small beach community located at South Carolina's border with North Carolina. My place is on a backwater creek that connects with an

388

inlet. It's perfect for making runs offshore if that's what you're suggesting might be a better way?"

"Our trawlers travel as far north as the Carolinas. East of Cape Hatteras to be exact. The *Paso Seguro* still supplies a mixed cargo of marijuana and cocaine but the *Gran Pretendiente* only stocks cocaine now. She's currently working the coast from south to north. If you can be ready in eight days, I can give you the lat-longs for meeting with her about sixty miles out."

"Consider it done, Juanita."

"I'll discuss this with Luis. It's a done deal only if he says so. Please accept my apology, but I have work to do. The brother of the girl kidnapped works with us in Florida. Like Luis, he left for Colombia with the news of her abduction. Leaves me pretty busy keeping our operations up and running."

"It's been a short but great meeting, Juanta. Thank you! Wish Luis could have been here."

"We stay in close touch by phone. Call me the day after tomorrow. I'll have his answer for you."

"Perfect! Gives me time to make the preparations necessary for connecting with the *Gran Pretendiente*. Can Juan give us a ride back to the airport?"

They were barely airborne when Jessie asked, "Trevor, you're a multi-millionaire?

"I told you I was pretty rich. The answer's 'yes' and I plan to be a lot richer if we can pull this deal off. You too, Jessie, but not without both of us taking chances. We go to jail if we're caught. Not to mention, I'll lose just about every penny I have."

"Yeah, but this beats the hell out of anything I've ever dreamed of doing. No kidding. Exciting as hell! And Juan, the big fellow that left us at the airport. Scary dude! I bet he does more than just drive?"

"You think? If they could, Dicey and Lavern might be able to help answer your question. Get my meaning?"

"Yeah, sure do. Are we going back to Miami?"

"No. Settled back and relax. This is a direct flight to Walterboro. Another four hours of flying. We've got work to do. No time to waste."

Monday morning, Luis phoned Freeport from his office in Colombia. He preferred checking in with Juanita at his convenience. That was especially true with the situation Don Fabio Ochoa Restrepo and family were currently confronting.

Juanita had proven herself on many occasions able to manage operations in Luis's absence. His call was a formality for the most part. Her update this time included Trevor's request and his explanation of how the opportunity in South Carolina had come about.

Juanita was confident Luis would agree to Trevor's proposal. Pablo Escobar's labs were processing cocaine at record levels to meet U.S. demand. However, Edward Ward's arrest and subsequent plea-bargain had significantly decreased Carlos Lehder's flight capabilities. The organization was experiencing an over-supply just when smuggling the drug into the country was becoming more difficult. The DEA's staff and resources were growing as were successful interdictions. Adding cocaine and removing marijuana from the *Gran Pretendiente's* cargo was a partial solution. But there was a strong disincentive among competent runners to meet with the trawlers. Reagan, the newly elected president in the U.S., was pushing for even harsher penalties when offenders were apprehended with hauls of cocaine or heroin.

Luis's approval of Trevor's plan came with a slight change. "I like Trevor's resourcefulness, Juanita. We could use more like him in our operations. With his abilities, odds are he will succeed in this enterprise. As you know, it couldn't come at a better time for us."

"My first thoughts too, Luis. We can certainly spare him two hundred kilos."

"He's proven himself more than once. As evidence of our confidence, instead, let him have 300 kilos. I'll inform Jorge and Pablo of the transfer."

"Is there a message or some instructions you would like for me to give Trevor?"

"I'll have to leave our arrangements with Trevor in your hands. The persons who kidnapped Marta are a paramilitary group demanding a ransom for her release. I'm told 12 million in U.S. dollars. I'm already late for a meeting with her brothers. Pablo Escobar and his cousin Gustavo will be attending. They've offered to help secure her rescue."

"Understood, Luis. Be careful. Juan and Diego have asked if you need them for your security.

They can be on a flight today."

"That's not necessary. Jorge has men watching after me. Tell them I appreciate the offer."

The meeting with all the principals in the organization was once again held at Las Margaritas hotel. Luis was assigned the job of arranging for negotiations with the kidnapers. A guerilla militia known in Colombia as M-19. His role as the negotiator was suggested by Fabio. The real purpose was nothing more than a delaying action.

In the meeting, Pablo and Jorge decided together that a severe response was required. Any conciliatory actions, including ransom, were completely rejected. They just needed a little time for a show of force. Luis's phony mediations were to provide that.

Within weeks, under the supervision of Pablo Escobar, a retaliatory force named, Muerte a Secuestradores was formed. MAS! They began to slaughter M-19 members. Families of that paramilitary group were threatened with the same fate. Marta Nieves Ochoa was eventually ordered released by the leader of M-19, Ivan Torres. No ransom was ever paid. MAS grew into its own paramilitary and continued to provide protection to local elites from kidnapping and extortion. Unfortunately, and in due course, MAS began to be used for political assassinations.

At a Murrells Inlet dealership two days after returning to South Carolina from the Bahamas, "Thomas Boyce" paid cash for a new Bayliner 3270. Trevor's familiarity with the craft in Port Saint Lucie was a primary reason for the choice. That same afternoon, he and Jessie took it for a maiden offshore cruise thirty miles north to Hogs Inlet. Trevor had timed the trip for the tides. Unless you stayed perfectly within the inlet's channel, the Bayliner's draft along with two Volvo Penta inboards required a high tide to navigate through without stranding on a sandbar.

Once they cleared the inlet into House Creek, Trevor's Cherry Grove waterfront home was a mere half mile south.

Earlier that day, Trevor's call to Juanita was more successful than he had hoped for. Luis had agreed to front him and Jessie initially with 300 kilos of cocaine. Juanita provided a location for tying up with the *Gran Pretendiente* in just five days. The meet was to take place at 7 a.m. sixty miles offshore. Trevor checked the tides. Weather permitting as always, he and Jessie would need to leave Cherry Grove in the Bayliner four hours before daylight with high tides starting to fall.

Trevor figured the distribution of that much cocaine the first go-round would take several months. It took just over two.

To cover the state for an initial distribution attempt, Trevor picked three of his and Kenneth's past and most reliable marijuana dealers. He chose them because of the area they worked, and because all three had once asked about adding cocaine to sales. Two years had passed. Even so, each of the three men were still in business and sounded elated to hear from TB, their old connection. Names and locations were Ricky Hardin in Charleston, Cecil Jordan in Spartanburg, and Todd Hager in Columbia. They became especially excited when "Thomas" explained he was switching from weed to coke. In less than a week, the absence of supply by Higgs and Topcoat had begun to panic those city's junkies. Todd had already started asking around Columbia as to where he might lay his hands on some quality coke. A lot of money could be made quickly if a new source came into play. It was exactly the way Trevor had described the opportunity to Juanita.

Unlike marijuana, coke could be packaged and sealed without the slightest odor emitted. Also, a couple of bales of marijuana required weighty bulk distribution. The same amount by value of cocaine could be carried in a plastic pint jar.

The old method of payments and deliveries while remaining completely anonymous had to be modified for working with cocaine. Very large amounts of money were involved with each transaction. In person management of the upper-level staff was necessary to avoid any temptation to cheat. The consequences of that action had to be made crystal clear.

Trevor never intended to replace the way the Higgins brothers ran their South Carolina drug empire. He ended up copying their procedures almost to a T. Abraham and Isaac appeared as normal but wealthy citizens of Columbia. Higgs and Topcoat, their aliases, were far from being such pillars of society. The two men were brutal drug bosses and easily capable of being a threat to any member of their staff. To achieve and maintain that along with the appearance of total control, regular meetings were required.

Trevor arranged for a meeting in Columbia with his former dealers. The purpose was to discuss a transition from marijuana to cocaine. Prior to that assembly, he was only known to Ricky, Cecil, and Todd as the mysterious TB. He planned to introduce himself as Thomas Boyce. Jessie would play the part of Richard, his younger brother. Trevor Lamont Dunbar and Jessie Talbert would remain anonymous. Trevor's management skills were copied from Luis and Juanita. His ability to intimidate subordinates was learned from Juan and Diego. It was not the reason for the meeting, but both Trevor and Jessie made sure it was an important part of it.

As instructed, Jessie had booked a top floor room at the Hilton Columbia for the gathering. Greetings were cordial but once everyone was seated with refreshments, a serious business tone followed.

Trevor began politely by saying. "Ricky, Todd, Cecil, thank you for coming so promptly. It's great to finally meet you in person. I believe the timing of our becoming better acquainted could not be more important. Perhaps all of you already know, but I've only learned of late that the persons formerly responsible for supplying cocaine in our state were killed during a robbery. Being from Columbia, Todd, you would be more familiar with their operations than I or Richard."

Todd shook an affirmative nod and said, "It's worse than you might think, Thomas. Their names were Higgs and Topcoat. They controlled the whole state's supply of heroin and cocaine. Dealers of those drugs are beginning to look around for a new source. Street prices are going up."

"Same thing is happening in Charleston," Ricky added.

"Good!" Trevor continued. "Let me lay out a proposition for you to consider, but understand it comes with serious requirements. My former source of marijuana is now capable of supplying cocaine instead. As much as South Carolina needs and more through Richard and me. We're prepared to make it available to you wholesale. $60,000 per kilo! That price leaves plenty of room for you three and your street pushers to make a bundle of money. Maybe even more than Richard and I will make."

An almost comical response appeared on the faces of the three seated guests. They looked around at each other, apparently astonished by what Trevor had offered. Ricky started to speak but stopped when Todd raised his hand towards him and then looked back at Trevor. "Let me get this straight. You're saying the three of us in this room will be in charge of distributing all of South Carolina's cocaine? Just we three?"

"Yes and starting next week."

Cecil leaned back in his chair, folded his arms and asked, "What's the catch, Thomas? Something like this sounds too good to be true."

Trevor acknowledged Cecil's skepticism. He stood, turned first to Cecil and then to Todd and Ricky before answering. In a direct and serious manner, Trevor replied, "The 'catch' is this! The people that supply me have zero tolerance for mistakes. So do Richard and I. Zero!"

Ricky knew but asked anyway. "What are you implying, Thomas?"

"Simply saying if one of you somehow gets caught, none of the rest of us exist. Hire a lawyer and keep your mouth shut. No plea deals. Say nothing! Anything other than that will get your ass killed. If not by my brother and I, for certain by my sources. Even if you're locked up, they have ways. Is that clear enough for you?"

Ricky complained, "We were in the marijuana business with both of you for a very long time. "Now cocaine. None of us then or now would ever turn on you. That's a promise. Our word on it!"

"Ricky, out of a crowd of my former marijuana dealers, Richard and I carefully chose just you, Todd and Cecil for exactly that kind of loyalty. You were my best and most reliable. And now, as compensation, all of you will become very rich in an unbelievable short period of time."

Ricky nodded his appreciation. "Your confidence in us is reassuring, but I think we deserve it. Speaking for myself, I'm in! Todd, how about you and Cecil?" Both Cecil and Todd nodded in as well."

"Okay, here's how we're going to proceed. We'll divide the state into three parts starting with Charleston and Georgetown for you Ricky; Todd has Columbia; Spartanburg and Greenville are yours Cecil. Go home and put the word out. Santa Claus is coming to town!" Trevor knew with his last comment a little humor at this stage of the game never hurts. He was right. All the men around the table grinned and relaxed a little.

Trevor continued. "By next week I'll have a safe place ready for pick-ups and deliveries. I'll call for another meeting here and provide the location and methods."

Todd asked what he, Cecil, and Ricky were all wondering. "Thomas, we've all made out pretty good with marijuana. Still though, and I mean no offence. $60,000 a kilo is one hell-of-a-lot of money. How much cash do you expect us to bring this first time around?"

"Saving the best until now that you've decided to join us. The good part. Your first supply of cocaine will be coming to you next week up front. No charge. Pay me back when you come for more. We'll adjust the cost of resupplies based on your success. Very soon, we'll get to pay as you go."

"Wow!" Todd remarked. "Thanks. Takes a lot of pressure off our backs when even a couple of kilos comes to $120,000."

Trevor pointed to Jessie for a reply. "Richard, I've been saving the last part of this meeting for you. Clue our partners in."

Per Trevor's instructions, Jessie had waited patiently for a turn in the conversations. He knew these guys weren't prepared for what he was about to tell them. Savored the moment for a few seconds. "Gentlemen, this is not going to be a small operation. Each of you will receive 25 kilos. Bring Thomas and I back $1,500,000 when you're done with it."

Twenty-five kilos were ten times what any of them had imagined. Ricky managed the only comment, and it was very short. "Damn!"

Trevor had watched for their reaction. A realization was beginning to dawn on them. They really were going to become incredibly rich. It was the proper time for what he said next. "I have some instructions for each of you to follow. Not advice but instructions! Orders, if you get my meaning! Generously share the profits with your dealers on the streets. Keeping them happy and ready for more is the safe way to do this. Don't get greedy. You'll still make more money than you've ever dreamed. Comprender?"

Ricky, Todd, and Cecil were well educated in the business of dealing drugs. At a price of $60,000 a kilo for cocaine, following Trevor's orders to share returns was like slicing a pie. They could more than double their cost to street traffickers and still leave room for those taking that biggest risk to make tons of money. In quantities of 10 grams or more, cocaine in South Carolina sold to users for $300 a gram. Even $400 per gram up north. Pricey, but demand was incredible in the early eighties. Estimates were that 15% of the U.S. population had at least tried the drug. Unlike heroin, cocaine carried little or no social stigma. Conventional use by "snorting" was often accepted in some communal circles.

Three days before their first run offshore, Trevor phoned Whitfield. If there were any new developments in the case of the Higgins' murder or the farmers market bust, he thought his attorney might have some insider information. Whitfield was prepared to answer his request for an update.

"Funny you should ask today, Thomas. I just inquired this morning. Two things really. Billy says three of those arrested at the market are singing like birds. The driver of the semi, one of the shift workers, and best of all, the supervisor."

"If they lawyered up, the DEA must be offering them deals to talk."

"You guessed it, Thomas. Like you said, the drugs came from Mexico. They crossed the border from Juarez and traveled all the way here by interstate. Billy thinks they supplied mostly the southern states. It probably won't be released to the newspapers, but he's pretty sure they have the name of the kingpin. An indictment for him will probably be added to the list."

"With what they found in that semi, it had to be an organized operation with considerable management somewhere."

"Estimated street value came to $100,000,000. It'll eventually be disposed of, but there may be a huge bonus coming to the state besides the six million they found."

"How so?" Trevor asked.

"Those drug bosses that were found murdered. The robbers left a safe wide open in their Heathwood home. Records inside showed that between the two of them, they owned stocks, bonds, and property all over the damn country. Rich as hell. Incredibly rich!"

"Does South Carolina somehow get all of it?"

"Looks like it so far. They had a lawyer here in Columbia. I know the guy. Bit of a crook himself. Name's Eugene Howell. At SLED's request I checked out his clients, Abraham and Isaac Higgins. The brothers died without a will. It's what we call 'intestate.' No living heirs according to this lawyer. It'll take some time in court, but in those circumstances by South Carolina law, the property escheats to the state."

"Serves them right. Payback! This makes you a hero, Charles."

"No, Thomas. We're both heroes."

"Yeah, but we have to remain 'unsung heroes' unless we want some Mexicans to get even by killing us."

"You may be right about that. To be safe, I think I'll stay in touch with Billy."

"Good idea. Thanks again and have a great day."

Mexican drug capos expected the occasional interdiction of shipments crossing from their border into the U.S. In the seventies and eighties, it almost always involved marijuana. That was more of a short-term inconvenience rather than a problem because the country literally had an unlimited supply of the stuff.

Cocaine and heroin were different. Even small amounts were quite valuable. For that reason, shipments were generally spaced and limited in size. Semi-trailer trucks hauling Mexican produce long-distance were an exception. Larger cargos destined for multiple points of distribution along the eastern seaboard were carried by them.

Florence's farmers market had served as a profitable and safe dispersal point for years. Luckily for the person responsible for that facility, the drugs seized represented considerably less than one simi's concealed load. Well over half had already been distributed. Still, an overnight loss of this size required an explanation.

On Wednesday morning four days following the raid, Nicolas Estrada boarded a flight in Ciudad Juarez for Guadalajara. He was "invited" there to meet with

Caro Quintero, a partner and capo within what had evolved by far into Mexico's largest drug cartel. Quintero's position in the organization was second only to Felix Gallardo, its recognized jefe. Estrada was a lieutenant assigned to the Juarez territory and supervisor of operations from there into the U.S. His invitation was actually a summons.

Guadalajara's metropolitan area is second in size to Mexico City. At Don Miguel Hidalgo Costilla International Airport, Nicolas was met by two of Quintero's security personnel. His escorts chauffeured him for thirty minutes through the city to an impressive casa grande in the effluent neighborhood of Zapopan. It was one of several homes the capo owned in Mexico. This place was built like a fortress with only an expansive garage facing the street. There was additional security watching from its roof.

Caro Quintero greeted Nicolas with a smile and handshake. "Welcome, amigo. Let's have a seat. Make yourself comfortable. I hope you had a nice flight?"

"Yes, Patron. Quite nice."

"I'm sure you've guessed the reason for your visit, Felix, and I need to understand what happened. Unfortunately, it was not something we could discuss with you over the phone."

Nicolas knew why he was there. Came prepared. "Our facility and methods were compromised by someone. Possibly a rival in the business because two of our best dealers in the state were murdered the night before the raid. The papers suggested their death was part of a robbery. An impossible coincidence, I think. Both men's throats were cut."

"Assassinated!"

"Absolutely, Caro! But by who? I knew both men well. Worked with them for years. They had a reputation. Nobody in their right mind would cross them. They had bodyguards plus protection provided by some local authorities."

"Somebody did, Nicolas. An enemy maybe? We all make them in this business. This time, I want you to find out who and for more than just the usual reasons. The loss of the cocaine came as an embarrassment. We recently negotiated an agreement with a group out of Colombia. They seemed desperate for new routes into the U.S. We cut a highly profitable arrangement for ourselves. They bring it through Panama to Mexico. We take half what they deliver free of charge, but once it's on our doorsteps, the deal comes with our being responsible for all of it."

"Half of what was confiscated was theirs?" Nicolas asked.

"The cocaine was, and Felix says we have to make good on it."

"How much, Caro?" Nicolas hated the question.

"Roughly, twenty million. So, you can understand our concern. This can't happen again!"

Until now, Estrada felt his meeting with Quintero was going well. However, the meaning of his statement about a recurrence was perfectly clear. And unnerving! His jefe was known for intolerance of mistakes. Best now to lay everything on the table and buy some time for discovery. "Patron, there were nine arrested that night. By the time they had legal representation, three had cut deals and confessed everything they knew. My name included."

"How do you know this?"

"The information comes from an attorney representing some of those arrested. My name could have only come from the market supervisor. He was one of those talking, so the attorney told me."

"Does this lawyer have a name?"

"Eugene Howell. He's been on my payroll for years. Long before I worked for you and Felix. A few court cases that generally just involved bail. He's mostly a legal advisor, but I plan to use him to find those responsible for our loss. Let him hire some local detectives to ask questions and report what he learns back to me."

"I like your plan, Nicolas, but don't stir things up right away. We don't need the attention it might bring to us. The U.S. government is still a 'sleeping dog' when it comes to cocaine. Let the dust settle some. Let the culprits think they got away clean. When the time comes, deal with them the same way your friends died."

"Thank you, patron. I'll proceed but quietly. When I have something, you will know."

Nicolas arrived back in Juarez after 10 p.m. His position as a lieutenant in the chain of responsibilities there had been made considerably more difficult by the DEA's market assault in Florence. The simi had passed into the U.S. from Juarez where dozens of trucks laden with produce came from Mexico each day. Still, for a period at least, any attempt to use the same method at the same border crossing was south of stupid. When smuggling, a truck's trailer typically carried 500 kilos of cocaine. Occasionally, twice that much. Another loss of that size and Nicolas was history. Caro Quintero had politely made that clear.

It would take time to replace the Florence farmers market. For that, South Carolina was not a consideration. A shame too because of the convenience of its central location. Now it was out since whoever had betrayed them was still a mystery, and the state's law enforcement was alert to their "modus operandi."

Nicolas already had falcons supervising activities in Atlanta. Georgia was a close alternative to South Carolina and its rural areas were agricultural in nature. Establishment of a new "hub" someplace in the state would require the least amount of time. Instructions were issued to the head of his team there for that purpose. It was a distasteful but necessary priority now. Establishing a new place and route for distribution took precedence over any personal vendetta Nicolas carried.

Quintero had ordered Nicolas to find the finks that informed the DEA about the Florence facility's drug connection. If they were the same butchers that had killed Abe and Isaac, all the better.

Eugene Howell received a long-distance call from Ciudad Juarez, Mexico Thursday afternoon, March 19th. The caller was his principal business benefactor, Nicolas Estrada. "Mr. Howell, how's your weather in Columbia?"

"Clear and sunny, Nicolas." The reply was code for a convenient and safe time to talk. An answer implying poor conditions would have ended the conversation.

Nicolas continued, "Have there been any new developments since we last spoke?"

"Nothing of consequence. As you instructed, I posted bail for the six men who are not cooperating with the police. The supervisor of the market was placed under the protection of federal authorities. His whereabouts are a mystery. The truck driver and the shift worker remained in custody. In court, I'll be representing the driver and several of the others if they appear. My guess is that some, maybe all, will not show up."

"When that happens, Eugene, will I be indicted?"

"Unfortunately, I think so. My advice is stay in Mexico."

"Until it's safe, I'm not traveling out of my country. In the meantime, I have an assignment for you. An investigative one."

"Nicolas, I'm glad to provide my assistance. Just name it!"

"Do you know a good private detective? One that can probe around without drawing attention."

"I do Nicolas, and he is very private. He can be totally trusted. We've worked together on occasions that required that type of loyalty."

"Hire him! Cover his expenses and double his normal fee. If your detective delivers, promise him a substantial bonus. Very substantial!"

"With that type of compensation, I guarantee he will be at your service. What do you want from him?"

"Something the police will never do. Find out who killed your clients and my friends, Abraham and Isaac."

"Okay, but what do you want from him afterwards? He's capable of additional services if properly compensated."

"Nothing more! Have him report to you and you report to me. His and your job will be finished. In time when all of this is forgotten, my associates and I will take it from there. Comprender?"

"Perfectly," Howell replied. Their conversation ended. Less than a minute later, Eugene phoned private investigator Robert Macklin.

Monday, March 23rd at the Cherry Grove beach house, Trevor and Jessie were up at one in the morning. Leann was staying there with them but slept in as usual. Both men were alert and a little excited. They were making their first offshore run. The schedule was to leave at 3 a.m. The timing would allow them to pass through Hog inlet an hour after high tide. Shallow sandbars would be covered with six feet of water. Fully loaded, the Bayliner drafted only three and made for its easy passage.

In case they were ever forced to return when the tides were unfavorable, for two prior days Trevor had practiced using a compass heading to navigate the inlet at low tide. The trick then was to stay within the five-foot-deep unmarked channel. At places, it was barely 20 feet wide. If you weren't careful, you could be grounded for hours on a sandbar.

Trevor and Jessie cruised slowly out of the inlet just after three and revved up to15 knots with a due east heading. Jessie was having a ball enjoying the light wind with a little sea spray in his face. For him, another memorable part of this first trip out was watching the sun rise dead ahead. Spectacular he thought. An exhilarating experience in his life that he would never forget. He was about to become a smuggler!

Four hours and sixty miles later, they tied up with the *Gran Pretendiente*. In ten minutes, three hundred kilos of cocaine were loaded aboard the Bayliner by the trawler's crew. Untied, Trevor started a slow route towards shore at about 7 knots. Their speed would place them back at the inlet's mouth an hour before high tide. His learned seamanship with Russell and crew out of Port Saint Lucie was obvious. Exposed gear across the stern of the Bayliner made it appear as though they were returning from an early morning fishing trip out in the Gulf Stream.

Three hundred kilos of cocaine powder are no small amount even for two men to unload. After docking the Bayliner, Trevor and Jessie used large cooler's packed full to carry up the boat ramp into the garage beneath the beach house. Parked inside was a 1980 Winnebago LeSharo. After purchasing it in Columbia for the occasion, Trevor had driven it to Cherry Glove. His plan was to use it for transferring the cocaine to his cabin on Lake Wateree. Once there, use the cellar concealed in the floor of the pump house for storage.

There had not been enough time to modify the Winnebago's interior in a way that would conceal over 600 pounds of cocaine. That would come later. It was a small risk, but one they would have to take this first trip inland. The cocaine was evenly stacked along its floor and covered with a tarp. Fishing rods, tackle boxes, life preservers, and a couple of suitcases were placed on top. The disguise was made to look as if the occupants in the RV were going on vacation. It wasn't needed. The trip to the cabin was uneventful.

Late the next day at the Hilton Columbia, Trevor's new team of dealers met with him and Jessie. Thomas and Richard to them. The who, where, and how transfers of cocaine were discussed. For both safety and convenience, Trevor had selected the Clearwater Cove Marina's parking lot on Lake Wateree for staggering deliveries. It was located off state highway 97 and only a few miles north of his cabin. So as not to attract attention, Todd, Cecil, and Ricky would arrive one hour apart. Identical keys were given to each. Their key would open the trunk of a 1976 solid tan Chevrolet Impala parked at the far back right side of the lot. The Chevy's cargo space would contain three separate 25 kilo satchels of cocaine. Todd, Cecil, and Ricky would each take one and leave for home. All three men understood that Thomas and Richard would be watching the conveyance from a distance. Sort of a necessary precaution. The street value of each satchel was roughly $7,000,000. An incredible amount of money in 1981.

At the cabin the following morning, Trevor and Jessie were up at seven. Over coffee with a side of muffins, Trevor went over safety procedures. "Jessie, you and I will remain more or less disconnected from the actual transfers today. Innocent bystanders if anything goes wrong."

"Okay with me but exactly how?"

"I'll leave here in the Pontoon boat at nine. It'll take ten minutes for me to reach the marina and check it out. If I'm not back by 9:30, it means come on ahead. Drive the Chevy there and park where we decided. Lock it and walk down to the marina's dock carrying your rod and tackle box. I'll be tied up to the dock and waiting for you. Look the part. We're just two guys going fishing. You and I can anchor out in the cove and watch the Chevy. I'll have the binoculars on board. Cecil should arrive first, then Ricky and finally Todd. Once they leave, I'll take you back to the marina and you'll drive the Impala back to the cabin."

"Empty and safe," Jessie said. "Seventy-five kilos delivered to them while we're sitting around and watching. No way any of them will even spot us. Maybe we should drop a line and hook in the water while we're observing. Got to 'look the part' Trevor."

"I'll have some jigs rigged and ready. If we can catch a few crappie, we'll celebrate a successful day with a fish fry this evening."

One hour apart transfers from the Chevy's trunk went smoothly. Unfortunately, the fish weren't biting. Trevor dropped Jessie at the marina so he could return the car to the cabin. He offered an alternative to the fish fry. "What say we settle for celebrating with steaks at Lake Murray Jessie.? Leann should be there by now." Relax with some bourbon and maybe a joint to wet our appetite."

"Sounds good to me Trevor. I'll race you back to the cabin!"

Four hours later, they arrived at Trevor's Lake Murray home. Jessie had phoned Leann from the cabin asking her to pick up some steaks for grilling. She wasn't expecting them until the next day but was glad they had decided to come home early. They all spent a pleasant family-like evening together. Everything was perfect. Leann turned in early leaving Jessie and Trevor on the patio. It was a clear night with an outside temperature in the low seventies. Nice weather for a middle of March evening.

Jessie had lots of questions and the timing seemed right. He started off with compliments. "I have to tell you something, Trevor, but it might make you even more cocky than you already are. You're one talented SOB. Where the hell did you learn all this stuff?"

"Truth?"

"Yeah, the truth! It doesn't make sense. Black, and raised poor in the south with little or nothing going for you. We met up. Next thing I know is you fly planes, sail boats at sea, speak a foreign language, and you're a millionaire."

Trevor grinned with an acknowledgement. "The answer's simple. It's been luck-of-the-draw so far. Link and I started off together in marijuana. You saw how he ended up. Could have just as easily been me, instead. He's an example of how things can go wrong in this business."

"I don't see how. Everything you try seems to work smooth as silk. Looks like 'we're in the money now,' and thanks for letting me in on this."

"Don't get ahead of yourself, Jessie. Remember, we're in debt to people who expect to be paid. Mistakes don't count. We owe $9,000,000. One little slip up and it's over."

"Yeah, but so-far, so-good. Maybe a downhill ride from here.

"Sure hope so. Just in case, I'll have to stay in contact with our new partners. In a month or two, they'll be ready for fresh supplies, and we should receive our first returns from them."

"That adds up to $4,500,000 for you and I."

"No. That and then some Jessie because those guys don't get another free ride on us. Each of them will have doubled their money when they come for more. We'll give them another 25 kilos each but at half price up front this time."

"So, when they want more cocaine, they pay us back for all of the first load and half again for the next.?"

"That's the way it's going to work, Jessie. By the third time around, we'll be even. From there on, they'll be paying up front."

"When they bring all that cash to us, what do we do with it? Can I buy myself a beach house too?"

"Sorry, but no. Maybe later after we've paid back our friends in Colombia. Until then, you and I will return every penny of it to them."

"I suppose we'll be taking more plane trips to Freeport for that?"

"No way, Jessie. We would be risking a customs inspection. You can't hide millions in mixed bills. About 300 pounds worth in cash. It takes a couple of strong wooden boxes for that much."

"How do we get them their money?"

"We're going to have to make regular trips offshore. The organization we're working with keeps one of their trawlers operating off the coast. They cruise back and forth from the Florida Keys to Cape Hatteras. We meet up and deliver when one is passing by Cherry Grove."

"Okay, I like hearing that. Sorry, but I get a little nervous flying with you. The trip out to the *Gran Pretendiente* was a lot more fun"

"Good thing, Jessie. We'll be taking the Bayliner out for offshore fishing trips often. Our disguise. Just fishermen enjoying the sport. Let the locals and any authorities out there get used to seeing us. On occasions, we'll bring in a catch of cocaine."

"What about Aunt Leann? She's already suspicious we're into something illegal."

"Yes, and she's bound to figure it out sooner than later. I think it's better if you and I sit down with Leann and confess our business enterprise. Together, convince her we're careful and will not get into any trouble. Another reassuring point to make is once we have enough money, our game's over and done. Take a permanent vacation. Travel some, maybe like Europe."

"I'm good with that, Trevor. We need to come clean with Aunt Leann. She cares about both of us, so we can trust her completely. I bet she would really like the part about traveling. If you're serious though, how long before we can retire?"

"I'm not sure. If all goes according to plan, a couple of years. Have to wait and see."

Lying in bed that night, Jessie imagined himself in two years. He would be twenty-one years old and a millionaire. Only wished his mom and dad could be there with him to enjoy his fortune. Still, it was a nice way to fall asleep.

By eight the next morning, Leann had breakfast ready for her "boys." With an opportunity provided at the table, Trevor and Jessie took turns explaining their new business. Near the end and worried it was not going well, Trevor added the part about traveling someday. Jessie also said something trying to reassure her with how careful they were. When finished, both men stared at each other with raised shoulders and eyebrows, then back at Leann hoping that she wouldn't be too pissed.

Leann had listened quietly with obvious tight lips. She thought for a moment, folded her arms, looked at Trevor, then Jessie and said, "Thanks both of you for finally telling me. About time! What part of Europe will the three of us visit first?"

Two men sitting at that table were suddenly relieved and laughing. Lots of hugs all around came next. Trevor and Jessie had been so damn caught up in their activities, they had totally misjudged Leann. Probably because of her cocaine addiction. Even with it, she was still both smart and observant.

When breakfast was finished, they all joined together in the living area with a cup of coffee. Leann explained that she had become suspicious since their trip to Florida. After that, her two men became inseparable spending days supposedly fishing in Cherry Grove on a ridiculously big new boat; taking it in the middle of the night out to sea; buying a Winnebago for the garage? And sometimes disappearing together for business meetings without saying where. Added up to running drugs.

Trevor was enlightened by Leann's description of his and Jessie's behavior. Basically, Trevor realized he wasn't so smart after all. Good thing it was Leann noticing and not someone else. He and Jessie had better be more careful if they planned to do this for two years.

27.

THE SEARCH

Early Friday morning, Robert Macklin came to attorney Eugene Howell's office. Eugene first spelled out why he had called the detective. "Bobby, I have a very important client who needs assistance. Understand from this moment on, my client prefers not to be connected to what he requires. It's a very private matter. You will report only to me and he remains nameless. If you can pursue this under those circumstances, it will be a profitable investigation for you."

"Just tell me what you need? Depending on the job, I don't give a damn who it's for as long as the compensation is appropriate. Just how much is your client willing to pay?"

"Whatever it takes. Consider your normal fee doubled. Deliver and you'll be well rewarded with a bonus."

"I'm hired," Macklin replied with a smile.

"Good!" Howell continued to explain the part leading up to Bobby's assignment. "There's a reason he insists on remaining detached. It's because he has recently been accused of being involved with drugs simply because of some business acquaintances. Those who made the accusations were part of a smuggling ring working out of Florence."

"I read about it in the papers. A big bust at the farmers market."

"I represent some of those arrested. One of them remains incarcerated and has named my client as a co-conspirator. I'm telling you this so you'll understand how confidential your investigation has to proceed. I'm riding a fence but doing it for my best client."

"Don't be concerned. It comes with my title. 'Private Investigator.' Let's get down to business. What does your client want from me?"

"It's right up your ally, Bobby. Find someone or somebody for him. Did you read about the murder of three men in Heathwood the day before the raid on the farmers market?"

Before he answered, Robert leaned back a little at the mention of "murder." Howell had baited him with money before getting into some serious crap like drugs and murder. "I did. Front page stuff when some robbers kill two upstanding Columbia citizens. It's especially big news when the victims turn out to be major drug dealers."

Eugene decided not to tell the detective that he had for years been retained as a lawyer for the Higgins brothers. Instead, he said, "They were friends of my client. He wants you to find out who killed them."

"Then what?" Bobby asked.

Howell knew the reason for the question. If paid for it, Bobby was willing to provide additional services. Not this time though. "Nothing more! Report to me and you're through." Eugene took out an envelope from his desk drawer and handed it to Bobby. "Your retainer. Find the killers and there's considerably more where this comes from."

Most lawyers retain private detectives for proof of spousal infidelity. It's a living but barely. It was not a common occurrence, but during his career, Macklin had subsidized his income by providing punitive actions against someone's offender. Once, that deed had involved a permanent but deserved solution. For that type of extreme service, he was handsomely rewarded.

Not even in a blue moon does something like this Howell assignment come along. It's a chance to get ahead and then some without getting your feet wet. From years of experience, Macklin was well acquainted with crimes committed in Columbia. He knew that it's incredibly rare for a well-planned robbery to turn into a triple homicide. Also, the brutal methods used by the killers suggested more. Perhaps a revenge killing made to look like a robbery. Abraham and Isaac Higgins had made lots of enemies as drug bosses. In all likelihood, their history as drug dealers would be the key to his success.

Robert's reputation with the city's police department was less than bad. Making matters even worse, rumors were that the Higgins brothers had paid some of its officials for protection. Obtaining any inside information from them was unlikely.

Newspaper accounts of the murder victims were most often limited to whatever the authorities chose to release. On the other hand, television coverage of the story might be helpful. Their accounts generally included televised in person and on-site descriptions of a major crime. Robert was well acquainted with one of the individual reporters. Julia Grant. She worked crime scenes for Columbia's CBS channel 10 station.

Robert made a phone call promising Julia a potential story. She joined him for an after six drinks at a Five Points bar. Years ago, they had been in a relationship. Ended amicably when each decided their occupations were not an appropriate fit. His methods of work, in particular!

They settled in a booth after being served. He asked out of courtesy, "How've you been, Julia?"

"Real good, Bobby." She placed her left hand out across the table showing off a sizable engagement ring.

"Wow! Congratulations. Anyone I know?"

Julia smiled. "Not very likely! You said you might have a story for me? What is it? I've got just an hour, or I'll be late to meet with him."

Robert began his questioning with what was partly true. "I'm investigating a recent crime for a client. You covered it on TV."

"The two brothers in Heathwood?" Julia guessed.

"Yes, and the person that retained me was a friend of theirs. He thinks the cops will get nowhere. Julia, this pays well if I can find the bad guys for him. Since you were there that morning, I hoped you might have seen something or someone. A clue to get me started."

"He's right about the cops. They're not chasing this like a major crime for some reason. If I help you, what's in this for me?"

Robert knew to lie. "Maybe an exclusive! If I find out who did this, you'll have a breaking news story the same day. That's a promise."

"Deal! I'm pretty sure I can help. When we arrived on the scene, the police wouldn't let the cameras inside the house. Bloody mess I'm told. I can see why but that can wait. Aside from those killed inside the home, there were two permanent residents present in the servants' quarters above the garage. Both were asleep when the murders took place. One was a security guard. The other one lived there as the men's housekeeper and cook. Seemingly I should say!"

"You have their names?"

"Yes but let me finish. The coroner reported it happened around midnight. The maid found the bodies the next morning. About 6am. She screamed for the guard, and once he came inside, he called the police. The two of them spent the rest of that day and half the night being questioned at the station by detectives. Without a lawyer, I might add."

"The cops must have thought they had something to do with it."

"Maybe at first because they figured the killer or killers might have had inside help. There was no sign whatsoever of a break-in. A wall-safe was left open with some money scattered around. I'm told by a friend in the department it was around twenty thousand in $100 bills."

"That's a hell-of-a-lot left behind! Maybe they had to leave in a hurry. Julia, this might help me. It does sound like an inside job. I was way off base with this. Thought perhaps they were killed by somebody who hated them. Let me have the names of these two people. I might be able to get more out of them than the cops."

"With your methods of interrogation, I'm sure you could, Bobby. That's if they were involved. I can absolutely assure you neither of them were. Would you like to know why?"

"If you're so certain, Julia. Hell Yeah!"

"When they were finally released that night my camera crew had left already. I had stayed at the station hoping for an interview. No luck with the guard though. He took off like a scared rabbit. The maid was in a different situation. Pretty and only 24. Her name was Amanda."

"You must have learned something from her. I'll pay you back somehow if you'll share it with me?"

"I'll do that and more before I'm finished. Her story is pathetic. Amanda is Mexican. Her mother died when the girl was in her early teens. At the age of fifteen, the father gave her away to satisfy a debt he owed. She was sneaked into the U.S. by a drug dealer and kept by him as a sex slave in Atlanta until she was eighteen."

Robert was far from an angel himself, but never abusive to women, much less a young kid. "My God, Julia. This is bad stuff. How the hell did she end up in Columbia as a maid?"

"Her story gets worse. The drug guy in Atlanta was named Nicolas Estrada. He must have gotten tired of Amanda because he made a gift of her to Abraham Higgins. She was used for sex briefly by him. Afterwards, the security guards. Amanda has been a housemaid and sex toy at that Heathwood home for six years, Bobby. The girl had never been off the grounds until now."

"Unbelievable. It's America! Do the cops know about this?"

"Some of it, not all. When SLED busted the Florence farmers market, two or three of those arrested talked. The name, Nicolas Estrada came up as the dealer Abraham and Isaac Higgins worked with."

"Amanda might be the key to solving their murder. I've got to talk with this girl. She's bound to be able to help. Do you know where she is?"

"Sure do, but only if you swear to god not to tell another soul."

"I swear, Julia. Trust me on this one."

"Amanda had no place to go after the police finished questioning her. The house in Heathwood was taped off. I took her home, Bobby. She's staying at my place with me. Now you, I, and my fiancée are the only ones who know that."

"Can I come see her?"

"Yes, but only if I'm there with you. The girl's scared to death of men. Since she was fifteen, she's been exploited for sex by a bunch of perverts. Consider this. Amanda was punished if she didn't perform."

"I didn't expect any of this from you, Julia."

"I'm helping you for a reason, Bobby. Amanda's story needs to be told! I'm putting together a special report for my station. Wake some of our worthless people in government up about what's going on at our border. They're bringing poor young girls here from Mexico with the promise of well-paying employment. Instead, they're forced into being whores. Complete this one girl's tale for me. Find whoever murdered those asses that used and imprisoned her for years. Imagine going through what she endured for eight years! Maybe when you find the killers, they'll be punished, but I plan to pin a metal on them."

With that small tirade, Robert realized his former girlfriend was on a mission. Even a vendetta! "Okay, Julia, when can I visit with her?"

Robert Macklin was in his early fifties. He had an above average history of relationships with different women. Nonetheless, the next night when Julia introduced him to Amanda, he was a little stunned. The girl could have easily won any beauty contest. It was an unforgivable sin that someone so blessed in appearance would have been mistreated by men the way she was.

Amanda Ramirez spoke English well enough, but she hesitated and looked to Julia before answering Robert's questions. Several times, Julia had to reassure and encourage her to respond.

As a detective, Robert instinctively knew his query wasn't going well. The night of the murder she was asleep. No help there. If the Higgins brothers had enemies, Amanda knew nothing about them. Robert had focused questions on that part to the point that the girl began to tear.

His interview was almost at a dead end when Julia asked Amanda about her abuse by the brothers. A significant revelation came about with her reply. "Only Mr. Abe, Miss Julia. Mr. Isaac was different."

Julia was initially surprised, wondering if maybe one of the two men might have been less terrible than the other. "What do you mean by 'different'? Was Isaac nice to you.?"

Amanda signaled a "no" with a shake of her head, folded her hands against her chin, pointed to Robert and said, "He liked to sleep with men. No girls."

Despite his excitement, detective Macklin asked in as calm a voice as he could manage, "Was Mr. Isaac with someone that night?"

"Si"

Robert turned to Julia. "How could the cops not know about this? You said they questioned her for hours."

"Just like we almost missed it. You see how rough this is for her. They asked all the wrong questions. Accusing type of an interrogation thinking she was in on it. They blew it! No surprise there."

"What about the security guard?"

"Clammed up, I'm told by my friend. The guy was scared of cooperating with the police. If he knew anything, he wasn't saying."

Macklin had one last question. "Was the person with Mr. Isaac's that night a regular visitor or a new friend?"

Amanda shrugged her shoulders. "I don't know sir. I was asleep when Mr. Isaac and Mr. Glenn came back home."

"Did Isaac go out often looking for friends?" Julia asked.

Amanda managed her first smile of the evening and answered in Spanish. "No. No tanto. Solo los Viernes."

In 1981, Columbia had three bars that were patronized by the gay community. During that period, South Carolina drinking holes still remained mostly segregated. The city had only one such bar where blacks of that persuasion congregated. Robert figured a white detective asking questions there would be as welcome as a fly in a bowl of soup. He needed the help of a friend. A black friend.

As young men in the mid-fifties, Quiney Simon and Robert Macklin had enlisted in the US army a week apart. Both trained in the same platoon at Fort Jackson and afterwards served together in Korea.

Neither stayed in the service but because of the experiences they shared in that war, the men remained good buddies.

Quiney worked part time as a night watchman for the Richland Mall. The pay was irregular and poor, so he was always out to make a buck or two. Robert had used him in the past to help with surveillance. This time he simply needed Quiney for his color.

Robert explained his racial dilemma to Quiney the day after he had questioned Amanda. His old war buddy enjoyed every word. "I know the place you're talking about, Bobby. Called The Shady Side and you wouldn't fit in. Not just because you're white either, if you know what I mean? You going in there alone might be asking to come out with a very sore butt. I can help if you don't mind me asking, what will a couple of hours of my time pay?"

"I'm familiar with the bar's reputation, pal. It's one of the reasons I'm requesting your company. The other is if someone there knows anything, they're not likely to tell a white detective poking around."

Robert hesitated a second for Quiney's response. Nothing, so he continued with what was likely his friend's main concern. "You're going to like the answer to your question. I'm on expenses. Let's say $300 if we strike out and twice that if I find the guy I'm looking for."

Quiney replied immediately. "Meet you at the front door tonight at eight." The amount was several times what he expected. He earned a minimum wage at the mall. $3.45 an hour. Three hundred bucks equaled almost a month's take home pay.

They entered The Shady Side lounge together. It was dimly lit, but Robert was impressed by the scene inside. It was furnished with leather lined booths along the walls, round marble top tables with cushioned chairs in the central area and a 20-foot-long Cherrywood bar near the back. Perfectly clean and neat. Everything was first class unless you were offended by an exceptionally long wall mural behind the bar featuring cowboys dancing together. If you looked closely enough, two or three of the couples in the picture were even kissing. Pretty much sent a clear message to the type of patrons catered there.

There were twenty or more all male customers and Robert was relieved to see two white men among them. Quiney noticed how his friend was staring around at everyone and sort of ushered Bobby towards the bar in the back. "Good thing I'm with you. You acting star stuck! Let's have a drink and get on with why we're here."

Robert recovered and held out a C-note to the man behind the bar. "Good evening, sir. Could we have a couple of scotch whiskeys?"

Quiney added, "Make both of those a double on the rocks."

When the bartender returned with their drinks and change, he asked quietly, "Are you two cops or something?"

Quiney answered, "No sir. Far from it. I'm a night watchman at the Richland Mall. My buddy here is a private detective hoping to find someone."

Robert could see this guy serving their scotch was not impressed with Quiney's description, so he took the conversation from there. "First of all, if you'll just here us out, keep the change."

The bartender's expression remained stolid, but he placed the 90 dollars in change into his pants pocket. Nodded his head and said, "Okay, tell me who it is you're looking for and why?"

Substantial gratuities work wonders with bartenders. Robert acknowledged the nod with one of his own and began to answer the question. "A frequent customer of your lounge was recently killed. Isaac Higgins. Because the cops are getting nowhere with solving the crime, a friend of Isaac has asked for us to help. If he was here the night of his murder, we want to find the person he left with. There's another 'Benjamin' in it for you if we do!"

The bartender looked around to see if anyone was watching. "Mister, you remind me of Isaac in a way. He never paid with anything but hundred-dollar bills. Isaac came in and left with a young looking 'cowboy' I'd never seen before. They sat and drank together in a corner booth for about two hours. That's about all I can tell you, but you might talk to Kerstian, his server that night."

Both Robert and Quiney turned and surveyed the place. Slightly puzzled, Quiney asked, "Is she working tonight?"

That finally brought the barkeep's smile. He raised a hand and motioned to one of the waiters. Kerstian strolled over. She was a "he." The barkeep explained what the two men standing there wanted to know. Robert handed over a twenty and said, "Can you tell us anything about the person Isaac was with?"

Kerstian accepted the "tip" and replied, "Not much, I'm afraid. He was new here and good looking. The two of them got along well, especially before they left. I haven't seen him since. Sorry."

Somewhat disappointed, Robert handed his card to both men. "If the guy comes again, phone me. Anytime, day or night. If I get that call, it pays $100 to each of you."

Robert and Quiney shook the bartender's hand and started to leave. Kerstian tapped Quiney's shoulder. "By the way sir. When I brought the tab to Isaac, I heard him say, 'Are you ready to leave, Thomas?' Does that help?"

"Did you get a last name?" Robert quickly asked.

"No. Just Thomas."

Macklin figured his search had been narrowed significantly by one night's work. He was looking for a young, black, gay man whose first name was Thomas. The population of Columbia was approximately 350,000 but only 25% black. He and Quiney wasted two weeks driving around black neighborhoods asking around. They chased down a half dozen leads that were worthless.

Discouraged, Macklin had to ask himself what now? He hated the answer. The city of Columbia's phone directory. First names followed surnames. Columbia was ninety percent segregated. List all the Thomases along with their addresses. Then exclude those living in white communities. Sounds simple. It turned out to be laborious as hell and took another two days. There were 612 names listed as Thomas. Only 104 of those resided in black neighborhoods. Robert was confident that finally he was getting somewhere. It turned out to be another dead end.

Out of 104 with the name, Thomas, the probability of being both young and gay was maybe two percent. It took a week to check out the listings. He and Quiney came up with three possible suspects. They managed to take their photographs. Back at The Shady Side lounge, both Kerstian and the bartender agreed none were the "Thomas" Robert was looking for. Total waste of time!

A month-long investigation seemed to have produced little. The identities of whoever killed the brothers that night was still somewhat unknown. Robert provided a written review of his investigation to Eugene Howell and a verbal to Julia. The unsolved clue to the mystery was who the hell was "Thomas?" Almost for sure, he was the killer or one of the killers. Howell reported his detective's results back to Nicolas Estrada. Julia Grant kept notes for her planned CBS expose.

Estrada was not pleased with his South Carolina attorney's report. The sum of it was that someone named Thomas probably killed his dealers. With not much in the way of another option, he told Howell to stay on the case.

Reluctantly, Nicolas would have to tell his jefes in Guadalajara some progress had been made, but more time was needed to solve the "who-dunit." Thankfully, when he did, both Felix and Caro were more interested in his progress with setting up the new distribution facility. That was going extremely well. They had purchased a small, unprofitable fruit Cannery in upstate Georgia. It would serve as a perfect excuse for semi-trailer trucks bringing produce from Mexico. Nicolas's goal was to have it fully operational by June.

Friday, September 4th, AUSA Albert Turner placed a long distance, station to station call from Jacksonville, Florida to Freeport in the Bahamas. A male voice answered. It was Diego. Albert simply said, "I'm calling from Jacksonville. I have a message for Ms. Aguero. Please have her return my call."

The number Turner had dialed was provided by Juanita. Alias, Juanita Aguero. The Freeport phone itself was in an apartment used for nothing more than concealing contact information made by telephone. Albert's message was passed on to Juanita by Diego using a separate phone in the same apartment.

When moving their office from Miami to Freeport took place, Juanita had instructed the AUSA to keep track of upcoming federal indictments arising out of Edward Ward's testimony. The Feds moved slowly and methodically. Months had passed prior to any charges being handed down by the court. Days before that would take place, Albert was to notify Juanita with any details. The advanced warning would give associates of their organization, if accused, basically time to get-the-hell-out-of-town.

Juanita returned Turner's call thirty minutes later. It was good news and bad news. Carlos Enrique Lehder Rivas and Jack Carlton Reed were named as defendants in a drug smuggling criminal enterprise via the Bahamas. That was the bad news. The good news was surprising. Fabio Ochoa and Luis Castillo were not included in the indictments.

Immediately after she ended the conversation with Albert Turner, Juanita phoned Luis.

He best not admit it, but Luis was elated. Sorry for Carlos and Jack but somehow, he and Fabio had escaped being accused. There was no time to waste, however. For the time being, Reed was safe in Colombia, but Lehder was still working out of Norman Cay. Luis phoned Jorge and Pablo for a meeting.

Three hours later in Escobar's Medellin home, Luis informed his jefes of what was soon to be a criminal indictment of Carlos. Since his little brother Fabio was in the clear, Jorge was beside himself but still asked,

"You're confident your information is correct Luis?"

"Very confident, Jorge."

"How much time does Carlos have?" Pablo asked.

"The weekend most likely because federal courts rarely hold sessions then. Afterwards, I can't say. To arrest him, they need to have the co-operation of officials in Nassau. Still, it's best not to underestimate the DEA. They may have already accomplished that. If so, Carlos needs to leave right away."

"Let's not worry so much about Carlos," Pablo argued. "I'll have Fernando fly him here by Sunday. Jorge, if they come after Carlos, they're going to find five or six thousand kilos of our cocaine that's backed up and sitting in Norman Cay. Can we get it on one of your trawlers by Monday?"

Luis answered instead. "Probably not, Pablo. Even if we could, it's too risky. The DEA has eyes watching Norman Cay. They would more than likely spot the transfer."

Escobar was becoming a little frustrated, "Can Fabio handle a load that large at one of his landing strips in Florida?"

Jorge answered with a negative nod. "It would be foolish to try and fly that much at once, Pablo. Most likely we would lose it all and bring a lot of attention to ourselves."

Six thousand kilos were nearly $200,000,000 worth. Little wonder Escobar was more concerned about it than Lehder. "Then first thing in the morning, have our men on Norman Cay load it up on the DC-6 and fly it here."

Jorge agreed with the decision but cautioned, "We have no choice Pablo, but without Norman Cay our cocaine will start stacking up in the warehouses."

Pablo Escobar didn't need to be told about the surplus. U.S. demand for cocaine was not the obstacle. The stumbling block was how to transport enough into the country. He practically welcomed any newcomers to smuggle his cocaine. George Jung was no longer connected to Carlos, but he was still flying some for Pablo. Luis's apprentice, Trevor was another recently welcomed entrepreneur. He was using the Ochoa's mother ships. The trawlers were responsible for smuggling twenty five percent of Pablo's production. Still, without Carlos and Norman Cay, Pablo required new routes and fast.

The now recognized head of Colombia's cocaine empire did not relish his reply to Jorge. "I know our problem, Jorge, and now it's even worse. You and I decided months ago the solution is very unfavorable, but I think we have little choice now."

"The Mexicans?" Jorge said even though he knew the answer.

"Yes, unfortunately. It's the only way unless you have a better idea."

It was not just unfavorable, Jorge thought. Even though there was no alternative, Pablo was putting it much too mildly. Mexico was damn costly. The bastards demanded half of whatever was delivered because they knew they could get away with their ultimatum. There's was the only country that shared a southern border with the U.S. Two thousand miles of it and permeable as a sieve. "Okay, Pablo. With the Cali brothers again?"

"Maybe not. We already have enough middlemen holding their hands out. I'll have Gustavo contact Juan Ballesteros directly. Let him arrange a meeting for us with Felix and his partners. It's time to know just how much they can handle. Maybe we can increase our volume and make up for their take. Fly our DC-6 there loaded to the hilt!"

Jorge changed the subject. He was thinking about his little brother. "Luis, is it safe for Fabito to stay in Miami?"

"For the time being, I believe so.". "At least from the DEA boys. I'd worry more about the competition. It's starting to get nasty. Some of those Cubans Castro shipped were hard ass criminals. To them, Florida is a cake ready for slicing. They have little respect for established territory."

Pablo Escobar was not about to share Florida with anyone besides the Ochoa brothers. "Luis, I'm going to have Griselda start taking care of that piece of business. She's highly qualified for that type of work." Then respectfully because he had answered for Jorge. "I'm certain you would rather Fabio remain focused on distribution, Jorge. It's best he doesn't get mixed in with any correctional measures that have to be used."

"I'd prefer Blanco for that too, Pablo. Just make sure she looks after Fabito. David and I promised not to let any harm come to him."

Luis reminded them of the indictments against Reed and Lehder. "We still have to let Carlos know it's time to leave Norman Cay. He'll only accept instructions from you, Pablo."

Escobar reassured them who the jefe was. "He will be on a flight with Fernando before the weekend is over. Either that or I'll have some of his guards pack him in the DC-6 along with our 6,000 kilos of coke."

Losing Norman Cay required just the type of decisive action Pablo and Jorge were implementing. Luis still had to inform Jack Reed of his indictment. He preferred to do that in person. Fortunately, that would require a flight to Cartagena.

Jack was staying in a nice, rented home not far from Michelle's. His companion, Sheldon, had joined him there. She and Mitch quickly developed a close friendship. Once Luis arrived back in Cartagena, he told Mitch the news about probable indictments being brought against Lehder and Reed. She was delighted her sweet husband was not included but wanted reassurance this did not change his decision to stay out of the U.S.

Luis's legal experience provided Michelle relief of her anxieties. "If anything, Mitch, it convinces me I've been right all along not to take chances. I'll never return to Florida. An occasional trip to the Bahamas is required of me now. Nothing more! Staying safe here in Colombia with you and Daniel is my only ambition."

"What about Jack? Have you told him yet?"

"No, not yet. I'll call and invite them over for drinks. It's better to hear bad news coming from me in person. I'm just glad we were warned six months ago this might happen. If Jack stays in Colombia, he'll be hard to find. Even if by chance the DEA does, it's unlikely they can extradite him. The family has considerable political influence if needed."

Luis was not aware that Jack and Sheldon had already made contingency plans to leave Colombia. They both seem to take the indictment news in stride and Jack explained why. "You guys are the only ones we can share our secrets with. You know I've flown to Panama several times since we arrived here in Colombia. Sheldon came with me on occasions. We bought a retirement home there, Luis. Used assumed names of course. It's a beautiful place set in a cove, very private and perfectly safe. We're wealthy emigrants from Canada with documents to prove it. There's no way in that setting anyone can connect me back to Carlos and Norman Cay."

Michelle hugged Sheldon. "Can we come visit someday?"

"Sure, and vice versa I hope."

The rest of their evening ended with pleasant goodnights at the door. Luis and Michelle tucked five-year-old Daniel in and then spent an even more pleasant hour together in their bedroom.

Carlos Lehder practically exploded with anger when Fernando arrived with Pablo's orders to pack and leave Norman Cay. At that time, he had single handedly built the most successful smuggling operation ever imagined. In three years, his flights of cocaine had shipped over 100,000 kilos of cocaine into three southern states. Florida, Georgia, and South Carolina. Carlos had personally grossed more than two billion dollars in sales. Now he was being told, not asked, to give it all up.

Sunday morning, March 7, 1981, Carlos Lehder watched as 6,000 kilos of "his" cocaine were loaded aboard the DC-6. Fernando Arenas watched with him. When the DC-6 barely managed to lift off the runway carrying its cargo, Fernando gave a whistle of relief and explained its flight plan. "She has to fly to Nassau to refuel Carlos. No way they could have made it off the strip with her tanks full."

Lehder's irritability was magnified by an earlier overindulgence of cocaine. He was still confident the DEA could not have gotten to him in the Bahamas. Being forced to abandon his island and all he had built there was too much "The sons-of-bitches are stealing my coke, Fernando. I don't give a shit if they crash in hell. I'm going back to the house and take care of some things there. Meet you back here in an hour or two."

"I'll be here waiting," Fernando told his jefe. "The weather looks good all the way home."

A little more than an hour passed before Carlos returned. They boarded the Cessna Citation II for the trip to Colombia. Fernando left the 3,300-foot runway with 600 feet to spare. As he came around to a south heading, he glanced back toward Norman Cay. Pillows of black smoke were coming from one of the island homes. Fernando knew without asking but turned an inquisitive look to Carlos in the right seat. Carlos confirmed the smoke's source with a spaced-out attitude. "Screw the damn place!"

Norman Cay's demise as a cocaine smuggling hub for flights into the U.S. ended with Carlos Lehder's departure. He never accepted any of the blame for its termination. However, his history on the island eventually revealed a personal accountability. Lehder's infamous activities there included many Bahamian officials. As a result, the place attracted the attention of the U.S. Drug Enforcement Administration. Still, the Bahamas were an independent country. That required considerable protocol by the agency. Any related defendant facing criminal prosecution that could provide solid evidence of the island's involvement in drugs became a prize asset. Namely, Edward Hayes Ward! He was a minor player but an instrumental one in the naming of a self-appointed kingpin. Carlos Lehder!

28.

HIGH TIDE IN CHERRY GROVE

Nine days into November, Trevor and Jessie made their third offshore cocaine run. This time it was a meeting with the *Paso Seguro*. Several times before in the past eight months, they had met up with one or the other trawlers, but only once to replenish their supply of cocaine. Five other trips delivered large amounts of cash in plastic storage containers. Each was packed with tightly bound ten-, twenty-, and one-hundred-dollar bills. In eight months, Trevor and Jessie had returned to the Colombians $18,000,000 in payments for six hundred kilos. It was a relatively easy financial task since they had netted the same amount for themselves. This time out, they were carrying $9,000,000 to pay up front for their next 300 kilos. The money was not a heavy load for the Bayliner. Ten containers placed in the boat's cabin weighed about one hundred pounds each. It was smooth sailing all the way out.

High tide that afternoon in Hog inlet was at 5:07 p.m. At a slow speed of about five knots, Trevor let his now experienced crewman, Jessie Talbert, take the Bayliner in. After tying to the dock, they carried six ice coolers filled with cocaine up the ramp and into the garage. The renovated cabinetry of the Winnebago was used to conceal the drugs. Once all 300 kilos were stored, Jessie laughed and asked, "Do you smell fried chicken?"

"You bet the hell I do. Let's get upstairs and give our cook a great big hug."

Leann accepted a warm greeting from both men. "You two are back right on time. I'll be another half hour or so before dinner is ready. Just one more pan to fry. Go wash up and make yourself a drink. When the table's set, I'll yell."

Trevor acted like he would obey but waved a kiss saying, "Aye, Aye Captain Fox," and tried to reach around her to a plate of fried chicken.

She shoved him back smiling. "Not yet, old man! Wait like a good boy. I'm the boss in the kitchen, remember?"

Trevor looked back to see if Jessie had left. He had, so Trevor leaned against her with a right hand on her rear and replied, "Maybe the kitchen but I'm the master in the bedroom."

Leann smiled again. "Especially tonight, sweetie, I hope you are!"

Early the next day, Trevor and Jessie left together in the Winnebago for the cabin. Leann stayed behind to finish house cleaning. Afterwards, she would drive alone to Lake Murray. It was pretty much a routine the three of them had started to follow. Her "boys," as she referred to them, would take care of business at Lake Wateree, then join her for dinner at the lake house. Usually a steak, baked potato, and salad. Perfect too because she needed the time to herself. It was a three-hour trip and difficult for her to make without stopping for "refreshments!"

Halfway to the cabin Jessie asked about his aunt. "Did you notice Aunt Leann was already on a cocaine high when we got back yesterday?"

"Sure did, but it gets worse after dark. Things were looking good for me last night, but by the time I climbed in bed, her mood swing had turned bad. She becomes so obsessed with her next hit of coke, she gets angry and starts fidgeting. Nothing else matters if you get my meaning?"

"We've got to do something?"

"I'm working on it, Jessie. A first-class rehab place for women like your aunt is being built in California. I hate the thought of sending Leann for something like that, but it may be the only way to get her clean. Sometime next year I'll try and convince her to go there."

"Well, it damn sure can't hurt. The timing might be right too. Are we still planning on calling it quits in a year?"

"I had a goal all along. When we reach $50,000,000 in profits, hang it up! To get there, we'll need to make four more runs like yesterdays."

Jessie corrected his instructor. "Your math's off. Twelve hundred more kilos added to what we already have comes to $54,000,000."

Trevor smiled. "Carrying around a little change never hurts."

The exchange with Todd, Cecil, and Ricky went smoothly. Only now, each of them left with 35 kilos. It allowed regular exchanges of cash for new stocks once a month, but these relatively new partners all began to share a common problem. Demand was exceeding their supply. It was an unanticipated event on Trevor's part. His plan had been to replace the Higgins brothers in South Carolina. Something more was taking place.

Trevor received $60,000 per kilo. Each of his three distributors charged a little more than twice that to their street dealers; the idea being to keep them overly content since they were taking the greatest risk. The margin between a wholesale cost of $130,000 and the price of street sales was too great. When cocaine was broken down and sold by the gram, a kilo was worth $400,000. Some of those who had formerly been "street dealers" graduated themself to "distributors" by outsourcing beyond the state's boundaries. Why not? Simply load a few kilos in a car, drive to Newark, New Jersey; and sell it at a much higher but still wholesale price to dealers there. Some of Trevor's cocaine was unintentionally going as far as New York City. If he and Jessie had chosen to, they could have become another Fabio. Luckily, it was their past that prevented a choice.

Often the sunsets on Lake Wateree were remarkable. Jessie photographed one for his godmother the evening of February 4th. "Aunt Leann would love to see this, Trevor. Has she ever come here with you?"

"Sorry to say but no, she hasn't. If our stay at the cabin involves business transactions at the marina, then I'd rather Leann not be here. Today is different. The Winnebago is gassed up and loaded for our trip to Florida. She could have joined us tonight and then, when we leave tomorrow morning, just driven back home."

"I wish she were enjoying seeing this setting sun. Whole damn sky is lit up in red."

"Blame the damn coke for her absence. It's why these days she stays mostly at home. Glad to see that bright sunset though. It's good news for our cruise out of Port Salerno. You've heard me say it before. I think the old saying is more dependable than any weatherman. 'Red sky at night, sailors delight.' It's a day from now, but we should have smooth waters over to the Bahamas."

They locked up the cabin and left for Florida at 7am. Jessie drove the first half. When Trevor took over, Jessie talked most of the way during the second half. "Funny thing, Trevor, but I never knew money could be such a damn problem. Just carried a few bucks and a condom in my wallet until we met. Not much of a loss if either went missing. Can't help but worry some with this haul. How about you?"

Jessie was referring to the Winnebago's cargo. Over a half ton of U.S. currency was packed in twelve plastic storage containers. Twelve million dollars. Impossible to conceal, so they were just stacked on the floor in the back and covered with a tarp.

"I'm not going to kid you. We're taking a chance moving our money like this. Not much of a choice though unless you want to bury it in the back yard. Have to be pretty stupid to do that."

"What about all the money we carry out to the fishing trawlers? Much safer way to move it, I think. Why not do the same with ours?"

"Maybe so, Jessie? But that money wounds up in Colombia. God knows where in South America it goes from there. I prefer the 'hands on approach.' Consider this. It may help you not to worry so much. I've driven to Florida and back more than a hundred times. Been stopped once. Pretty good odds and even ten times better when going to Florida."

"Why? What's the difference between going and coming?"

"Anyone smuggling drugs on I-95 is leaving the state. Cops watch out for traffic carrying narcotics north, not south."

They were six hours into their trip and had just passed by St. Augustine. Trevor noticed Jessie was quiet for a change. "Something must be bothering you, Jessie. First time we did this, you seemed to enjoy it.

"Just that I think. First time, you're excited about becoming rich as hell. Second time, you're worried you could lose it all."

"Comes with the business we're in." Trevor had repeated what he remembered Luis saying. "Two more hours to Port Salerno. Once we get on our way in the morning to Freeport, our moneys in the bank."

"When you say that, I wonder how you can be so sure. What makes the Bahamas different?"

Jessie's questions were beginning to make Trevor feel like he was the wise old guru teaching an apprentice. Had to keep telling himself his partner was barely a year into the business. One hell-of-a-fast learner and inquisitive to a fault. Reminded him of himself.

"For one thing, it's a sovereign nation only a hundred miles off the U.S. coast. Aside from being a tourist attraction, the country's financial sector is dependent on its offshore business activity. Consequently, the banking laws are favorable for what we do. Clients and deposits remain confidential. Some refer to the Bahamas as the 'Switzerland of the west.' Does that answer your question, Jessie?"

"Some, I guess. But if the banks in the Bahamas are safe, why do you transfer everything we earn to Switzerland."

"Good question. It's something my pilot friends taught me. Swiss banks are even better. Laws there keep international depositors very private. You're one of those now."

"Yeah! And it wasn't too long ago that I thought it would take two years to get where I'm at now. You made me an equal partner. Never expected that! I just turned twenty and already a damn multimillionaire. At least that's what my Switzerland bank account says."

"I consider you and your aunt as family. You're much more than just my partner."

Trevor had purchased a Bayliner 4050 Bodega in Vero Beach last July. He purposely kept it docked at a marina in Port Salerno because he knew the waters there from his experience with Russell. Hours before daylight, he and Jessie transferred the Winnebago's cargo to the 40 foot Bayliner's cabin. Then, the two of them easily cruised to Freeport.

Once arriving in the Bahamas, Juanita had arranged for their safe harbor with the authorities. At the appropriate time that afternoon, Juan and Diego came aboard. With their guidance, Trevor slowly motored to the western most end of Freeport. Juan took the helm from there. At an idle speed they entered Old Bahama Bay. There were large, beautiful homes on cut canals at the back of the bay. They docked at one of the nicest. Juanita was on one of its two patios and waved as they arrived.

Juan and Diego assisted with unloading their cargo. Twelve million in cash was stored temporarily in a down-stares locker room. Later, in smaller parcels, it would be deposited in one of three banks Juanita worked with in the Bahamas. For a nominal fee, the banks would wire transfer deposits to Trevor's and Jessie's numbered accounts in Switzerland. Multi-digits there replaced the actual identity of the holder. The transactions were surprisingly simple and commonplace in the early eighties. Even so, Juanita's connections in the Bahamas were essential for Trevor to in effect "launder" the money safely.

Once work was finished, Juanita inquired, "I assume you two will stay the night here with us?"

"If it's not too much of an inconvenience, yes we would like to," Trevor replied. "But it has to be my treat for all of us at the restaurant tonight?"

Diego chimed in. "Juan and I are up for that."

"I'll make reservations for seven, Juanita said. And Diego, bring Lucia with you. I'm sure she'll enjoy a night out after staying all day in the apartment waiting for a phone to ring. Trevor, you and Jessie come upstairs. There's someone there waiting for you two."

Trevor wondered who Juanita might be referring to. Without asking, he and Jessie obediently followed Juanita inside and up a curved stairwell to a closed door at the end of a back hallway. Juanita knocked softly. A moment later, Luis stepped out.

Nice surprise for Trevor. The two men had not seen each other in a year. Big smiles along with handshakes came with Luis's saying, "Really good to see you again, Trevor. We apparently have a lot to catch up on. You've come a long way fast since flying for Carlos. First though, introduce me to your partner."

"Sure will! Jessie, meet my friend and teacher, Luis Castillo. The person we owe all our good fortune to. Luis, this young man is Jessie Talbert, my partner and like a brother to me."

Luis replied approvingly. "Welcome to our company, Jessie."

The introduction was a formality. Juanita had already told Luis of the close relationship between Jessie and Trevor. As well, she approved of this newcomer's politeness and quiet demeanor. In short, Jessie had received her blessings. That was more than enough for Luis. "After you two get settled in, Trevor, let Jessie relax with Junita and beverages on the patio. We've got some time before dinner, so join me here in my office and let's go over a few things."

Trevor did as instructed. Still a bit salty after the trip, he showered, changed clothes, and returned. He and Luis spent the better part of an hour alone discussing events. The loss of Norman Cay was an important segment of the conversation, especially with the account that both Carlos and Jack had been indicted. Theirs and the island's fate led to a compliment from Luis. "You deserve a lot of credit for bringing South Carolina into the fold, Trevor. The state has been a soft spot in our distribution since we started. Smart move too and great timing. The DEA is watching for any movements coming off Lehder's island, so your contributions have helped a little. The persons we work for in Colombia are appreciative."

Trevor knew better than to keep secrets from Luis. Only the absence of any time together had prevented him from telling the details of how he came up with the idea of supplying cocaine in his home state. Now was as good a time as any to set the record straight. "There is something important you should know, Luis. It's the circumstances that brought about our takeover there."

"Are you referring to the deaths of the two narcotics dealers in your state?" Luis asked. "Juanita has already explained that to me."

"The short answer is yes. It's the reason why they were killed that I hope you'll understand. You've never met my companion, Leann. I'm no angel when it comes to women, but my relationship with her is solid. She has some problems but always remains devoted and loyal like you wouldn't believe. Deserves payback!"

"Sounds familiar," Luis replied thinking of Mitch. "How does she fit in with all this?"

"She's Jessie's godmother. Both his parents are dead. He lost his father in 1978 and his mother died in a car accident just a couple of years later. That's how he came to live with Leann and I in Columbia. Thing is, he came back there for a reason. He wanted revenge!"

With that one word spoken, Luis performed his customary leaned back, folded his arms, stared straight at Trevor and said, "I think I'm beginning to see what you're leading up to. The drug bosses?"

It was an obvious cue from Luis for Trevor to continue, so he did. "Higgs and Topcoat were their names. The two men were brothers with real bad reputations. For years, they used intimidation, and more often brutal force to maintain control in South Carolina. Jessie's dad worked for them until they blew his brains out on a street corner. Cops didn't care. Assumed it was a drug deal gone bad. Everyone, including Jessie, knew the truth."

"Are you about to tell me Jessie killed them?"

"No, we did!"

"Trevor, you never cease to surprise me. As you know, I leave things like that up to others."

"Early on, Luis, I tried to talk him out of it. No way! Jessie loved his dad so much, he wanted justice no matter the consequences. I grew up in Columbia. Nobody in their right mind would mess with Higgs or Topcoat. Those two men deserved to be taken out, but he didn't stand a chance against the two of them on his own. They always had bodyguards. Besides that, they had a dozen street enforcers working for them. Jessie is family, so I had to get involved."

"Is there any way the police can tie you in with their murder?"

"No! Caught them completely off-guard in their home. We left a safe open to make it look like a robbery. Worked too! That's the story reported by the newspapers. Also, some narcotic officers may have been tied in with them which explains what my attorney learned. The investigation has already been moved to a back burner."

"Thanks for keeping me informed, Trevor. Be careful though. The heroin and coke those brothers sold came from Mexico. You can bet the

Mexicans are not moving the loss of drugs and dealers to a back burner. They're a violent and ruthless bunch with long memories. They'll come after you if they find out what you just told me."

"We were careful, Luis. Still are too in our new business venture. Thomas Boyce, not me, bought the beach house on the border with North Carolina. The Bayliner we use there to connect with your trawlers and the one we came here in are also registered in his name. Jessie assumed Link's old alias, Richard Boyce. Even the guys we sell to don't know our real identities. TB and RB were the marijuana distributors in South Carolina. Now they've changed to cocaine."

"Disguise works. Yours was one of the things that impressed me when we first met. Along with that, I have to say you and Jessie have the potential to grow your business. Next trip out, figure on 400 kilos instead of three. Demand is incredible. If possible, by this time next year we would like to have you make twice your current runs to the trawlers."

Luis's suggestion was not something Trevor expected. He replied with a hint of argument. "Twice as many runs next year at 400 kilos each adds up to 3,000, With that much, we'll be supplying half the country."

Luis shook his head. "You have no idea how large the market is. Even if you double down, your share of U.S. imports will only be five percent. The labs in Colombia are producing 80,000 kilos annually. We need people like you and Jessie. With the loss of Carlos and Norman Cay, our transit is hurting. Out of necessity, we're starting to fly the cocaine to Mexico. We're working with the biggest outfit in that country. It's taken from there into the U.S."

"I'll do all I can to help, Luis. In this line of work, I suppose it's better to have the Mexicans as partners rather than competitors. It's not likely, but in case you hear any of them complaining about the new guy that took over in South Carolina, give me a heads-up please."

"Count on it. There's a hungry crew waiting on us. Enough of this business. Let's go have some fun."

Dinner that evening was like a class reunion. Everyone laughed a lot and drank too much. Jessie seemed to easily fit in with the group. Trevor noticed that Diego and Lucia were now close companions. Juanita quietly whispered to him confirmation of their relationship. The party ended with Luis inviting him and Jessie to stay over a few days. Trevor declined saying, "Wish we could but not this trip. I promised Leann we'd be home for Valentine's Day. There's no way to make it in time unless we leave tomorrow."

"Maldita!" Luis exclaimed. "Thanks for the reminder. I completely forgot. I'm leaving on the first flight back to Cartagena. Michelle counts on me being there for special occasions."

Early Saturday morning, Trevor and Jessie left Port Salena for the return to South Carolina. The Winnebago was perfectly clean carrying only luggage and sporting equipment. Didn't matter. The only stop required was for gas and snacks.

Jessie was in a great mood the whole trip. The transfer of money had gone smoothly, and meeting with everyone in the Bahamas during an overnight stay was exciting and memorable. He commented to Trevor while driving. "I've said this before. I'm getting used to this lifestyle you've introduced me to."

Trevor thought for a moment before answering. "In our meeting together, Luis asked that we increase the amount of cargo we carry from the trawlers to 400 kilos."

"Not a problem, Trevor. The Bayliner can cruise with that and then some. Todd, Ricky, and Cecil have been asking for more too."

"That's not all he wants from us. Next year, you and I have to make twice as many runs offshore. Luis thinks our part in the organization's annual cocaine distribution should increase to 3,000 kilos."

Now it was Jessie who hesitated before responding. "That's almost $100,000,000 worth in a single year and just our share. Nice round figure but scary too! What did you say to him?"

"What I had to say, Jessie. That you and I would help all we could."
"Are we?"

"No! For one thing, by the end of this year, I will have reached my goal. When that's accomplished, I promised myself and your aunt Leann we'd hang it up. Remember? Retire and perhaps travel to Europe."

"Aunt Leann can buy half of Europe with a hundred million, Trevor. Cut her in for a third and my guess is she wouldn't complain if we added one year to your plan."

"No amount of money would make any difference to her. She'd stay loyal to the end even if we said it was going to take another ten years. But Leann has got to have help. I want her off of cocaine by Christmas."

"Okay, I'm listening. How?"

"Try something new. Remember, in California, the first lady to former President Ford is opening a special rehabilitation facility for drug addicts. You and I are going to convince Leann to go there for treatment. From what I'm told, a few months there, maybe more, and a person can come out clean. Any outside financial assistance they receive is considered a charitable contribution. If we provide the right incentive, I'm pretty sure they will accept her as a patient."

"Can she be out by Christmas?"

"Hope so. I'm timing it that way for our end game, Jessie. I started running drugs in 1973. Marijuana at first and now cocaine. Nearly ten damn years of taking chances is enough. I learned something from my first boss. His name was Kenneth. He was smart for a white man. Straight out of Vietnam, he started dealing marijuana. After several years, he became rich. Then, he escaped."

"By 'escape,' you mean he got out of the business?"

"Clean as a whistle. Link and I worked for Kenneth. A little over four years ago, he turned everything over to us and simply walked away. God only knows where he is now. After this Christmas, Thomas and Richard Boyce will do the same thing. Turn their part of the business over to Ricky, Todd, and Cecil and get the hell out. Disappear! Leave South Carolina! It'll be like they never existed. Trevor Dunbar and Jessie Talbert will be two honest and very wealthy black men seeing the world."

"Have to say, Trevor, they'll sure love taking over our end of the partnership, especially if it's 3,000 kilos next year. Both smuggling and distribution for them will be no small problem though. Those guys will have to bury all the money someplace."

"Yeah. On the surface it sounds too good to be true, but greed can get you in trouble. It's already risky bringing in a ton of coke off the trawlers every year. Smuggle twice as much and you triple the risks. You only have to get caught once. A lot of money can be made, but it's not worth spending ten to twenty in a jail cell."

"Hell, I'm only twenty. I'd be old when they let me out. Working with you has made me overconfident. I'm ready to say 'adios' whenever you are. Aunt Leann, you, and I will all sail away into the sunset. Wave goodbye while smiling and counting our money."

"Christ, Jessie. Optimism is one thing, but there's nothing romantic about dealing cocaine. We're still criminals in the eyes of the law."

"I've watched the sun set too many times from the deck of our Bayliner not to see the romance in what we do. Beats the hell out sitting on your butt in some office. It's going to be tough to give this up."

"Yeah, but office work is leagues better than a prison. Luis told me Jack Reed, the person that taught me how to fly, has become a wanted outlaw in the U.S. Convinces me that sooner or later everyone that stays too long sneaking drugs into this country gets caught or must hide somewhere. By this Christmas, we're out-of-here!"

Valentine's Day with Leann was celebrated at Lake Murray. Her two boys made sure she was showered with cards, boxes of candy, and assorted gifts. It was an enjoyable occasion for everyone. Trevor decided it was best to wait until the Betty Ford Clinic was fully operational before suggesting she go there for treatment.

Jessie had an original idea concerning their future European travels. He enrolled as a day student at Columbia's Benedict College just to take French. A foreign language had been a required course his senior year of high school. He had chosen French then, and now at Benedict, he hoped to become as fluent in it as Trevor was in Spanish.

Windy weather during the first week of March prevented a scheduled run offshore to bring in their fourth load of cocaine. Ten days later with the return of calm seas, Trevor and Jessie met with the *Gran Pretendiente* seventy miles east of Myrtle Beach. This time they carried 400 kilos ashore.

The men made their usual trips to Lake Wateree in the Winnebago followed by distributions to partners at the Clearwater Marina parking area. The lot was large and inconspicuous. There were occasional visitors to the adjoining recreational campgrounds, but it was fenced and reserved for authorized military personnel. Each transfer of cocaine during the next two months went without the slightest signs of trouble. It was as though the methods they employed for exchanging coke for cash were made increasingly perfect with practice.

The month of April brought the necessity of transferring cash and making another trip to the Bahamas. It was an uneventful ride both on the road and on the sea. That is, if you can call sailing to an island paradise to deposit $12,000,000 into your bank accounts "uneventful." Once Trevor and Jessie arrived in Freeport, the safety factor quadrupled in their favor. Luis was not there this time, but his presence wasn't required. Juanita and her crew took care of the visitors and the money.

The drive home in nice weather was long but pleasant. Trevor drove and Jessie practiced his French all the way. They left the Winnebago at Lake Wateree and switched to their car for the ride back to Lake Murray. Trevor had tried to phone Leann from the cabin to say they would be home for dinner. She hadn't answered. The reason why became clear when two hours later they pulled into the driveway. A sheriff deputy's car was waiting for them. A uniformed deputy got out, walked over and apologized for blocking the driveway. He asked Trevor his name and afterwards said, "Sorry, but I may be bringing you a little bad news. A lady whose driver's license lists this address as her home has been in a car accident. Her name is Leann Fox."

Jessie gasped and before Trevor could reply, immediately asked, "How bad? Is she okay?"

The deputy raised an open hand to answer Jessie's questions. "Calm down son. The ambulance took her to the Baptist Medical Center.

While waiting here, I checked on her condition not more than an hour ago. Doctor there is sure she's going to be fine."

Trevor let out a deep breath. "Thank god for that, deputy!"

The deputy shook his head in agreement. "I have to say, that's one lucky girl! She must have been coming home because it happened on highway 378 only a few miles from here. Looked like she may have run off the road and then overcorrected. Flipped a new Chevy Malibu over several times. Completely totaled it and then some."

Trevor thanked the deputy and then quickly backed out of the driveway. The Baptist hospital was in downtown Columbia. Still, in only thirty minutes, he and Jessie were both standing bedside with Leann. She was sound asleep with a head bandage and some obvious arm and facial bruises.

Leann's doctor came in and introduced himself before explaining her condition. "She may have suffered a mild concussion. Bruised a bit as you can see but the x-rays showed nothing broken. Unfortunately, we had to sedate her."

"Why?" Jessie asked. Trevor already knew the answer but let the doctor explain anyway.

"One minute she was talkative and then suddenly overly anxious and extremely irritable. Even cursed one of the nurses. Along with the nosebleed and dilated pupils, I can tell you I've seen this before. Maybe you know, but in case you don't, she's a drug addict."

Trevor nodded an affirmative understanding. "We know, doctor, and it's probably the reason for the accident. Recently, I've made arrangements for Leann to enter a drug rehabilitation facility. It's new but you may have heard of it. The Betty Ford Clinic in California."

The doctor raised his eyebrows along with wide eyes. "Of course, I've more than just heard of the place. It's in the news. Staffed with the best professionals I'm told. Great, if you can get her in!"

"She's already been accepted," Trevor replied. "Within a week of leaving your hospital, we'll have her on a plane to the west coast. That's a promise!"

The doctor thought for a moment. Wondered who the hell are these two young black men? Stared hard at Jessie with an expression of recognition saying, "You're Jessie Talbert! The great freshman lineman for USC that was hurt the year before last. I was here at the hospital when they brought you in. How's the knee?"

"I played defensive end," Jessie corrected. "Thanks, but the injury was a severe enough tear that my career in football was over."

Leann's hospital stay lasted three days. She spent another week recuperating at home. In a way, the car wreck proved helpful. It brought an awakening to her drug problem. Even with that realization, it took a few days for both Trevor and Jessie to talk Leann into trying the rehab clinic in California. Convinced her it was almost a resort. Trevor didn't mention a recent six figure donation to the clinic Charles Whitfield's law office had made in her name. No questions were asked regarding her admittance. $600,000 did the trick. It was no coincidence that the amount was his half of what had been removed from the Higgins brother's safe.

Friday, April 16th, Trevor, Leann, and Jessie boarded an American Airlines non-stop flight out of Charlotte, N.C. to Los. Angeles, CA. They drove a rental from there to the resort city of Rancho Mirage. Their appointment for checking Leann into the rehab clinic was set for 10 a.m. Saturday, so Trevor had made reservations for the night at the Ritz-Carlton. Dinner that evening included quite a few tears shed by Leann. Both the "boys" assured her she would be home before Christmas. Leann had accepted the necessity of coming off cocaine. Still, the parting was a sad and difficult occasion for all.

The third week of May, another cocaine delivery accompanied by receipts was made at Lake Wateree's Clearwater Marina. As usual, Trevor and Jessie observed the exchanges from their anchored pontoon boat in the cove. Of the three partners, Todd was last to arrive and leave because Columbia was the nearest city to the drop point. Each man had left with 35 kilos of coke. As payment, each had placed two military duffle bags in Impala's trunk and back seat. Even though Trevor now required settlements to be made in nothing smaller than twenties and preferably hundred-dollar bills, it was not a light load. Roughly 500 pounds. Trevor dropped Jessie at the marina's dock and motored the pontoon boat back to the cabin. Jessie drove the impala filled with cash there. The Chevy's duffel bags of money were transferred to six plastic storage containers and concealed beneath the pumphouse floor. Trevor glanced at the remaining space, smirked and said, "Good thing we're meeting with the *Paso Seguro* next month. There's not enough room left for another batch of this stuff."

Jessie had to laugh. "I never imagined my biggest problem would be where to store money. No worry, Trevor. The payoff at the trawler for 400 kilos comes to $12,000,000. There'll be plenty of space here once we do that. Work here's finished. A stay at the cabin tonight sounds good. With Leann not home expecting us, there's no hurry to get back."

"Sounds good to me too, Jessie. There's a great pizza house with draft beer in Camden. Let's clean up and go."

Later, and after having enjoyed too much pizza and way too much beer, Jessie commented, "I miss Leann, but it sure is nice not worrying about her."

"Miss her too, Jessie but time flies bye. Before you know it, she'll be back home. Think about this, instead. We're coming to the end of our business here. After this next run, only two more to go. I'm planning on meeting this September with Ricky, Cecil, and Todd. They'll need a few months of preparation for the takeover. I'm certain the organization in Colombia will welcome their help. Luis told me they need newcomers because of a big shortage in distribution."

"So far, everything you've tried has gone without a hitch. Take today for instance. Not even a hint of any problems. Almost boring! I'm positive everything will go smoothly in the short time we have left."

Jessie's reassurance could not have been more wrong. An old saying would have been accurate. "What-goes-around-comes-around." Neither he nor Trevor knew, but Todd's transfer of coke and cash that afternoon had been under surveillance.

As a detective with a successful investigative record, Robert Macklin could not have been more discouraged with his ongoing assignment. Once every month he had to report negative results to Eugene Howell. His search for the mysterious "Thomas" had met with nothing but dead ends. The only good part was that a substantial cash retainer came with each visit along with instructions to keep at it.

Halfway into the spring season, he got a promising break. It came from his army buddy.

Quiney Simon had continued to visit The Shady Side lounge. His friend, Macklin, had tripled the reward to $1,800 if he could help locate the gay cowboy named "Thomas." Quiney considered the amount a damn fortune, so he put up with the occasional approaches made by friendly men at the bar. A guy who introduced himself as Herb had twice offered to share a line of coke with him. The second proposal caused Quiney to give his first name before saying, "No thanks, Herb, but tell me, how much does that stuff cost you?"

His suitor smiled and said, "Nothing! Otherwise, I wouldn't be offering you a freebee."

The reply was totally unexpected, so Quiney continued the conversation out of even more curiosity. And, on purpose, in an overtly polite manner. "No offence, but I've heard that coke is horribly expensive. Probably the reason for my not trying it before now." The lie worked!

Herb sensed an opportunity to become more personal. He had noticed Quiney had recently become a Shady Side bar patron. Closet gays were common. Herb had surmised Quiney might be looking for some very private companionship. "It's anything but cheap. Cost around $400 per gram on the open market. Comes to about $50 or $60 a line unless you're a heavy hitter."

"What's an open market?"

Herb smiled. "You know? Sales on street corners, alleys, sometimes in restrooms."

Quiney knew a lot more about drugs than he was pretending. He was playing Herb along just to see where it took him. "Well, that settles it. Stuffs way beyond anything I can afford."

"Maybe so, but it's not a problem if you're interested. Wouldn't be telling you any of this but I checked you out with the bartender. He says you're a night watchman at the mall."

"Just part time, and only when they need me. Minimum wage too, so you can see where I'm coming from. I'm pushing my finances just coming here for a drink. But you said your coke was free. How do you manage that?"

Herb wrongly figured the question was his opportunity to impress Quiney. "I deal a little."

With that answer, Quiney thought maybe he should have been an actor. For whatever reason he wasn't sure, but he was reeling this guy in "hook, line, and sinker." With a broad smile plus a soft handshake, he asked Herb one more "baited question." "Well, I'll be! Any money in it?"

Some men can resist a chance at self-esteem. Not Herb. "You bet there is and a lot if it's coke. Years back, I started by selling dime bags of marijuana. Got by but that's about all. Risky too! I passed an ounce to a college kid who turned out to be a young-looking narc. He busted me, but it wasn't a big deal."

"Did you serve time?"

Herb laughed. "Hell, no! Not for a measly ounce. Todd's lawyer bailed me out the same night. I had to appear in court a week later. The judge gave me six months of probation and a $100 fine. White man, so of course I had to promise him I'd be a good 'boy.' You know the drill."

"Yeah, sometimes we all have to do a dance for them. Sounds like you had a good lawyer. Who's Todd?"

"He's the 'man' here in Columbia now. Same race as us too. Todd and I go way back. He flipped from supplying marijuana to cocaine right after those two drug bosses got themselves murdered. That's how I got started with it. He supplies me with cocaine at a price that lets me make some real dough."

Quiney immediately knew he was on to something or someone, so he continued to play dumb. "Seems to me a little over a year ago I read about two brothers being killed during a robbery. It came out later in the papers that they were involved in narcotics."

"Involved my ass! They controlled the whole damn state. Powerful, and mean as hell too. Whoever took them out did us all a great big favor. Especially me and Todd."

"Maybe it's wrong to ask, but I could sure use some extra money. I barely get by as it is. Stay broke most of the time. Is there any chance for me to get my hands on some coke to sell?"

Herb sensed an opportunity, smiled and said, "Maybe, but we'd need to know each other much better before that can happen. Even

I have to go through channels instead of dealing directly with my old friend. Suppose we go out to dinner one evening later this week. I'll mention the possibility to one of Todd's assistants. They're bringing a new supply over to my place tomorrow night. Either way though, it'll take time."

"I'm okay with that, Herb, and dinner would be nice."

"Great! Do you know Groucho's Deli in Five points?"

"Yes"

"Okay. Let's meet there at about seven on Thursday."

"Herb, I'm already looking forward to our becoming friends. But if I have to work, can I have a raincheck?"

"Sure. Just call me and we can make it another time." Herb wrote his number on a paper coaster and gave it to Quiney.

Looking at his watch with a slight show of alarm, Quiney said, "Damn! Wish I didn't have to leave so soon, but I'm working tonight. Until we meet again at the Deli then."

The two men shook hands. Quiney tried to pay his bar tab, but Herb insisted he'd take care of it. Quiney thanked him and left. His work was a perfect excuse to leave, but not the real reason.

Quiney Simon believed there was more than a slim chance his persistence might be about to pay off. This Todd fellow's takeover as the city's supplier of drugs right after the Higgins brothers were killed was too much of a coincidence. Damn convenient timing! And, it was possible the server, Kerstian, might have gotten the name wrong. Perhaps what she overheard said in the booth was "Todd," not "Thomas." There was a way to make sure. Find Todd.

Quiney waited in his car a block down from The Shady Side lounge. Herb came out half an hour later. Staying well back, Quiney followed him for six or seven minutes to a nice Craftsman style home in Old Shandon, a predominantly white community. Dammit, Quiney thought to himself. Here I am pinching every penny, and some guy half my smarts is obviously well off. When I'm through helping Robert with his search and get my money, maybe I'll try selling some coke myself. No place to go but up from where I'm at now.

Right around nine the next morning, Robert Macklin arrived at his office. Quiney was there waiting. He carefully described his meeting with Herb the night before and emphasized the circumstantial part of Columbia's new cocaine supplier.

Macklin agreed the timing of Todd's replacement of the two Higgins was unlikely to have been fortuitous. "Did you get his last name?"

"No, but I may have a way of getting it. I pretended to be interested in selling some coke myself. Tonight, at his house, Herb plans to bring that possibility up with someone that delivers for Todd."

"Do you know where Herb lives?"

"Yeah. I followed him after he left the lounge."

Macklin grinned. "Seems to me Herb is pretty careless Quiney. No pun intended, but are you sure he's not just stringing you along for a ride?"

"I'll try to forget you said that, Robert. If this works out, I definitely earned my bonus last night. Maybe you should double it. The guy wants to take me to dinner. Hopefully, I can avoid doing that. My plan is to follow the delivery boy when he leaves Herb's house. If it's an exchange of cocaine for cash, then he will probably return the money to his boss."

"I'll be coming with you. Remember, I'm a private investigator. Safer too. I'm licensed to carry a firearm."

"I'm not licensed but just in case, I'll bring one along too."

"I'm driving, Quiney. Pick you up at five. Where does Herb live?"

"The Old Shandon neighborhood."

"Christ! That's where the lawyer we're doing this search for lives. Hell, they're probably neighbors."

"Sounds about right. It's an upscale part of Columbia with almost all white people. Good thing you're joining me. A black man waiting alone there in a car invites attention."

Private detectives perform a lot of wait and watch details. On this occasion however, Macklin and Simon were fortunate to have arrived two hours before dark. They parked on the street nearly six houses down from Herb's home. About 6pm, a grey Ford sedan with two white occupants pulled to the curb outside of his house. The right front seat passenger got out, looked around, and then walked to the front door carrying a small tote. He entered without knocking. Not more than a minute later he came back out carrying a case instead of the tote.

Robert commented, "Do you realize we just witnessed a drug transaction take place?"

"So far, so good," Quiney said. "Stay back but don't lose them. This plan of mine is working. I'm already counting my money."

The advice wasn't necessary. Robert was experienced at tagging along behind another car without drawing suspicions. That ability was needed. The two men in the Ford took highway 378 from downtown Columbia to a rural area called Horrell Hill. The distance covered 12 miles of mostly countryside. They left 378 onto a gated driveway leading to a ranch style home set 300 yards back. The entire property was fenced and well kept. Robert had followed but stayed a half mile behind. When he came to the drive, he continued at 50mph without slowing.

Robert, "Did you see that big mailbox at the gate?"

"Yeah. I saw it,". "The name on the box was T. Hager. Congratulations, Quiney. I think we just found Todd. Maybe we also found our Thomas. Let's go home."

Macklin needed to confirm it was Todd Hager that accompanied Isaac Higgin from the bar the night of the murders. It should have been an easy task for a good detective. Take a photograph of Todd and show it to Kerstian and the bartender. Bingo!

About a hundred yards down 378 and on the opposite side of Hager's driveway, there was an abandoned tobacco barn. Normally, it would have offered the perfect place to hide and wait for taking a picture. Robert's camera was a Canon fitted with a 100-300mm telescopic lens, but the ranch house was set 300 yards back from the road. For a facial close-up, the distance was too far. He'd have to sit behind the barn and watch for a better opportunity.

There was an awful lot of money coming Macklin's way if he was successful. Howell had more than double the original bonus to $15,000.

For that amount of money, the detective was up at 4 the next morning and concealed behind the tobacco barn before daylight.

For two days, over and back, the Ford sedan with its white driver and passenger left and returned. On each return, they carried a case inside the ranch house. Even when they were gone, at least two men remained inside the home. Judging by the number of trips Robert observed the men making, he realized this was no small operation. Some serious drug dealing was taking place.

Robert was looking and waiting for a black occupant to come out of the house, not always these two white dudes. They were obviously just employees making the exchanges. Finally, late on the morning of the third day, the garage door opened, and a SUV backed out with a single driver. The windows were tinted but with the telescopic lens, Robert could tell the person behind the wheel was black. This had to be Todd. He left the driveway heading west. The grey Ford sedan with the usual white men followed behind. Staying way the hell back, so did detective Macklin.

Still tailing a half hour later, Robert knew this was not just some morning's outing. They had taken 378 west for ten miles, turned left on 601 and continued another twenty miles through the town of Lugoff. There, Robert nearly lost them at a stop light where they avoided Camden with a left turn for the 521 bypass. Four miles later, they turned left again onto highway 97 north. A sign at that intersection with arrows pointing read "Liberty Hill 20" and "Great Falls 31."

Highway 97 was a winding road and hilly. Perfect for closing up his tail which he did. They stayed on it for about 12 miles, then turned left at the top of a hill where the arrows read "Clearwater Cove Marina," and underneath, "Wateree Recreation Area." Robert realized with that turn he had been to this place before. In fact, it was with Quiney at the campgrounds for a fishing trip. Only then, they had come from Columbia through Great Falls and turned south on highway 97. The recreational area was reserved for those who served or still served in the military. His familiarity with the grounds helped him to watch what came next.

Todd Hager parked next to a Chevy Impala at the far end of the marina's lot. His coworkers in the Ford continued pass and stopped at the Marina. Both men exited their car, looked around and waved back an apparent all clear to Todd. It was anything but "all clear!"

Robert had gone through the gate to the adjoining recreational area and stopped by the side of a large trash dumpster. From about 80 yards away he watched and photographed Todd Hager open the Impala's trunk and swap two heavy green duffle bags for just one from the Chevy. The trade took no more than 30 seconds, but Robert's Canon equipped with the telescopic lens had shot four good pictures of Todd.

Todd left in his SUV followed by his Ford companions. Robert debated what to do next but decided to continue the surveillance of his prime suspect. Had he waited five minutes more, he would have seen a pontoon boat pull up to the marina's dock, Jessie Talbert hop out of it, walk across the parking lot to the Impala, open the driver's side door, get in, start the engine, and leave.

The SUV and Ford were returning back to the ranch house by the same route as before. Robert had the pictures he wanted and stopped tailing as they passed through Lugoff. In Columbia, he dropped off his film at a Fotomat where they offered overnight development. Once home, he called Quiney.

Hoping the person phoning was Robert with news, Quiney answered on the first ring. "Hello. Who's calling?"

"An old army buddy with good news. I have pictures of Todd Hager being developed. Are you free tomorrow night for a visit to The Shady Side?"

"I'm working an 11-to-7-night shift at the mall. Does that work?"

"Yeah. Pick you up at eight tomorrow night. The show and tell at the bar shouldn't take more than a few minutes. I think we have our man, Quiney. I watched him make a switch of money for drugs in a parking lot. You wouldn't believe how much!"

"Maybe you and I are in the wrong business. I've been giving it some thought. Both of us deserve more after what we went through in Korea?"

"It's a coincidence for you to say that. I had eyes on something today that may provide the perfect kind of financial opportunity for the two of us."

"I'm listening?"

"It's a chance to retire rich but definitely not open to discussion on the phone. Plenty of time for that in the car tomorrow night after we've confirmed our search. I'll see you at eight."

Disappointments are always worse when you're so very sure of an outcome. First the bartender and then Kerstian were absolutely certain the photos of Todd Hager were not "Thomas."

The bartender explained to Quiney. "Not even close to the same guy. This 'Thomas' was in good shape. Tall too. Maybe six feet or more. The guy in your picture looks short. And he has a gut on him."

Macklin and Simon left the lounge not even talking. Depressed with the results, particularly from Quiney's perspective. In the car he said. "I'm finished with hanging out in that place trying to find your killer, Robert. Sorry, but I can't take any more Herbs coming on to me."

"Okay," Macklin replied and changed the subject. "Maybe it's a good thing he's not our man. Do you still have your old M1?"

"Yeah, but don't tell anybody. I claimed to have lost it. Why?"

Macklin described the transaction that took place at the Clearwater Cove marina. Ended the story with a strong hint at what he was suggesting. Quiney, you and I have been there. We know the place. It's in the middle of nowhere. Hardly anyone around. A little risky but a piece of cake compared to Korea."

Quiney knew exactly what Robert was leading to. "How much money do you think Todd put in the trunk?"

"Two duffle bags full. A million at least."

"I'm in! We'll take them out and split 50-50?"

"That's a messy possibility but maybe not necessary since there are two of us. Here's my plan. Todd makes the switch and leaves. His guards obediently follow their boss. If you'll watch my back from the campgrounds with your M1, I can jimmy the car door and hot wire the Impala in sixty seconds."

"Great idea! Clean as a whistle and you'll take off down the road."

"No reason in hell why it shouldn't work, Quiney. You'll follow me in my car. Pick someplace off 97 that's secluded and transfer everything.

Leave the Chevy where we do that. Drive back together through Great Falls to Columbia. We'll be two men returning from a fishing trip. Only instead of fish, we'll have a million bucks in our coolers."

"How often do you think they make the swap?"

"No idea. Give it at least a week. Then we'll have to go and watch from the campgrounds every day. Fish a little to blend in and not look suspicious. If we spot the Chevy, we'll know Todd's not far behind."

"No way I'll sleep between now and then. I'll clean up the M1 and practice some at the firing range. I might be rusty, old buddy."

"Damn sure hope not if it comes to counting on you. You were one hell of a marksman in Korea."

"Don't worry, Robert. I still am."

"I wish I hadn't made an appointment to meet with Eugene Howell in the morning. Got ahead of myself. I told him about the photographs of our suspected killer. Hope he's not too pissed that I was dead wrong thinking it was Todd."

"If we pull off this heist, who the hell cares about the lawyer? It's the perfect crime. We're stealing a drug dealer's money. It can't be reported to the cops. Way I see this at the finish line is that we're free and clear once it's done."

As Robert had anticipated, his meeting the next morning with Eugene Howell did not go well. The lawyer was expecting to learn the last name and whereabouts of "Thomas." Finally, too! But when Macklin arrived, the expression on the detective's face told Howell something was wrong.

Robert's bowed head confirmed what he had to say. "Bad news, Mr. Howell. It's not him."

"You seemed so certain when you called. What happened?"

Robert carefully explained the events that led to his wrong conclusion. He emphasized the part where Todd had taken over as Columbia's drug boss right after Isaac and Abraham Higgins were killed. It seemed to him and his assistant in the investigation that the timing of Todd's takeover could not have occurred by chance. Robert ended with the photographs of Todd Hager making an exchange of what he suspected was money for drugs.

"Mr. Howell, I thought we had our man until we showed these pictures to the bartender and a server. Both were positive Hager was not the person Isaac left with that night. This Todd fellow is short and pudgy. They said Thomas was in good shape and at least six feet tall. I'm discouraged. If you fire me, I'll understand."

"Saying I'm disappointed would be an understatement, but you're not fired. Keep working on the case. Nice photographs of this dealer. Maybe someday, I'll have to defend him in court."

"Keep the damn things. They're yours bought and paid for."

Leaving lawyer Howell's office still employed was good news for detective Macklin. He had become used to being paid double his normal day rate. Whoever the client funding his investigation was, he had to be wealthy. Robert smiled to himself thinking some irony was about to take place. He had been hired to find out who had committed a robbery of two drug dealers. Now, he and Quiney were planning to do exactly the same thing. Well, maybe not exactly he hoped. If Todd and his watch dogs left after making the transfer to the Chevy, there was no reason to kill them. Comforting to know Quiney would be there with his M1 just in case. In Korea, his buddy could shoot a gnat off your shoulder at fifty yards.

Robert drove home with imaginations of travel while being rich. Even had thoughts of becoming a Caribbean playboy. Another Jimmy Buffett. He had no idea what he had left behind on the lawyer's desk would prevent any possibility of his dream from being a reality.

Eugene Howell sat in his office contemplating what he could say to Nicolas Estrada. Thinking he had good news to share and soon, he had called his client the day before. Now Estrada was expecting a report and not in any way the one his lawyer had to make.

Eugene stared at the photographs wishing this Todd dealer really had turned out to be the murderer. He noticed something on one of them that aroused his curiosity. Apparently with the exchange of money for drugs completed, Todd had closed the Impala's trunk. Eugene removed a magnifying glass from his desk drawer. Using it, he could make out the Chevy's license plate.

A criminal lawyer always wants to know who drove the getaway car. Especially if it was full of cash! Eugene thumbed his rolodex to Emily Harrison's number at the South Carolina Department of Motor Vehicles. Three years before, her nineteen-year-old son had been charged with DWI in a car crash that resulted in the bodily injury of an underage female passenger. With the discreet help of a well-paid juror, Howell successfully defended her son in court. It all ended with a fine and probation. As part of his compensation, Emily had offered him payback if he ever needed anything from DMV records.

The conversation with Ms. Harrison was brief. Eugene read the plate's numbers from the photograph and requested the registration information. Emily said she would call back shortly. Five minutes passed before she did. The Chevrolet Impala, South Carolina plate number ARM 176 was registered to a Thomas Boyce with an address in North Myrtle Beach. Emily had taken the liberty of checking the DMV's driver's license records. Mr. Boyce was a 6'1" black male born January 20, 1954.

Eugene Howell could not believe his luck. All the pieces of the puzzle came into place now. Macklin had been right about the coincidence between the Higgins brother's murder and Todd Hager's timely replacement of their operations in Columbia. But the detective should have carried his investigation deeper. Had Robert done so, he might have come to the realization that Todd was nothing more than a middleman. Thomas Boyce had taken over as boss of distributions. An accomplishment he most likely achieved after he killed Isaac and Abraham.

The phone call to Nicolas Estrada lasted fifteen minutes. Howell went over every detail of the investigation. For the most part, his Mexican client had remained silent but attentive. Eugene ended his side of the conversation with a conclusion. "Mr. Estrada, I don't know if this Boyce fellow acted alone or had help. For certain though and from day one, he planned the whole thing in order to take over Isaac's and Abraham's business. Now he's running things in Columbia. Maybe South Carolina."

Nicolas replied in a calm but appreciative manner. "As always, Eugene, thank you for your services. The compensation we discussed in return for a successful investigation will be forwarded to your bank account in the Bahamas."

"It's a pleasure to work with you, Mr. Estrada. And I might add, if you require punitive measures to be applied in this case, I have in my employ just the right person for that."

"I'll keep your suggestion as an alternative, Eugene. As you might imagine, we have our own people for situations like this. For now, please consider your investigation over and completely confidential."

Nicolas Estrada declined his lawyer's offer to help with the disposal of Thomas Boyce for good reason. This was not a job for some amateur. Caro Quintero's instructions were over a year old now but still very clear. He had said, "Let the dust settle, then deal with the culprits the same way your friends died." Higgs and Topcoat had their throats cut. Thomas Boyce would meet an identical fate but only after experiencing so much pain he'd wished for death.

The name Thomas Boyce itself rang bells. During the sixties and early seventies, Estrada's Carolina drug sales consisted of heroin. Cocaine came later. Marijuana in the state was mostly managed by another dealer. Locals knew him only as TB. Connecting the initials now was simple. Apparently, Thomas Boyce had decided to change from marijuana to something more profitable. His only way to accomplish that was to remove not only Higgs and Topcoat but also the competition. Once the farmer's market was eliminated, he could take over.

A lieutenant's position in the Guadalajara organization was second only to that of the jefes. In that role, Estrada had command authority over his sicarios. If he issued them an order, the instructions were never questioned. But if anything went wrong, the responsibility was his. A safer way for Nicolas to carry out the assassination of Thomas Boyce was to make sure his jefes agreed with the directive. Make any unintended or damaging outcome a shared liability. Nicolas called Caro.

By 1980, what had become the first major Mexican drug trafficking group to warrant the title of a cartel was formed. Three men were responsible for its origin. Miguel Angel Felix Gallardo, Rafael Caro Quintero, and Ernesto Fonseca Carrillo. Together, their "Cartel" soon controlled most of the narcotics operations in Mexico. During the late seventies, marijuana and heroin were the incredibly profitable products they exported to the U.S. Early 1981, they started working with Columbian cocaine producers. In a short period of time, the shear popularity of the drug in the states caused its value to match that of both heroin and marijuana combined.

Caro Quintero received a precise report from Estrada regarding the identification of who had assassinated their South Carolina dealers, and more importantly, exposed the organization's methods of delivery into the eastern portions of the U.S. Nicolas ended with requesting permission to proceed with an appropriate retribution.

Caro's response was slightly cautious. "Nicolas, ready a couple of your best and most trusted sicarios for the task. The results of your investigation convinces me this Thomas Boyce is our stoolie. As such, he has shown a total lack of respect for our territorial claims. Before you proceed, however, I will discuss this with Felix and Fonseca. Our cooperation with the Colombians is going well. Incredibly profitable. Any interruption, no matter how trivial, would be costly."

"I'm not sure if I follow you, Caro. How are the two connected?"

"He's distributing Colombian cocaine in the eastern part of the U.S. It's unlikely, but Thomas Boyce could be a respected member of Pablo Escobar's organization in Miami. For all we know, maybe one of his associate's relatives.?"

"If they're our partners, why would he have done this?"

"Partners now, but mostly just in the past year and a half. Before that, we competed with them along the east coast. Especially in your Carolina's. Last September, the DEA closed a big part of their smuggling routes out of the Bahamas. Now they're forced to work with us. Keeping good relations is making a big difference in our revenue"

"Okay, we wait but how long?"

"Maybe soon. Felix and I will meet with Gustavo Gaviria and Juan Ballesteros in two weeks. They come as Pablo Escobar's negotiators. Actually, it's just an excuse to check records and return to Colombia with Pablo's share of the profits."

"You think one of them might know who Thomas Boyce is?"

"Positive, unless he's a nobody. Gaviria is also Pablo's cousin and second only to him in their operations. We can bring up Boyce's name and offence to see if there is any objection to his removal. Decide on our actions depending on Gaviria's response."

That afternoon, Caro went over Nicolas's report with his colleagues, Felix, and Fonseca. Neither hesitated sentencing Thomas Boyce to a painful death unless the Colombians objected. Felix insisted, "They better have one hell-of-a-good reason to protect this rat fink. Remember, we reimbursed them for their part of the loss. Twenty million. That's the price they'll have to pay back to save his ass."

Monday morning, June 14th, Roberto Gaviria, Gustavo Gaviria, and Juan Ballesteros arrived in Guadalajara. Typically, they stayed at the Hotel Americas where their Mexican counterparts maintained a spacious office for conference meetings. This trip, business discussions lasted only an hour and ended amicably. Partly because Pablo's brother, Roberto, was present, Felix invited all of them for an evening's dinner at his estate followed by an overnight stay instead of the hotel. The invitation was graciously accepted.

It was an evening of dining poolside with multiple courses of Spanish food. Juan Ballesteros suspected Felix was being overly courteous for a reason. A correct assumption. Their host had decided to bring up the Thomas Boyce matter in a polite atmosphere should he have to request a return of $20,000,000.

Gallardo began with an apology. "Forgive me gentlemen, but I have a delicate situation to discuss with you. Someone who works with your organization in the states has caused us a great deal of harm. He murdered two of our dealers and informed the authorities where one of our successful distribution centers operated. Our loss was significant."

Since Felix began by saying the offence was committed by one of their stateside employees, Gustavo was quick to understand the jefe was about to request punishment. "Felix, like you, we do not tolerate disloyalty. I can promise you the severest penalty will be administered. Who is this ratfink?"

"Thank you, but since his treachery was committed against us and in a particular manner, I prefer my own response. Unless, of course, he's not a close friend or a part of your family. His name is Thomas Boyce."

In reply to the name, Roberto Gaviria shrugged his shoulders. Acknowledging he also had no idea who the person was, Gustavo did the same along with open hands. He was thankfully relieved Griselda Blanco was not the perpetrator. "If this Thomas Boyce works for us, Felix, he's far down on our list of dealers. I've never heard of him. Do Roberto and me a favor and kill the snitch any way you see fit?"

Felix accepted their consent saying, "Very well my friends. Your understanding is appreciated. I'll let Caro settle this problem on behalf of all of us. Not right away though. This is not something that will be allowed to interfere with our relationship. Pablo needs to be informed of our intentions in case he feels differently than the two of you. If he has no objections, we'll proceed."

Only a half dozen people connected to the Medellin organization knew that Thomas Boyce and Trevor Dunbar were one in the same. And that link was contained entirely within the Bahamas. Luis, Juan, and Juanita were acquainted with both names from the start of their association with Trevor during the late seventies. Later, Diego and Lucia. That evening when Felix Gallardo provided only Trevor's alias to Roberto and Gustavo, they honestly had never heard of the man.

With a resolution agreed on that night, nothing more might have been said about the matter when Roberto and Gustavo arrived back in Medellin. Except that, Felix wanted Escobar's approval as well as theirs. When they told Pablo, the jefe saw no reason to get involved since the Mexicans intended to settle with the offender. And like Gallardo, Escobar would have wanted to deal with it personally if someone had exposed one of his operations to the authorities. Still, courtesy and precaution required Fabio to be advised. He instructed Gustavo to acquaint Luis with the situation. Let him pass it on to Fabio.

Luis, Mitch, and Daniel were returning to Colombia on Wednesday after an enjoyable one-week cruise to the Mexican Riviera on the MS Tropicale. It was a small delay in communications that nearly cost Trevor and Jessie their lives. That same Wednesday Caro Quintero had received clearance to proceed with the murder of Thomas Boyce. Felix cautioned him to make the disposal in a quiet manner so as not to draw attention to the cartel. Caro assigned the task to Nicolas Estrada.

Nicolas had two of his best sicarios in Juarez fly to Atlanta the very next day. A falcon from the upstate cannery in Georgia was there to meet them. His name was Andres Rojas, in his mid-twenties, and young for the level of responsibilities he managed at the cannery. It was a position assigned simply because he was a second cousin to Fonseca Carrillo.

Andres' instructions were straightforward. Ask no questions, make reservations for the three of them at a North Myrtle Beach hotel, drive there, provide his passengers with weapons, and follow their orders once they arrive. He politely introduced himself at the airport. Neither of the sicarios returned the courtesy!

Andres' personal car was a 1979 Mustang coupe and unsuitable for the occasion. To make the trip to the beach, he had requisitioned one of the canneries' much roomier vehicles. A solid blue 1981 Ford Bronco XLT. A case behind its back seat held three of the newly emerged Glock 17 handguns chambered for the 9mm Parabellum cartridges. And for reasons not explained to Andres, he had included two heavy duty box cutters and a blow torch. The sicarios knew the purpose of both items!

The first month of June is peak tourist season for the South Carolina beaches. Normally it was a seven-hour trip from Atlanta to Myrtle Beach. It took nearly nine hours due to congested traffic. And hotels were booked solid. With the short notice given, the nearest accommodations Andres could find with three vacancies was a Days Inn just across the Intracoastal Waterway from North Myrtle Beach. One of the sicarios made a derogatory comment directed at Andres about staying at an out-of-the-way inn. Had the assassin known that their chauffeur was related to one of the Guadalajara cartel's jefes, he would have shown him a great deal more respect.

They arrived at the motel just after ten that night. It was late after signing in, but the sicarios wanted to check out an address in Cherry Grove. Andres knew better than to argue. Once in Cherry Grove and with a map of the area taken from the motel's office, they drove north on Ocean Boulevard to 59th avenue and turned left. Then two blocks later, took a right on Channel Avenue. At the street's dead end, there was a huge, impressive home lit up to beat all hell. Obviously occupied. Flood lights at the back illuminated a large boat tied to the dock. Both Mexicans got out of the Bronco and stared at the house and the surroundings for a full minute. Then they returned to the car and instructed Andres to take them back to the motel.

Basically, that night the two assassins were just surveying the layout. They had to be careful completing the assigned task. Orders from Estrada were to combine brutality with silence. No witnesses and leave nothing behind that might implicate the cartel. To follow those instructions, both sicarios agreed a quiet entry into the home a little before sunrise would be best. Most vacationers were still asleep then. Their victims too!

After disembarking from their cruise ship in San Diego, Luis and family had flown to Bogota and taken a shuttle flight to Cartagena. Several messages were left for him on his recorder. The last was from Gustavo asking that Luis return the call when he arrived home, regardless of the hour.

It was after dark, but Luis understood there was a slight sense of urgency. Gaviria answered his phone politely. "Who's calling please?"

"Luis. Is there something important you need to tell me?"

"Sorry, Luis. Maybe it could have waited until tomorrow."

"Timing's fine. Just arrived in Cartagena. Go ahead. What is it?"

"Bear with me and I'll explain. It's slightly complicated. Yesterday, Roberto and I returned from a meeting with Felix in Guadalajara. We're not certain, but one of Fabio's cocaine dealers may be an informer for the DEA. Gallardo identified him, and they know where he lives. Said this person killed two of their workers and disclosed one of their most important facilities to the authorities. Since they were the ones offended, Pablo and I consented to his removal by the Mexicans. We both agreed that anyone in our organization who talks to the feds, even if it's against a competitor, is a risk to us as well. Pablo wants you to explain all of this to Fabio, in case he's close to this guy. Hope not though."

Luis had to ask even though he knew the answer. "Who did this?"

"His name is Thomas Boyce. A lowlife I think because I've never heard any of our people mention him. Doesn't matter now. Once Felix received our okay, he ordered the execution. My bet is this little ass of a drug dealer has only a few days to live."

"I'll notify Fabio in the morning. If he has anything to say about this, we'll pass it on to you and Pablo."

Luis didn't debate what to do next, and it was not Fabio he intended to phone tomorrow. His hands would have been tied except that it was Thomas Boyce and not Trevor Dunbar named for the treachery. Thankful for that small bit of grace, he placed a call to the Bahamas. Lucia answered. "This is Luis. Have Juanita call me at my number in Cartagena. It's an emergency!"

If he could help it, Luis would not let some lousy Mexican drug lords kill a friend. That was his relationship with Trevor almost from the day he recruited him. And only until this pathetic incident, Pablo and the others appreciated Trevor's contributions to their efforts, particularly with the loss of Lehder's island routes. Screw the Mexicans. Thomas Boyce could die but not Trevor.

Fifteen minute later, the phone rang. It was Juanita. She listened carefully to every word Luis spoke. He described Gustavo's understanding of the situation and added what he already knew from his discussions with Trevor months earlier. Luis ended with, "Juanita, get in touch with Trevor right away. There may not be much time. They're coming for him and there is nothing we can do to stop them. Tell him to disappear. At once!"

"Trevor should be easy to reach, Luis. He and Jessie will be meeting with the *Paso Seguro* on Friday."

"He needs to forget making another run onshore for us. Carrying on business as usual is a 'death wish' for both of them. But Juanita, the timing for meeting the *Paso Seguro* may be a blessing. If they can get to the trawler, instruct them to stay onboard. There's no safer place on earth for them to hide. It's completely out of harms' way. Hell! Make it an order from me!"

After hanging up the phone with Luis, Juanita immediately placed a call to Trevor in Columbia. Almost always an answer there, especially this late in the day even if Trevor was away. Not this time because Leann was now in California.

Juanita called Trevor's other secure phone at his beach house. Crap! Still no answer. She left messages on both recorders and phoned her results back to Luis. They were hundreds of miles away and there was nothing more to do but wait. Luis thanked Juanita for her efforts and asked that she let him know when Trevor responded. Hopefully, it would not be too late?

There was a reason for no answer of the phones at Lake Murray or Cherry Grove. Trevor and Jessie were at the cabin preparing the Winnebago for a trip to the beach the next morning. Preparations required loading the motorhome's concealed compartments with $12,000,000. Modifications had been made for that purpose, but even then, it was not an easy task. The money was to be payment for receiving 400 kilos of cocaine when they met with the trawler Friday.

A fixed habit afterwards on these occasions meant enjoying some Jack-on-the-rocks and grilled T-bones with sides. Trevor and Jessie complimented their dinner and drinks by sharing a joint of Colombian as an appetizer. The combination made for an incredibly pleasant evening.

Full and still a little stone, they called Leann at the rehab center in California. Trevor always asked Jessie for some privacy and spoke first, so Leann had answered with a knowing response. "Hello, sweetie. How's my lover boy?"

"Missing the hell out you girl. In lots of ways if you know what I mean."

"Well, big boy. We'll have to make up for lots of lost opportunities when I come home, 'if you know what I mean,' sweetie?"

"Watch out." Trevor chuckled. "I'll be counting on it. Maybe wear that little 'tush' of yours out!"

Leann laughed and repeated him again. "I'll be counting on that too."

Their conversation went on for another five minutes. Got better with some details added in. Finally, Trevor called for Jessie to take the phone.

With Jessie, the chit-chat was more of a respectful and appreciative adopted son talking to his godmother. Of course, he asked how she was fairing at the center. Leann replied she loved the place and how thankful she was to be there. Aside from that, back and forth exchanges of events were the main part of their talk. Pretty normal stuff except that towards the end, Jessie mentioned that Thomas and Richard were going offshore fishing Friday.

The statement was purposely out of context, but Leann was very familiar with what it meant. She responded in an innocent code. "Well, do wish those boys lots of luck. Tell them I hope they catch some fish but to be careful out there."

"Sure will, Aunt Leann. And you hang in there too. I know it has to be rough sometimes but remember we both love you. Just call if there is anything you need. Anything at all."

"I will. And I promise to get well, Jessie. It's working for me here. Until our next call, take care. I love you."

Jessie and Trevor left the Lake Wateree cabin at eleven Thursday morning. The Winnebago was stored with nearly 800lbs of cash. Normally they could make it to North Myrtle Beach in a little more than two hours. Traffic was backed up on highway 501, so they took an alternate route north through Marion and Nichols and then south on highway 9. Less traffic but still required three hours.

Jessie was in an obvious good mood singing along with the radio playing beach music. Trevor asked, "What's got you so stirred up?"

"Mostly just happy about Aunt Leann. She's clean, Trevor, and plans to stay that way. I think she'll be coming home by the end of November."

"Me too. Timing works for us because we'll have made our last run offshore by then. In between, we'll make a couple of cruises to the Bahamas for bank deposits. By the end of the year, Todd and the rest will take over. It'll be a 'clean-getaway' just like my old friend, Kenneth."

"Good thing we're bringing in another 400 kilos tomorrow. It's been over a month since the last transfer with them. They're probably scraping the bottom of their coke barrel by now."

"Yeah. No worry though. I've got it set up with them for early next week. Only a few more months of work ahead, so not much can go wrong now. Instead of beach music, Leann, you and I will be singing Christmas songs all the way to France."

France?

"To keep our promise, Jessie, I've been studying up on its south coast. The Mediterranean there is perfect for us. But don't go and say anything about this to Leann. My plan is to make it her welcome home present."

Trevor pulled into the garage of the beach house at 2 p.m. Parked next to the Firebird Trans Am. Jessie preferred to keep it at the beach instead of Lake Murray. It was a great ride for impressing the girls when cruising Ocean Boulevard.

Normally they would load the Bayliner at night so as not to draw the attention of other boaters. Plenty of time for that since high tide allowed for leaving at 5:30 the next morning. There was a subtropical storm in the Gulf of Mexico, but that posed no problem to the Carolina coast. The schedule was to rendezvous with the *Paso Seguro* at 10 and return to shore by early afternoon.

Once they were upstairs and inside, Jessie checked out the fridge and Trevor went to the phone to see if there were any messages on the recorder. There were two. The first was from Leann and left several days before, but he listened to her five-minute one-way conversation anyway. The second call came Wednesday night from Juanita. The message was short and disturbing. "This is Juanita. Urgent that you call me right away. Say again. Urgent!"

Even though he was in the kitchen, Jessie had overheard the message. Trevor looked at him as he dialed. "Something must be very wrong. Maybe the DEA? We'll see."

In the apartment set up for communications in Freeport, Lucia most often was there acting as the receptionist. Not this time. Juanita answered instead. "Trevor returning your call, Juanita."

Her reply was scary. "Glad you're still alive, Trevor. We were worried. Where the hell have you been?"

"Out of touch for a day or so. We've been getting ready for a run tomorrow. We're okay though. Jessie's here with me, and I've got you on my speaker. What's happening?"

Juanita described the details of her conversation with Luis. She ended by saying. "He's convinced that if they hadn't already, the Mexicans will kill both of you before the weekend is over. They think you're Thomas Boyce from North Myrtle Beach, but that doesn't matter. Trevor, these people don't mess around. They're coming for you. The assassins could be there already just waiting for the right opportunity."

Jessie turned and looked around the room. Walked to the hall closet and came back with two 12 gauge Browning semi-automatic shotguns, handed one of them to Trevor and asked, "Does she know how in the hell they found us? It's been a year!"

Trevor nodded an appreciation of the weapon and said, "Who knows how? Sons-of-bitches never give up, I guess. Stay away from the windows and watch the stairs. Give me a minute to think this through." Trevor wiped his forehead twice before continuing. "Juanita, we could take Jessie's Firebird and make a run for it to Walterboro. Fly my Cessna to Freeport. But we're sitting here with $12,000,000 in cash that we would have to leave behind. No damn way I'm going to do that."

"Flying here is not what Luis wants. The *Paso Seguro* will be on location for a meeting with you tomorrow morning. Bring your money. His orders are to stay onboard once you reach the trawler. Understand this Trevor, I said 'orders.' It's not a request. You'll be safe on the ship."

"Comprender, Juanita. Tell Luis gracias from both of us. If we're not on the *Paso Seguro* tomorrow, it's because we're dead!"

"Are you and Jessie armed?"

"Yeah. To the teeth and loaded for bear. If they come for us tonight, we'll be ready and waiting."

Juanita ended the conversation with three words. "Buena suerte, Trevor." But she thought to herself maybe the two of them had at best a 50-50 chance against trained professionals.

Trevor and Jessie stood in the upstairs living area holding shotguns and staring at each other. Jessie broke the silence. "What now, partner?"

Trevor walked to the window facing House Creek and looked out. Everything was normal with six or more fishing boats scattered along the backwaters. Next, he went to the front window facing Channel Avenue. Tourist season was in full gear with cars parked at every beach house. A few sunbathers were coming and going along the street. He turned back to Jessie and said, "Lots of people out there. If they try anything, it'll be after dark. Late, probably when everyone's asleep. It's safe to load the Bayliner now. Start her up and check everything. Make sure all we have to do when we leave in the morning is watch our backs and take the hell off."

Jessie replied, "Okay, but it's broad daylight out there. Some of those fishermen might notice. Hard to disguise loading 800 lbs."

"Yeah, but they're all trolling for flounder and drifting with the tide. We'll space five minutes between trips. That way, never the same boat out front. We'll make it look like we're getting ready for some serious fishing in the morning if anyone asked."

"Then we better get to it. Even with the two of us, unloading the Winnebago and packing ten of those plastic containers will take time and lots of sweat."

They finished an hour before sunset. Not a peep made by anybody when loading the Bayliner. Back upstairs, they made tuna sandwiches and had them for dinner along with pickles and chips. Jessie griped, "Dammit! I was looking forward to some good seafood in Calabash. If those bastards come tonight, they'll have to pay dearly for making me miss my shrimp and oyster platter."

Trevor smiled at the attempted humor but replied in a sober tone. "Just when I thought nothing could go wrong, this crap has to happen. Changes everything. As of today, we're out of the drug business. If we make it through tonight, Luis said we'll have to disappear permanently. He told Juanita some of the people in our own organization don't trust us anymore. I'm thinking we'll move our European vacation up by five months."

"What about Leann?"

"It'll be dark soon, so let's eat our sandwiches and then call her. We can't be sitting around talking on the phone tonight."

Leann was not expecting a call after one just a day earlier. With the boy's trip scheduled for the offshore, she wondered right off if something had gone wrong. Her worries came from past experiences. Confirmation came next.

Trevor recognized Leann's apprehension when she answered, so before going into a discussion of events and potential consequences, he reassured her they were both fine. During five minutes of his explanations for the call, Leann never said a word. Trevor ended with, "we're shutting down, Leann. By tomorrow morning, we'll be deckhands on a fishing trawler. Very rich deckhands too!"

Her initial reply was short. "When will I hear from you again?"

"Probably not for some time, but don't be concerned. For a while we won't exist. Just stay put and get well. Remember the trip we promised you. When Jessie and I get ourselves safely relocated, we'll send an unmistakable message. Count on it!"

Leann accepted the bad news incredibly well considering. She repeated several times to Trevor how much she loved him and to please be careful. Finally, she asked for Jessie. Much of the same followed with him. After they hung up, Jessie said, "I could tell. Aunt Leann was crying."

Trevor shook his head. "Yeah. Same with me. Getting dark Jessie. Lock and load time. We don't sleep tonight. You watch the back stairs. I'll watch the one up front and the road outside. Turn the outside flood lights on. In fact, let's turn all the lights on in the house. Make it look like there's a crowd of people inside."

Jessie didn't question his orders. After lighting up everywhere, he placed himself at the stairway; eased the breach back on his Browning to make sure it was chambered with a round, looked back at Trevor and said, "If you see anybody, say something."

Coffee is a great stimulant. Jessie had made two thermos jugs for the surveillance. Added to adrenaline, your brain can be focused to a maximum.

Evidently the case because both remained at their stations for several hours without speaking. Outside, all had stayed pretty normal. Then at 11 p.m.,

Trevor watched a SUV turn off 59th avenue onto Channel, dimmed its headlights, and slowly idled down the street. Suspicious as hell he thought. With an unnecessary low voice, he whispered, "Jessie, get over here! This could be it."

The driver stopped twenty yards short of the dead end. Two men got out, looked around for about a minute, then got back inside. The SUV made a U-turn and left. Trevor confirmed his thoughts. "You saw Jessie. Neither of them was white or black. Gotta be Mexicans!"

"But they left. Must know we're here with the lights on. Did you see any guns?"

"No. Not from here. Good thing we lit up! Otherwise, my bet is they might have tried to come in. Sneaky SOBs will be back when they think we're asleep. Can't leave either. It's low tide now and too windy to try and navigate the channel at night. We'd run up on a sandbar for sure."

"Now we know for certain it's tonight. Are you telling me we're going to sit here and wait for them to come murder us? Hell, even if we survive, the cops will be all over the place!"

"That's it! You're a genius, Jessie's. What we need is the cops. Just wish I'd hadn't put my binoculars on the boat, dammit! We could have gotten the license plate."

"You're going to call the cops? That's crazy man! We'll wind up behind bars and probably in the same cell with those two Mexicans."

"An anonymous call from Thomas Boyce. Lie! Then we're out of here. Turn all the lights off and leave. Anchor in the creek way down and wait for high tide. Watch the window. I'm calling the cops."

Trevor dialed the operator and asked for the police department. Possibly because the beach was packed with visitors, a watch commander answered. Trevor gave his address and false name before explaining it was not an emergency. He reported having seen three men who looked to be Spanish driving slowly up and down 59th avenue and Channel Street. "Sir, they stopped near my place, two got out to look around. I'm 100% sure they were holding guns."

"Did you get a license number, Mr. Boyce?"

"No sir, but they were driving a blue Ford Bronco. Looked brand new too. Not many like that cruising around in Cherry Grove. Anyway, it's late and past my bedtime. It's just that my wife insisted I report this to you."

"I can assure you we'll be on the lookout for them, Mr. Boyce. And thanks! We depend on citizens like you to keep North Myrtle Beach safe."

"Glad to be of service sir." Trevor replaced the phone on the receiver. "Let's get the hell out of here, Jessie. Take our guns just in case. And that bottle of Jack Daniel's too. It'll help pass the time until the tide changes."

The Jack Daniel's was a godsend. They had to wait while anchored in the creek for six hours. At 5 a.m. and still an hour before high tide, Trevor slowly motored the Bayliner through Hog Inlet and out to sea. It was an unusually difficult passage due to waves. Winds were picking up, but the 32-foot Bayliner was a highly capable craft in 4 to 6 foot sea swells. As the boat's bow rose and dipped with each wave, Trevor saw Jessie's apprehensive expression and assured him there was nothing to worry about. "I've been in worse seas, Jessie. Bit bumpy but that's not a problem. We're going to be ahead of schedule too, so hang on and enjoy the ride."

The *Paso Seguro* was on location to meet with the Bayliner at 9 a.m. the 18th of June. An hour early on this Friday morning because Captain Rene Perez was concerned about a tropical storm that reportedly had moved across Florida from the Gulf of Mexico overnight. To escape its path, he had decided to sail north as fast as possible once his passengers and their cargo were onboard. Rene was happy to see the Bayliner arriving early. Seas were now 7 to 9 feet making for a tough transfer of its ten plastic containers of cash. Each weighed approximately eighty pounds. Thanks to his experienced crew there were no mishaps. The trawler was underway in less than twenty minutes. The Bayliner was abandoned at sea. Trevor came on the bridge where Rene quickly briefed him on the weather and commanded him to go below and join his friend. Trevor obeyed!

Andres Rojas received a wake-up call at 5 Friday morning. Right out of bed, he did a line of coke. Twenty minutes before sunrise, he checked himself and the two sicarios out of the Days Inn. They left for Cherry

Grove in the SUV. Occasionally they passed by another car on highway 9, but as anticipated, the streets were pretty much absent of any traffic. The quiet but very windy morning suited the sicario's purpose. At least they thought so.

Andre caught the stop light at the corner with Ocean Drive. When the light changed, he turned left. A few hundred yards further he carefully passed around a city garbage truck making its collections. Afterwards, he glanced back in his rear-view mirror. Nothing behind but the truck and no cars ahead at all. Their timing seemed perfect for the mission. Except!

Beginning with Memorial Day, the population of North Myrtle Beach grew by ten-fold and remained that way throughout the summer. To meet the temporary security demands the city contracted police officers from other municipalities in the state. And instead of eight-hour shifts, the department requested them and it's regulars to make twelve hour patrols. Most readily accepted the opportunity. Anything over eight hours in a day paid time-and-a-half and double-time if working more than a forty-hour week.

Daytime and night stretches ran from seven to seven. There was a much needed and favorite "watering hole" on main street when ending a day's shift. To begin a 7 a.m. shift, lots of the officers gathered first at Cherry Grove's IGA's breakfast cafeteria. It was located at the corner of Sea Mountain Highway and Ocean Drive. Because of its police patronage every morning, there was no safer place in the state.

After a long night on patrol, Officer Rosa Lee Roberts arrived in the IGA's parking lot a little after 6 Friday morning. She was one of just two females that worked street duty for the NMB force. Looking forward to a $2 breakfast special, she waited in the lot for a fellow officer working the day shift to join her. His name was Hollis Stokes. He and Rosa had been "dating" for six months.

Hollis arrived on time, waved, and then parked several spaces down. Out of habit, as she was about to exit her patrol car, Rosa checked her side mirror, frowned, then swiftly twisted around to looked over her left shoulder. The stoplight had turned green and a blue Ford Bronco, Georgia plate, with three men inside was making a left onto Ocean

Drive. The vehicle's description and occupants were on her watch-list as suspected thieves and possibly "armed and dangerous."

Officer Roberts started her car and backed out to pursue while blinking her lights on and off at Hollis. She stopped for a moment, lowered her window, and yelled twice to him before taking off. "I need back up! I need back-up!"

Not more than twenty seconds after the sighting, Rosa was turning left onto Ocean drive. One quarter mile ahead was a damn city garbage truck smack in her way. Unless it had turned off onto one of the side streets the Bronco must have passed it, but she had to be sure. Consequently, she slowed and stared left at each of the next four avenues before rounding the blockage. About one half mile ahead she spotted them. Rosa floored her patrol car with Hollis now coming up fast from behind. A half a minute later and a hundred yards behind, she lit up the Bronco. Hollis did the same.

The North Myrtle Beach Police department had a modern Communication center. Rosa had radioed in her pursuit. Right out of the movies, the dispatcher was "calling all cars!" The IGA's parking lot was packed with them and only two miles from the action that followed.

Andres was caught completely by surprise. It was light enough that he had been concentrating on the street signs so as not to miss his 59th avenue turn. When suddenly blue lights started flashing close behind, he panicked and floored the Bronco. It was one of several incredibly bad choices Andres made. Beginning with, Ocean Drive would come to a dead end in another half mile as it reached Hog Inlet.

Every officer in the IGA's cafeteria responded to the call for assistance. In less than sixty seconds, another half dozen police cars raced north on Ocean Drive with turret lights flashing and sirens sounding. One hundred feet short of the dead end, Stokes and Roberts had used their patrol cars to block the street. Both were crouched behind them with guns drawn and pointed at two men standing in front of the Bronco. The driver had taken off running north towards the inlet.

Andres continued to the left when he came to the beach. Forty yards further and he was facing the Inlet. At high tide, it was 300 yards wide with crashing waves and a very strong outgoing current. He looked back and nobody had followed, so he decided to try and cross. Another mistake. An Olympic swimmer may have had a slim chance. Andres was fully dressed and wearing shoes. He alternated for a short distance, partially swimming between wading chest high on sand bars before realizing there was no way he was going to make it. He was totally exhausted once he returned to shore where five cops were waiting now. They cuffed and searched Andres, finding mistake number three. Still tucked under his belt in back was a fully loaded Glock 17. A spare clip was in his right pocket.

The South Carolina Law Enforcement Division was notified about the arrest in North Myrtle Beach of three Mexican nationals. SLED's investigative assistance was requested because, among other things, the apprehensions involved both "narcotics violations" and "potential crimes of violence." Weapons seized were box cutters and three Glock 17 handguns with spare clips. Beneath the driver's front seat of the Ford Bronco, a carton was found containing 46 one-gram baggies of cocaine. Chief J.P. Strom immediately assigned two experienced agents to the case. One of them was lieutenant William Mozingo.

Billy Mozingo and another agent did not arrive at the Horry County Detention Center until 4in the afternoon. Their delay in driving there from Columbia was the result of a subtropical storm now located 65 miles southeast of Myrtle Beach. Terrible weather to be on the roads.

Horry county detectives brief them on the circumstances of the arrest and the status of the detainees. Two had pretended to only speak Spanish and then remained silent, apparently aware of their Miranda rights even though they were not U.S. citizens. When arrested, both had wallets, each stuffed with $5,000 but no identification cards.

The third person was much younger, scared, and still a little wet from fleeing. After his rights were read to him, he continued to talk claiming to be an innocent driver for the others. With more questioning, he admitted that the coke found under the car seat was his. Andres' wallet only had about eighty dollars but also contained a Georgia driver's license, an American Express credit card, an employee ID, and a condom.

The county's detectives had begun an investigation of sorts on their own. Andres Rojas' license address was in the town of Ringgold, a small city about one hundred miles northeast of Atlanta. His employee ID showed that he worked at a nearby fruit cannery. The Bronco was registered to the cannery as a company car. And finally, the three Glock 17 pistols were registered to a security firm also located in Ringgold.

Billy Mozingo thought to himself. Unless lighting does strike twice, there's no way I could be this lucky? Christ! Everything fits like a glove. Mexicans working in a cannery requiring shipments of fruit, a local security firm armed with the very latest issued pistols that somehow made it into the hands of these three men, and 46 grams of cocaine in the Bronco. He turned to the chief Horry County detective and asked, "May I have a moment alone with this kid?"

They brought Andres to an interrogation room. Billy introduced himself, asked if he was comfortable, being treated properly, offered him a cigarette, and assured Andres he would come out of this mess okay. The change in tactics from the way the other detectives had questioned Andres worked. Andres and Billy exchanged some polite comments before the SLED lieutenant inquired, "Andres. I have to know one small detail, and I hope you'll answer truthfully. When the semi-trucks arrive at the cannery, do you help with unloading the drugs?"

Rojas answered defensively without thinking. "No sir. I have nothing to do with that part of the business." His denial was the final confirmation Mozingo had hoped for.

If there was one thing that Chief Strom appreciated in an agent, it was one's willingness to take an initiative. Described Billy Mozingo to a tee. The lieutenant walked out of the interrogation room and requested a secure office phone. Moments later he was talking to a friend and counterpart, Gerald Blanding, within the Georgia Bureau of Investigations.

After receiving a briefing, Gerald said, "I've got to be honest with you, Billy. I was a little jealous when you pulled off that drug raid in Florence. Got you a promotion. Maybe it'll be my turn to be the hero."

"There's a small difference, Gerald. That market was a state-owned facility. No search warrant was required. A delay could have cost us."

Lieutenant Blanding laughed softly. "You remember I once told you I'm no fan of Governor Busbee, but I'll say one thing for the man. He hates drug dealers with a passion. I'll have a search warrant within an hour. The place is a two-hour drive from Atlanta, so I'll be there personally sometime tonight. We'll see if they're canning something besides fruits."

"Good luck, Gerald. Let me know how it turns out."

Friday night, June 18th, Gerald Blanding and eight other GBI agents passed through the cannery's gate and served a search warrant to the plant's manager at the front office. No semi-trucks with trailers were present, but hidden within the refrigerated portion of a warehouse, the agents seized 500 kilos of cocaine and 120 kilos of heroin. Without question, the cannery was being used as a distribution hub. And the raid's bonus was discovered when agents opened a walk-in-freezer. Its back wall was packed to the ceiling with crates of cash.

Eight persons on the grounds at the time were all arrested. Several more arrests followed the next morning. It turned out to be the largest drug bust ever to be made in the state by Georgia's authorities. And, as agent Blanding enjoyed thankfully bragging to his friend, Billy, slightly larger in both drugs and money than the Florence raid.

Subtropical Storm One made landfall 50 miles north of Tampa on June 18th. Contrary to normal, it strengthened as it moved overland and then rapidly headed northeast along the U.S. coast. Hours after the GBI Friday night drug raid at the cannery in Georgia, the *Paso Seguro* was riding out the storm 70 miles off the northeast shores of Cape Fear, North Carolina. Usually, a fishing vessel would seek a safe harbor inland, but that option was not available to Captain Rene. The trawler's hole was empty of fish of course, and instead contained 8,000 kilos of Pablo Escobar's cocaine. Exposing $250,000,000 worth of his drugs to U.S. territorial waters was considerably more dangerous than the weather.

The *Paso Seguro* was a 68-foot, steel hulled, wet fish, stern trawler. Her captain was exceptionally capable from having sailed twenty plus years in the Caribbean Sea, Gulf of Mexico, and the Florida Straits. During some of those voyages, Rene had experienced much worse storms. And in this storm with him at the helm, the ship's bow was easily "trimming" with tips forward and backward. Winds were 55mph and would gust up to 70mph. At times on the bridge, Captain Rene appeared to be enjoying the challenge.

There's a "saying" that if anywhere, it often applies to being at sea in bad weather. "Shit Happens!" The *Paso Seguro* was a fishing trawler that rarely fished. For show and disguise, they would occasionally let out the ships netting and pretend to trawl. The seldom practiced procedure may have been the reason why the netting on the right side was improperly secured by one of the crew. As the ship's bow dipped low and tilted from a large wave, the net loosened, leaned far off to starboard, caught the water, and then dragged beneath the hull. It quickly fowled the propeller and its shaft.

Panic below deck nearly followed. The ship began to list hard to starboard and take on water. Without propulsion, its capsizing was inevitable. And a captain on the bridge without power was useless. Definitely not his seamanship though. For a full minute, he radioed a SOS with his position. Rene ordered all hands to come on deck in life preservers.

The *Paso Seguro* was equipped with a Viking IBA 16-person, low profile, life raft. Stored in a container, it weighed 300lbs and required several crew members to deploy. Captain Rene supervised by yelling orders. Any mistake handling it as the trawler listed hard to port and then starboard and all aboard would either have drowned or died of hypothermia.

In still rough seas on June 19th, the United States Coast Guard out of Cape Fear's Oak Island station rescued fourteen sailors 76 miles off the North Carolina coastline. All hands survived after they had abandoned ship for an inflated life raft. Their 68-foot trawler capsized, then sank beyond the continental slope in waters over one mile deep. The crew were Honduran Hispanics. Only the captain and the ship's navigator spoke English. As instructed by their captain, Trevor and Jessie played their roles well.

Nine of those rescued by the coast guard were placed in the station's holding center. Five others appeared to be suffering from moderate hypothermia and were transported to Wilmington's New Hanover Regional Medical Center for an overnight wellness stay. All were issued hospital gowns for the occasion. For their return the next day to the Oak Island station, the clothes they had arrived in were washed, dried, and hung in their room's closet. Personal items such as a watch or wallet were stored in a plastic bag and left for each inside a bedside table drawer.

Because of the storm, high winds continued into Sunday morning when the coast guard's van arrived to retrieve the five sailors. Two were missing! The hospital had minimal security, so around midnight they had simply dressed, left by the front entrance, and hailed a taxi for a ride to the bus station. A Greyhound bus had left Wilmington's Padgett Station at 5 a.m. for Columbia, South Carolina. The two "Hondurans" had boarded it for the trip. Just over three hours later in Columbia, the pair took another taxi to a home on Lake Murray. Trevor and Jessie thanked the driver and paid him with a hundred-dollar bill.

There were reasons they had to return home. Mainly, to retrieve passports and coded Swiss bank account numbers. To hasten their departure, Trevor was issuing orders like a jefe. "We won't be back, Jessie. Pack just one large suitcase and your leather overnight bag. I'll do the same. Between us, that will max out the storage space in the Cessna."

"How much time do I have, Trevor?"

"Two hours and we should go. I have no way of knowing for sure if the Mexicans connected Thomas Boyce to me. Wish we didn't have to take our chances coming here, but I never figured on leaving like this. Before we go, I'll make some calls and wrap up some loose ends. Let's get packing!"

An hour later, they had loaded Leann's Maverick with their luggage along with personal items and keepsakes. If they left the car behind at the Walterboro airport, it was still registered to her. Trevor was hoping to make their getaway difficult to trace. He also took all of the cash he kept in an attic safe. $34,000 in one-hundred-dollar bills.

Still there were the necessary phone calls. His first was Charles Whit-field. The secretary answered and put him through to a familiar answer. "Good morning, Thomas. As always, it's great to hear from you."

"Thanks, but I'm afraid this may be our last conversation. Regrettably, our association may be coming to an end."

"What's wrong, Thomas! Surely your lawyer can help."

"They found me, Charles. The sons-of-bitches that ran drugs from the farmers market know it was me that reported them. I don't know how. They just did."

"Are you certain?"

"Absolutely certain. The one person I trust most in my line of work told me so. Thanks to him, I'm still alive. They sent killers to my home in North Myrtle Beach. I saw three of them coming and managed to make it the hell out of there before they could get to me."

"You said North Myrtle Beach. Two quick questions. Were they His-panics and is your place in Cherry Grove?"

"Yeah, why exactly?"

"Where the hell have you been? It's all over the news. Three Mexicans armed to the teeth were arrested there by police early Friday morning. If those were your bad guys, you're safe. They're behind bars and that's just half the story."

Trevor wanted to hug that police watch commander. At least the immediate danger may have been removed. "I've been completely out of touch, Charles, but they have to be the same ones that came after me. This gives me a little breathing room. Even so, I got to disappear. More will come. What's the other half?"

"A lot of it is in this morning's paper, but I got the scoop from my SLED contact. He was involved with questioning them. One talked! Thomas, they busted the same outfit again just like they did in Florence. This time it was at a cannery in upstate Georgia. The way things are working out, you could get a job with the DEA."

"Not likely. Even some of the people I worked for don't trust me any-more. Seems they've decided to get in bed with these Mexicans. Means I don't have a prayer in hell. It's the reason I'm calling. I'm leaving the country. Permanently! But I want it to look like I'm dead."

"Just how the hell do you do that?"

"Already have. I left Cherry Grove's inlet in a 32-foot Bayliner Friday morning."

"Just when that storm was coming?"

"Yeah, and it was one hell-of-a-storm too. Sixty miles out, I secretly switched to a ship and abandoned the Bayliner. It probably sank."

"You're trying to make it look like you were lost at sea?"

"Yeah, and damn nearly became shark food for real. If you can help with this, Charles, there will be a substantial compensation coming to you."

Whitfield loved to hear Thomas suggesting a payment for services. Never had any other clients even come close in that category. "Without a body it may take some time, but as an attorney for your estate, I can definitely have you declared 'legally dead.' Your trip to sea in a storm exposed you to what the courts call 'imminent peril.' When you fail to return, those circumstances can accelerate the presumption of death. I'll need a few details from you. That's all."

Trevor answered Whitfield's questions over the next several minutes. The principal data the lawyer needed were Thomas Boyce's Cherry Grove address, phone number, deed and title information, bank accounts, and registrations of the Winnebago, Firebird, and the Bayliner.

When his notes were completed, Whitefield said, "Since I probably will not be in communication with you again, make out and sign a will as to how you wished your assets allocated. Mail it to my office with me named as executor. I'll take care of having it witnessed and notarized."

"I'll send it once I'm safely out of the country. Afterwards, I might continue to use you as an intermediary here in the states under a different and confidential name. For example, the young lady you arranged to have placed in the California clinic may need your assistance later this year. Also, maybe some updates on your progress. Would that be appropriate?"

"Of Course."

"Well then, when Thomas Boyce is officially declared dead and everything is settled, withdraw half of the trust fund for yourself. Will that be sufficient, Charles?"

Whitfield had to allow the question to fully register. The amount would be in the low six figures. "Much more than adequate, Thomas. Thank you!"

Next on Trevor's to phone list was Todd Hager. But Thomas Boyce was supposed to be dead or missing. So instead, after giving instructions of what to say, he let Jessie call as Richard Boyce. There was no answer, but while Jessie was leaving a call back message, Todd picked up.

As best he could without revealing the history of reasons for shutting down everything, Jessie told the dealer some of what had happened. "Todd, the Mexicans are back! The bastards are taking over and anyone that gets in their way is dead meat. They sent assassins after Thomas at his beach home, but the cops stopped them. Read the papers and you'll understand. My brother tried to make a run for it in his boat during the storm. I haven't heard from him since. Nobody knows yet, but he may not have made it. Either way, it won't make a difference to the Mexicans. More will be coming and maybe for all of us."

"What do you want me to do, Richard?"

"Close up shop and tell Cecil and Ricky to do the same. Make it into a permanent vacation. We've all made lots of money, but its worthless if none of us live to spend it."

"I'm on this right after we hang up. Anything else?"

"Yeah, Todd. Even if Thomas comes out of this alive, you'll probably never see either of us again. Understand?"

"Yes, my friend, but I hope your brother is okay. We all owe him."

Trevor had listened to Richard's conversation with Todd, and he appreciated the last comment. When they hung up, he complimented Jessie on the call.

Trevor phoned both his mother and Juanita before they left. The conversation with his mom required ten minutes of telling half-truths and lies. The one with Juanita was brief. He explained that they would be arriving by boat in Freeport the next day. She was glad he was coming and safe. Juanita still had not received a report on how the *Paso Seguro* was lost. One was needed. 8,000 kilos of Escobar's cocaine were lying on the bottom of the Atlantic. Making the event even worse, the ship also sank with an estimated $100,000,000 in cash. Trevor's $12,000,000 included. The DEA never knew, but in the history of east coast drug interdictions, nature's contribution to the effort that 18th day in June was one of the very largest.

Trevor and Jessie drove from Columbia to Walterboro, flew the Cessna to Port Salerno, then completely exhausted, spent the night at a motel. Except for a three-hour nap on the bus from Wilmington, neither had slept in over two days. Monday morning, Florida's weather was perfect. They left Port Salerno in the Bayliner 4050 Bodega two hours before lunch time. Cruising at 20 knots, they made it to Freeport in under five hours. Juan was there to meet them.

Later that evening, at what Juanita now referred to as her "home," Trevor furnished an account of the circumstances leading to the sinking of the *Paso Seguro*. Afterwards, she phoned Luis with the explanation. When finished, Juanita handed the phone to Trevor. It turned out to be the last time the two men would ever speak. Apparently, the danger of reprisal by the Mexicans and perhaps Escobar remained. Luis reiterated he and Jessie should vanish. Depart Freeport right away and cease all communications.

After dinner that night, Trevor gave the keys to his Bayliner to Juan and Diego explaining it was a long overdue gift of appreciation for their assistance in Key West. Both men understood and expressed it with an understanding reply. "Gracias, Trevor. Mantente segura."

Tuesday morning, June 22nd, Trevor and Jessie boarded a shuttle flight in Freeport for Nassau. That afternoon they flew first class on an international flight arriving very early the following morning at Charles de Gaulle Airport, Paris, France. To cover-their-tracks over the next few weeks, Jessie's French proved to be a considerable help.

A phone call from Ciudad Juarez to Eugene Howell was made by Nicolas Estrada asking that he represent three Mexican nationals arrested in North Myrtle Beach. A day later, the lawyer secured the two sicario's release conditional on their immediate deportation to Mexico. When the police stopped the Bronco, both had surrendered peacefully. Neither the weapons nor the cocaine found in the car was connected to them for certain. As the vehicle's driver, Andrea was not so fortunate. At his hearing, he was deemed a flight risk and bail was denied. Charged with multiple offences including "possession with intent to distribute," he bargained on the advice of his lawyer for a reduced sentence. Andrea Rojas received between two and five years served. Then deportation.

The loss of another distribution center, its stores of drugs and cash, combined with the incarceration of Fonseca Carrillo's cousin, was unacceptable to Felix Gallardo. A week after Andrea was sentenced, Nicolas Estrada's body was found in a ditch on the outskirts of Juarez. He had been shot pretty much to pieces.

In anticipation of the heist of a lifetime, detective Robert Macklin and Quiney Simon staked out the Clearwater Marina for nearly a month. The Chevy Impala with its cocaine never came. Neither did Todd, Cecil, or Ricky. Out of frustration, the two would-be robbers decided to go directly to Todd Hager's Horrell Hill ranch home. Maybe take on the whole bunch if they had to. The place looked deserted. Out front was a realtor's "For Sale" sign with an attached note beneath reading "Sale Pending." For Macklin, it was back to being a private detective. For Quiney, it meant returning to his mall security job.

The second week of July a noteless postcard featuring the Eiffel Tower was placed in Leann Fox's box at the Betty Ford Clinic. For something without a single written word, she was thrilled. In August, another card arrived from Italy, and of course it displayed the Roman Colosseum. This time she was jealous. Even more so when in September, one with the Rock-of-Gibraltar showed up. "Dammit!" she said aloud. "I love this place, but now I can't wait to get out." The timing of that opportunity came by federal express in early October. Inside the package was her passport and a first-class ticket booked for November 3rd with Pan American Airways connecting in New York City for Paris, France. A note included this time said, "Love Forever! Pack to stay for the same!"

A week before she was to check out of the clinic, a priority mailed envelope came from a law office in Columbia labeled Strictly Confidential. The return address was that of Charles Whitfield, Attorney at Law. Enclosed was a copy of Thomas Boyce's will. It named her as sole heir to his estate in the event of his death. Mr. Whitfield was designated as executor. He had included a copy of a petition submitted to the South Carolina courts requesting that Thomas Boyce be declared legally dead. A brief handwritten note from Charles to Ms. Fox explained why the request was made. Also, he was very sorry for her loss but that she keep her position as heir apparent confidential.

With her departure imminent the last of October, the clinic's staff had declared Leann completely well of cocaine. Hers was a perfect rehabilitation and worth every penny contributed. A celebration party was scheduled for the day before she left. On that occasion, Leann cried. So did several others.

Leann landed at Charles de Gaulle Airport early on the morning of November 4th. She had packed two large and one middle size suitcases for her "stay". The luggage required a few extra minutes to go through a brief customs inspection. While standing in line for her turn, she had anxiously looked ahead for a much anticipated welcoming. Beyond the custom's gate there were quite a few people waiting for arrivals. Trevor nor Jessie were part of the crowd. Leann cleared customs.

With a porter trailing behind, she passed through a still congested waiting area constantly glancing forward and to both sides. Just seconds before her excitement was about to turn to disappointment, there he was!

Leann shook her head with an approving smile. A tall handsome black male with a wide grin and hands placed on his hips had stepped from behind a column. Trying hard for a romantic welcome to Paris, Trevor wore polished leather shoes, pressed dark pants fastened at the waist with a gold buckled belt, his favorite silk shirt complimented with a matching ascot at the neck, and a black beret slightly tilted to the right side of his head. He had also added to his appearance a neatly trimmed mustache.

What followed next was right out of the movies. Leann and Trevor almost trotted towards one another and embraced with she being lifted a little off her feet. Then they kissed. A long and warm kiss. More than two dozen individuals standing around had watched their reunion. All smiled and half clapped! Finally, Leann asked, "Where's Jessie?"

Trevor replied. "He wanted to give us this moment." He pointed over her left shoulder towards the next column. Jessie was there with arms spread wide as he came to her. Now it was his turn to hug.

Trevor had stepped back to watch their reunion. For a moment, a bit of a ruckus at the custom's gate drew his attention. Three Air Transport Gendarmerie were carrying out an arrest of a backpacking teenager. One of the officers was holding a one-ounce plastic bag of hashish he had taken from the kid's pants pocket. Trevor's head shook a negative disapproval thinking to himself. Poor guy. And they're arresting him for a lousy ounce of marijuana. A damn ounce! When will they ever learn? Trevor was referring to the authorities!

Trevor turned back to Jessie and Leann. It was time to leave. A limousine was waiting to transport them to Le Meurice for a five-night stay. It was reported to be the finest five-star luxury hotel in Paris. For the three of them, this was the beginning of a wonderful new life in Europe!

29.

EPILOGUE

Trevor Lamont Dunbar….. Trevor was 28 years old when he left the U.S. He never returned. Within six months of arriving in France, he had purchased a villa in Porto-Vecchio, Corsica. Soon after, he added a 35-foot Arcoa Yacht to its harbor. A year later, he and Jessie together bought a nearby 267-acre property east of Sotta. It came with riding stables and a small vineyard. Leann and Trevor still reside in Porta-Vecchio. They never married or had children but instead have traveled all of Europe the years since. Annually, they also visited Switzerland for fun in the snow and bank transfers.

Jessie Talbert married and eventually settled in Marseille, France. He and his wife, Celeste, have four children. Three girls and a boy. Leann and Trevor are considered their grandparents. As family, Jessie, Celeste, and the kids often visit Corsica to join "Gramps" and "Nonie" either at the vineyard for horse riding or Porta-Vecchio for sailing the Mediterranean.

Kenneth Bayne…..Kenneth and Patricia still reside in Lafayette, Louisiana. They have two children. Over a period of sixteen years, Kenneth and Pat's family venture into oil and gas exploration proved very successful.

In 1994, they sold the company's Louisiana and Texas properties for $112,000,000 to Petrofina's U.S. subsidiary Fina Inc. Kenneth retired and became an avid sportsman. Patricia splits her time between raising the kids while also working as an active and devoted member of Lafayette's First Baptist Church.

Jacobs Morgan..... Jake made Naples, Florida his home. He married and divorced twice in less than ten years. His third try proved to be a winner. He never had children until he and his present wife decided to adopt a girl and a boy. Both kids were Jamaican and acquired simultaneously from the orphanages in Kingston that Carl Bayman had constructed.

Peter Ingram..... For the rest of his life, Pete remained in Jamaica's Montego Bay and enjoyed every day there came rain or shine. He never married but had several companions over the years. Pete was in apparent good health at the age of eighty-five, but then suffered a massive and un-explained heart attack. Among many others, five close friends attended his funeral service in Jamaica. Hank, Jerome, Buck, Jake, and Kenneth.

Bucky Givens..... Buck and his wife, Wanda, are living in a large house that he built on the Negril River just across from the Bayman's Marina. As anticipated, they needed the space. They have seven kids.

Hank Bayman..... Hank and Martha never moved from their beautiful Jamaica home in Negril. Hank manages the family businesses and Jerome still works for him. And now he and Martha have lots of grandchildren to manage as well. The kids visit often!

Juanita Macarro.....Juanita kept the Freeport beach house for herself. She became Aunt Juanita after Diego, Lucia, and their son moved in with her. All still live in Freeport but have nothing to do with smuggling.

Juan Valencia..... Juan fulfilled his dream of having his own hacienda. In 1986, he immigrated to Brazil where he purchased a 1200-acre ranch in the southern state of Rio Grande do Sul. Today he looks and plays the part of a "gaucho." For appearances to go with a little conceit, he rides horseback wearing a "silk pocket square neck handkerchief" set off by a white "Stetson."

Luis Rojas Alfonso Castillo..... Luis continued his association with the Medellin Cartel in Colombia through representation of Don Ochoa Restrepo's three sons. In 1992 as they were leaving his office, Luis and son, Daniel, were abducted by a vigilante group known as Los Pepes. The kidnappers were enemies of Pablo Escobar. Both Luis and Daniel, with bullet riddled bodies, were found stuffed in the trunk of a car three days later. Michelle Linville grieved their loss for two weeks before taking her on life with sleeping pills.

Carlos Enrique Lehder Rivas..... In 1987, Carlos Lehder was captured in Colombia and extradited to the United States where he was tried and sentenced to prison for life without parole.

Jack Carlton Reed..... By an unexplained coincidence, a week after Lehder's arrest, Jack Reed was apprehended at his home in Panama. Reed was convicted of conspiracy to distribute cocaine and operating a criminal enterprise. He was sentenced to two consecutive life terms of imprisonment. He was granted a Clemency Release after 23 years but died shortly afterwards.

Edward Hayes Ward..... Ward, because of a plea-bargain agreement, served only four years of a 20-year term before being paroled into a witness protection program. In 1988, he became one of two key witnesses for the prosecution against Carlos Lehder. The other was George Jung!

George Jacob Jung.....Jung was arrested twice in 1987, but released soon after he testified against Carlos Lehder. He was arrested again in 1994 for possession of nearly 800 kilos of cocaine. He received a 60-year sentence but was released in 2014. Soon afterwards, he served an additional two years for parole violation. And by then of course, his infamy came with his character played by Johnny Depp in the movie "Blow."

Albert Turner.....Shortly after the conviction of Carlos Lehder, the U.S. Attorney General for the middle district of Florida launched an internal investigation of its Jacksonville office. There was a credible report of "leaks" pertaining to the indictments and prosecution of drug defendants. Three days after being questioned and scheduled for a lie detector test, Albert Turner took his own life with a 38-caliber revolver. Tony Mathis attended the graveside funeral for his "friend." Tony wept the entire service!

Captain Rene Perez..... One week after the loss of the *Paso Seguro*, Rene Perez and crew were returned to Honduras. Apparently, Captain Perez retired. His whereabouts today are not known.

Raymond Grady Stansel.....Captain Ray Stansel was scheduled to be tried January 5, 1975, in Daytona Beach, Florida for smuggling marijuana. He did not appear. The lawyer for the defendant explained his client was reported to have drowned while scuba diving off Roatan, Honduras. Few in law enforcement believed the story. On May 26, 2015, 75-year-old Dennis Lee Lafferty died from a traffic accident in Daintree, Queensland, Australia. His loss was mourned not only by his wife, Janet Wood Lafferty, but their children and the entire Daintree community. Janet later revealed that her husband was actually 78-year-old Raymond Grady Stansel, the legendary smuggler of marijuana in the early 1970s.

Pablo Emilio Escobar Gaviria.....Pablo Escobar became the world's most powerful drug trafficker in the 1980s. He accumulated wealth into the billions. He was imprisoned June 1991, escaped July1992, and fatally shot in a gunfight with police December 2, 1993.

Gustavo de Jesus Gaviria Rivero..... Pablo's cousin, Gustavo Gaviria was killed in Medellin by Colombian police August 11, 1990.

Griselda Blanco…..Noted in the drug trade for her ruthlessness and nicknamed La Madrina, Griselda Blanco attempted to escape rivals by moving to California in 1984. She was arrested there a year later and ultimately imprisoned in the U.S. for nearly twenty years. After returning to Colombia, she was shot by gunmen on the streets of Medellin September 3, 2012.

Roberto de Jesus Escobar Gaviria….. Pablo's brother surrendered to Colombian authorities in 1993. He was released in 2006. To this day he remains alive and well.

Fabio Ochoa Vasquez….. In 1991, Fabio and his brothers turned themselves in to Colombian authorities. They were released in 1996. Fabio was arrested again for trafficking and extradited September 2001 to the United States. He was convicted and sentenced to 30 years in a U.S. federal prison.

Juan David Ochoa Vasquez…..David rejoined the Ochoa family after his release from prison in 1996. At the age of 65, he died of a heart attack while at a private clinic in Colombia.

Jorge Luis Ochoa Vasquez…..Based on a U.S. warrant, Spanish police arrested Jorge in Madrid November 15, 1984. He remained there for two years although both the U.S. and Colombia had applied for his extradition. Spain eventually did extradite him July1986, but on charges of illegally exporting Spanish fighting bulls to Colombia. There he received a suspended sentence and disappeared only to surrender with his brothers to Colombian police January 1991 in return for the promise of a reduced prison sentence. All three were released in July 1996. Jorge Ochoa currently lives in Medellin.

30.

ADAGE

Except For The Stakes, Dealing Drugs Is Like Gaming The Slots In Las Vegas. Lots Of Players Come To The Machines. In the Long Run, Only A Very Few Ever Win. But Hoping to Score Big, More Keep Coming. The Slots Will Always Be Spinning. It's The Same With Drugs. Dealers Will Always Be Dealing!

Today, The Street Value Of A Kilo Of Cocaine Sells For An Average Of $200,000. Half What It Cost In The Early Eighties. Colombia Is Still The World's Largest Cocaine Producer. The United States Is Still The World's Largest Consumer.